DEATH AT PARADISE PARK

ROSS GREENWOOD

B

Boldwood

First published in Great Britain in 2023 by Boldwood Books Ltd.

Cover Design by Head Design

Cover Photography: Shutterstock

A CIP catalogue record for this book is available from the British Library.

Paperback ISBN 978-1-80549-673-1

Large Print ISBN 978-1-80549-669-4

Hardback ISBN 978-1-80549-668-7

Ebook ISBN 978-1-80549-666-3

Kindle ISBN 978-1-80549-667-0

Audio CD ISBN 978-1-80549-674-8

MP3 CD ISBN 978-1-80549-671-7

Digital audio download ISBN 978-1-80549-662-5

Boldwood Books Ltd
23 Bowerdean Street
London SW6 3TN
www.boldwoodbooks.com

To Gary Bainbridge

Thank you for your time and talent.
The pictures of Hunstanton are wonderful.

NORFOLK MAJOR INVESTIGATION TEAM STRUCTURE

Detective Superintendent
Zara Grave

Detective Chief Inspector
Vince Kettle

Detective Inspector
Vacant

Detective Sergeants
Ashley Knight – Bhavini Kotecha

Detective Constables
Hector Fade – Barry Hooper – Salvador Freitas – Emma Stones –Jan Pederson

Family Liaison Officer
Scott Gorton

Twinned Detective Team Sergeant
Ally Williamson

Forensic Pathologist
Michelle Ma Yun

1

Alfie Hook squeezed himself into the driver's seat of the red Ford van and pulled the door shut. He sucked in his potbelly to fasten the seat belt. When he could hold his breath no longer, he puffed out, which left his stomach resting on the steering wheel. Alfie smiled as he checked his mirrors. Jackie had been saying if he put the seat back any further, his feet wouldn't reach the pedals.

He pulled out of Paradise Leisure Park, drove straight up the road for half a mile, turned left at the roundabout, left again and cruised into Vegas Fish Bar's concealed car park, which only locals tended to use. Despite it being near Hunstanton seafront, spaces were always available.

Kiosks and stalls were stored there in the off season, but as it was June, they were out making money on the promenade. There remained one large, high-sided catering vehicle rotting under a tree in the far corner. Alfie reversed between it and the fence with a squeak of his van's brakes.

The sea breeze blew frying smells through the cab's open windows, and his mouth watered. He didn't bother to wind the windows up or lock the door because he'd be back in five minutes. It would air the cab of him, too.

Alfie had finished his deliveries early. There was a moment when he considered going home and having the salad Jackie said she'd make for him when he returned at ten, but a quick glance at his watch confirmed he had plenty of time. Perhaps he'd eat the green stuff as well when he got back, or at least the wedge of cheese she often placed on the side.

He stepped down from the van, and his foot pulsed with discomfort. The extra pounds he'd gained bearing down on it wouldn't have helped, but the major cause was the resurgence of his gout from a few years back. Alfie tried to ignore it, but the soreness was excruciating.

A gust of wind brought another wave of hot grease over and he grinned. There were few joys nowadays, but this was one. Alfie reckoned the Vegas did the finest fish and chips in the country, and he was a man of considerable experience. For a short while, he would forget the pain.

There were a couple of parking spaces outside the amusement arcades further up, but he preferred it around the back. With the size of his belly, he always imagined people judged him when they saw him eating a takeaway.

The chip shop shut at nine, and there were only two other customers queueing inside so, before he opened the door, Alfie took a moment to cast an eye over at the fairground three hundred metres away at the seafront. It was where he and Jackie had enjoyed their first date, nearly half a century ago. They'd only taken enough money for two rides, but wandering around in circles for hours together had been the greatest evening of his life. Few had come close since.

Alfie pictured Jackie pulling him towards the donut stand, her short flowery dress blowing in the breeze, bra straps on show. It was as if that night they'd invented kissing. The guy gave them a donut each for free and said get lost because they were putting his customers off.

Alfie put his fingers on his lips, and for a few seconds they felt tender again. He could almost taste the sweet dough as if he'd bitten into it.

With closed eyes and a growing smile, he saw those two teen lovers laughing together on the roller coaster, until a series of screams, perhaps from the Sea Dragon ride, jolted him from his nostalgia. But the cries were screeching gulls fleeing from the approaching weather front, and Alfie knew those youngsters were long gone.

After a heavy breath, he pushed the door open to let a customer out, and stepped into the shop. A spotty kid, the only one left waiting to be served, ordered two saveloys and a portion of chips and was soon away.

Alfie adjusted his jeans, which had chafed the inside of his leg raw in the four short delivery walks from the van that evening, and shuffled forwards.

'Alfie!' said the owner, Joe. 'Your usual?'

'Please.'

Joe winked at him. 'I was saving this for myself.'

Alfie laughed as the friendly bald man with the big glasses slid a gigantic piece of battered cod out of the warming oven and rested it in a box. Grease glistened under the shop's bright lights.

If gurgles were trains, Alfie had a fleet of InterCitys thundering through his stomach. Joe was waffling on about how bad the weather was for June, but apparently next week was supposed to be Mediterranean. Alfie wasn't taking much notice. He was quietly focused on preventing his jaw from opening for that heavenly first bite.

'Hotter than Rome,' shouted Joe, with a huge smile and an Italian accent.

'Save you going home for your holidays,' replied Alfie, despite having heard Joe came from Madeira.

'Too right,' said Joe with a laugh.

Alfie paid and wandered back to his van. Even though it was a fresh night, his thighs were hot and his armpits damp. He knew his health was getting to be a real problem. His GP told him at his last check-up that if his blood pressure had been one point higher, she'd have immediately rung for an ambulance.

That was unwelcome news, but it was the gout in both big toes that affected his standard of health and happiness. The agony was indescribable, and with him always. The doctor had asked him to score it out of ten, but it was off the chart. In the winter, he'd been worried about getting frostbite down there. They rarely had enough credit to put the heating on, and the blistered skin was so tender, he couldn't even bear to cover his feet with a bedsheet. He'd told Jackie many times since she'd returned home, his quality of life was terrible.

Alfie slid back in the van's cab but left the door wide to let the air cool him while he tucked in. It would hopefully dry the sweat that poured from him these days whenever he ate anything warm. With a grunt, he reached over to the glove box and removed his salt and vinegar shakers. With a flick of the thumb, he popped open the takeaway container, rested it on his stomach, and covered the contents with both.

Alfie lifted a thick, heavy chip from the container and blew on it. With a sigh, he nibbled at it and blew out breaths as the sumptuous flavours hit his taste buds. Gazing seaward with the sun setting behind a bank of grey clouds, he enjoyed his brief moment of rapture while he could.

Alfie knew he wasn't long for this world. He'd known for

certain after he saw his medical notes contained an awful phrase. Imminent heart failure. Men like him didn't make old bones, so, overall, sixty-five seemed acceptable. His dad and brother had died in their mid-fifties.

If there was an afterlife and pearly gates, Alfie considered he had an outside chance of sneaking through them. He'd raised his grandsons and kept them and himself out of jail, which was more than his wife could say to either. Laws had been broken along life's journey. There'd even been a few women when Jackie first went away, but he hadn't strayed too far from the righteous path.

Chuckling to himself, Alfie struggled to remember when he last visited a church. Cousin Margot's wedding, probably, around the millennium. Perhaps he'd better put in another appearance, slip a few quid in the collection tray, like a backhander ahead of Judgement Day.

He reached into the glove box again and pulled out a set of metal cutlery. There was no point paying for quality fish and chips, which weren't cheap nowadays, then poking them to death with a small wooden fork.

Alfie's mind strayed to his wife. Jackie was back, and boy had he missed her, but she was much changed. She hadn't been an amiable woman at the best of times, but she'd come out of prison hardened, yet strangely lacking in confidence. Hopefully, she would calm down. Sometimes she stared at him, and he'd get goosebumps. Not the good kind, either.

At present, she was on a knife's edge, as though the violence of prison had been released at the same time, and, like an unwelcome cellmate, followed her home.

He supposed not wanting to visit busy places was natural after everything she'd gone through. Alfie, on the other hand, believed his job was done. These last few years had been tough health-wise, and he'd been hanging on until his wife returned and took over.

Alfie held on to the idea of heaven. He'd die happy if it meant seeing his son again. Barely a day went by without a memory blindsiding him, leaving him feeling as though someone had whipped away the ground he was walking on. Ten years Lennie had gone. Still no peace.

The part of Jackie that was most human had also died that night. Afterwards, she'd taken too many risks. A woman with little to lose. Sometimes Alfie wanted revenge, but how does the jackal kill the lion? Only with cunning or numbers, and Alfie was neither genius nor leader. It was Lennie who'd had the brains.

Alfie burned his lip on a fat chip as he grinned at the thought of Lennie aged six sitting on his knee in an armchair, reading out loud, then peering up at Alfie's proud face for confirmation, even when Alfie's reading was no longer good enough to check for mistakes.

Lennie would have known what to do, but he was dead. Alfie's wife's intelligence was a different beast. More the savage instinct of a cornered rat than the strength and stealth of a hyena, but she was a survivor. When she went to jail, it left the family with no one capable.

Alfie was placing the first bit of fluffy white cod into his mouth when he noticed someone striding towards his van. The sun had begun its final descent, lighting up the fairground in the distance and filling his windscreen with a burst of bright orange light, which cast the approaching figure into silhouette. Alfie squinted and was unable to distinguish if it was male or female.

They must be heading for him, because there was no other reason to make for this quiet corner of the yard. Maybe Alfie had forgotten his change. He closed his door so they could reach him.

Cursing, Alfie moved the container of food off his stomach to the passenger seat. If there was one thing he hated, it was an interruption to his eating.

Moving swiftly, the person scraped their coat as they slid between Alfie's wing mirror and the back fence to reach his window. They materialised beside him. Alfie's eyes widened when he recognised them. Without pause, they climbed up onto the van step, so they were at eye-level.

'What are you doing here?' he spluttered, bits of batter spraying over the dashboard.

His visitor raised a brown-gloved hand, which held a black handle. Before Alfie could make a sound, there was a solid click, and a dark blade leapt into view. He knew instantly it was no toy.

The last throes of light glinted off the steel and blinded him for a brief moment. Hot breath warmed his ear. Edging away as far as he could, a horrified Alfie glanced deep into the eyes of his assailant and found them devoid of questions or mercy. His face collapsed with the understanding there would be none of either.

It occurred to Alfie, as the hand drew back to strike, that he cared about dying, after all.

2

Detective Constables Barry Hooper and Hector Fade had been arguing and winding each other up all afternoon. They'd been through sport and cars, and Ashley suspected they were coming to the end of politics. Any *Guardian* or *Daily Mail* readers listening in would have been deeply insulted.

Ashley had smiled as DC Salvador Freitas slid his choice of newspaper into a desk when Hector started on the fascists who read it.

As far as she was concerned, the only subject left to fall out over was women. Barry, who reminded Ashley of Zac Efron, but squatter, and Hector, who resembled a tall Eddie Redmayne, would then, despite their good looks, both be out of their depths on the topic. Hector would know this, Barry would not.

It was always this way when it was quiet. Since the incidents on Cromer Beach two months ago, it had been a particularly peaceful period. Bhavini was off with a family problem, although strangely she hadn't shared the gritty details with Ashley, just mentioned it was serious and that it concerned her parents. The other two in the team, Jan and Emma, were at Suffolk HQ assisting with a hugely complex fraud case. Hector and Barry should have been in fabulous moods, having been saved any involvement.

Hector was in his early twenties on the Fast Track programme, and with them for just over six months. Barry was mid-thirties, experienced, and a typical example of male officers of that age. Hector had proven himself a cool, somewhat aloof character in his brief spell with them, but Barry's special power was being able to get under the skin of every single person on the planet, and probably most of the animals.

'So, hotshot,' said Barry. 'It's Friday night and what you up to? Warm cocoa with the parents? Bit of tennis with the butler? I suppose there isn't any point in you going out.'

'And why is that?'

'I heard through the grapevine you're a virgin.'

Ashley's fingers froze over her keyboard. Sal, who was in his mid-fifties and was as round as he was tall, reached into his drawer, retrieved his newspaper, and placed it over his head.

There'd been a drunken bonding session on a Sunday at The Wellington public house a few months back. Hector, being new, had found himself invited, despite it traditionally being women only. After a few drinks, those present had each shared a secret. Hector had surprised them all by saying he'd yet to have sex.

Ashley believed there had been an unwritten rule that day, where their revelations would go no further, but someone had blabbed.

Hector's already pale complexion paled further. Barry's grin widened upon realising he'd hit a home run. Hector rose from his seat.

'You seem to have an extremely healthy interest in my sex life. Some might say an unhealthy interest.'

Barry shook his head. 'I'd rather shag Sal.'

'I shall take that as a compliment,' replied Sal. 'You need to give me a couple of weeks' notice, though. I'll have to up the cod liver oil tablets to loosen my hips.'

Hector laughed, but his fists were clenched in front of him.

'My wife's celibate,' continued Sal, trying to ease the tension, 'which pretty much makes me the same way. We used to enjoy nookie before bed, then we had children, so we did it in the morning, until we adopted a dog, so we take it in turns to walk him instead.'

'Don't give me that bollocks,' said Barry. 'You've got five kids. I bet you're at it like nasty rabbits.'

Ashley was opening her mouth to restore order when DCI Vince Kettle hustled into the office.

'I'm glad you four haven't left yet,' he growled.

Ashley allowed herself a small grin as Barry's face fell. There went his Friday evening.

'We received a misper call this afternoon,' said Kettle, 'from a woman panicking. Her husband didn't return home last night and still hasn't shown. He's a delivery driver, so our call handler contacted the company he worked for, Stones Builders Merchants. They have GPS tracking on all their vans. The vehicle had spent eighteen hours in the car park of a fish and chip restaurant in Hunstanton. Our responder found him lifeless in the driver's seat.'

'I assume by your manner he hasn't had heart failure,' said Ashley.

'Kind of, but only after being stabbed.'

'Oh, dear. Does the wife know yet?'

'No, the officers on scene only just called it in. They're securing the area, but the victim's nearly twenty-four hours cold, so the perpetrator will be long gone.'

'Have they ID'd the victim?'

'Yes, that's the complication. It's Alfie Hook.'

The name didn't register with Hector, but Sal's, Barry's and Ashley's eyes widened. It was Sal who commented first.

'No way.'

Kettle nodded.

'Yep. The better half of Jackie Hook, who's only been out of prison for three months.'

3

Ashley realised Hector's blank expression was because he'd have been at school when the events happened. Considering what Jackie had done to a police officer, though, and the fact Hector's father had been high up in the Met, it was still a little surprising that he was unaware.

'She can't be out already,' said Barry. 'Didn't she get twenty years?'

'Yes,' said Kettle. 'But she received a quarter off for a guilty plea at the first stage of proceedings, which meant sixteen. That was a little over eight years ago, so she's served half and will be out on licence.'

'Wow,' replied Barry. 'I wonder what an eight-stretch has done to her. She wasn't too far off sixty when she went down.'

Ashley had still been in CID and involved with the case at the beginning as they'd closed in on Jackie's operation, but when they'd realised the volume of money and the scope of the crimes, the Major Investigation Team had taken over.

Jackie was a tough, aggressive woman. It seemed doubtful

prison would have mellowed her. Yet Ashley had got on okay with her because she was a realist and had a sense of humour.

Jackie's problem was she was an illogical person when it came to offending. Her actions damaged many people's lives, but Jackie considered it more or less okay because she was providing for her family. Simply put, she was a criminal through and through. Ashley believed people like Jackie deserved to be locked in the dark until they learned otherwise. Most of them died having never seen the light.

Would serious time under lock and key have got the message across to Jackie? Or would she return to the only career she knew the moment she arrived home, to make up for lost time?

'Who is this Jackie Hook?' asked Hector.

Kettle chuckled.

'Everyone in the force knew Jackie. She and her son were a crime wave in Hunstanton and surrounds. At one point, the commissioner reckoned their family was responsible for over half of all stolen goods in the area. She was active for decades.'

'And she evaded justice all that time?' asked Hector.

'No, she did a few short sentences, but she wasn't daft. Jackie the Hook, as she became known, used people she knew who would never drop her in it to deliver and store the goods. If anyone got caught, she paid them off and didn't use them again. In the same way county line operators use children to deal drugs nowadays, she later involved her grandsons and their friends, who were all sixteen and under. It was mostly electrical items, phones, consoles, and small-scale drug dealing, but, as things tend to do, they escalated.'

'I was in uniform at the time,' said Barry. 'I was first on the scene when we found her son's burned-out car in a field not far from Snettisham. Lennie and his girlfriend were sitting in the front seats.'

Kettle nodded.

'We still don't know exactly what happened, but we think the Hooks trod on the feet of a bigger operator. The family organisation fell apart without the son. The grandkids had to move in with Jackie and Alfie because both their parents died in the fire. Jackie either got careless or desperate when a traffic officer attempted to pull her over in a car shortly afterwards with nearly two hundred thousand pounds in cash in the boot and a pistol in the glove box.'

'Oh, God. Of course, I remember,' said Hector. 'She ran him over.'

Ashley shot from her seat as anger from the memories resurfaced.

'Jackie swore she tried to drive around Alan, who was a good copper. She made no comment on arrest, but after a week on remand, she asked to return to court. As I said, she was a practical person. Jackie pleaded guilty to death by dangerous driving and possession of a firearm. The money was confiscated.'

'Interesting,' said Sal. 'I'm not looking forward to seeing her again. So, who's going to the seaside?'

'Everyone,' growled Kettle.

Barry and Ashley grumbled good-naturedly. Hunstanton was over an hour away with reasonable traffic.

'I know,' said Kettle. 'Overtime should make it an easier pill to swallow, but, Ashley, I want your guys at the scene. There'll be support back here from the other teams. If Alfie and Jackie were selling stolen goods again, or were moving money or drugs, it'll have ramifications for crime all over North Norfolk. If Alfie's been killed, there could be a syndicate involved. This wants snuffing out before anything gets out of hand.'

'My money's on Jackie killing Alfie,' said Barry.

If it was a joke, Kettle didn't smile.

'Or it could have been someone he was dealing to,' said Ashley. 'You know the addicts sometimes turn up desperate with no money, then take what they need.'

'Give me the heads-up when you arrive,' said Kettle. 'Scott Gorton attended a course today and the other FLO is ill. This is Jackie Hook we're dealing with, so you'll have to deliver the news.'

Ashley was partly relieved and partly perturbed. She and Scott almost had a fling a few years back, but she'd pushed him away. She still felt they had a chance, but it never seemed the right time to explore it. He was brilliant at his job, though, and she enjoyed working with him.

'A death message to Jackie won't be a pleasant task,' said Sal. 'Are you sure we won't need armed officers?'

'I'll do it,' said Ashley. 'Hector can come with me. If I recall correctly, she had a thing for handsome young men.'

'That's reassuring,' said Hector as he grabbed his coat.

Ashley's mind was already whirring as they left the station. Kettle was right. This could have dangerous repercussions. At least travelling in the same vehicle, the detectives could discuss the case while they were en route.

What concerned Ashley most was the phrase Kettle had used about Jackie. He'd described her as panicking when she called in. Jackie just wasn't the type to panic.

Unless something had terrified her.

4

Sal Freitas booked a Volvo XC60 out and offered to drive. He had a nickname of The Freitas Trainus, which was based on his stature and the fact he was slow and steady in most facets of life, apart from his driving. His diligent nature was more suited to the office, but he enjoyed stretching his limbs every once in a while, and he was also one of the few detectives who kept his driving qualifications current.

'I remember reading up on the Jackie Hook case,' he said as he pulled away. 'But it was a done deal, and her plea kept the gory details out of court. So, it could only have been one of two things.'

'Spell it out for Hector, please,' said Ashley.

'Sure. Jackie's old school, so highly unlikely to grass, but when you're found with a huge quantity of money and a gun, the sentence is going to be significant, which loosens most tongues. Jackie didn't flinch and took a cool week to think about it. So, it was either her cash, which is doubtful, or the person she was moving it for wasn't the kind you upset.'

'Had to be the latter,' said Ashley.

'Agreed,' replied Barry. 'Her son and his partner were already dead, so unless she fancied a similar fate, she didn't have a choice. If someone super rich really wants you taken out, you've had it. You can't run, and you can't hide. With such a big piece of bird, she'd end up with lifers. Most have little to lose, and someone always takes the money.'

'So, Jackie took the fall,' said Sal. 'Pleaded guilty and threw herself on the court's mercy. She was late with her plea, so didn't get the full third off, but any discount is a chunk when you're talking decades.'

'Couldn't she have got witness protection?' asked Hector.

Barry chuckled. 'People like Jackie don't trust that sort of deal, and it doesn't appeal, anyway. They want to stay in their own communities.'

'It'll be interesting to see what happened to the rest of the family while she was inside,' said Ashley. 'If they aren't on hard times, it's probably the person Jackie didn't mention who kept them sweet for her staying shtum.'

'I suppose eight years served isn't too bad. A life sentence must have been on the cards,' said Hector.

'The papers were calling her a cop killer,' said Barry. 'But the judge's hands were tied because there was no prior planning or obvious intent, and she stopped after she'd run him over and rang for an ambulance. The judge slammed her by giving her a consecutive sentence for the handgun.'

Barry and Hector settled into discussing the Hooks' history as they drove. Ashley had something else to say on the topic, but wondered if Hector would come up with it. He'd only been with them for two months, but he missed little. They were on the outskirts of Hunstanton at 7 p.m. when he twigged.

'If the massive haul of cash wasn't hers, whose was it? Someone would be furious.'

'Exactly,' said Ashley.

'Is there a main gang who control the trade in the area?'

'That was the two-hundred-thousand-pound question. Back then we suspected a Betty Brown of running a considerable number of growing rooms in Norfolk rentals, as well as farm buildings, but again, nothing connected to her. We had all sorts of finds. Vietnamese immigrants were commonly brought over and forced to cultivate crops for years to work off the cost of being smuggled into the country.'

'So, you think it was her cash in Jackie's van, and Jackie decided upsetting this Betty Brown was a risk too far.'

'We simply don't know. There were rumours of VAT fraud and corporate embezzlement, even contract killings. As far as I'm aware, we haven't heard another thing about Betty Brown since, although most of the drug cases tend to be dealt with by Ally Williamson's team. We can check with him after we find out what we're dealing with.'

'Okay,' said Hector. 'I've never been to Hunstanton before. What's it like?'

'You've really missed out,' said Barry.

'Didn't you grow up here, Sal?' asked Ashley.

'Yep. If you can believe it, I attended the same school as Betty Brown. She was two years above me, but she was a real trouble-maker, even then. My parents still live in Old Hunstanton, so I return a lot. I guess you could say people either love or hate Sunny Hunny.'

'Or Peterborough-by-the-sea.' Ashley laughed.

'I went on a training course recently in Peterborough run by an Inspector Barton. He was a top bloke. When I told him I came from Hunstanton, that's what he called it. It's only an hour or so from Peterborough, so it's their closest seaside resort and gets a lot of day-trippers and caravanners.'

'Sunny Hunny's non-holiday population is similar to

Cromer's,' said Ashley. 'But Hunstanton is a bit more kiss-me-quick hats and donkey rides on the sand. It also has a Sea Life centre and a decent fairground.'

'I'm not surprised I haven't been for a visit,' said Hector.

'Snob,' said Barry.

'I love donkeys,' said Sal.

'Maybe we could buy Barry a straw hat,' said Hector. 'Take him to the beach and make a few quid.'

'Ha ha,' said Barry as the others laughed.

'If you've got young kids,' said Sal, 'it's a good day out. The beach isn't great, but Old Hunstanton further up is dog friendly and has a fabulous wide sandy stretch, so the area caters for everyone as long as you know where to go. I love it for nostalgic reasons, which I think is half the pleasure for many who return.'

'I'm not sure if someone your age will enjoy what I enjoy most about Hunstanton, Hector,' said Ashley.

'Okay, what's that?'

'It's the sunsets. Cromer's hard to beat for sunrises, but Hunstanton is one of the few resorts in Norfolk that face west across The Wash, so on a cloudless day the sun sets over the sea. It's like watching a golden ball light up the horizon, then plunge straight down into the water.'

'Can't twenty-four-year-olds enjoy that?'

Ashley smiled.

'Maybe. I guess I wasn't bothered about them when I was your age, but as I get older, I find their beauty inspiring and de-stressing. A good sunset slows down time.'

Barry chuckled from the back. 'Sick bag, anyone?'

'How about you, Barry?' asked Sal. 'Enjoy a nice sunset?'

'I'd prefer a football match.'

Sal took the roundabout that led into Hunstanton at speed. The road sloped downwards, so the caravan parks, seafront and fairground appeared below them. Raindrops pattered against the windscreen. Thick grey clouds filled an ominous sky as far as the eye could see. Above the waves, heavy rain was falling.

'It's supposed to be hot on Sunday,' said Sal.

Ashley wasn't listening because they'd reached the turning for the car park next to Vegas Fish Bar. A uniformed PC held his hand up to stop them entering the busy crime scene, which was lit up by the flashing lights of the emergency services. Ashley got out of the car and showed her warrant card.

'DS Ashley Knight,' she said.

'Park further along, please, then you can walk in,' he replied.

It had been obvious to Ashley straight away that things here didn't add up. Why wait until the afternoon of the next day to report a man in his sixties missing? Why wasn't the delivery company more concerned if they could track his vehicle and saw it was parked in a public car park? How come nobody noticed the body for nearly a day?

Whenever there were so many unanswered questions, Ashley always suspected the danger was far from over.

5

Ashley was familiar with the row of businesses next to the car park, having been in most of them. They included a chip shop, an ice-cream parlour and two big arcades.

She remembered Alfie's fondness for food, so there were no prizes for guessing which he'd come for.

'Barry, have a word with the staff in the chippy, please,' she said as Sal parked up in front of the first arcade and they got out.

'Yes, Sarge.'

Ashley, Sal and Hector approached the outer cordon again, gave their names to be recorded, ducked under the tape and walked up the path. There was an inner cordon separating off most of the car park, making a corridor to what Ashley guessed would normally be an undercover eating area, but was now filled with police and CSI. Ashley recognised the crime scene manager, who Barry had nicknamed Dracula due to his looks: stooped, dyed black hair and pasty. It also meant Ashley struggled to recall his actual name. A uniformed sergeant called Frank Levine was present. She strode over to them.

'Hi, Ash,' said Frank. 'Come to take over?'

'We're mostly here for the sea air. You know Sal. Barry popped in the chip shop, and this is DC Hector Fade. He's here to learn. Hector, do you remember the crime scene manager from Cromer beach?'

'Of course. Hello again, Gerald,' said Hector, shaking his hand.

'Pleasure,' said Gerald.

Frank gave Ashley a smile. He was pushing fifty and knew the job backwards. Frank would recognise a youngster in MIT on the Fast Track, but he also understood everyone needed to learn. He shook Hector's hand.

'Welcome to Hunstanton,' said Frank. 'How long you been in?'

'Good to meet you. It'll be two years in November,' replied Hector. 'Who discovered the body?'

Frank's eyes crinkled.

'I like a man who's all business. You're in luck because it was me. We were told about the misper and that the van was here. I drove over suspecting a crime scene and approached the vehicle from the front. The windows were down, so I popped gloves on and opened the passenger door. Mr Hook, whom I know from old, smelled very dead. I gave him a poke, and he was stiff.'

'Hector. Do we need a pathologist to attend to tell us approximately how long Alfie Hook's been deceased?' asked Ashley.

'I might need reminding,' said Sal.

'Over eight hours, but less than thirty-six,' replied Hector, having remembered their force's pathologist, Michelle, telling him that during his first post-mortem.

Ashley slipped into full detective mode. Even though Hector was learning fast, she still spoke aloud for his benefit.

'Many murders are assaults gone too far, but this doesn't sound like that. It's doubtful the perpetrator is nearby, but it's still probable they were acquainted with each other. The deceased is married to a known criminal who was tardy in reporting him missing, so that's where we'll head next.'

She glanced at Gerald.

'How long to process the scene?'

He gestured to the large car park.

'Most of the night. Luckily, due to Frank's quick thinking, the location was preserved and might still have secrets to give up, but it's a car park which has had twenty-four hours of visitors, so we'll see. I can send you a picture of the victim if you want, save you from approaching him. The doctor has been and gone. He had a peek at Alfie's NHS notes. The guy was walking dead. He had more problems under his bonnet than a Robin Reliant. We'd be ticking boxes on forms and going home early if it wasn't for the small puncture wound in his chest.'

'Single?'

'Yes, under the ribs. As you were hinting at earlier, it seems clinical. No murder weapon found. Nothing obvious for us to focus on, either. There are fingerprints on the windows of the van, so those are a possibility.'

'The body's not been moved?' asked Hector.

Frank and Gerald chuckled and shook their heads.

'Alfie Hook's a large man,' said Frank. 'Even Hercules wouldn't stand a chance.'

'He'd only touched the fish, so that gives you a great focus for your time of death,' said Gerald. 'He didn't seem the type to order and not eat pretty quickly.'

Ashley glanced around the area. The covered eating section needed a lick of paint, and the ground was worn with broken tarmac. There were no CCTV cameras she could see or any overlooking properties.

Normally a uniformed officer would give the deceased's relatives the news if there was no FLO, but not for Jackie Hook.

'Okay, Sal. You carry on here. Barry, Hector and I will visit Alfie's wife.'

'I'll ask the guys to check for doorbell cams in the surrounding streets, but I doubt we'll get much from the area,' he replied. 'There's a massive car park over the road and another caravan site, so hardly any residential housing.'

'Great,' said Ashley. 'Let's hope the amusement arcades have cameras looking out onto the street, or the chip shop does. The suspect could have walked past either.'

Frank cleared his throat.

'I hope I'm not stating the obvious, but there are four large caravan parks around here, all within a five-minute walk, all full of people who are arriving and leaving. There's a rotating cast of thousands, so time is important.'

Ashley looked down the side of the van. PSST! Bricks was painted on as a company logo.

'Brilliant,' said Ashley. 'We've only been here ten minutes, and I'm already concerned. Frank, ask your guys to knock on any residence, including caravans, which look over this part of South Beach Road. Ask them about this van. It's likely they'll remember it. Perhaps they'll recall other details from the same time. I'll let Kettle decide if he wants the cost of a full search team, but I assume he'll wait until we hear what Alfie's wife has to say.'

'The murderer might have been in the van with him,' said Hector. 'Co-worker, maybe.'

'True. I'll see if we have a contact for the delivery company while you're gone,' said Sal. 'Ask what kind of employee he was, where he was delivering to, was he alone, and so on.'

'Excellent. Frank, you're local. Are the Hooks back up to no good?'

'Alfie hasn't been heard of since Jackie went away. For a while after she was banged up, the streets here were full of desperate addicts who couldn't buy what they needed, which proves Jackie was dealing locally, but Alfie never picked the business up.'

'Did Betty Brown leave town as well?'

'Gone legit, apparently. Not a peep from her, either.'

Barry sauntered over, yanking a large paper package from inside a white plastic bag, and started to unravel it while he spoke.

'The owner confirmed he knew the guy and served him last night. Said he was one of his best customers.'

'What about Alfie's vehicle being left overnight?' asked Ashley.

'Joe said Alfie often slept in his van here.'

'CCTV?'

'Yes, but only pointing at the counter. I've asked for it, just in case. He told me it was quiet last night. And no, he can't think of anyone memorable who might be involved.'

'I don't suppose Joe's the murdering type,' said Hector.

'Nope. He's beside himself. Really devastated, as are his staff.'

Barry had opened his chips by that point and stuffed one in his mouth as they all stared at him. Steam came from his haul, bringing a divine aroma.

'What?' said Barry. 'He insisted, and I got a big portion.'

Ashley smiled at Hector, who was curling his top lip at what he no doubt perceived as Barry's lack of professionalism, but she and Sal moved next to Barry to help themselves.

It was going to be a long night.

6

Ashley, Hector and Barry returned to their vehicle knowing it was blindingly obvious they were likely to struggle for witnesses. Alfie had been dead in a public car park for nearly twenty-four hours, and, apart from his wife reporting it the next day, nobody had contacted the police. Ashley rang Kettle and he agreed to sign off a press release that night to ask for people to come forward if they'd seen anything suspicious.

Even though Sal had booked the car, they were all insured to drive, so Barry took over after Hector had confirmed Jackie Hook's address. It was only a five-minute drive to Willow Road, which was one of the less expensive parts of town. The house was a standard three-bed end-of terrace council house. It was still only eight o'clock, and, despite the weather, the lounge windows were open. A light was on upstairs. The battered Vauxhall Astra on the drive had a smashed passenger window, which had been covered with a black bin bag.

'Before we head in,' said Ashley, 'let's have a think. Guilty or not, Jackie's just lost her husband. If I remember right from her trial, she was caring for her son's two boys. They were sixteen or so at the time and involved in the family business, so they might be here and are now grown men. I'm not sure what to expect when we arrive, so let's go easy and see what she says.'

'Jackie hates me,' said Barry. 'I nicked her son a few times before he died, and she always gave him an alibi, even if it was a blatant lie.'

Ashley smiled. There was no love like a mother's love, even in the face of solid evidence.

'What were her children like?' asked Hector.

'Jackie only had that lad,' replied Barry. 'If you mean the grandkids, they weren't what you'd expect. A lot of these street kids are tough, wise beyond their years, heartless and quick to anger. These two were kind of flabby and docile. I suspect they were just doing what Dad and Granny told them. They wouldn't have the nous to run anything themselves so that's probably why we haven't heard from them since.'

'So,' said Ashley. 'Jackie's been in jail for eight years after losing her son, and now her husband. Compassion and calm are needed, at least at the beginning. Stay in the car, Barry, and join us after ten minutes.'

Barry nodded and checked the time on his phone. Like Jackie, he was also a realist and knew his presence might not help at first.

Ashley and Hector left the vehicle and walked up the path, which was the tidiest bit of an otherwise unloved front garden. Ashley rang the doorbell.

As they waited, Hector couldn't stop himself from having a little dig at Barry.

'It makes sense not to bring Barry in,' said Hector.

'You might not believe it, but DCI Kettle told me Barry was considered quite modern when he first joined up. That was nearly fifteen years ago. Woke wasn't even in the dictionary, but life is a conveyor belt. If you stick around for a while, Hector, soon enough the new recruits will be laughing behind your back and calling you a Stegosaurus, while sniggering or cringing at your outdated clothes and views. That's simply the way it was, is, and always will be. You're just too young to know it yet.'

Ashley watched Hector's response to her comment. When he first arrived, he'd have taken the bait, but he was learning. Hector even ignored the jibe about hanging around long enough, which was directed at him having mentioned a job offer in the private sector. He had until the end of October to decide.

'Aren't you worried Barry will mess up an investigation with his attitude?' he asked.

'As I've said before, this is a game we're playing. Nobody confesses when we show our faces at the door, whether we're polite or rude. We need to unsettle people. Knock them out of their comfort zones, make them annoyed even. Others we use sweet talk and humour. Remember, if you kill someone and are found guilty of murder, the judge has no option other than to impose a life sentence, whether you've admitted to it or not. You might as well have a go at evading justice.'

Jackie had been a large, bouncy, forceful woman. Ashley almost didn't recognise the slim old lady who opened the door. Jail must have agreed with her in that regard, whether that was time spent in the prison gym or just the lack of junk food and booze. She still had the eighties frizzy dirty-blonde hair, but that was it. Her red eyes rested on Hector for a second, then her gaze strayed to Ashley. Jackie raised an eyebrow, and Ashley nodded.

Jackie's chin wobbled as she put a hand to the wall. She turned and lurched away, leaving the door wide.

Ashley followed her in. She immediately sensed the heavy stillness of a home waiting for the imminent arrival of devastating news.

Ashley found herself in a reasonable-sized lounge with an

enormous TV on the wall. Jackie sat looking insignificant on the sofa with her head in her hands. The other two occupants must have been the grandchildren, but they'd grown and filled the armchairs they were in. Hooded eyes switched from the TV to see who'd turned up. One of them picked up the remote, but only muted the set as opposed to turning it off. Jackie glanced up.

'Where?' she whispered.

'I'm afraid he was discovered in his van behind Vegas Fish Bar. He was dead in the driver's seat.'

'Bloody twat. I said that place would kill him.'

Ashley knew Jackie's family had moved from Ireland to Canada, then to Norfolk, so she had an unusual accent. For a moment, Ashley wondered if she meant *plaice*.

Ashley suspected these boys hadn't attained their troll-like proportions by eating too much fruit and veg, either. Ashley tried to check Jackie's expression, but her head was back in her hands. Was she playing, or did she really believe her husband had died from natural causes?

Hector walked past them all and stood at a doorway through which Ashley could see a kitchen.

'Tea, anyone?' he asked.

'At least he hung on until I got out,' said Jackie, shaking her head at him. 'Silly sod, never did look after himself.'

'Mrs Hook,' said Ashley. 'We think Alfie was murdered.'

7

Jackie slowly stood and pulled her hands away from her face, which was a storm of emotions. There was shock, sadness and anger, and possibly blame there. Ashley walked over to Jackie, who trembled as though she might collapse, and gently held her upper arms. She let Jackie pull her into a hug.

Ashley peered over Jackie's thin shoulders at the boys, but their expressions had hardly changed. These young men had experienced tough upbringings and lost both parents. Perhaps the blows no longer had any impact. Ashley half expected them to put the sound on the TV back up.

There was plenty in the rulebook on how to give news like this, but dealing with people was never straightforward. Ashley rarely hugged her friends, but this woman had lost her life partner.

Jackie recovered fast.

'Who? Who's fucking murdered my Alfie?'

'Please try to stay calm. That's why we're here,' said Ashley. 'To find out what happened.'

Jackie's immediate route out of her pain was rage.

'That's your job. Do it!'

'Jackie, please take a seat.'

Jackie, still bristling, sat down. Ashley perched on the sofa next to her, then nodded at Hector, who took his pocketbook out.

'Look, Jackie, you were away for a long stretch, so Alfie kept his nose clean. These boys appear well cared for, and they're off our radar. We want to find out who did this as much as you do, but we know little about Alfie's recent life, so we need you to tell us.'

Jackie visibly wilted at the thought of being honest with the police.

'Nah, I can't do that. Goes against everything I believe in. I'll sort it.'

'That's great. You're on probation for another eight years. One step out of line and you'll be serving the rest of your sentence inside. Who'll care for these lads?'

Jackie glanced across at Ashley, then at her grandchildren.

'Lazy fuckers could find jobs.'

Ashley smiled. 'Come on. Tell me what Alfie's been involved in.'

Jackie's face twisted in pain. 'Nope, can't do it.'

Barry chose a good moment to enter the house. Jackie recovered her prickly nature in seconds.

'I remember you, Barry. Just when I thought today couldn't get any worse, you arrive.'

'It's nice to see you too, Jackie. We're here to help.'

'Fat chance you've got of nicking anyone.'

'Nicked you and yours, didn't I?'

'Pinned it on us, more like. Here to arrest me again, are ya?'

Barry held her gaze. 'Everyone's a suspect at the start, you know that. Do we need to look at a copy of his will?'

Jackie couldn't help herself. 'Alfie invested for our futures all right, but mostly on slow horses.'

Barry's eyes wandered over to the two youngsters, who still hadn't moved. He kept a straight face.

'I love what you've done with the boys. Is taxidermy expensive nowadays?'

'Piss off, Barry,' said Jackie, but there was the ghost of a smile. 'I ain't got nothing to say to you.'

'Worried about what the neighbours might think?'

'Too right.'

'It'd be a shame if I had to return in a marked vehicle with a huge grin on my face. Perhaps come out laughing afterwards, shouting thanks for your help.'

Jackie's eyes became flinty.

'My Alfie was clean. He kept these two out of jail. He was a hero. Had to raise them on his own. I have total respect for him keeping this family together. He had to go straight, and so did they. Our criminal days are over.' She jutted out her chin. 'It's me and the boys now. We've lost everything, but we'll fight on.'

Ashley was smiling inside at the charade playing out in front of her. Barry was brilliant at dealing with people like Jackie. He understood them. She suspected Barry's upbringing had been on rough streets, although he rarely mentioned his family.

'Was Alfie involved with anything dodgy at all while you were gone?' she asked. 'He needed to keep putting food on the table. The odd bit of easy money would have come in handy.'

'I told ya. Straight as a die, he was. Alfie couldn't risk going away himself with me not being here. I was lucky to have a man like that. Few would've stepped up the way he did.'

'Why did you wait so long to report him missing?'

'It wouldn't be the first time he'd nodded off in his van.'

'Was it the company vans he slept in?' asked Hector.

'Yes. There's two. A blue and a red. Both with PSST! on the side.'

'We found him in the red one.'

Jackie shrugged. 'He had a bike to get to the warehouse. If you try to imagine the exact opposite of Lance Armstrong, that was Alfie, so he often brought home whichever van he was in.'

Ashley nodded. 'This is obviously the beginning of the investigation. Is there anything else you'd like to make us aware of at this point?'

Jackie shook her head while avoiding eye contact.

'Jackie. A family liaison officer will be appointed to you. They'll be in touch tomorrow. If you give me a mobile number, he can arrange a visit to Alfie at the mortuary.'

Jackie told them her phone number in a monotone.

'I can't believe he's gone. It doesn't feel real.'

They questioned her for a bit longer, but she'd slipped into a distant state and Ashley knew there was no point in continuing.

'We're going to head off,' she said, rising from her seat.

Hector stopped in front of Jackie on his way out.

'I'm sorry for your loss.'

Jackie smiled up at him. 'You seem a good lad. Don't finish up like them others.'

Ashley took in the room for a moment. The sofa was in an acceptable condition, and the TV was high end, but the curtains and carpet weren't up to much. It was spotlessly clean, though, and probably would have smelled that way if it weren't for the stale smoke. Folk like Jackie were bundles of contradictions. Ashley suspected even they were confused by the criminal code.

Jackie had sat back down and finally seemed to take in that Alfie was gone. Barry beat Ashley to what she was going to ask.

'Do you still hear from Betty Brown?'

Jackie's head snapped up, her mouth split into what could have been a smile or a grimace. 'You always were sneaky, Barry.'

'It's a delightful place you have,' he replied. 'Your family were clearly looked after whilst you were away, so your sacrifice wasn't in vain.'

'Get out, you lot,' she said, getting to her feet swifter than Ashley would have expected. Jackie's eyes flashed. 'This is all ours. Alfie had to fight for it. He grafted.'

Barry coughed.

'Doesn't it pay to keep your mouth shut?' he asked.

Jackie bared her teeth.

'That fucking bitch left my family on life support.'

8

The team returned to the car and began the drive back to Vegas's car park.

'What do you reckon, guys?' asked Ashley.

'I think that proves who owned the two hundred grand Jackie got caught with,' said Hector.

'I meant about whether she had anything to do with Alfie's death.'

'You can't trust a word out of that woman's mouth,' said Barry. 'As for Dumb and Dumber on the armchairs, they're barely capable of independent thought.'

'Succinctly put,' said Hector. 'I detected genuine remorse, but she was erratic. I must say I haven't had loads of experience with that sort of person.'

'Do you mean someone without a trust fund?'

Hector ignored him. 'What were this Alfie Hook and the son who died like?'

Ashley left Barry to answer. He'd worked the area longer than her and had been involved with the family for the years when they were active.

'Those grandkids' brains came from Alfie. Their father, Lennie, inherited Jackie's nous, her lack of morals, and her thirst for money. Lennie was also as aggressive as Jackie used to be, but more physical.'

'That's right. He had a rep for being hard as nails,' said Ashley.

'But he was smarter than Jackie and had bigger plans,' said Barry. 'I bet it was him that caused them problems by expanding their operation, which ended up with him and his girlfriend getting smoked.'

'Charming,' said Hector. 'So, this Betty Brown was suspected of owning the money Jackie had on her. Surely it wasn't her who organised the hit that took out Lennie.'

'Rumours abounded. One was that Betty Brown did it.'

'That makes no sense,' said Hector. 'Why knock out the son, then still work with the mother?'

'We're not dealing with normal people here,' said Ashley. 'They're ruthless and amoral. They steal children's bikes. Take from the vulnerable. Burgle old folks' bungalows. Betty could have done it to make Jackie desperate, so she would work for her, believing Jackie would never find out.'

'We'll probably never know,' said Barry. 'MIT took the case, and I've not heard a dickie bird since. Ally Williamson had just started in MIT, so he might know, but I don't think she's resurfaced. Maybe Betty realised how close she was to going down for decades and retired on what she had.'

'Not many of Betty's type can accept the loss of that amount of money,' said Ashley. 'If she retired, she'd have more time to stew over it.'

They pulled up at the murder scene. The arcades and fish shop were shut, and the flashing blue lights had gone.

'You two, find Sal,' said Ashley. 'I'll call Kettle.'

Vince Kettle had worked his way through the ranks to DCI but was still known as Kettle to everyone, even his boss, Detective Superintendent Zara Grave. He would have been a DI when Jackie was sent down. He picked up on the second ring, and she updated him.

'Did CSI find anything obvious?' he asked.

'Nope, Gerald or Sal would have called me.'

'What's your plan?'

'We'll do what we can here while you get the wheels in motion back at OCC, then we can call it a night, but I want to return tomorrow morning with Barry and Hector. I'd like a chat with this Betty Brown. She's a link in all this, even if just a cold one.'

'I haven't heard that name in a while. She shacked up with a guy by the name of Abraham Englebert who owns farmland close to where you are. Rich as hell.'

'I assume she was questioned at the time?'

'Of course. We had nothing, though, and she lawyered up.'

'What about other drug outfits in the vicinity?'

'Ally Williamson's team deal with most of those cases. I'll send him a message to expect a call from you in the morning, but the drugs market in Hunstanton has been fragmented for years, so I wouldn't pin your hopes on it.'

'Okay. Sal and Jan can visit Stones Builders Merchants tomorrow. That might give us an angle because the van wasn't Alfie's. Sal can check the route he took and get a feel for whether they're legit. To be honest, we don't have much at this point.'

'Do you need a door-knocking team?'

'It depends on whether you want to knock on thousands of caravans.'

'I'd rather not. Speak to Betty Brown and the van company. Michelle offered to do the post-mortem first thing tomorrow. We'll have a meeting here at midday and set up the incident room.'

'Make it 1 p.m. Hunstanton's an hour away, remember?'

Ashley cut the call as Barry, Sal and Hector returned with glum faces and got in the car.

'No joy?' asked Ashley.

Sal shook his head.

'Gerald's found a few partial footprints, but little else. The fingerprints will be run tomorrow, and the PM might help, but there was nothing immediately helpful. Gerald has taken samples from the back of the van, which resembled dusty grass cuttings, but he said it could be a different type of grass. Other than a few boxes of tiles, it was empty.'

'Interesting. He'll be able to test for cannabis in the morning, too. We'll do the necessary here, then get home and be fresh tomorrow.'

'There goes our weekend,' said Barry. 'The women of Norwich will be devastated when Hoops doesn't turn up.'

Hector caught Ashley's eye and smiled. 'Surely the anticipation is half the fun,' he said. 'The ladies of Norfolk will just be keener when they see you next.'

'You're probably right,' replied Barry, deadpan.

Two hours later, Sal took the driver's seat and drove them out through the dark streets.

'I had a good chat with Joe at the fish shop,' he said. 'He seemed a really friendly chap. He's known Alfie a long time. Alfie sold him a reconditioned iPhone once, which lasted two weeks, but other than that he spoke highly of him.'

'When was that?'

'A few months ago.'

Ashley's mind ticked over. At the least there was some criminality. Would Jackie have been aware of what Alfie was up to? Yes, she decided.

'Did you ask him about drugs in the area?'

'I asked him about the scene in Hunstanton. He runs a chippy, so he sees a lot of those with the munchies. There are quite a few potheads, the odd heroin addict who begs outside for money, but that's it.'

'I suppose it's not the kind of place for a rave club or fancy cocaine bar.'

'Perhaps the suspect brought Alfie here and killed him after they'd parked up,' said Hector.

'But thought he'd allow Alfie a final bit of battered fish as his last meal,' said Barry.

'Oh, yeah, sorry.' Hector laughed. 'It appears I'm past my best.'

'No, that's possible. Alfie would have been distracted by his meal,' said Sal.

'We'll have clearer heads tomorrow,' said Ashley. 'Screw the fraud case. We need Jan and Emma back. If Barry, Hector and I visit Betty first thing, Sal, you take Jan, and grill Alfie's manager at the builders' merchants. Any other thoughts from spending time at the scene?'

'I don't see this as a desperate theft. It was the end of the day, and the van was likely to be empty. This is hardcore. A single stab to the heart, no witnesses. It seems as if a spirit appeared, knifed him, then vanished.'

They drove back in silence. Most detectives need peace and quiet to organise their thinking. Sal dropped Ashley off in Cromer at her address on Mill Road. She was beat. Lately, she'd been putting her life back together after a series of blows, and things were improving.

Working with Hector had helped. He had unusual ways and thought processes, but perhaps because of that she'd found it easy to open up to him.

Ashley was also focusing on her health, now she was approaching her mid-forties, so she ignored the lure of a glass of wine and made herself a salmon sandwich. It barely hit the spot, so she went to bed to stop herself eating anything else.

As she lay down, Ashley's mind kept drifting back to the murder. People were rarely killed for no reason, so it raised one question.

Who gained from Alfie's demise?

9

OVER FORTY YEARS AGO, TEXAS

The young man lurched out of the bushes on stiff legs. He hadn't seen a soul for two hours, so the omens were good, and few ventured out at dawn on such grim days. Old Cliff Stanley would, though. He'd visited every morning for the past week. It seemed spending time on his boat first thing, drinking coffee, watching seabirds and tinkering were his simple pleasures. Cliff's poisons to cope with life's worries were mild.

The youth glanced around him. A few of the other boats had lights on, but the curtains were drawn, as they had been at dawn yesterday. It was now or never, and he pulled the brim of the Stetson, purchased at a thrift shop the previous day, further down his forehead. The damp collar on his windcheater chafed his cheeks as he strode forward.

Lifeless grey clouds drooped overhead. Speckles of rain drifted in the breeze. He reached Emerald Bay's furthest jetty and noted movement on Cliff's motor yacht, which had pride of place on the final mooring.

His boots tapped out a rhythm on the wooden surface as he ambled towards the boat. Consequences tugged at his resolve.

Told him to go home. A smile threatened on his face, but instead a scowl formed. To think he imagined himself a cowboy, striding to confront a wicked man, right hand hovering at his side.

His hand was at his side, but it was holding the carrier bag they gave him when he bought the hat. There was nothing cool about this.

No smoking guns, no pale riders, no damsels in distress. Simply hard business.

It would have helped if Cliff were a terrible person, but the biggest insult proffered when he'd asked around was that Cliff was ornery. Did that crime fit the punishment?

Yet, the boat was new. The ranch where Cliff lived hollered luxury to all who approached. He clung to the fact that Cliff must have done something wrong for them to have sent him.

As he neared the end of the jetty, the youngster forced himself to put on the rolling gait he'd used around the place when getting background on Cliff, even though half of him wanted to sprint the other way. A few people had stared at him, but he'd been nonchalant enough.

What was bugging this cowboy was who had bought his own debt? His poison had always been poker. Owing a losing hand to crooks in Wyoming was hardly good news, but they'd been letting him pay the interest off with local jobs. None of which had so far needed violence. There had been no prospect of him clearing the actual loss, though, which had kept him worried.

Maybe this task had been on the cards the whole time because the Wyoming crew had told him that his slate would be clean upon completion. Then he was to leave town. Perhaps the game had been rigged.

He'd politely declined the offer of this job, but they'd explained he didn't have that luxury. Judging by the concerned looks on those tough men's faces, they'd been given no choice, either. Now he was at the boat, his options were gone. The time for decisions was over. Only action remained.

'Excuse me, sir. How are you today?' he asked the man's back.

Cliff turned slowly; his tired face twisted into half a smile.

'Old and cold, but it's invigorating out here. As always.'

'I'm headed up the coast this afternoon. Do you know these waters well?'

'Sure do, and it's a dark day with a shifting forecast.'

'I don't want to take any unnecessary risks.'

Cliff nodded.

'Seventy years I've sailed these beaches. Hop on and have a coffee. I'll give you the lowdown.'

The man in the Stetson stepped onboard. When Cliff turned to lead the way, his guest slipped the rolling pin from his carrier bag and clonked Cliff around the top of his head. Not too hard. He didn't want to kill him.

Cliff staggered towards the side of the boat. The cowboy gave him a firm shove, and the old guy toppled over. Cliff made no sound, nor did he struggle. He just sank out of sight.

The murderer tried to imagine he was returning his weapon to its holster as he strode back along the jetty, but he'd committed a terrible sin, from which there would be no going back. The black stain on his heart would never leave.

That day, he knew, two lives had been destroyed.

10

PRESENT DAY

At 6 a.m. Ashley woke naturally. She could hear the rain tapping on the window, but she wouldn't let that put her off exercising. That was until she stepped out of the front door and saw water bouncing off the pavement. She was about to retreat when her neighbour's door opened. Ashley recognised the paramedic who was leaving and stepped out under the porch as concern for her elderly neighbour hit her.

'Morning, Joan,' shouted Ashley, arching her neck to peer up the road for the ambulance. 'Is Arthur okay?'

'Yes, he's fine. Gotta fly. I fell asleep on his sofa after some amazing port and Stilton.'

Ashley noticed Joan had casual clothes under her waterproof work coat. For a woman in her early sixties, she soon scampered away. Just before Joan was out of sight, she stopped and waved back at Ashley. Ashley realised Arthur, who was in his early seventies, had come out of his house. He was the intended recipient of the wave.

'Beautiful morning,' he said with a contented smile, before closing his door.

Ashley suspected wine and cheese were the last things they were remembering from the previous evening.

She went back inside, took a slow shower, and tidied the house while waiting for Hector and Barry to arrive. Hector lived nearer Norwich, so he'd offered to pick up a pool car, then collect Barry in Sidestrand, which was about three miles from Cromer, and then head to Ashley's. Barry knocked on her door looking like a drowned rat.

'Did you swim here?' she asked as they got into the Audi that Hector had collected.

'My street's full of parked cars, so I came out to the end to save Hector any hassle. He was late.'

'By thirty seconds,' said Hector.

Ashley hoped these two weren't going to make it a long drive. Norfolk's roads were mostly single lane, so leaving early was better than getting stuck in traffic or behind a procession of farm vehicles. She decided to make a few calls. First up was the family liaison officer, Scott 'Flash' Gorton.

'Scott speaking.'

'Hi, Flash. Barry, Hector and I are on our way to see Betty Brown. Just giving you the heads-up on your call to Jackie Hook this morning. You obviously know Jackie, but I thought I'd say be on your toes.'

'Yes, I do. I assume she won't want me there.'

'Alfie dying won't have helped her demeanour, but time inside seems to have taken the wind out of her sails. My nose is twitching at something, though.'

'Sounds like Barry's let some wind out of his sails.'

'That's certainly possible.'

'Okay. It seems a push to think Jackie would be involved. Maybe Betty's back on the scene, although I haven't heard of her in years.'

'The case is wide open, but there might be an organised crime angle.'

'Okay, I'll see what's what with the Hooks.'

Ashley finished the call.

'I saw Flash out with a real beauty last weekend,' said Barry. 'He's about your age, isn't he, Ashley? His date looked about thirty, so he was swaggering. Assuming, of course, she wasn't a hooker.'

Ashley felt a twinge in her gut. She hoped it wasn't jealousy, but there was no point dwelling on it. If she'd wanted to go out with Scott, she should have asked.

Hector tutted at the driving conditions. The rain had stopped, but a mist had formed in the countryside. They drove through pockets where visibility kept dropping to metres so Hector slowed right down.

Ashley wondered if she'd get a signal, but her call to DS Ally Wilkinson connected immediately. She found Ally odd but suspected that was because he was in his fifties and still sported a Shane Warne beach-boy haircut.

'Hi, Ash. What's up?'

Ashley updated him on the case, which took a while with all of his questions.

'Okay, Ally. Two major questions. Tell me about Hunstanton's current drug scene, and are there any players who would consider murder?'

'At the moment, we think there are two gangs who control most of Norfolk. A group of mostly third-generation Italians, who are a tight crew, some family, but predominantly young friends. They fancy themselves as being Mafia-like and call themselves the Romans. The other bunch are Eastern Europeans. Serbians, Romanians, Albanians, bit of a mishmash. Their moniker is the Vampires. The Romans operate out of this side of Norwich, but the Vampires are all over. Great Yarmouth,

Norwich and across to Ipswich. We suspect they're unenthusiastic bedfellows.'

Those places were the three largest population centres. Great Yarmouth had around a hundred thousand residents, Ipswich about a hundred and thirty thousand, and Norwich two hundred thousand.

'So, they operate mostly near the biggest urban areas and therefore where the money is.'

'Exactly. Hunstanton's too small for them to bother with and, being almost out on a spit, the access is bad. Out of season, anyone new sticks out like a sore thumb. The national drug teams are on the ball. They tell me it's just a few local players over there. Betty Brown could have been moving serious weight back when Jackie went down, but if Betty's involved now, she's perfected the art of stealth.'

'Any murders with a single stab wound?'

'No. We suspect the Romans are more into the cocaine trade and seem to run it as a business with threats rather than actual violence. They have a nightclub, and there's a sleazy escort business, which we think is the link to the Vampires, because the exploited workers are from Eastern-Europe. The Romans are clever, and while we pick up the dealers, we can't lay a finger on the top men. The Vampires are much more chaotic. It's old-school discipline. People go missing all the time, a few turn up dead, but there's been nothing your side of Norwich.'

'Is it rival dealers who are dying?'

'Both the people who cross them, members of their own team, and the trafficked, who are sometimes disposed of when their use has gone. There was a girl found in some woods last year who might have been connected.'

'Bastards.'

'Yep, and you know how porous our borders are, so it isn't easy.

I work closely with the drug squad, and they're trying every angle.'

'Perfect, Ally. I'll see you at the one o'clock meeting.'

Hector stopped for coffees at a petrol station. After an hour, the satnav instructed him to turn right down a road that was barely wide enough for two cars to pass. They were still nearly ten miles from Hunstanton. Ashley leaned forward to look at the satnav screen. There were no features on it, just the road they were travelling on.

Out of the window, the mist hung heavy over the land and trees. Thoughts of spectral beings flickered through her mind as they turned right again and trundled along another road, which narrowed further. They'd need to pull over if a car came the other way. The fields were full of crops, so there was clearly a functioning farm nearby. They reached huge black wrought-iron gates, which reminded Ashley of an entrance to an asylum. Hector pulled over and stared up at them. The metre-deep stone wall on either side of them was high and layered with razor wire.

The gravel path beyond the gates led between two rows of well-established trees before it disappeared into the fog.

'Get your garlic and crosses out,' said Hector, picking up on the gothic theme.

'If a headless horse arrives, I'm staying in the car,' said Barry.

'It was the rider who was headless, you heathen,' said Hector.

'Trust you to know. Too much reading instead of riding.'

'Barry, shut it,' said Ashley.

'No, it's okay,' said Hector. 'Barry, why is my celibacy so troubling for you?'

'It's not. I can fix it. The Gingerpuss would be right up your street.'

'Isn't that typical? When you tell someone you're celibate, their first reaction is to try to set you up. If I explained I was teetotal and straight, would you immediately offer to take me to a gay biker bar?'

'I'm just pulling your leg.'

Ashley blew out a breath, told Barry to update Control on their location, and left the car. To her surprise, there was a state-of-the-art intercom built into the stone wall. There was one button above a blank screen with a flashing green light. She pressed it and, thirty seconds later, the screen came to life and a male face appeared, who said slowly and deeply, 'Abraham's'.

'Hi, I'm here to speak to Betty Brown.'

Ashley raised her ID to the screen, but it had gone dark again. Another half a minute passed. Ashley peered up into the nearest tree and saw a CCTV camera. There was another disguised in the top corner of the gate as part of its design. She was about to press the button again when there was a clunk.

The gate creaked and groaned, then began to open.

11

Hector drove cautiously through the gate. A large ivy-covered cottage materialised out of the gloom. The mist clung to the roof where a few tiles were missing, and the paint was fading on the front door. It was smaller than Ashley expected, but there was an array of aerials. A satellite dish sat high on one side.

A young man in a smart black coat, black trousers and shoes stepped from the property and walked towards them. Ashley wondered whether he was armed by the way his coat bulged.

The rules in the UK stated that apart from a few hunting and sports licences, nobody could carry a firearm unless they worked for the Crown. As he crouched at Hector's window, she could see it was a radio.

'ID, please.'

Hector showed his warrant card. The man glanced at Hector's face, then at Barry's, then Ashley's. He stepped back.

'Mrs Englebert will see you at the main house.'

Hector turned left and trundled up the drive, which stretched around into another wooded area. When they cleared that, Hector drew in his breath and Ashley did the same. They'd reached a magnificent Georgian mansion with a huge ornate front door. There were statues and large potted trees placed along a wide porch. On that stood a slim, perfectly made-up woman in a sharp business suit. Next to her was a man in fatigues carrying what appeared to be a rifle case.

The woman pointed to a huge, paved area in front of a triple garage where three high-end, gleaming cars were already parked.

Hector swung in, turned the engine off, and they left the car. The lady and gunman had gone, and the butler stood in their place. The sound of a deep-chested dog barking furiously echoed from behind a number of smaller dwellings on the right. The beast sounded hungry. Ashley was quietly relieved she wasn't alone.

'Mrs Englebert will receive you in the library,' said the butler.

Barry and Ashley exchanged a glance. They trudged into the house and followed the man to a double door where he gestured for them to go inside. The library was just that, with walls of filled shelves. Ashley had easily recognised Betty outside because she was almost unchanged, which was surprising considering so much time had passed.

Betty was seated behind a modern black desk, and a few logs were crackling in the fireplace in the middle of the back wall despite the time of year.

'To what do I owe this pleasure?'

Ashley looked around for somewhere to sit, but there wasn't anything close to the desk. Three chairs had been stacked in the corner behind Betty. There was a barrel-chested man in the other corner, whose jacket also bulged, but, judging by his Desperate Dan jaw, she suspected it was muscle. He reminded Ashley of Oddjob from the James Bond films due to his stature and tight suit, but he was hawk-eyed and fair-skinned.

'We've come for a chat, Betty,' said Ashley.

Betty gestured to the phone on her desk using a finger that had a gold ring with an enormous twinkling stone on it.

'I wanted to see you in person,' said Ashley.

'It's Elizabeth now. I've not been Betty for ten years.'

'Eight years,' said Barry. 'You look well.'

Elizabeth squinted at him. 'Barry Hooper. And your name is Ashley Knight. I rarely forget names, even from a different lifetime. What is it you want?'

'It's about that different lifetime,' said Ashley.

Elizabeth slowly raised an eyebrow.

'That period has no interest for me now.'

'Alfie Hook has died.'

'The only shock is that he wasn't dead years ago.'

'Murdered,' said Ashley, abruptly.

Elizabeth didn't even twitch.

'Thanks for letting me know,' she said.

'When did you last see Alfie Hook?' asked Barry.

Elizabeth laughed. It was a natural sound and almost ended in a giggle. She seemed for those few moments a completely different person. Still attractive, especially with such perfect make-up and clothes, she now exuded a calm confidence. After rising from her seat, she walked towards them with a warm smile.

'Time's up,' she said.

Ashley half expected a trapdoor to open up, but instead she was ushered from the room.

'I got with a multimillionaire seven years ago. Do you honestly think I'd have anything to do with the Alfie Hooks of this world?'

'Jackie wanted to say hi,' said Barry.

Yes, thought Ashley. There was the slightest movement at the edge of Elizabeth's eyes.

'You must tell her hello back,' she replied, but any warmth was gone.

The butler was outside the room, but so was an old man. He was slim in a perfectly fitted navy suit, and his expression was keen, but he shuffled towards them.

'Who are these people, darling?' he asked.

'Police. They are leaving,' stated Elizabeth.

Ashley detected a look pass between them as she stepped forward and held out her hand. The man didn't even glance down at it.

'Pleasure to meet you, Mr Englebert,' she said.

'My name is Abraham,' he said softly. 'Don't come here again without an appointment.'

'We could come with a warrant,' she said.

His right cheek twitched.

'I wouldn't recommend that, especially if my pooch is loose.'

'Money doesn't put anyone above the law,' said Barry.

Abraham gave him a look that Ashley had seen parents give their children when they were being silly. 'I'm not sure I'd entirely agree.'

Ashley watched as one of the hands of the frail man before her trembled at his side.

Despite that, she felt a shimmer of concern.

12

The three detectives left the building and returned to their car. To Ashley's surprise, Elizabeth followed them out and stood next to it.

'Honestly,' she said. 'We wouldn't sink so low.'

Ashley recalled the brassy person this woman had been before. The plummy accent was new as well.

'I have the feeling you were expecting us.'

'Only coppers and thieves come here unannounced. If you were the latter, you'd have been taken care of on the drive.'

Elizabeth chuckled again, which made Ashley wonder if she'd had an early sherry.

'Just kidding,' Elizabeth said.

Ashley didn't believe her. About any of it.

She got back in their vehicle, and Hector crunched the car away through the gravel.

'Nice to see an old friend,' said Barry.

They laughed to break the tension, but something wasn't right.

Ashley made a few more calls while Hector drove them back

to the murder scene in Hunstanton. She spoke to someone she knew who dealt with higher net-worth individuals and corporations, but Abraham Englebert wasn't on his radar, so she rang Emma back at the Operation and Communication Centre (OCC) in Wymondham, which was around ten miles from Norwich, and asked her to chase it up.

The rain stopped as they approached the coast, and the sea breeze had cleared the moist air from the countryside, but it was still a grim day. The tape hung limp at the entrance to Vegas's car park, with only a solitary CSI van hinting at the dark deed that had occurred. Sal and Jan were at a bench with Gerald, who was out of protective clothing.

'Finished?' she asked.

'Yes,' said Gerald. 'Last night's rain has done for the scene, although there wasn't anything much here. There's a storm coming, but we'll have time to finish the van. We'll need to take it with us, but the business wants to collect a hundred tiles from the back because it's a specialist order, which took two months to come from Italy. They can come down now and get them. We got nothing from the fingerprints.'

'Pity,' said Ashley.

'There is some good news for you. I had that sample found in the van tested first thing. It was cannabis. There was only a small amount, but it was present.'

Ashley let the fact wander around her head for a moment until Sal interrupted her.

'I've got something interesting, too. The company employed Alfie for the past seven years. He's a character, but popular. He was slower than the other guys, but he's never sick or late in. There's the odd bout of falling asleep in his van, perhaps a dozen times over the years, but they aren't delivering medical supplies, so it's not the end of the world.'

'What are they delivering?'

'Bricks, paving slabs, slates and tiles.'

'Commercial or domestic?'

'Both. Not too much high end, except the order like those tiles. People read the catalogue. If it's a minor job like a kitchen or bathroom, they request it online, then Alfie drives it over. He also delivers samples if it's for larger projects like patios or extensions. For big orders or heavy loads, they use a lorry.'

'And it's always their van he uses.'

'Yes, they have two vans and four drivers, including Alfie. The other three guys also do shifts, packing and loading, and they share the deliveries depending on what's needed.'

'So, any of them could have dropped the drugs?'

'Yep.'

'Brilliant.'

'There is one intriguing angle.'

'Go on.'

'Alfie started his round half an hour early. That wasn't unusual for him, and he finished his last pick-up well before nine.'

'Doesn't the chippy shut at nine? Maybe it's his Friday evening treat.'

'Perhaps, but remember, the vehicle has a tracker. That's how they knew where it was parked all night and why they weren't worried.'

'And?'

'They showed me his route that evening. You can see him enter Paradise Leisure Park a little after eight thirty. The van drives right the way to the top, then it's stationary for three or four minutes. He heads back out and comes here. I took a picture of the screen.'

'So?' asked Ashley.

'He had no drop-offs in Hunstanton.'

13

Ashley grinned, but Sal hadn't finished.

'And it's not the first time he's been there. They don't do much business in Hunstanton because there's another popular builders' merchants here.'

The plot thickened. Ashley checked her watch. Being over sixty minutes from OCC was annoying in cases like this. They could use local stations for interviewing and a few closer by had custody units, but it was better to have everything and everyone in the same place with the best facilities. The Operations and Communication Centre was a shiny new glass building which fulfilled that purpose.

'Did the company seem in any way dodgy?'

'Not at all,' said Sal. 'They want their van back, but they are a super-friendly family firm. They even had a dog in their office.'

'A snarling Rottweiler?'

'An enormous love-sponge Bernese Mountain Dog called Frankie. I was at medium-risk of being drowned in slobber.'

'Okay,' said Ashley, checking her watch. It was approaching

ten. 'Let's speak to the park manager and see if anyone there has seen Alfie's van before.'

Ashley walked over to the vehicle Alfie was killed in. The rotting van beside it had been moved, so she could take clear photos with her phone. There would be no missing this vehicle. It was a bright red Ford Transit with PSST! Bricks written in huge letters on each side in yellow and under that in small black writing was Paving, Slabs, Slates, Tiles, Bricks. At the bottom was written Stones Builders Merchants.

The team headed to their cars and set off. They turned right at the roundabout, then drove for half a mile before Hector slowed down.

In front of them was a huge sign above freshly painted white gates. 'Welcome to Paradise' was written in large golden letters above an image of a modern play area, which was filled with colourfully clothed children running around. There were happy couples holding hands and smiling people walking dogs.

It should have been the antithesis of the gothic entrance to Abraham's estate, but rising above the sign was the largest black cloud Ashley had ever seen. The insides of it churned and it felt like dusk. As Hector drove into the site, a squall blasted up the lid of a large wheelie bin and lifted out a newspaper. It flapped and flew over the parked cars next to it. There were kids running all right, but to escape before the sky fell in.

'Paradise,' said Hector, flatly.

'I'm not sure religion would have taken off quite like it did if eternity was going to be spent here,' said Barry.

Heavy drops thumped on the roof of their car as Hector slid the Audi into the last space outside Reception. They waited for Sal to trot across from the spaces over the road where he'd parked.

The reception was empty apart from a teenager with blue-streaked black hair at the front desk. He was sniggering and obviously chatting to a friend on the phone, holding it with his chin against his shoulder.

There were two desks with computers behind the reception, which Ashley guessed was an admin area, and a similar desk on the right, which had a 'Sales' sign above it. A closed door with 'Manager' written on it was at the rear. Ashley stood at the counter and waited for the young lad to look up at her. He was in a uniform that reminded Ashley of fast-food restaurants. His name badge was nameless.

She slid her warrant card onto his desk. He glanced at it, shrugged, then spun away in his chair.

Barry's arm reached over and cut his call. The kid spun back to find Barry pointing at him.

'Chatting to your friend.' Barry hooked a thumb back at himself. 'Busy police. Where's the manager, please?'

'He's in a meeting.'

They all heard a burst of male laughter from the office, a female titter, then another guffaw from the deeper voice.

'We'll go straight through,' said Ashley.

A short middle-aged balding guy with a protruding belly looked as if he'd been caught with his trousers down when they knocked, opened the door and strolled in. The other occupant of the room, a woman not much older than the teenager outside, blushed and slipped past them.

'Leave those files in the usual place, please, Gail,' said the man. He opened his arms wide to welcome them. 'I'm Percival. How can I help you?'

Percival had the beginnings of a Bobby Charlton comb-over. The style fascinated Ashley whenever she spoke to a person with one. The only other resemblance to the England World Cup hero was his light-brown hair colour, or perhaps the football Percival had hidden under his V-neck sweater.

'We're investigating a murder,' said Ashley.

The man's face fell. 'On this site?'

'In Hunstanton.'

'Oh, you mean the incident near the Vegas. That's a relief. Murders aren't good for repeat business.'

'The victim came here before he was killed,' said Sal. 'A delivery around 8.30 p.m. at one of the caravans was his last call.'

'No, we don't have vans racing through the estate. We have two hundred caravans and lodges here with children and elderly people wandering all over. Packages are left at Reception and the recipient comes and collects them. It's much safer.'

'I can assure you he went directly to the caravan,' said Sal.

'Oh, no, no, no. There are many expensive luxurious lodges where they expect peace and privacy. No large vehicles drive around the park unannounced. Your source is wrong.'

Sal grabbed a chair, pulled it up beside Percival, and sat down. 'The company's vans have accurate trackers using the latest technology. We've watched the driver's route. He drove through your entrance and wound through your campsite, which appears complicated to navigate if you don't know the way. He proceeded straight to the back of the site and parked up.'

'Perhaps he came here by mistake.'

'He's been here numerous times in the last few months.'

Sal took his mobile out and showed the image to Percival, who went redder than when they first walked in. He followed the map on the phone with a finger.

'That's to a section of Diamond, our most select estate,' said Percival.

'We need to chat to the residents there.'

Percival picked up his pen. 'What's your email address? I'll ask them to get in touch.'

Ashley smiled.

'You misunderstand. This is a murder enquiry. We'd like you to accompany us there, explain how the site works, and generally be incredibly helpful.'

'I'm free this afternoon.'

'I'll come back then, bring lots of uniformed police, flashing lights, maybe sirens, and rolls of crime scene tape. Shut the entrance for a while until we've spoken to everyone here.'

Percival scowled.

With a wide smile, Ashley held her hand out for him to precede her. 'Or you could cooperate with our investigation.'

Percival trudged to the door.

14

A MONTH AGO

Pip left her lodge and walked across to Jasmine's place. As was often the case, she was met by the sweet smell of incense from the joss sticks that her friend burned. Jasmine was already in the hot tub with a dubious-looking cigarette in her hand.

'You didn't hang about,' said Pip.

'I wanted to stretch out before anyone else got in. Want a drag?'

'It's a bit early for me. I'll have one of those San Pelligrinos I brought over.'

'They're in the door of the fridge.'

Pip nipped inside and grabbed a bottle, then stood next to Deniz, who was leaning on the railing. He hadn't acknowledged her arrival, but that wasn't unusual. She watched the gentle breeze lift his hair and got a glimpse of tanned neck.

'Penny for them?' she asked.

He turned to her, but Ray-Ban sunglasses hid his expression until he removed them. Deniz's eyes shone as he took a second to look over her face.

'I thought I saw something out there, beyond the reeds.'

'A person or an animal?'

'I got a sense it was a man. Watching. Or waiting.'

'It's probably the groundsman.'

'I don't know. I got the feeling he didn't want to be seen.'

'Maybe it was the duck-poo monster, wondering if he's invited to the barbecue.'

Deniz gave her a grin and ran a hand through his locks. Pip managed to stop herself from beaming up at him.

Pip looked past his shoulder at the pond. It was the first lovely day of the year, and the air shimmered above the water. Gusts moved the reeds in a gentle dance, but she couldn't see anything. A dragonfly hung in the air and then was gone. High in the sky, the odd cloud formed, then broke into wisps.

As the wind dipped, the sun was briefly hidden by one of those fleeting clumps of cotton wool. The salty sea breeze was replaced by the whiff of decay from the never-ending cycle of decomposition that came from the brackish water. The rays soon warmed her skin once more, but she still experienced a moment of unease.

'It's funny you should think that,' said Pip. 'Glory said it felt as if a pervert had his eyes on her when she was having a cocktail here last week.'

'That sounds like Glory,' said Jasmine, chuckling in the hot tub.

'Is she coming over?'

'Later. I suspect she has a hangover from yesterday.'

Jasmine smiled at Pip, then rested the back of her head on the hot tub and stared up as a huge gull, fat and prosperous, drifted above them. Its beady eyes peered down as though surveying the battlefield before letting out a cry as if all was lost. Jasmine closed her eyes after it flapped its wings and was soon gone, but Pip felt drawn to gaze back across the pond.

She felt a pang of guilt when she then took the opportunity to look up into Deniz's handsome face, but Deniz was staring over the ripples that spread across the water at whatever was out there.

His eyes were steeled as he replaced the Ray-Bans.

15

PRESENT DAY

Percival led the detectives from the site's reception as if they were heading to the gallows. He was already huffing and puffing by the time he clambered into the back of Hector's car. Ashley edged away from him. It was hard to describe the man as anything but slovenly and unhealthy. His suit was new, but it hung all wrong on him. Ashley detected a faint whiff of body odour and dreaded to think how he'd smell by day's end.

Percival directed them down a tarmacked single-lane road that wound through the park. There were static caravans as far as the eye could see. It was like a maze full of huge white bricks. Hector almost went the wrong way, even with the manager directing him.

'Does every caravan have a number?' he asked.

'We're going to Diamond, which has what we call lodges, but yes, that section of Diamond has six lodges, so Diamond One, Diamond Two, and so on. It's at the far-end of the site and next to a small lake. There's a meadow beyond for dog walks, and it's all rather splendid.'

'How many homes in each area?'

'A little over fifty vans in Bronze, Silver and Gold. Forty in Diamond.'

They passed a sign for Diamond and reached a pretty roundabout filled with shrubs and flowers. Around it were several massive caravans with wide decking and plenty of space either side. One had a large solid hot tub at the front of their deck overlooking what Ashley would classify as a big pond rather than a lake. It was full of tall reeds with ducks sitting at the edge.

Despite the rain, which was pounding on their bonnet, it appeared exclusive.

'Wow,' said Ashley. 'It is nice. How much are these?'

'Upwards of a hundred thousand new. We do deals if they upgrade older lodges, and there's a vibrant second-hand market.'

'They look like two caravans glued together,' said Hector.

Ashley caught Percival's scowl.

'In a way, they are. They need to be transported here from the factory. A police escort is needed if the lorry load is over twelve feet wide, which would be prohibitively expensive. So, they usually come in two ten-feet-wide units, and we link them on site.'

'Can you live in one all year?' said Ashley.

'The licence rules state that's forbidden. We're open eleven months. All residents must have another place as their home. We check everyone has their names on the council tax somewhere else.'

Ashley noticed a slight wobble in his voice, which indicated Percival probably wasn't too thorough around that.

'People live here almost permanently, then?' she asked.

'Yes, plenty do. Helga and Hans in Diamond Three are a lovely German couple. They've been with us for over forty years. This is their fourth lodge. They have a flat in Swaffham which they rarely use because they're here. They go back to Germany for January, which is the month we're closed.'

'It seems a lot of money for two caravans nailed together. Is there a healthy mark-up?' asked Hector.

Ashley definitely caught a glare before Percival replied.

'The landlord of the site has to turn a profit,' he said. 'There are many overheads in a place like this.'

'Don't the caravan owners pay site fees, too?' asked Ashley.

'They do.'

'How much are they?'

'Five hundred pounds.'

'Oh, that's good.'

'Per month. Plus energy bills.'

Ashley whistled. 'Right, so in summary, you need to have a few quid to own one, or I suppose people can rent them for the week.'

Percival sneered.

'Rarely in Diamond. People here treat it as a home. They make friends, form relationships. It's a supportive little community. Some renters aren't our favourite kind of people. There's rubbish left, noise, uncouth behaviour. Bronze is our main rental area.'

'So, Bronze has the worst vans. Silver is better, Gold nicer still, then Diamond. Don't people mind knowing they're in the least desirable part?'

'Not at all. It was my idea. It's aspirational. Many can't wait to pay more for an upgraded holiday in a quieter, more salubrious part.'

Ashley, Hector and Percival got out and braced themselves in the wind, which had picked up from gusts to being almost constant. The clouds overhead had lowered, but the rain wasn't as heavy as it sounded on the car's exterior.

Ashley took in the immediate vicinity. Five hundred pounds a month seemed expensive when you'd already spent a wedge buying the lodge. The place was deserted as well, but she supposed it wasn't a day for taking a stroll. Three of the lodges appeared to have lights on, which looked dim in the gathering gloom, but that was it. A line of ducks mournfully quacked past as they vacated the pond, as though warning them to abandon all hope.

Sal and Jan left the warmth of his car, too. Sal walked over with his phone out, wiping the screen, but Jan gave Ashley some paper.

'Gail from Reception came out and gave me a map.'

Ashley looked at the piece of A4. The site was roughly the shape of a coat of arms. Gold and Diamond section were top left and right. Bronze and Silver were lower left and right, with Reception in between them and the entrance at the bottom. In the centre was a play park, laundry, tennis court, and the clubhouse.

'I believe this is the spot from the map,' said Sal, pointing with a finger. 'The roundabout is there, but the lodges aren't detailed. I'd guess it was one of these,' he said, indicating One and Two Diamond.

'Do you think Alfie knew he had a tracker on his van?' asked Hector to Sal.

'Yes, all the drivers were aware. Whether an older guy like Alfie understood what that implied is up for debate. He could have had a friend in Diamond, or maybe he enjoyed coming here for a peaceful nap next to the pond, before deciding there was still time for chips.'

The surrounding breeze slackened for a moment, and they all got a strong whiff of something unpleasant. Even Percival's nose twitched.

'What the hell is that abhorrent stench?' asked Hector, glaring at Barry.

'Assuming that means nasty, it's probably the ducks,' said Percival.

'You better ring for a vet if they're responsible,' said Barry.

'They poo everywhere. I'd shoot the lot of them, but the guests love to see them waddling around.'

A strong gust returned, but the unpleasant odour lingered now their noses had registered its presence. The sound of wind chimes ominously carried over to them.

'Okay. This might be a wild goose chase, so let's get a move on,' said Ashley with a sniff. 'Sal, you take Percival back to the office. Ring Stones Builders Merchants and tell them their tiles in the van are ready for collection. Secure any CCTV the site has. Find out how things operate here. We'll need a list of who owns the caravans, so have Emma start on the paperwork. Percival, you are not to leave the park today until we have this information. We're going to knock on some doors.'

'I'll need to speak to the owner of the site before releasing any of those details.'

'Call him then. Has there been any unusual behaviour on the site lately?'

'Like what?'

'Arguments, drunkenness, undesirables.'

'Of course not. Well, nothing outrageous.'

'No unexplained deaths.'

'The average age on here is around seventy. Naturally, people occasionally die unexpectedly.'

Ashley could tell by his lack of eye contact and flowery language he wasn't being honest again.

'Anyone recently?'

'Not that I recall. No heart attacks or strokes, anyway.'

Ashley imagined throwing Percival into the pond. She took a deep breath, then regretted it. Percival's lake was more like the black lagoon.

'When were the police last here?'

'Not for a while.'

'When?'

'Not this week.'

'This year?'

'Yes.'

'What for?'

'A suicide.'

'Wouldn't you describe that as suspicious?'

'There were pills. It was an overdose.'

'Why would anyone kill themselves when they lived in Paradise?'

'Must have been a problem from elsewhere.'

Again, the manager was no card player.

'Percival. Was it on Diamond?'

'No, it was near the start of the year on Silver.'

'Where is that exactly?'

Percival pointed down the road beyond a picket fence at a single caravan which was more aged and had no balcony.

'She died in that.'

16

Ashley sent Sal and Jan off with Percival before she strangled him. Hector knocked on number one and took out his pocketbook. The decking was immaculate but empty. With a storm coming, Ashley guessed they'd taken the deckchairs inside. The person who opened the door surprised her.

The man was tall and rangy, with a full head of longish hair, resembling a deeply tanned David Ginola. After a few sleepy blinks from pretty blue eyes, he pushed his locks to one side.

'Can I help?'

'Yes, I'm DS Ashley Knight,' she replied, flashing her warrant card. 'These are my colleagues, DCs Fade and Hooper. I assume you already know Percival. Is this your lodge?'

'Yes.'

The lodge groaned under the weight of the wind, which luckily was battering the other side. The clouds had darkened further.

'Can we come in?'

He crossed his arms.

'Sure,' he said after a pause.

They trudged into a hall with six closed doors. The guy opened one and directed them into a roomy lounge. Huge windows looked out onto some trees behind the lodge. It was so cosy and warm inside that Barry took his jacket off. He and Ashley wandered to the back, where there was another door out to the decking and a view of the pond. The kitchen area, which was spacious and modern, was the only part in a mess with a sink full of cups, plates and glasses.

'Any chance of a coffee?' asked Barry.

'I'm going out. What can I help you with?'

Ashley hid a grin. It was a common ploy to see if a person was keen to get rid of them.

'Can I have your name, please?' asked Hector.

'Deniz Turner.'

'Thank you, Dennis. We're trying to trace the movements of a red van.'

'My name is Deniz. It's Turkish. I don't have a red van.'

'Have you seen one?'

'What, like a Royal Mail van?'

'No. Bigger. A panel van for a brick company.'

'Why would anyone get bricks delivered here?'

'They do slabs and tiles, too.'

Deniz shrugged.

'Where were you on Friday night around eight?' asked Hector.

Ashley watched Deniz wrack his brains for somewhere to say, but he came up wanting.

'I was here.'

'What work are you having done?' she asked.

'None. This is only a few years old.'

Ashley stared at the kitchen table and the expensive Apple laptop and tablet on it. Ashley's toast this morning had been thicker than the TV, which was on a nice glass stand in a corner.

'Is that new RAV4 out the front yours? I've always fancied one of them,' she said.

Deniz gave her a charming smile and ran his hands through his hair again. This lifted his short-sleeved white shirt to show a tantalising glimpse of tanned midriff. He must use a salon or had been on holiday. Ashley also noticed a smudged blue tattoo on his upper arm.

'Yes. I got a good deal on it.'

He was in great nick. The only sign of ageing being a few strands of grey.

'How old are you?' she asked.

His eyes narrowed.

'Forty.'

'You must have a great job to afford this.'

'I do. I'm a programmer, so I can work where I like. Hunstanton has a lot of family history, so I choose to live here. I know I'm lucky.'

'You've never seen a red van?'

'Nope.'

'How about in the last few months?'

Deniz shrugged.

'Apparently, they drop parcels at Reception, but this one didn't.'

'Ah, right. Look, all this doesn't pay for itself. I stare at my computer for most of the day, not out of the window.'

His gaze lingered on Ashley, which made her stomach twitch.

'Any odd neighbours around here?'

'A few,' he said, flashing perfect teeth.

'Isn't the vibe a bit old for you?' asked Barry.

'No, you'd be surprised. The clubhouse is popular, and there's usually decent people about. I'll talk to anyone.'

'No Mrs Turner, Mr Turner?' asked Hector. 'Or another Mr Turner?'

The same disarming smile appeared.

'Just my stepdad. I occasionally bring him here, but my mum died some time ago, and he's pretty frail and easily confused.'

'Which means you have the place to yourself,' said Ashley. 'Nice. How long have you been living here?'

'About a year full time.'

Ashley waggled a finger at him.

'You're only allowed eleven months.'

Deniz grinned.

'My home's in Sheffield. I might downsize it now I'm spending my days here. I love seaside life.'

They left Deniz smiling in his doorway and trudged over to the lodge with the hot tub, which was secured tight in the far corner of the decking. Deckchairs had been lashed to the fence where a barbecue had been pushed. There were no lights on inside, and nobody came when they knocked, giving it an air of the Mary Celeste.

'I choose to live here,' mimicked Barry. *'I'll talk to anyone.'*

'Are you jealous because he isn't losing his hair?' asked Hector.

Barry jerked his head towards Hector.

'I'm not losing my hair.'

'He was quite dashing,' said Ashley. 'I might have to come back this evening in a cocktail dress to interview him. Although perhaps he was a touch too charming.'

'He looks the type to wear a cocktail dress,' said Barry, who gave number two a heavier knock but there was still no answer.

They were about to leave when Ashley crouched down, took a pen out of her pocket and poked at a few scattered dog ends that were by the doorstep.

They all had roaches in the end of them.

17

Ashley considered the find for a moment. Someone at lodge Two smoked weed, or at least a visitor did. Ashley put gloves on and went to the wheelie-bin cupboard at the back of the lodge, but it was locked.

She returned to the decking and peered through the window. The inside appeared lived in due to the pile of crumpled clothing on a worktop, and she could make out a cup on the draining board and one on a table. Ashley rang Sal.

'Sal, can you ask Percival for the contact details for number two? Seems like somebody enjoys a spliff or two, but there's nobody here. Number three's lights are on, so I'll chat to Hansel and Gretel from Germany. Maybe they'll know if the owner of Two was about yesterday.'

'Okay. Percival told me more about the suicide. The police came, and there was a Coroner's Inquest, then nothing, so he assumed that was it. He's on the ball with it, because the site fees aren't being paid. The victim's solicitor explained to him she died intestate without a close relative, so it's taking a while to sort.'

'What was her age and name?'

'Percival's getting all arsey about what he's allowed to provide. I'll organise the paperwork with Emma to make sure it's watertight.'

'Okay. We've uncovered nothing solid here yet, so you and Jan can head back to the office for the meeting. We won't be far behind.'

As she cut the call, her phone rang. It was Gerald.

'Hi, Ashley. The bosses of the delivery company arrived to collect those tiles. They're ready to leave. Do you need to talk to them?'

Ashley heard excited deep barking in the background. 'Whose dog is that?'

'They brought their hound. Frankie. Massive great thing.'

Ashley recalled Sal's comments about them having a Bernie. She was about to say the owners could go when she received another whiff of decaying fish.

'Actually, wait. Do Bernese Mountain Dogs have a good sense of smell?'

'Any dog's is about a thousand times sharper than ours.'

'Ask the owners if they mind bringing the hound down here. There's a pond here and the closer you are to it, the worse it smells.'

'I bet they'd love their dog to plunge into that, but I'll send them down.'

Barry was already knocking on the Germans' door and Ashley caught up as Hector and he were entering. She followed them into the hall. Again, she was amazed by how modern it was. Ashley had taken a few caravan holidays with her dad when she was much younger and before he stopped wanting to leave the house. She recalled concrete shower blocks with freezing floors, collecting their own water from a standpipe, and draughty windows dripping with moisture. These lodges reminded her of high-end apartments.

Barry was talking in the kitchen, but he was out of sight.

'Get yourself a seat, please, Hans,' he said. 'We'll talk to you in the lounge.'

'I'm all right. Don't think I tire easy just because I'm getting on a bit.'

Ashley caught a glimpse of Hans as he entered the lounge and sat. She choked back a laugh. He made Yoda look like a boy scout. Hans noticed her.

'Ooh, wow!' he said. 'The talent's turned up. You can sit next to me.'

Hans's face crinkled up, and he laughed and gasped so hard she struggled to feel insulted, even after he put his hand on her leg when she took a seat beside him.

'She's single,' said Barry.

Hans beamed at him.

'We just have a few questions,' said Ashley.

'Pardon?'

'Some questions,' she shouted into his ear.

'No, I don't have any. Do you?'

Ashley nodded.

'Fire away, then.'

'Are you friendly with your neighbours?'

'The person of colour or the woman with mental problems?'

'Erm. Who's the one next to the pond?'

'Jasmine.'

'Does Jasmine have mental health issues?'

Hans leaned so close she could smell his heady cologne.

'They both do, but Jasmine's are worse.'

'Does she smoke cannabis?'

'Yes, all the time. The scent reminds me of my youth, but my wife moans about it. I'd have a few puffs, but Helga reckons I'd never wake up again.' Hans scratched his chin. 'She's probably right.'

'Do you know where she is?'

'Helga?'

'Jasmine.'

'She was here a little while ago.'

'Today?'

'I'm not sure. It was after Easter.'

'It's June now.'

'Yes, so it was after Easter.'

'Was she here a few days ago, or a week? An estimate is fine.'

'Perhaps a week.'

'Have you seen a red van around here lately?'

'Yes, a few days back. I mentioned it to Helga. She reckoned I was drunk and dreamed it.'

'Why did she say that?'

'I was drunk. It was unusual because I thought someone had written piss on the side of it in capitals. I can remember seeing it a few times before.'

'Could it have been PSST!? Like when you try to grab someone's attention?'

'That would make more sense. My eyesight's pretty poor now. I had to give up my licence and car last year.'

Ashley showed him a picture of the van on her mobile. He blinked, stuck his tongue out of the corner of his mouth, then nodded furiously.

'And you think the lady on the other side of you has mental health issues as well?'

'Pip in Four, yes. She drinks a lot. Sometimes I hear her

shouting and arguing, but I don't know who with. Maybe she's on the phone. They're all a bit crazy on this part of the site. Normal when they arrive. Mad when they leave.'

'Where's Helga?' asked Barry.

'Who knows? She has more energy than me. Younger, you see, and no doubt up to no good. A looker, too. So, keep your hands off when she arrives, young man.'

'I'll try, but no promises,' said Barry. 'Hans, I assume it doesn't always smell so bad here.'

'It's that bloody pond. Things crawl in there and die.'

'Do you mean people?'

Hans laughed his head off. His hand came up to stop his teeth falling all the way out.

'Probably, son. When the quiet drives them to it. The ducks die in there every now and again, and swans. There's a cat around here that kills stuff. A heron eats the fish and leaves a mess, too. Don't think we've had any humans in there yet.' Hans scratched his head. 'It has stunk worse of late, but my sense of smell is going. It whiffed like that when I worked on Hamburg docks in the sixties.'

'Was it the same foul fishy stench?'

'The docks always stank, whatever the weather. No, one particular afternoon we found a dead fox floating in a huge container, which had filled up with rainwater.'

'Trust me. You're lucky your ability to smell has gone.'

'Only thing I've got left is my hearing.'

'What age are you, Hans?'

'What?'

'How old are you?'

'I'm good, thank you. Still life in me yet.'

Ashley stood.

'Excellent. Thanks for your help, Hans. I'm going to speak to Pip. See if she knows where Jasmine is.'

'Why don't you ask Jasmine's pothead boyfriend?'

'Who's that?'

'The pretty kid next door. Dennis.'

18

A taxi drew up as they stepped off Hans's decking.

'This is Helga now,' said Hans.

Helga carefully exited the vehicle with two full carrier bags. She appeared to be around eighty. Barry held the gate open for her and gave her an obvious wink, which made Hans at risk of losing his dentures again. The detectives left the couple to put their shopping away.

Sal was next to pull up and leave his car. Behind him was a blue van that had a couple in the cab and PSST! on the sides. Sal beckoned them to get out. They were both around fifty, wearing black jeans, and white T-shirts bearing the company logo.

'This is Mr and Mrs Stone, which is appropriate for their commercial activities.'

'Thanks for coming,' said Ashley. 'Sal, they've got that dog you met at their office with them.'

'I see what you mean about the stink,' said Mrs Stone. 'Weirdly cloying. Smells worse than my husband after a boys' night out.'

'Would you mind letting your dog sniff around to see if there's something obvious?'

'I suppose, but he's only three and boisterous still. I'd rather he didn't go in that water.'

'No problem. Just keep him on the lead and circle the pond.'

Mrs Stone went to the side of the van and a few seconds later a gigantic black, tan and white beast leapt out of the back. Ashley had never seen a male Bernese Mountain Dog close-up. He had a huge lionlike head and must have weighed more than her. Mrs Stone put him on a thick lead and braced herself. Ashley could see the dog's nose flaring.

Getting a police dog was unlikely without a solid reason, so this was worth a try.

'Sit, Frankie,' said Mr Stone, coming over to join them. Frankie sat down, but his haunches quivered. 'Where would you like us to search?'

The dog drooled as he stared lovingly up into his owners' faces.

'Walk him around the pond,' said Ashley. 'I suspect it's a dead something. If we can see where he's interested, it will help. It's just so windy, I can't tell where the smells are coming from.'

Mr Stone swallowed, presumably having realised it might not be dead fish the detectives were looking for. He clicked his fingers in front of the hound to catch its attention, then held eye contact.

'Wherezit! Wherezit, Frankie!'

Frankie tried to shoot off, but Mrs Stone held on. The dog strained at the lead and eventually she was pulled onto her arse. He dragged her across the wet grass for a few metres, so she let him go. Loose, he thundered towards the swamp.

'Stop, Frankie. Sit!' bellowed Mr Stone.

Frankie stopped at the water's edge with his nose in the air. He wandered further away from them, then stopped. There was a lull in the wind. He stared into the water, turned to look at Ashley, and made a loud 'ruff'. His nose flared again as he ambled back towards Jasmine's lodge, following a line of scent. After another sniff, he jumped up and rested his front paws on the railings next to the hot tub. Slaver quivered from his maw as he released a low howl.

Ashley walked over and grabbed his lead. In the lea of Jasmine's lodge, the smell was overpowering. The dog scrabbled at the fence, trying to get through. Mrs Stone had picked herself up and took the lead back, so Ashley returned to the decking. She put booties over her shoes, just in case.

Ashley opened the gate and strode over to the hot tub where the heavy stench filled the air. She was about to lift the cover when a maggot dropped onto the wood from the edge of the tub. Then another. Ashley loosened the cover and, when the wind next died, she began to peel it off.

Lying on top of the control panel was a large rotten flat fish. It was hard to say what species it had been. Up close, the stink was incredible. The water was murky and foul, but there was a dark object concealed by the scum that sat on the surface. She yanked the cover all the way off, and the bloated face that burst through the grey froth was unlike anything she'd seen before.

Ashley was putting her hand to her mouth as Mrs Stone shrieked.

The mystery of Jasmine's whereabouts was over. Ashley turned away from the gruesome sight to compose herself just as Deniz appeared at his door. From his elevated height and angle, he could see what had arisen from the depths.

His eyes met Ashley's as he retreated into his lodge. They were full of guilt.

19

A WEEK AGO

Jasmine checked herself out in the mirror. It must be over thirty years since she'd last worn a bikini, and she hadn't felt confident then, despite the fact she should have been doing her shopping wearing one. It had been downhill since. She held her tummy in, but that seemed to make it wobble more when she moved.

Her swimsuit was a nice style and fit the night Deniz made love to her in the hot tub, but there had been an element of unwrapping a pork shoulder joint as he tried to romantically peel it off.

Deniz had been rather distant since. There was one night when he came over and they had sex, but he wasn't anywhere near as loving as when they first started seeing each other. Afterwards, she'd asked him about his recent visitors. He'd dressed, then barely said goodbye. She should have kept her mouth shut.

Deniz had definitely waved to her today, though, and he ran a hand through his hair, which always made her legs weaken. God, she was a teenager again.

Jasmine scowled at her lined face. She was beginning to look and feel old. Smoking was clearly to blame, but without the peace and distraction that habit had given her while she was married, she'd have killed herself years ago.

Jasmine had believed men ceased to see her as someone to be interested in sexually. She could just tell, so it was a major surprise when Deniz was keen. Chuckling, she thought it would be exciting to do the deed again, even if it was the last time.

Jasmine had felt many eyes on her that night. It was so unlike her, but knowing heightened it to an experience that would linger in her mind for the rest of her days. As she recalled the lovemaking, she surprised herself by shivering. Did those watchers' eyes glitter with interest, disgust, arousal, or was it jealousy?

She laughed quietly and wrapped a towel around herself as she noticed her messy lodge. She'd just smoked a spliff, and her limbs were lovely and heavy. The last thing she fancied was tidying. It was doubtful Deniz was going to come over when half the single women in the vicinity were interested, so she couldn't see the point in making the place presentable.

Besides, she thought with a giggle, one glance at her bikini, and surely he would ravish her in the water again anyway, with his manly urges forcing him to do manly things. She was laughing out loud as she stepped outside and pulled the cover off the tub.

'Nice evening, Jasmine,' said a beaming Hans, who was feeding the ducks next to the sign saying not to.

'I'm waiting for the sunset,' she said, giving him a sloppy smile.

Judging by Hans's roaming eyes as he departed, the bikini was working on him. It was a shame he wasn't 250 years younger. He only left when she wrapped a towel around herself.

Jasmine wheeled the BBQ out from behind the lodge. She'd felt pathetic when she nipped out and bought ribs and burgers in case Deniz wanted something different from the fish that she'd taken out of the freezer. She'd bought it last time after he said it was his favourite, but he'd cancelled. It wasn't cheap either, with her having to get it from a friend of hers who knew someone.

Jasmine opened the barbecue lid and gasped. Six mice burned alive. She faintly remembered cooking veggie sausages a few nights ago when she was wasted, but couldn't remember eating them. She decided to clear them up later if necessary and closed the lid. It would be better if he wasn't watching when she fired it up.

Jasmine put the hot tub on the highest setting. It would take a while to warm up, but she'd forgotten to get the fish out of the freezer early enough. She rested it on the side, briefly contemplating putting it in the water, but the liquid was as murky as the pond. It needed a clean, but that was a shit job as well. She squirted a quarter of a bottle of bubble bath in for good measure. Only she would know the liquid below the froth was more soup than spring water.

After lighting three patchouli incense sticks, she coolly glanced around while pretending to talk on her mobile. Out of the corner of her eye, she spotted definite movement at Deniz's kitchen window. Excellent. She rested her phone on the side of the tub, took a deep breath, then let the towel slide from her body and stepped into the water as daintily as she could manage, while trying not to snigger.

After thirty minutes, Jasmine had almost forgotten about Deniz. She found it so amazing being at Paradise knowing her arsehole of a husband was no longer in her life, and no money worries either because of his demise.

With eyes closed, her other senses took over. Warm scents rising, the bubbles on her skin, birds tweeting their evening songs, and the ducks quacking contentedly as they waddled home for the night.

Lavender from the bubble bath was the dominant smell, but

there was also a hint of various lotions, make-up, perfume, baby oil, and possibly beer from when she knocked a glass of Budweiser in when she was cooking those mice.

The sun had just dipped out of sight when she heard her gate click. A gentle breeze blew the spicy sweet aroma of patchouli over her. She loved it. The same sticks were burning when Deniz brought her dreams alive that night, making her feel at one with the earth.

There was embarrassment the next day about the brazenness of it, but only Bertie had raised an eyebrow at her, and he was regularly up to no good on his decking.

When her flooring creaked, goosebumps immediately materialised. Jasmine attempted regal, lying with her arms outstretched and her head resting on the edge. The tub shifted slightly as the person approaching depressed the planks next to it. After a few long seconds, Jasmine remembered the fish next to her head and opened her eyes. She stared into an earnest face.

Time slowed as she recognised the expression of intent. A solid object descended out of the dusk and thudded into her skull. Her vision went black. She slipped beneath the surface.

For a moment, Jasmine drifted away. A strong survival instinct kicked in and she shoved her head up through the bubbles.

Jasmine's assailant grabbed a shoulder, hit her again, then pushed her back down.

20

PRESENT DAY

Ashley gagged now the corpse had risen to the surface. Helga and Hans had come out of their lodge and walked over without being noticed. It was Helga who shrieked. Ashley loosely returned the cover as Hector herded the Germans back inside. Both were open-mouthed.

Mrs Stone had dropped the lead and staggered backwards. There was an almighty splash as her dog leapt into the black pond.

'Frankie, no!' bellowed Mrs Stone, a second too late.

Frankie wallowed around for a bit, then clambered out of the swamp, resembling a hippo who'd spent all day relaxing in there.

'Ring it in, please, Barry,' said Ashley, stepping away from the muddy monster, but the liquid was so thick, little came off when the animal shook himself. Mrs Stone was close to tears as she put Frankie in her van. Her husband's eyes were fixed on the hot tub until she drove off.

Ashley sent Sal back to Reception to fetch Percival and the details of who owned the six lodges in this section of Diamond. While Jan and Hector ensured Deniz didn't sneak out of the rear of his lodge, she rang Kettle. The wind and weak signal made the call difficult.

'Did you say you've found a body in a hot tub?' he asked.

'Yes.'

She shook her head as she overheard Barry use the term 'floater' during his call to Control.

'Any chance it's natural causes?' asked Kettle.

'Not likely. Someone's put a large fish on the side, possibly to create a stench, so the remains would be recovered quicker.'

'How long do you reckon it's been there?'

Ashley approached the hot tub up wind and had another look at the disfigured face. The skin had come away.

'It's hard to say, but a while. It's bloated and decay has begun. Blood has drained from the top of the body. Less than a week maybe, but certainly more than a few days.'

'Any suspects?'

'Yes. We had a chat with the owner of the caravan next to hers, Deniz, and he was shifty. Nothing I could quite put a finger on, but it turns out the victim was his girlfriend.'

'It's usually someone close to them.'

'Exactly. The body obviously isn't in the best condition, but she seems a tad on the old side for him. He's a handsome guy. Might be a money angle. He's in his lodge, and when Sal returns, I'll see what Deniz has to say, but we'll be bringing him to OCC under caution.'

Ashley watched as a car cruised into the drive for lodge Four. It seemed there was also someone in Five with lights having turned on inside.

'Hang on. There are more people in the dwellings nearby now. I'll send Barry, Jan and Sal back with the boyfriend. If he's volatile, I'll ring for a van, but he doesn't seem the type. Hector and I will interview the other neighbours. See if we can get a feel for what's going on here. I assume Deniz isn't going to confess, but it seems he's the link to both deaths.'

'Perhaps Alfie Hook was having an affair with the victim, and the boyfriend found out.'

Ashley thought back to Alfie and smiled.

'Stranger things have happened, but not many. Besides, she was already dead when Alfie came here yesterday, so he either didn't know, or he visited someone else. It appears the deceased, Jasmine, smoked cannabis, so she could have been getting it off Alfie, and that's why he was here. We'll have that checked out. I'll talk to CSI when they arrive, and hopefully they'll process Deniz's lodge first. The quicker we get the body to the mortuary, the better. They'll have to search inside a big pond, too. Push your meeting to 6 p.m. I'll be back well before then and I'll have had a chance to talk to Deniz.'

'Okay. Try to see the likely cause of death. It'll be important if it's a knife wound.'

Ashley strode over to Jasmine's decking. She put another pair of gloves and booties on but stood on the other side of the railing so she didn't need to walk across the decking. She took a deep breath, then leaned over the tub. The water was a murky reddish brown. She suspected it was blood that had caused it, but there was no visible injury on the exposed part of the bloated body.

'She's in a bikini, but there's nothing obvious, although the water probably contains some blood. I'm guessing not a stabbing because there'd be more of it. CSI won't drain the tub until they've finished with all their photographs, sampling and fingerprinting.'

Ashley heard vehicles behind her and turned as the first response vehicle drove swiftly into Diamond. Ashley was glad they hadn't put their sirens on as that would have only drawn interest. Another police 4 x 4 arrived. Hector strode over to assist with securing the scene.

'Make sure the residents of Four and Five don't leave,' she shouted to Hector.

'I'll ring if there are any developments,' she said to Kettle, and finished the call.

Sal returned with Percival, who craned his neck to see inside the hot tub before turning a shade of yellow and looking unsteady on his feet.

'Is she really dead?' he said. 'Terrible shame.'

'Okay,' said Sal, passing her a sheet of printed paper. 'The lad at Reception has provided us with a list of names for the owners of the lodges on Diamond and their home addresses.'

'Great. I'll have a chat with Deniz now. We'll see what he has to say, but I suspect we'll end up arresting him. If that's the case, I'd like you, Jan and Barry to escort him back to Norwich and start on the paperwork. I'm going to talk to the owners of Four and Five, assuming they aren't renting, of course. I also want to have an idea about how Jasmine died before I leave.'

Barry came over, and they stood outside Deniz's lodge. The smell of death lingered in the air. Ashley's ears strained to hear if there were any sounds coming from inside but there was nothing and the lights had been turned off.

'Wait a minute,' said Ashley as Sal raised his fist to knock.

She called over the two constables who'd left their 4 x 4.

'Just in case,' she said to Sal and Barry.

Ashley briefly explained the situation to the response officers. Sal knocked, and they all took a step back.

A gust howled around the edges of the lodge. Jasmine's wind chimes jingled madly in the background but Deniz didn't come to the door.

Ashley stared down at the list of names she'd been given. Number two belonged to Jasmine Green. Number one was owned by Dorothy Turner with an address in Sheffield. She recalled Hans using Dennis instead of Deniz.

Ashley tensed as a shadow approached the door and it opened.

Deniz came out with bright white trainers on, and a black baseball cap pulled down low.

'Sorry. I was getting dressed.'

'We need some questions answering, please, Deniz,' said Sal.

'Okay,' he said, still looking down so his face was concealed.

'Your actual name is Dennis, isn't it?' asked Ashley, suspecting deceit from the beginning.

Deniz lifted his head so they could just see his eyes under the brim of the cap. They were bloodshot.

He briefly caught Ashley's gaze, then nodded.

21

Dennis Turner appeared to be in a weakened mental state and Ashley wondered whether he might confess on the spot.

'We're here to talk to you about Jasmine Green,' she said.

Dennis lowered his cap again, so his eyes were concealed, but his voice was stronger.

'I won't say anything without my solicitor present.'

'If you're responsible, then co-operate now.'

'I can't say any more.'

Sal stepped forward.

'I'm arresting you on suspicion of the murder of Jasmine Green.'

Ashley watched as Sal finished cautioning him before Barry cuffed Dennis at the front, led him away to Sal's car, and put him on the rear seat. Dennis didn't utter a word, remaining stooped and docile, even as Barry slammed the door. No denial, no anger, nothing. He didn't glance over at the murder scene.

When he arrived back at OCC, Dennis would be under incredible scrutiny. Fingernail scrapings would be taken, and his clothing would get rushed to the lab. The location records and contents of his phone, and the drives of his laptop, would be analysed. CSI would start a fingertip search of his dwelling, car and any other addresses he might have. For a few days at least, his life would be under a microscope.

'Thoughts?' asked Hector.

'I don't know,' replied Ashley. 'People who kill never fail to surprise me. Some of them turn themselves off like he's doing, but there's something odd going on. He might have killed his partner, Jasmine, in the heat of passion, but why would he murder Alfie up at the chip shop?'

'Two killers?'

'It's a bit of a coincidence.'

Ashley exhaled deeply, then tutted.

'They're a strange pair to be murdered. Lodge-owning, dope-smoking Jasmine sounds pretty harmless, and Alfie doesn't appear to have been a significant threat to anyone.'

'Yet Dennis didn't come out and deny the accusation.'

'Which means...' said Ashley with a smile.

'He's probably got previous.'

'Good, you're learning. Did you clock the prison tattoo?'

Hector shook his head.

'Jail tats often end up as smudged blue marks.'

Ashley called Barry over. 'Do a name check on Dennis Turner in case he's wanted for killing officers in escort vehicles.'

Barry smiled because all transported prisoners were treated as if they were going to do that. She also wouldn't need to remind Barry to stay in touch with the team back at OCC and Control. Nor would she need to prompt him to keep making entries in his pocket notebook, which she occasionally had to do with Hector.

'Will do.'

The area was filling fast with the necessary teams. An ambulance was pulling in, and two CSI vans had arrived. More police units were parked at the entrance to Diamond. When he arrived, the doctor would be there for minutes, but processing the rest of the scene would take days. The swirling wind and intermittent rain would also make it an unpleasant task.

'Come on, Hector. Let's have a chat with whoever's in Four. It should be a Patricia Dilley. Hopefully, at least one person here is of sound mind.'

They knocked on the door, and a slim black woman in trendy, tight spandex quickly answered it. She appeared in a surprisingly upbeat mood.

'Hi, officers.'

'We have some questions if you have a few minutes.'

'Okay, no problem.'

'I'm DS Ashley Knight and this is DC Hector Fade. And you are?'

'Patricia Dilley, but call me Pip, cos I'm small but full of energy. Come on in.'

Ashley stepped inside and got a whiff of liquorice and herbs. She suspected Pip might also be full of alcohol.

The layout was identical to Dennis's lodge.

'I've always been envious of these,' said Ashley. 'Could you give me the tour?'

'Sure. There are three bedrooms, one with an en suite, a main bathroom, the lounge and kitchen area, although it's open-plan. It's like a bungalow but, instead of being on an estate, we're surrounded by nature, and I can walk to the beach in fifteen minutes.'

'Or Vegas Fish Bar,' said Hector.

'I don't go there. I suffer from IBS, so greasy food races through me.' Pip giggled. 'Too much info?'

'And you live here on your own?'

'Yes. I was a doctor at King's Lynn hospital for thirty years.

Owning one of these was always my dream. I thought it was my husband's, too. When I retired a few years ago, I bought it with my tax-free lump sum. Turns out my husband wanted to do different things, so I live here on my own now. I love the peace and quiet, but, most of all, I adore the sunsets.'

'My colleague's going to take a few notes, if that's okay?' asked Ashley.

'Of course. Sit down. I've had a Negroni cocktail, which is so naughty. I didn't even make it to midday.'

'I suppose it feels like you're on holiday all the time here,' said Hector. 'Although doesn't alcohol upset your digestion?'

'Negronis don't for some reason, but I only have one or two. I never drank spirits, but a guy I was seeing introduced them to me as an aperitif. It's Saturday and I treat myself before having a nice piece of salmon with salad. I suppose you aren't allowed on duty. How about tea or coffee?'

'Nothing for me, thanks, Pip,' said Ashley. 'Now, how close were you to Jasmine?'

'Is she, you know, dead?'

'I'm afraid so.'

'Murdered?'

'We're not certain of anything at this point. I'm sure Hans or Helga will tell you we found her in the hot tub.'

'What a terrible shame.'

'Yes,' said Ashley, realising it was the exact same phrase Percival had used.

'She loved that tub and was always chilling in it and watching the sunsets.'

'Did she tend to relax inside it with other people?' asked Hector.

Pip laughed. 'What is he like? No, Jasmine's not that way at all. She invited me over to try it out, but it's not my thing. I wouldn't climb in the bath with her, so why get in her tub? Her boyfriend was sometimes in it when he wasn't being a wanker.'

'Dennis.'

'He calls himself Deniz, but yes. They'd split up, though. He's a complete player, and he was mean to her.'

'How so?'

'He'd often agree to go around for dinner. She'd buy all the ingredients, cook, then he wouldn't show. Just cruel, thoughtless stuff. He's been seeing a real corker lately. I said Jasmine was better off without him, but she was vulnerable.'

'In what way?' asked Ashley.

'The usual, I guess. She had an abusive marriage.'

Ashley's ears pricked up. 'Go on.'

'Sounds as though her husband was a psychopath. One of those men you read about in the paper who's super successful but devoid of emotion. He ran a FTSE100 company, loads of cash. She was stuck at home in London where she didn't know anyone.'

'I assume she finally summoned enough courage to leave, and he didn't like it.'

'No, not at all. She was well and truly stuck. He'd done the whole thing. Controlled all the money, her friends, investments. They had a son, who she didn't want to leave, but they aren't close now. Then her husband had a sudden fatal heart attack a few years back. She inherited everything and purchased this place. Her son lives in the house in London, but she doesn't return much, and he's only been here once. We all heard the row they had.'

Ashley checked her sheet of paper.

'I've got an address for Jasmine in Barnes.'

'That's it. Her son will be there. Works for an investment bank as a trainee in the city. HSBC, I think. Training to be just like his dad, by the sounds of it.' Pip chuckled. 'Sorry, look at me making jokes when Jasmine's been killed.'

'Would you say Jasmine and you were close?'

Pip tipped her head to one side.

'No. We're all nice and friendly here, but you have to be careful not to get too pally. If you fall out, there's trouble in Paradise, if you know what I mean. It's like prison. You can't avoid them if they live next door. So, I'd say Jasmine and I were chatty, nothing more. I'm closer to Glory in Five. She enjoys a drink and a gossip in the evening, and we play tennis, even though she always kicks my arse.'

'Were you here on Thursday night?'

'I was at an Indian restaurant on Thursday, in Lynn and, unusually, I was back at Lynn all last weekend, too.'

'Do you have anyone to corroborate that?'

'Lots of people.'

'Okay,' said Ashley. 'I think we have enough for the moment. Please try not to go anywhere today while they process the scene. The officers will help if you must leave. Will you be here next week?'

'I was planning to be. Should I be worried? I heard someone was killed last night up on South Beach Road too.'

Ashley wasn't sure how to reply.

'Be vigilant, Pip. We're taking Dennis in for a chat at the station, but I can't say more.'

'I'd doubt he'd have the balls to do it, drippy sod, although it's dangerous being his ex-girlfriend.'

'Why do you say that?'

'The woman who took her own life earlier this year went out with him too.'

22

Ashley left Pip's lodge wondering who the hell was handcuffed in the car outside. Barry was waiting for them.

'Okay, we're off,' he said. 'Lover boy here has a history as long as your arm.'

'Anything serious?'

Barry checked an email on his phone.

'No, that's the strange part. It's mostly low-level, although there are two counts of arson when he was a teenager. There's a lengthy juvenile record of petty stuff, but the adult years are mainly acquisitive crime. Theft from shops, but also commercial burglaries, one aggravated domestic burglary, fraud, quite a few drunk and disorderly offences, multiple aliases including Donald Taylor, Darren Turner, and, of course, Deniz Turner, and various vehicle offences, the most serious being dangerous driving and taking without consent.'

'A car crash of a record, if you'll excuse the pun. What are the details of the violent offences?'

'The aggravated burglary only led to a suspended sentence, so I assume he was caught with a weapon to break into the house, like a crowbar, but not a knife. I doubt he threatened anyone with it either, or he'd have got custody.'

'Any others for violence?'

'Just one. Fifteen years ago. Assault with intent to resist arrest.'

'That doesn't sound promising for your drive to Norwich.'

'He only received a conditional discharge so he was probably drunk. He'd already been to prison twice, so anything serious and he would've gone back down.'

'Wait a minute. No record for drugs?'

'No. Not even possession of small amounts.'

'And the arsons?'

'The last one was when he was nineteen. Again, no custodial stay for either.'

Ashley updated Barry on what Pip had told her. Barry twisted his head to stare at the car with Dennis in but didn't comment.

'Has he said anything?' asked Ashley.

'No. He's zoned out. Gave his date of birth and confirmed his home address in Sheffield, but that's it. There's another odd thing, though. There's no offending for the last three years.'

Ashley leaned into the breeze as another gust rocked her.

'Can you or Sal give South Yorkshire Police a ring and ask them about this guy? Check what sort of house it is. Sheffield is a horrific drive from here.'

'Three-hours at least, and it'd be worse by public transport.'

'It seems unlikely he'd be driving back and forwards for six hours to hide anything incriminating. Call Emma at the office to check ANPR, and let's see where his Toyota's been.'

'Bank account check in case he's rented a car out?'

'Yep. Let's keep looking at every angle. Phone mast analysis for his and Jasmine's mobiles. Pip said Dennis and Jasmine had split up, but we'll hopefully know if they were both here at the same time, so it at least puts Dennis in the vicinity.'

'Michelle's going to give us a huge window for time of death.'

'Yep, anything else before we visit the next lodge?'

'Percival has changed his tune and is sending all the records we asked for, which makes me suspicious.'

'Let's hope Dennis is honest with us or this could be tricky,' Ashley said with a wry smile.

Barry laughed. 'We'll get going. See you back at OCC.'

Another CSI van was arriving as she and Hector approached the next van and Ashley studied her list. Gloria Trubell. Home address in King's Lynn, which was only sixteen miles away.

While Hector knocked, she compared the six lodges. They looked well built with double-glazed windows, so they might not have heard all the vehicles arriving, but she reckoned if it had happened in her back yard, she'd have been out of her lodge asking questions.

The woman who opened the door to them was wearing tight leopard-print exercise shorts and a short crop top. She said nothing, just gave them a thin smile.

'Gloria Trubell?'

The woman nodded.

Ashley introduced herself and Hector, then explained why they were here.

They weren't invited in. Glory had a flushed complexion and drops of moisture on her forehead. She was noticeably older than Pip, so it was impressive she thrashed her at tennis.

'Can we come in?'

'I'd rather you didn't. I haven't tidied.'

'You ought to see my place,' said Ashley.

'And I'm a bit busy. Could you return this afternoon?'

'We can go to a police station if you'd prefer, and talk there.'

Ashley detected a small grin as the door was opened wide for them. The layout was the same. Gloria directed them into the lounge and herded them onto a sofa. She turned behind her and switched the TV off, which had been muted but still played a yoga class. Then she picked up the exercise mat and moved it out of sight to the kitchen.

Gloria had an amazing figure and athleticism for anyone of any age, never mind someone who appeared to be a pensioner. She had grey hair and a lined face with no make-up, which was quite a contrast to her toned body.

The lodge was more impersonal than Pip's had been, but there were a few pictures of a younger Gloria in front of the twin towers of the World Trade Centre and another on top of a massive dam. There was a picture of a young man fishing off a boat, arms bulging as his rod strained.

'We're here to talk to you about what's happened on the site and near here, Gloria,' said Ashley.

'It's Glory. Kids at school struggled with my name, and they kept cutting it short. Eventually it stuck.'

'Okay, I like it,' said Ashley. 'Do you have a partner, Glory?'

'Sorry, is Jasmine dead? I've been peering out the window. Even I know all these people don't turn up for nothing.'

'Yes, unfortunately.'

'How?'

'We're not sure. She was in the hot tub.'

'Was that the horrible smell?'

'Perhaps part of it.'

Hector pointed at the photograph of the fisherman.

'Do you enjoy fishing?'

'That's my husband. He did, but he had a car accident a few years back and is in a coma.'

'I'm sorry to hear that.'

Glory's jaw clenched for a second.

'Yes, it's a godawful thing. We hoped to retire in the sunshine.

He planned to write a book, but they don't expect much change now. The awful part is because he was so fit, he could last for decades.'

'Are you here on your own, then?'

'Yes, I visit my husband a few times a week. It's only thirty minutes if the traffic is light, and it's the least I can do. If the roads are bad, I'll stay at our flat in King's Lynn, then return like I did today.'

'Were you here last night?'

'No, I was at home.'

'Could anyone else confirm that?'

'Yes.'

'It's funny, some people call this their home.'

Glory chuckled, and this time her smile was genuine.

'This is a vacation spot for me,' she said. 'A place separate from my life in Lynn.'

Ashley realised Glory was also a local like Jasmine because only fen folk shortened King's Lynn to Lynn.

'Do you know an Alfie Hook?'

Glory shook her head, nonplussed.

'Were you aware someone died near Vegas Fish Bar?'

'No. When was that?'

'It was a delivery driver in a red van on Thursday evening.' Ashley paused to see if there was a change in Glory's demeanour, but there wasn't. 'Have you seen a red van around here recently?'

'You mean on the park or generally?'

'Here.'

'No, wait, maybe twice. You don't see many apart from maintenance trucks. I recognised it because it had PSST! on the side of it. That's what caught my attention the first time.'

'Did you notice who was driving it?'

'No, it was just a head in the cab. It was parked opposite in between Deniz and Jasmine's. Oddly enough, I can recall hearing a raised voice.'

'Male or female.'

'Male.'

'Was it the driver or someone else?'

'Sorry, I've no clue. It might even have been the guys next to me. They have the odd ruckus.'

Ashley checked her face for malice, but none was present. She seemed to have a clear idea of what went on in Diamond.

'Do you ever smell cannabis here?'

'Occasionally. Now, that is Jasmine. Was Jasmine.' Glory's chin wobbled for a moment, but she sniffed and carried on. 'She was always burning joss sticks and scented candles. I loved the citronella ones because they helped with the mossies in summer, but I've often noticed the warm smell of colitas.'

Ashley smiled at the line from 'Hotel California'.

'Does she smoke it with her boyfriend?'

'I never saw her current one, Deniz, smoke anything. He's into his fitness. We've had the odd jog together when we've bumped into each other around the site or on the seafront. Pip and I sometimes go running, but she drops out at five miles.' Glory cocked her head to one side. 'It won't be Jasmine's previous bloke either, seeing as it's illegal and therefore against his precious rules.'

'Who's the previous guy?'

'Pervert Percy.'

23

Ashley did a double take.

'The manager of the park, Percival?' asked Ashley.

'Yes. He was just Percy. Then Deniz arrived, they got friendly, and he became Percival. He hoped to be cool like Deniz, until Deniz stole his girlfriend.'

Ashley nodded at Hector. It was time to pop Deniz's bubble.

'We believe Deniz Turner's real name is Dennis Turner.'

Glory stared at Ashley, then laughed.

'That makes sense. The lovely couple at number three, Hans and Helga, always call him Dennis and he never corrects them. I thought he was being polite because they were old. Jeez, Percy and Dennis sure are peas in a pod.'

'How long has Dennis been here?'

'A bit over a year, I'd say. I think it was his mum and dad's place. I saw them once when I first bought my lodge, but she was on her last legs, and he didn't so much as smile the whole time he was here. I've not seen either of them for ages.'

'Do you speak to Dennis, or did you chat to Jasmine?'

'No, not often. Jasmine was a twitchy, quiet type. Nice enough, but a gentle soul. She offered to read my fortune once. I had a glass of wine while she did it, but she took it seriously. My reading was great, but then she told me they weren't Tarot cards, but another sort of fortune-telling card, which didn't have death and the other dark stuff in the deck.'

'Sounds as though she preferred to keep a positive outlook on life. Will you be here next week?'

'Yes, apart from the odd trip back to Lynn.'

'It's likely we'll have more questions. We've got your contact details. Anything else you'd like to tell us?'

'No.' Glory smiled. 'It's incestuous here, isn't it?'

Ashley smiled back. She'd been thinking the same thing.

'You can say that again.'

'It's *Love Island* for old folk. I avoid it all. I've always found it best to keep my distance because this isn't real life. When I visit my husband, I'm reminded of that.'

'Thanks for your time,' said Ashley.

As Ashley left, she realised Glory's place was spotless, which was at odds with what she had indicated at the door. She shrugged. Did anyone want the police in their home if they could help it?

The lights were on at Six, which was the last of the homes on this part of Diamond.

'I almost can't wait to see who's in here,' said Hector. 'It's probably Lord Lucan and Elvis.'

'Hi,' said a handsome man around sixty when he answered the door. 'Come in. We thought you'd knock.'

Ashley and Hector trudged in and went straight to the sofa and sat down. Another good-looking man, but slighter and pretty rather than handsome, came in with a tray of coffees and biscuits. He pushed a pouffe over and rested the tray on it.

'Help yourselves. Careful with those biscuits. I've already eaten three.'

'Thanks,' said Ashley, who was parched and hungry.

After they'd made their introductions, they didn't need to question the happy couple because they both loved to talk.

'I'm Verne,' said the older one who'd answered the door. 'This is Bertie. We've been married for eight years, and we've been here for six, so we've witnessed most of the comings and goings.'

'Have you noticed a red van?' asked Hector.

'I've seen the one that was here a few days ago before. There's another one the same in blue. We're at the end, so we notice more of who comes and goes, but we have our decking at the back.'

'That way,' joked Bertie, with a wink, 'we can sunbathe topless.'

Ashley chuckled. 'Good for you.'

'Ooh, is this anything to do with the incident up near the Vegas?'

'We don't know at this point.'

'I've just watched two officers hide the hot tub with a tent. She loved that thing, saucy little cow,' he said, with a mischievous look.

'Why saucy?'

'I was shutting the windows one night at the front, and I saw her in it with Studley Dudley over the road. Going at it they were, without a care in the world.'

'You didn't tell me that,' said Verne.

'I only watched for ten minutes.'

Verne raised an eyebrow. 'Now who's a saucy cow?'

Bertie chuckled.

'It's a shame. She was a nice, pretty girl, but we had little to do with her. Even though we're in the same section, there's plenty of space and we can go ages without crossing paths. We aren't here much because I'm still working. Although retirement beckons.'

'What do you do?' asked Ashley.

'I'm a theatre manager at King's Lynn hospital. We live in Thetford. There's a lot of pressure, but it's rewarding. The money's good, too. I want to buy a motorbike.'

'You'll do no such thing,' said Verne.

Bertie winked at Ashley.

'I'll also purchase a sidecar, and a huge Big Bird costume for him to wear, so we can make people smile as we drive past.'

Ashley and Hector couldn't help laughing.

'Have you heard any arguments? Or seen anything that might indicate trouble?' asked Hector.

'That's the thing,' said Bertie. 'Dennis has fallouts all the time, with different women.'

'Do you remember that car one of them had?' asked Verne. 'She was attractive, although she bellowed that he was a fucking liar. At least the motor was classy.'

'Did you see her or catch the vehicle type or reg number?'

'No, it was dark, but it had a throaty roar. Bit like its owner.'

'Dennis also rowed with Percy shortly after the loving in the hot tub,' said Bertie. 'I only overhead snippets. Dennis said he thought Jasmine was single, and asked Percy what he wanted him to do.'

'I assume they didn't duel for her honour.'

'Percy flounced off.'

'It's amusing these women fall for it,' said Verne. 'Besides, dating on your doorstep is silly, especially in Percy's case. He should know better.'

'With him being the manager?' asked Ashley.

'Oh, he is a wicked man,' said Bertie. 'Percy's not just the manager, he's also the owner.'

24

When Ashley was at the door to leave, she remembered what Glory had said. Verne and Bertie were grinning as she stepped outside, so she spoke bluntly to see their response.

'Someone mentioned you two occasionally argue.'

Verne's face fell.

'Who told you that? Bloody shit-stirrers. I bet it was that thieving prick, Percy. I always knew he'd rip us off at some point.'

'Shush,' says Bertie, softly. 'Now look what you've done,' he said to Ashley.

'What did Percy do?'

Bertie took a deep breath.

'We explained when we first arrived we might sell up in five years and go travelling for a while. Percy suggested he'd give us a decent price when the time came, but when we put out feelers last year, he wasn't generous at all. Blamed it on inflation.'

'Which is bollocks. Have you ever seen a poor park owner?' said Verne.

Ashley shook her head, but her mind was on Percival, who'd lied to her face. She confirmed the couple would still be around for the next few days and thanked them for their help. Bertie ushered Verne back inside, waved at the detectives, then closed the door.

Ashley and Hector returned to the cordon that had been set up at Two where Gerald, the CSI manager, was waiting.

'I wasn't expecting to see you two again so soon,' he said, remarkably chipper for someone who must have been on his way home from the Alfie Hook scene.

'Not sad you aren't snoozing on the sofa?'

'No, I like these kinds of cases. Poor Alfie was straightforward. But this one is a bit of a conundrum in an interesting location. It'll take us days to complete, and it's supposed to be warm tomorrow.' He smiled at Ashley. 'I've had my eye on some new fishing kit, so with all this overtime I can pay in one fell swoop without getting divorced.'

'Ah, you're a fisherman. Was that your turbot?'

'Not bad. It's actually a big sole. My first thought was it was put there to disguise the stench of the dead body.'

'So instead of smelling a rotting corpse, they'd smell fish and think it came from the pond.'

'That's right.'

'We wondered whether it had been done to draw attention to the tub. I suppose a fish would decompose a lot quicker than Jasmine.'

'Yes, without being surrounded by cold water, fish bacteria multiply much faster than in humans.'

'Any clue to how she died?'

'We've removed the body from the tub now, but it's not obvious. The barbecue was out on the decking with what appears to be incinerated sausages on it. She might have slipped and banged her head as she got out to check on what was cooking.'

'And as she fell back in to drown, she shoved the barbecue away and pulled the tub cover on top of her?' said Hector.

'Just running things through, young man.'

'Fair enough,' said Ashley. 'I assume you can catch sole around here.'

'Yes, but that's the intriguing part. Young sole feed at night close to the beach, but this one's too large. They live a hundred metres down so only a trawler would catch a fish this size, unless it was dead and washed up on the beach.'

'Which means someone bought it.'

'Yes, and it wouldn't have been cheap, either. If Tesco have a fish counter still, I doubt they sell a sole this size.'

'I suppose it's possible Jasmine purchased it a while back for the freezer, then took it out for the barbecue. Then whoever attacked her left it and covered the hot tub up.'

'Agreed. It would be significant planning to buy the fish prior to killing her. Keep in mind, not many places would sell this type of fish.'

'Okay. Was there much blood in the water?' asked Ashley.

'Some. I wouldn't have wanted a dip in this hot tub. If the liquid had been any thicker, it would have resembled gravy.'

'Gross.'

'Yes, so it's hard to say what the make up of it is. Jasmine has a lot of hair, which prevents us seeing, but I wouldn't be surprised if Michelle found a fractured skull underneath.'

'No weapon in the tub?'

'No, but a mobile has been recovered from the water and we're checking the drain now.'

'Excellent, so if the phone was on, we'll know when it stopped pinging the nearest mast and therefore have a reasonable guess at time of death.'

'Yes, but after a long spell submerged, the chance of getting information off it is virtually zero. It's an old model too, so any connection to the cloud is unlikely.'

'Have you been in her lodge?'

'One of my team had a quick look in case there was something of immediate importance. It's messy, but it doesn't appear there's been a tussle of any kind. She smokes inside.'

'Drugs?'

'Yes, and cigarettes. A tobacco tin on the kitchen worktop contains a pouch of baccy and what appears to be a couple of buds of marijuana. No obvious blood spills, no broken crockery, upended chairs, nor smashed windows. There's a good picture of her on the wall, seems recent. He took a photo of that for you, and the rest has been videoed to save you going in.'

'What about the pond and Dennis's place?'

'We'll have police divers here tomorrow. They'll need to do it by finger, which won't be nice for them. We've popped inside Dennis's place too, and there was nothing obvious like a murder weapon. We'll search properly after Jasmine's. I won't stay too long, but my team will work 'til late. I've spoken to Michelle. We'll get the body to the mortuary for her by close of play today so she can do the PM first thing in the morning.'

'Great.'

A uniformed sergeant appeared at Ashley's shoulder.

'We've got more bodies to help. Do you want door-to-door inquiries done on the next part of the site, or we could assist with the search?'

After allocating tasks, Ashley stared past the pond and through the trees. There were caravans as far as the eye could see. Kettle would need to request a proper search team. Any one of them could contain the suspect, or the person responsible could have easily left the park altogether without being seen. It wasn't like London here, where every third lamppost and house had CCTV.

Movement grabbed her attention as a CSI stepped off Jasmine's decking and strode towards his boss.

'Gerald. This was in the filter of the hot tub.'

Gerald took the bagged item off him and felt its weight. He held it up to the light. Ashley stood next to him.

'It's an earring,' he said, showing her. 'Just one. Big, but weighty for its size.'

Ashley admired the leaf design.

'If it's gold and those are diamonds, then I doubt it was Jasmine's,' said Gerald. 'Seems too extravagant compared to the style and décor of her lodge.'

'I checked,' said the CSI. 'The victim's ear piercings had closed up.'

25

Ashley said goodbye to Gerald, who confirmed he'd call with anything urgent.

'Shall we have a word with Percy before we leave?' asked Hector.

'I'm sick to death of all the half-truths we've been given. If Percy had been honest with us at the start, then we wouldn't need to talk to him again. We haven't got the time now, so he can come back to OCC.'

Ashley arranged for two uniforms to assist with a transfer to Norwich, and they followed her to Reception, where Percy was hastily leaving the office with his briefcase. A two-seater BMW's light flashed, then Percy clambered inside. Hector parked a few centimetres behind his rear bumper. Ashley caught the expression of total panic on Percy's face as he slipped from his car.

'I was just coming to see you.'

Ashley shook her head. 'You weren't, Percy, were you?'

Percy grimaced. 'No, sorry.'

'No problem,' said Ashley, leaving her vehicle. 'Nice of you to bring your briefcase, which I assume contains your laptop. Do you have your phone with you?'

Hector took gloves and an evidence bag out of the van and took Percy's phone and briefcase from him. Ashley concluded he was trying to flee, so, with his lack of earlier disclosure, decided she had enough to arrest him. She felt further validated when, like Dennis, Percy didn't protest in any way except for demanding to ring someone.

'Later,' said Ashley.

'It's my right to have a phone call.'

'No, you have a right to legal advice. I can let someone else know where you are if I don't think it interferes with my investigation.'

Percy quietened down and clambered into the back of the van without further protest. He seemed to be half asleep by the time she'd given the uniformed officers their instructions. Hector stared at the van as it left the park.

'Do guilty people usually sleep so easily?' he asked.

'Not unless they're drunk. I suppose he could have been exhausted by his actions, and expecting to be caught. Now he has been, it's a relief.'

Hector shook his head.

'This all seems rather convoluted to me.'

'I suppose, but it often is until we see the big picture. Dennis and Percy have serious questions to answer. How they reply will direct the rest of our investigation.'

They returned to their car and drove in silence for another ten minutes, then Ashley's phone rang. It was DS Bhavini Kotecha.

'Hi, Bee. How's things?'

She heard Bee sob before replying. It sounded as if she was outside.

'Ash, I need advice, or at least to speak to someone kind before I go crazy. Can we meet tonight?'

Ashley thought of the interviews she had to do. Bloody job, but these first few hours were so important.

'I'm not going to be home until eight at the earliest.'

'That's fine. I'll book us a table at The Red Lion. I'll see if the window one is free.'

Ashley briefly smiled. There was nothing like eating with a view of the sea. Then Bee started to weep.

'Bee. What's wrong? Do you want me to send someone to help?'

'No, I'm at my brother's.'

'Don't do anything daft.'

'I won't. I've just been so stupid. You know when we had our girls' day out?'

'Yes.'

'I felt empowered and took Himansu for a meal and told him I wasn't prepared to be second-best. He ghosted me afterwards, which wasn't nice, but my dad discovered what was going on and he's thrown me out. I don't know what I'm going to do.'

'Hey, it's okay. You'll get sorted. It's not the end of the world. I'll be at mine and ready to go at eight thirty. We'll walk into town, eat, and put the world to rights, okay?'

'Okay.'

Bee finished the call and Ashley blew out a deep breath.

'I take it that was Bee with man trouble,' said Hector.

'Yes. Her married boyfriend and her religious father being the men.'

'It seems our day at the pub caused many ripples in the universe.'

'How do you mean?'

'Everyone there took something from it and made changes to

their lives. Emma told me a few days ago she's fed up with her status quo.'

'She said status quo?'

'No, that's my term.'

Ashley almost pouted at the fact Emma had told Hector first. Hector smiled.

'Bee decided that being the other woman doesn't suit. You're getting yourself together with your fitness and direction. Everyone says you're more focused and happier.'

'It's true. I do feel fitter and healthier. The unhealthy drinking is under control. It'd be nice to have someone special to share my life with, but it doesn't matter as much any more.'

'Good for you.'

'I think the paramedic who came along with us is dating my neighbour.'

'Joan and Arthur?'

'Yep.'

'Wow. There must be ten years between them.'

'Yes, I fear for him.' She chuckled.

'How do you feel about your thing?'

Ashley grimaced.

At the meet in The Wellington pub, they'd all shared a secret. Ashley had admitted to them, and she supposed to herself, that she wouldn't be having children. Hector had asked her before if she wanted to discuss it, but she'd declined.

'Remember I told you about the airport disaster?' she said.

'Yes.'

'Well, after I knew it was over with him, I panicked and investigated freezing my eggs.'

Ashley swallowed as she thought back to the meeting with the company when they'd discussed her sample.

'Sounds reasonable.'

'It's funny how I homed in on that. I suppose it felt good to be proactive. Anyway, there was a problem. A diminished ovarian reserve was the diagnosis. I won't bore you with the maths, but basically I didn't have many eggs left, and the ones I did have weren't in the best condition.'

'Was there no possibility?'

'Well, there's always hope, but it was the slimmest of chances. So, I didn't bother as it was expensive. It was strange for a couple of weeks after I made the decision. Like someone had died. I suppose my hopes of being a mother in a natural way had perished.'

'There are many ways to be a mum.'

Ashley smiled at him.

'Did you talk to anyone about it?'

'Yes. I'm talking to you now. I needed to get used to the idea myself. It's not the end of the world. I love my job and I can focus on that, and it's a relief, in a way, to finally accept it.'

Ashley was again surprised why she found it so easy to open up to this young man.

'What did you learn from our day out?' she asked.

'Michelle has a crush on me. She asked me out for a drink.'

'Wow. Are you going to go?'

'No, I don't think so. Despite what I've just said, she's ten years older than me, and I think that matters when I'm twenty-four.'

'It's funny this has come up. It occurred to me when we knew Dennis had been dating Jasmine, and they had a significant age gap. Surely it's just a case of finding someone you enjoy spending time with and letting it flow from there.'

'Ah, I see. You're saying it's a clear path ahead, so don't put barriers up before you've walked it.'

Ashley laughed. 'Something like that, and Michelle might

teach you a thing or two. She's pretty, clever and has a well-paid job. It's not like you've been asked out by Myra Hindley.'

'There is a loose connection. Michelle manhandles dead bodies.'

'In the end, it's about enjoying spending time together.'

'"All you need is love,"' said Hector.

'Da-da-da-da-dar!'

As they continued their journey in companionable silence, Ashley realised she enjoyed spending time with Hector. The ebb and flow of a good detective team was often a balance of support and piss-taking. Hector was proving capable of both.

26

The incident room had been set up and was a hive of activity when they arrived. Barry, Emma and Sal were deep in discussion.

'How's our likely suspect?' asked Ashley.

'The usual,' said Sal. 'He's adamant he won't say another word until the family brief has arrived, and the solicitor said he'll be here at nine tomorrow.'

'I take it you explained to Dennis he's entitled to legal advice, not legal advice from someone twelve hours away which eats into the time we can hold him.'

'We did. He insists he'll tell us everything tomorrow.'

'Okay, give him the duty solicitor. Do the interview, apply pressure, but not too much. Assuming he doesn't give us anything, it's not the end of the world if he sings in the morning. We can keep him overnight while we wait for CSI to finish.'

'Yes, Sarge.'

'Have we spoken to South Yorkshire Police about Dennis's address?'

'Yep,' said Emma. 'The DS I spoke to was a bit surprised because Stumperlowe is one of the more prestigious addresses in

Sheffield. They've sent a team out to see if there's anyone home. They're doing background searches, too.'

'And the council records?'

'That's the thing – the property is in the name of a Cecil Dowd.'

Ashley frowned.

'Why is that familiar?'

'He was an MP.'

'Brilliant. Dennis gave a false address to Percy.'

'No. Dennis is down as one of the residents of the property, but there's no Dorothy Turner. Cecil must be Dennis's stepdad.'

'Perhaps Dennis and Cecil have a few issues, so that could be an angle for you at interview. Any progress with the suicide?'

'One of the other teams has taken it. They'll be ready to report at the meeting.'

'Anything with CCTV?'

'Nope.'

'Hector and I are off to talk to the owner, Percy. We don't have enough to keep him in, unless he gives us something. I should be finished and ready for the meeting with Kettle at six. I've sent you a recent picture of Jasmine, so let's have the boards set up and see if it helps with connections between Jasmine and Alfie. There's a vague drug angle, but I suspect it will come down to the usual.'

Even Hector didn't comment. It was usually sex or money.

An hour later, Dennis had refused the duty solicitor and declined to answer any questions. The duty solicitor then came and sat with Percy in interview room two, opposite Ashley and Hector. Hector went through the preliminaries. It was cool in the room, but Percy was perspiring heavily.

'You have quite a bit of explaining to do, Percy,' said Ashley.

She deliberately used the shortened version to see if he corrected her and gave them a hint of any vanity.

'I know, I know. Sorry, but I tell everyone I'm the manager so I can say that I'll ask the owner, then blame it on him when it's a no. Everyone's always after something or trying to break the rules, and nobody likes to be told no. You wouldn't believe the amount of people who grow things on their plots. It's not a bloody allotment.'

'I'm prepared to let that pass if you start by telling us about the woman who died earlier this year.'

Percy wiped his forehead to clear the sweat from it.

'We were dating for about six months, and it was going well. At least, I thought it was. Then Dennis Turner arrived. His mum, Dorothy, owned the lodge. I'd seen him a few times with her, but she became ill. Dennis moved here permanently, except for the month we close. I spoke to Dorothy's husband, and he said Dorothy wanted Dennis to use the lodge when she died.'

'Did Dorothy die?'

'I think so. Dennis never mentioned it. The bills keep getting paid.'

'Back to the lady who took her own life. What was her name?'

'Katrina Lake. We used to go in the bar together, and I'd show her off. She could really dance. We made a fabulous team.'

It was hard to imagine Percy tangoing around the dance floor, but Ashley humoured him with a smile.

'What went wrong?'

'Dennis started coming in the clubhouse, and next thing I know, Katrina was teaching him the foxtrot. I had my suspicions, but she denied it. Apparently, I was like a stuck record by going on about it, so she dumped me anyway. Then she dated him.'

'The police must have talked to you after the suicide.'

'Yes. A few months after Dennis started seeing her, he dumped her, so that's why some think she killed herself. I was secretly pleased the same thing happened to her, which I know isn't nice, but she broke my heart.'

'Did you try and rekindle your relationship after he broke it off?'

'No, she was in a foul mood afterwards, but I reckon the suicide was something else. She didn't seem the type to do it over a man, especially not a git like Dennis. Katrina had never married. She was a strong-willed woman.'

Ashley paused as she tried to get her head around how interconnected it all was.

'Then you started dating Jasmine,' said Hector.

'Yes. Now, she was a bit more delicate. She pursued me, if you can believe it. I was always kind to her, and I'd helped her find a hot tub when she wanted to buy one. That's how we started chatting. I never got to use it because we were shut for winter, but then Dennis split up with Katrina and started flirting with my Jasmine and she lost interest in me.'

'That must have made you angry.'

'It bloody did, but what could I do?' Percy's attempts at covering up his receding hair meant he had a bit of a floppy Mohican. That and his jowls moved around as he shook his head.

'He's younger, better looking. The women love him. In fact, I liked him. He always made it seem as if they were single by the time he dated them, and they chased him. I realised he should have rebutted their advances if he valued our friendship.'

Ashley raised an eyebrow at that slightly strange comment.

'You'd still describe you and Dennis as friends then?'

'We used to have a beer together in the bar.'

'Do you date a lot of single women on the campsite?' asked Ashley.

Percy calmed himself, then picked at his fingernails to avoid eye contact. 'A few.'

'How do you think that looks with you being the manager?'

'I'm lonely. Where else am I going to meet people?'

'How cross were you with Jasmine for splitting up with you?'

'You don't have to answer,' said the solicitor.

'No, it's fine. I was upset, but I'm kind of used to it. Seems to happen a lot to me, so I became the bigger person and even had a coffee with her last weekend.'

Ashley had been assuming that was approximately the time of her death. Percy picked up on it.

'You want to know if I murdered her. That's what you really want to know.'

'That's right,' said Hector. 'Did you?'

27

Percy leaned back in his seat and tried to put his hair into position.

'Do I look like a killer?'

Ashley had seen enough to know that was a moot question.

'Doesn't owning the park make you a rich man?' she asked.

'It's part of a family trust, but yes, I am wealthy. You'd think I'd be more popular.'

Ashley recalled his slightly greasy behaviour with the young girl from Reception.

'Why didn't you tell us about the suicide straight away?'

Percy nibbled his bottom lip.

'The whole thing made me nervous about being implicated. If there was anything dodgy, I'd have been the first person the police would talk to. Then Jasmine dying was similar, and you guys arrived.'

'You didn't know she was dead then,' said Hector.

'Sorry. I mean the man at the chip shop. I'm not crazy. Why would I kill people in my own park? I live a pleasant life with fine dining and good company, given half the chance. My cars are top of the range. Look at me. Prison would be a disaster. I doubt I'd be lonely in there.'

'Right, Percy,' said Ashley. 'We're going to leave it there for the moment.'

'Can I go?'

'Not just yet. I need to hear an update from the teams at the scene, which should be soon.'

'Please. I won't vanish. I've got a site to run.'

'One last question, Percy. You mentioned you and Dennis became friends when he first arrived, so you must know him well. How does he react when things don't go his way?'

Percy's eyes shifted from side to side. He appeared a simple creature.

'Do you mean does he get angry? I'm sorry to say that he seems quite decent. It surprised me when he stole my women.'

Ashley suspected the reason they dumped him was more to do with his unusual behaviour rather than Dennis's charm.

They finished the interview and returned Percy to the cells. The meeting with DCI Kettle was about to begin. Kettle preferred to keep the briefings formal because they had a variety of personnel in from all areas. Their contribution could be as important as a seasoned DS's.

Ashley's team trooped in at the back, but Kettle beckoned her to the front. He had a chair waiting.

Kettle cleared his throat.

'Thank you for staying late for those who are part-time.'

A brief chuckle went through the staff who were used to Kettle's style, knowing he would then go for the jugular.

'Let me sum up. Two murders less than half a mile apart in the seaside town of Hunstanton. The person we suspect died second was the partner of a recently released career felon. We believe that killing was around sunset on Thursday. Has the PM been done?'

Sal, who was near the front, raised an arm.

'Stand, please, Sal. Speak up.'

'Yes, sir. Single knife wound to the heart. The pathologist was doing more analysis this afternoon. She'll finish the second PM first thing in the morning and is already here tomorrow at midday for a meeting, so she'll attend our get-together if she has the chance and update us all.'

'Excellent. Okay, DS Ashley Knight will be deputy SIO for these cases. What progress have you made at the scene of the death of Alfie Hook?'

'Very little at this point,' said Ashley. 'You'd struggle to find a better location to kill someone, but we know when he likely died because he bought fish and chips and barely touched it, despite getting his own knife and fork out. His mobile phone and money weren't stolen. His wife, who recently finished an eight stretch for death by dangerous driving, was surprised and devastated, but not to be trusted. It seemed to me her family were at least partly taken care of while she was away, which fits in with the rumour that Betty Brown may be connected.'

'I heard Betty had married someone with money.'

'Yes. She oozed confidence that she wasn't involved, but, as we all know, these people could lie for England. Alfie's employers were helpful and provided the route Alfie drove, which included the caravan park, although the site wasn't on his list of drop-offs. We knocked on the caravans nearest to where he briefly stopped. Inside one was a man who told us a string of lies, including his name. We found his next-door neighbour, who was also his ex-girlfriend, dead in her hot tub.'

'I understand a phone was in the water, so we should be able to get the time it last connected with the nearest mast, assuming it was turned on. Who's dealing with that?'

A woman from another team stood up.

'The carrier is Three,' said Zelda, one of Ally's members. 'Which means we should hear by midday tomorrow at the latest. From prior experience with water damage, there'll be no data retrieved from the phone. However, we're contacting social media sites for information, and we've recovered her laptop. Her home address checks out. By council records, she lived with just her son in Barnes when she wasn't at the park.'

'And Mr Dennis Turner was using aliases, but hasn't explained why,' stated Kettle.

Ashley nodded.

'Apparently, he'll talk when the family solicitor arrives. Something doesn't stack up. We're checking to confirm if his mother, who owned the lodge, is dead. The address Dennis gave is also that of a retired MP in Sheffield.'

'I assume we've made contact?'

Ashley turned to Sal and Barry.

'No,' said Barry. 'South Yorkshire Police attended the address. Prosperous street, posh house, no reply. Landline rings out. We're trying to find a mobile number for Mr Cecil Dowd, but no luck so far.'

Kettle took his time as he pondered the next steps.

'This Dennis Turner can be linked to both of the deceased, but he was dating Jasmine, so his prints and DNA will be all over her property anyway. He owns next door, so his mobile will be in the vicinity. If he lives alone, there's no reason why he should have an alibi if he was at home. You say the CCTV in the park is patchy, and there's little where Jasmine died.'

'Correct, sir. This won't be easy if nobody cracks. Also, the man who runs the site, Percy Gray, dated Jasmine. He's a touch odd, also a liar, but an unlikely murderer. The evidence on him is weaker, but both Percy and Dennis dated a woman who killed herself six months ago.'

'I hadn't heard about that. Has anyone seen the coroner's report?'

Another person from Ally's team, Morgan, rose from his chair. 'We just got it back. Coroner's verdict was suicide. There was no note, but the way the body was found and the organisation of her ID and other personal items in the caravan indicated significant planning. There was a break-up, and her mother wasn't long deceased. Some tablets had been recently bought because the receipts were present. The only comment made was one pill type used was unusual.'

'In what way?'

'Two packs of paracetamol were purchased a few days before, but there was also heart medicine taken, which was prescribed, and something called hyoscine butylbromide. Commonly known as Buscopan, it's often used for IBS, but it wasn't prescribed, and she took a lot. It is also used during end-of-life care, and Katrina's mother died a year earlier, so the drugs could have come from then. Friends said they were remarkably close, and her mother's death hit her hard.'

'Right. It seems Dennis Turner has many questions to answer. I think we can wait until tomorrow to see what he says, by which time we'll have much more from the scene and the two post-mortems. Last thoughts, Ashley.'

'There's something not quite right here. I wouldn't be surprised if there was more than one person involved. Whoever was responsible knew that caravan park well, and they knew about the car park near Vegas Fish Bar, which suggests they're local or frequent visitors. If we ignore the suicide, we still have two murders.'

'I agree. We'll crack on in the morning. Everybody, you know the score. Phone records, social media, bank accounts, CCTV, friends, relatives, you name it. We'll have a meeting tomorrow at 1 p.m., which Michelle, the pathologist, will hopefully attend. Then I want bodies back at that scene, re-interview neighbours and every last person in that park if necessary. Let's search Katrina's caravan, assuming it hasn't been sold or cleared out. Speak to bar staff and cleaners. We're all aware of where cases like this go if those responsible don't think we're close to catching them.'

Every cop in that room knew what he meant – the killer might strike again.

28

Ashley returned to the custody suite to see Percy while he was given conditional bail. The one condition being that he didn't leave the county. He said he was happy for them to check his mobile phone records to prove his innocence. They were under no obligation to give Percy a lift home, but Hunstanton was an hour away.

Percy had a hangdog expression on his face and dropped his keys when they were returned to him. Ashley tried to see things from his point of view if he was innocent. She also knew having him onside might be helpful.

'Shall I ask if anyone's driving back to Paradise?'

'No, it's okay. I'll ask my son to pick me up.'

'I didn't know you had a son.'

'Stepson. Sort of. Hamilton. He was that young punk you saw at Reception earlier. His mother lives half a mile from here. We were really close, still are, despite what she did. I partly blame her for his behaviour. Fancy calling him Hamilton.'

Percy appeared ready to reveal more, then didn't.

'Okay,' said Ashley. 'I'll be back at the park tomorrow afternoon to check on progress as they finish processing the crime scene at Diamond. There's going to be a fair amount of disruption and intrusion while we talk to others on the site. I'm sorry for the aggravation, but these are very serious crimes, and we need to catch those responsible.'

'It's no good for business having ambulances and police all over the place.' Percy rubbed his eyes. 'I suppose it can't be ideal having an investigation so far from your main office.'

'No, and time is money at the beginning. I don't suppose you have any caravans vacant?'

'What do you mean?'

'We often situate mobile vans near scenes, so if members of the public or, in your case, the holidaymakers, know anything, they can easily find us. An empty caravan would do the trick.'

'Come to Reception tomorrow, and I'll sort one out for you. Do you want to be at the scene or the entrance? I'll put something up in Reception saying where you are. Everyone will be talking about it anyway. We've already had cancellations, although we've also had inquiries, which is a bit freaky.'

'Entrance, please. Thanks, Percy.'

Ashley watched him stagger down the police steps and thought what an unusual fellow he was before heading to her desk to tackle her paperwork. She was tired and had one eye on the clock.

'Want a lift, Ash?' asked Barry.

'Are you leaving now?'

'Yes. I'll meet you downstairs.'

Ashley got in his car five minutes later, and they began the drive back. When a case first kicked off, it dragged people and their vehicles all over, but there was usually someone to cadge a lift off. Barry was closest, and she often felt bad because she'd only ever dropped him off on a couple of occasions. She wasn't even sure which house was his.

Barry drove without talking, which let Ashley remember Bhavini and worry about her, but the things she'd seen that day kept interrupting her thoughts. Ashley thought at first Barry had picked up on her need for downtime, but his brow was furrowed.

'Spit it out, Barry.'

'So much for the weekend.'

'You get to spend it with me. What could be better?'

There was an uncomfortable pause.

'That's true. I've always liked you.'

This silence was longer. Ashley felt her eyes bulging with the growing tension as it continued.

'In a "let's give each other dead arms" kind of way?' she asked.

'I guess every way. Sorry, I'll shut up.'

Ashley considered his words and his general behaviour and couldn't resist commenting.

'You've a funny way of showing it.'

'I struggle with talking to people sometimes.'

'Do you mean you struggle to be polite?'

'Hilarious. I'm not the person everyone thinks I am.'

'Please don't tell me you're worse.'

'It's true. And I'm not bothered about having children.'

Ashley's head jerked to the side.

'Who told you about that?'

Barry pretended to be focusing on the roundabout he was driving around, but she almost heard the grinding gears in his brain.

'Nobody. But you must admit you're close to being past the age for it.'

'Jesus!'

'I said I wasn't good at these things.'

Ashley's mind churned as they drove the rest of the journey, wondering who had a runaway mouth from that drunken day out.

As they neared Ashley's house, Barry cleared his throat.

'Are you hungry? We could grab a bite to eat from that restaurant you're always talking about.'

'Bann Thai?'

'That's it.'

'We'd never get a table without booking on a Saturday night.'

'Is it that popular?'

'Yep.'

'Maybe we could book and go one weekend.'

Ashley froze, unsure how to reply.

'How about a takeaway tonight instead?' he asked.

'Tempting, but I already have a hot date. Maybe another time.'

Barry was frowning when he pulled up outside her house, but his expression changed when he saw Bhavini hugging herself at Ashley's front door.

'Is she okay?' he asked.

Bhavini turned towards them. Make-up was streaked down her face.

29

Ashley said goodbye to Barry, left the car and pulled Bhavini into a stiff embrace. Taking your police hat off when a shift finished, then putting on the one of friend or partner, was a struggle for many officers.

Ashley helped Bhavini inside, sat her down, and fetched a glass of water. She was such a strong character, it was odd to see her so vulnerable.

'Are you sure you want to go out?' asked Ashley.

Bhavini took a tissue out of her pocket and dabbed at her make-up.

'What can you rustle up?'

'Banana sandwich?'

'Not tempting. Anyway, I've booked, and the walk will do me good. Tell me about the case on the way, so I'm up to speed on Monday. I've only picked at food since all my drama kicked off, so I could eat a horse.'

They wandered into town, arms linked, while Ashley updated her on the murders. The wind had dropped away to nothing, and it was a mild night.

'Sounds complicated,' said Bhavini. 'I suppose a holiday park is like holidays abroad. If you put a load of humans together, add sunshine and alcohol, things will happen.'

'You mean they'll shag each other?'

Bhavini laughed, but she still held firm to Ashley's arm.

The bar at the front of The Red Lion was heaving. It had a genuine seaside-pub vibe and a range of real ales, so it drew in a varied crowd. Ashley breathed in the hoppy smell. Her stomach rumbled as they threaded their way to the restaurant area through a welcoming buzz of conversation and laughter.

'Hi, Bee,' said the waitress who greeted them. 'I saw you'd booked.'

'Hi, Jo. Yeah, I'm starving!'

'Come on. I know you like this table.'

Jo escorted them to one of the tables at the window. It was facing the wrong part of the beach for the sunset, but they had a sea view with a red tinge to the sky. Smiling, Ashley took off her coat and stared out over the calm water. As darkness blanketed the horizon, she imagined the rhythmic sound as the gentle waves lapped against the shore, a soothing reminder that the sea could be a source of comfort.

Cromer at night was a tranquil place. A sense of peace came over her as she sat down, but then she recalled Bhavini's plight.

They chose a mocktail each. Bhavini didn't drink and Ashley wanted to be straight for what would be a busy next day. They made small talk for a while as they soaked up the warm atmosphere, then Ashley cut to the chase.

'So, tell me everything.'

Bhavini puffed out her cheeks.

'After our afternoon out, it was clear I was putting up with being second choice. Himansu had the best of everything. I saw the pictures of his family life on Instagram, and all I got was a gym buddy and the odd, furtive hotel trip.'

'Shall I be blunt?'

'You often are.'

'That's your fault for being with a married man.'

'Oh, Ash. We met at the gym and he said they were getting divorced, but I reckon it was all lies. They haven't split up, and it's been eighteen months. He kept saying soon, but he was spinning me along.'

'At least you can see that now.'

'Yes. Anyway, I took him for a meal at Cromer Tandoori so I could recall our girlie afternoon together and be strong.'

'And you gave him an ultimatum.'

'No, I told him to do one. I felt like a veil had been lifted.'

Ashley sprayed a bit of her Mango Mule at Bhavini, who was in full flow and ignored it.

'He went mad. Started shouting horrible stuff, but family friends were eating there. It was obviously a lovers' tiff. When I got home from work a few days later, my parents were waiting for me. Their friends had told them what they'd seen.'

'I take it your dad wasn't happy?'

'He went crazier than Himansu did. Why can men be so aggressive and opinionated? Anyway, my mum cried, and he ranted. I had no choice but to tell them everything.'

'And he threw you out and made you homeless.'

Bhavini nodded, wide-eyed, then smiled.

'Well, he knew I'd just go to my brother's, who has a box room. My bro's very aware of my dad's tantrums about bringing shame to the family. It was horrible, though. My mum begged him to let me stay, but you know what I'm like, I stomped out.'

'Will he calm down?'

'I don't think so. Not when it was all made clear.'

Their food arrived. Ashley grinned at her home-made burger, which wouldn't be long for this world. Bhavini had gone for the closest thing to a horse: the rib-eye.

She was faster to get stuck in than Ashley. Apart from the odd McDonald's chicken product, Bhavini had been a vegetarian for the whole time she'd been with the team.

Ashley watched her stuff a thick slice of meat, dripping with garlic butter, into her mouth, and understood the real problem.

30

Ashley put her fork down with a chip still impaled on it.

'You're pregnant.'

Bhavini nodded but continued to chew.

Ashley watched mesmerised as Bhavini chowed down. *What baby wants, baby gets.* She glanced down at her friend's stomach. There was no discernible bump, but Bhavini's clothes were more loose fitting than usual.

'How far along are you?'

'Sixteen weeks.'

'And you didn't notice?'

'No. My periods have always been light and irregular. I was so thin when I was younger, I didn't have one for a year when I was twenty. Himansu and I used precautions, but you know how it is. The Cromer beach case was a distraction, although I have been unusually tired. Things were prickly between us because I kept grilling him about his supposedly failed marriage. You can imagine what my father said.'

Ashley's mouth dropped open.

'You told him that as well?'

'Yes, I was too stressed to lie, and his judgemental tone raised my hackles, so I shouted, *And I'm pregnant*!'

'Wow. Have you told Himansu?'

'Yes. He said to get rid of it.'

'Just like that.'

'He's a bastard. I'll never speak to him ever again.'

Ashley briefly reflected on the practicalities of that depending on what happened, but Bhavini was emotional, and the reality of her situation obviously wasn't clear to her.

'Have you considered your options?'

'God, it's hard. I know I can have a—' Bhavini grimaced. 'I don't even want to say the word. It seems such an awful thing to do. But I'm single with little money behind me, and nowhere to raise a child. I'm only thirty. I've just passed my inspector exams. So much for getting DI Ibson's old job. What a mess.'

Ashley felt a gremlin crawl from the depths of her soul and sit on her shoulder. It whispered in her ear. *Tell her you'll look after it.*

'They say there's never a right time to have a baby,' she finally said. 'Some people spend years trying to get pregnant and never can. Maybe it will end up a blessing.'

'But I can't afford it on my own.'

'Sergeants make a decent wage. What have you been doing with yours?'

'I owed £50,000 after uni, which I've thankfully now cleared. My car's expensive, and I've been paying my way at home.' Bhavini gritted her teeth. 'I bought everything when I was with Himansu. Holidays, hotels. I even lent him money.'

'Bee! Well, you won't be doing that any more. I'll help in any way I can.'

'Sorry, Ashley. I shouldn't be moaning to you, but the prospect of living alone and going through all this is terrifying.'

'No, it's fine.' Ashley had a thought. She blurted it out. 'Live with me.'

Bhavini finally paused eating.

'What?'

'Stay at mine. I've got a spare room. Rent free. It'll be good for me, too.'

'My God. That would be so amazing.'

Bhavini stared out of the window at the darkening sky. After a few moments, she turned to Ashley, who couldn't read her face.

'Let me think about it.'

They finished their meals and strolled back to Ashley's place. While the kettle boiled for a camomile tea before bed, she wandered around downstairs. Life could be so strange.

Perhaps these four walls would echo to the sound of children's laughter, after all.

31

The watcher carefully picked his way through the quiet section of the site, slipping between the caravans like a wraith. This was his favourite part of the day. People locked themselves in for the evening with relief, safe and sound in their little bubbles, as if everyone else ceased to exist.

When the weather was warmer, though, even the new lodges with air con left their windows open. Folk rowed and shouted. Outside, you could listen to every word. Didn't they care?

He smiled to himself. Others fooled around and forgot who could hear. One couple even did things in their hot tub, not bothering who watched.

He reached the area where he always stopped. It was different beyond this point. He imagined evildoers inside the dwellings, but, most of all, he felt exposed. The wind whipped across the pond, rustling the reeds as though an invisible giant strode through them.

A twig snapped, then another. Something scampered through the undergrowth. There was a louder cracking sound, but different, heavier. More stick than twig.

His heart moved into his throat, and he stepped backwards. There were always creatures in the night. Everyone knew that, but he'd thought he was the only one out there up to no good. It felt as though someone had breathed over his shoulder in the dark. He glanced behind, but saw only shifting silhouettes.

He had been the master as he pried into people's lives, but the watcher was now observed. Predator to prey. Of that, he felt certain. Shadows lengthened and closed in as he took flight. The game had changed. The stakes were higher.

Fear snaked up his spine, now death had come to Paradise.

32

Ashley woke on Sunday at 5 a.m. with another different bedmate. Bhavini was sleeping on her side and lightly snoring. Her breath smelled faintly of mint. Was it toothpaste or the mint chocolates that she'd eaten at the end of the meal? After a quick brush-up, Ashley left the house in her running gear. It was a beautiful, still morning without a cloud in the sky.

Ashley ran easily through the chalet park and up along the clifftops away from the town centre towards Overstrand. She slowed where the erosion was worst and edged past the bungalows that were getting closer to the edge. Never was it more obvious that nothing was permanent than on the eroding cliffs of Norfolk.

At the Cliff Top Café, she paused. A bacon sandwich in their front garden always hit the spot. The manager, Karen, waved to her from the window with the cloth she was holding. Ashley tapped her stomach and shook her head. Karen rubbed her belly and laughed. It was lucky they weren't open yet.

Ashley took the quicker route along the road back to her

house, where she ate a bowl of yoghurt-topped muesli, then popped upstairs for a shower.

Bhavini was still asleep so Ashley dressed quietly for work. As she headed downstairs, she heard an unusual knocking sound through the thin walls. Next door were having more than cereal for breakfast.

Ashley stepped outside and her twenty-year-old Vectra started as usual on the first twist of the key. She often got grief from people over her battered car, but it was dependable. Pulling away, she found herself peering over her shoulder to see where a baby seat might go.

Ashley put on her sunglasses for the drive to OCC and told herself to get a grip. The traffic was light, and she sang along to the radio. She hadn't been at her desk five minutes when custody informed her Dennis Turner's solicitor had arrived. By ten o'clock, he had deemed his client ready, and they faced Ashley and Hector in an interview room. Ashley ran through the formalities, then nodded at the solicitor, who had indicated he would make a statement.

'Dennis Turner would firstly state he hasn't hurt anyone. The reason for his failure to engage is because of his previous offending. I'm sure you are aware it would be easy to assume escalating patterns of criminality.'

The man smiled at Ashley. His suit was a perfect fit, and his black beard and short crown of hair trimmed to perfection. He reeked of wealth and confidence. Computer programming must pay extremely well if Dennis could afford this guy.

Ashley didn't mind brilliant lawyers. They kept the police on their toes, and they tended not to waste time.

'My client is not a flight risk. I understand the reasons for his arrest and the importance of you tackling a case of this magnitude in a thorough and professional manner. Therefore, Dennis is happy to answer any questions honestly. I will be asking for bail. I can't see a reason for any conditions. The lodge is his home. The victim, sadly, is dead. There is no additional danger there. If he must return here at regular intervals to confirm his lack of involvement in any part in this and to show full co-operation, that would be acceptable.'

Ashley nodded at Dennis. She bet he'd find all that agreeable. Hector and she had prepared. They had no smoking gun. His DNA and fingerprints would be present at the scene. The fact Dennis was happy to talk was good. It would give them chance to catch him out if he was lying.

'Right, Dennis. Would you mind explaining for the tape why you've been calling yourself Deniz?'

Dennis sighed theatrically.

'My father was a Turkish immigrant. Altan Taner. When he came here, the country was generally welcoming, but he got judged on his name. So, he changed it to Alan Turner. He met my mother in Sheffield, had me, and became a successful importer and exporter from that part of Europe and Asia. But he was never at home, and I turned into a wild kid.'

'Your record would suggest wild doesn't come close to covering it.'

Dennis shrugged. 'I suppose that's fair.'

'And that continued until you approached forty.'

'That's also true. My father and I banged heads. It was best to avoid each other, and I rarely saw my mother. I've drifted through life. Once you have a record, nobody wants to know. It hasn't been easy. I have a conviction for arson even though it's decades old, and you can't get housing because of it. When my dad died, my mum and I began to reconnect. She'd started seeing this politician, but she still invited me to live back at home. I was crashing on a mate's sofa, so I accepted.'

'This is the place you have as your non-park residence. Stumperlowe Park Road.'

'That's right.'

'Go on.'

'My mother became ill. She had a wasting disease. I wasn't working, so I cared for her. She'd remarried by then.'

'To Cecil Dowd. Did he mind you being there?'

'He could see it was what my mum wanted. She'd rather I looked after her than a team of strangers. She preferred to die at home, and that's what happened.'

'You mentioned you owned the house, but the council has it being under Cecil's name.'

'It passed to me in her will, but he has the right to live there until he dies. I also inherited the lodge and a trust fund.'

'That's quite a turnaround for you.'

Dennis nodded enthusiastically, revealing the beginning of dark roots in his hair.

'I've always wanted to be a computer programmer. I realised I could come here and be whoever I liked. My dad told me when I was young he would have called me Deniz if we'd lived in Turkey, so I thought, why not? I bought a nice car, new clothes, white teeth, and moved here. Quietly at first. Nobody knew me, but they were cautious because I was on my own.'

'Then you started dating,' said Hector.

'Yeah, I went to the bar in the clubhouse and met people. My past remained a mystery. They treated me well. No crappy assumptions around my record. They gave me a chance, so I seized it. I've been on my best behaviour.'

'Katrina was devastated when you dumped her.'

Dennis paused, then took a deep breath.

'It was shit, but I wasn't cruel. She was fun, offering to teach me to dance, because I had no idea how to. When she split up with Percy, we started a thing. I enjoyed it, until she nagged me to death about reliability.'

'Was she crushed when you split?'

'More angry. I don't think she was used to being dumped. I tried to be nice about it.'

'Could she have taken her own life over you?'

'Of course not. She'd never married, no kids. She was happy dancing and doing copy something-or-other to keep dough coming in. Perhaps sad her mum had died, but that's it.'

'How did her mother die?' asked Ashley, interjecting for the first time.

'Complications from hip surgery. It was really quick though, so it was a shock.'

'Then you stole Jasmine away from Percy,' said Hector.

'Did he tell you that? Percy's a bullshitter. She dumped him because he was forever in her space. She reckoned she wouldn't have been surprised if she'd lifted the toilet seat in the morning and found him staring out of it.'

Ashley managed to stop herself from smiling.

'What went wrong with Jasmine?' she asked.

'She was too chilled for me. I respected the hippy vibe to begin with, then it got old. She was a bit of a stoner, and that's never been my thing.'

'How did she feel when you broke up?'

'A little sad. She was into me. That's why I love it here, man. It was like, my time. All these chicks wanted Deniz.'

'Chicks? They were much older women.'

'So what? They were all in great shape. Yoga and Pilates and shit. They smelled so good, looked fine, and they all had money.'

'I thought you had money.'

'I do. It was nice they had cash as well, so we split bills and things.'

'How many people have you slept with on Paradise?'

The solicitor leaned forward and shook his head.

'That's superfluous.'

'You have to admit it is suspicious both of his ex-girlfriends are dead.'

'It's sad,' replied the man. 'Not incriminating.'

'What was your relationship with Alfie Hook?' asked Ashley.

Dennis glanced across at his brief, who nodded.

'When I first started dating Jasmine, she wanted some weed, because she'd been stressed by Percy's odd behaviour and some other bloke kept loitering near her lodge.'

'Who was he?'

Dennis shrugged. 'No idea. There's obviously not a dealer on the site, but I got chatting to a fella in town and he pointed a guy out.'

'Who was the guy?'

'Just a random I met walking past The Honeystone.'

'Can you describe him?'

'Pretty average, unshaven, with a baseball cap and sunglasses.'

'That's convenient.'

'We were outside. It was a bright day.'

Ashley made a note to get one of the teams to visit The Honeystone to see if anyone had been loitering nearby, but she suspected the guy didn't exist.

'You admit you purchased cannabis off Alfie Hook.'

Dennis again checked his solicitor, who gave him a thin smile.

'I didn't know his surname. Just Alfie.'

'And you're aware he's dead.'

'I heard.'

'How did that make you feel?'

'Kind of bad, but I barely knew him. He looked like he could have snuffed it any second.'

'Did you have a row with him the night he died?'

Dennis's right eye twitched, even though he tried to remain calm.

'Who told you that?'

'Is it true?'

'Yeah. I explained I didn't need any more weed because me and Jasmine had split up.'

'What did he say?'

'Moaned that I might have let him know sooner. He was always a bit grouchy. I think he found walking painful, but he was really grumpy. Think his wife was giving him some grief. He'd moaned about her before. Anyway, Alfie told me we'd never met if anyone ever mentioned it. Then he left.'

'That makes him the third person who's died after recent contact with you.'

'Can you get to where you're going, please?' asked the solicitor.

'We're closing in,' said Ashley.

'I doubt that. Show me the evidence implicating my client.'

'We're checking a variety of sources. I'd also like to speak to Cecil Dowd.'

Dennis leaned over and whispered to his brief, who whispered back. The older man nodded firmly before turning to Ashley.

'We can provide his mobile number. That should be enough to release my client.'

'We're waiting on reports,' said Hector.

'For what? He lives next door and dated both of the victims. His DNA and prints were there for months. Do you have either a weapon or motive?'

Unfortunately, Ashley had to agree they did not.

'Final question,' she said. 'Katrina killed herself with a drug that is used for end-of-life care.'

'So?'

'Katrina's mum died suddenly. Whereas you cared for yours at home.'

33

Dennis shrugged, but Ashley thought the comment had hit home.

'So?' he replied.

'Did you give Katrina any drugs?' asked Hector.

'I think that's enough wild stabs in the dark. Shall we call it a day?' said the solicitor.

Ashley terminated the interview and had Dennis returned to the custody suite.

'What are your thoughts?' she asked Hector as they walked back to the incident room.

'Mostly plausible explanations. But I don't trust him. A sharp solicitor gives him the illusion of credibility, but he lied to us. I'd put money on him having lied to him as well.'

'True.'

'Would you buy dope for your girlfriend?'

'Dennis would, but I'd be surprised if she took the habit up recently. Who was she getting it from before? Besides, if Dennis was so great, why would she still be so stressed out by Percy's behaviour that she needed some?'

'Exactly. Either he's lying or Percy is.'

Sal and Barry were in the office writing on the whiteboards, one each for Katrina, Jasmine and Alfie.

'What's new?' asked Ashley.

'Lots, but none of it good,' said Sal. 'Phone records seem normal. Text messages and social media again come up as par for the course.'

Ashley cursed under her breath. They were going to have to revisit all the witnesses, then spread their net wider. The first two days were key for investigations. If it wasn't solved quickly, they would still likely crack the case, but it would take much longer.

Ashley and her team went through to the meeting room. She wasn't fussed about letting Dennis go, but his turning-over-a-new-leaf rubbish didn't convince her. By the time they reached forty years old, the behaviour of virtually all the career criminals she'd ever met had been ingrained. Trouble followed them or they found it themselves.

Kettle arrived and summarised the progress so far. Michelle Ma Yun appeared at the back of the room near the end and confidently walked to the front. Ashley watched Hector's face redden. Michelle reminded Ashley of the actor Michelle Yeoh. She had the same gaze that fixed you in place.

'I'll talk to you about Alfie Hook's murder first,' she said. 'It's been a long time since I've seen such unhealthy organs which weren't the cause of death. The blade that was responsible for his demise was sharp and used with skill and force to find its way through the ribs and so much internal and external fat. Alfie died more or less instantly. Estimated time of death was as you suspected. No surprise there.'

She held up her notes and refreshed her memory, then lowered them.

'Jasmine would have died swiftly too. She has a minor fracture and a nasty bruise on the upper right side of her skull, probably from a blunt object, but maybe just a slip. I suspect she wasn't knocked unconscious because there are signs of struggling, namely a couple of split and damaged nails. However, there was nothing under the fingernails, so perhaps the assailant had thick gloves on, or she broke her nails in the fall. Either way, Jasmine didn't scratch her attacker.'

There were a few quiet comments as people digested those facts.

'If you recall one of the deaths on Cromer beach where bruising came up on the neck after the event, then there's a similarity this time, but on the shoulders. This bruise is smaller though, and could have been done in a multitude of ways. So, she could have been stunned, then held down. It wouldn't have taken much effort to drown her in this water, which had various relaxation products in it and that would have made the bottom and sides slippery. Date of death from her body is not easy, time of death impossible, but I would guess she was spending her Saturday or Sunday night chilling in the hot tub before she died. The fish complicates things. Its decomposition doesn't match the weekend timing. Any thoughts as to why?'

'It was out of the water?' someone shouted out.

'No. Moisture does accelerate decay in some cases, but air temperature is generally warmer at this time of year.'

'It was placed there later.'

'Possibly, or more likely it was frozen when left.'

Ashley heard a few sounds of surprise. Michelle explained.

'Perhaps the person who planned this lives nearby, and has a freezer, but that's your job.'

Ashley smiled and raised her hand.

'Can you tell us about hyoscine butylbromide?'

'Ah yes. The suicide. Emma rang me and gave me the details. It's a strange combination of drugs to overdose with. On its own, hyoscine butylbromide wouldn't have much effect apart from dizziness and a dry throat. That's one of its main purposes. You will all have heard of the death rattle when someone dies. More or less, it's the fluid from the body collecting in the airways. The body is breaking down and unable to expel these substances, which then gurgle and bubble in the throat. We think painless for the dying, but unpleasant for family to hear. This drug is used to dry the secretions and therefore lessen the rattle. It's medication for the living, given to the dying.'

Michelle peered around the room to see if there were any further comments.

'How is it administered and what are the effects?' asked Ashley.

'Injected or tablet form. It could be crushed and put in a drink or food. It's liable to make someone placid, pliable, and more easily influenced.'

Ashley wondered if someone had used it to sedate Katrina before giving her the rest of the drugs, which killed her.

'Two final points,' said Michelle. 'If Jasmine's death was premeditated, the killer was clever. She would have drowned quickly and quietly. I'm surprised the stench of human flesh and fish decay didn't alert anyone sooner. It would have hummed a few days before Jasmine was found. The delay makes timings hard and toxicology reports more unreliable. I haven't had the results back for cannabis, but I think it's safe to assume it was present.'

'There's a pond nearby,' said Ashley. 'It often smells a bit dodgy, and it had been breezy. Not to mention there was a cover on the tub. A mobile phone was in the water, though. Do we have timings from the provider?'

'Yes, the final connection to the mast was just after 9 p.m. last Saturday,' said Jan.

Michelle smiled at being proven correct.

'If you remember,' she said. 'I wanted to analyse the tissue that was damaged in Alfie's chest. As I mentioned earlier, he was killed by a razor-sharp knife, which was also quite thin. It cut through the body easily, but there were three slices in the heart. There would usually be three holes in the chest wall, not one. Think about what that means.'

Michelle had her audience rapt as she stared around.

'A volunteer, please. You will do.'

A red-faced Hector rose after being singled out. Michelle held an index finger up to the room.

'The weapon.'

She mimed stabbing Hector with three wild thrusts. Then she rested her hand on his chest and mimed three short, crisp ones with no lateral arm movement.

'Your killer was no wild amateur,' she said. 'This was no lucky, frenzied attack.'

Michelle looked around for a final time.

'It was a ruthless execution.'

34

Kettle closed the meeting, and the teams dispersed. Ashley and her team returned to the incident room. She had gathered Sal, Barry and Hector around a table to discuss Michelle's findings when a call came through for her. She listened intently, said goodbye, and tutted.

'Now what?' asked Barry.

'The computer guy has done a quick analysis of Dennis's laptop. If Dennis is a programmer, he doesn't do much programming. The only thing of note after an initial exploration is he's downloaded a lot of poker software. It appears he enjoys a flutter, which makes me wonder about the money angle.'

'No dodgy searches on how to drown neighbours?'

'Nope. Same for Percy's laptop. The guy said his is so lightly used, it's more for show.'

Emma came over after finishing the call she'd been on.

'We've had the lab on the phone after they've checked the earring that was found. There's no recoverable DNA on it after being immersed for so long. It has an expensive diamond in it, though, so someone will be devastated.'

'Are we saying it's worth thousands?' asked Sal.

'Yes, maybe tens of.'

'It could have been in the drain for a while,' said Ashley. 'Gerald will have checked in Jasmine's and Dennis's lodges for its partner, but I'll ask to make sure. We're also going to need to search Alfie's house, which might be a touch sensitive in light of his recent death. If Jackie kicks off, we'll take her to the nearest nick, which will be King's Lynn.'

'It's interesting Katrina died with unusual drugs in her system. Ones Dennis may well have had access to,' said Emma.

'Yes, but what would Dennis gain by killing her?'

'Perhaps he owed her money,' said Sal.

'Or he killed her accidentally and tried to cover it up,' said Barry.

'An average person would struggle to conceal these crimes. I don't see Dennis as a criminal genius,' said Sal.

'And yet we have three untimely deaths all within his social circle,' said Hector.

'What do you all think? We've confirmed Dennis is a liar, possibly even a pathological one. I say we release him. We could ask for an extension, but I still reckon there's something strange going on at Diamond. I wouldn't mind being there when Dennis returns. Perhaps see how he interacts with the others. The police divers will be in the pond today, and CSI should have finished in Dennis's lodge.'

'We have his stepdad's telephone number now, so maybe he'll give us some background. Maybe Dennis's mum is still alive,' said Hector.

'I'll ring him,' said Ashley. 'I'd rather visit him, but a six-hour round-trip doesn't appeal when we're so busy.'

Ashley picked up her desk phone and rang the number that Dennis had given them earlier.

'Cecil Dowd,' was the abrupt answer.

'Good afternoon, Mr Dowd. I'm Detective Sergeant Ashley Knight with the Norfolk police.'

'Oh, God. What's he done now?'

Ashley smiled.

'Dennis is assisting us with our enquiries.'

'Bloody hell. Surely he's not involved in those murders in Hunstanton.'

'I can't disclose anything at this point. He said the property in Stumperlowe is his, but you're allowed to live in it. Is that right?'

'Jesus Christ. If you haven't already realised, that boy is a compulsive liar. He doesn't have a single honest bone in his body. I married his mother and, when she died, I inherited the house and the lodge. Dennis was brought back to say goodbye when she was ill, but she rallied, and they reconnected. She left him a more than generous trust fund, which pays him five thousand a month.'

'So, he's set for life.'

'Yes, she knew him well enough to understand he would just spend it all if she gave it in a lump sum. Hence not leaving him the house.'

'I take it you aren't his biggest fan?'

'No, he'd have the change from the side of your bed given the slightest opportunity. My wife insisted I look after him, but I want to slap his face every time I speak to him, so I let him stay at the lodge for free. I pay the upkeep. It's worth every penny to keep him three hours away. He returned here when it shut last year, but I removed anything valuable and kept out of his way.'

'Does that mean you haven't seen him since February?'

'Correct, and I don't expect to hear from him until January when the park closes again. I even made him give me his key back.'

'He said his dad was Turkish. He's been calling himself Deniz Turner.'

'Jeez. He told me that he'd changed now he has money, and he was going to live an honest life. Dennis has used different names for decades. To be fair, he was decent to his dying mother, and his father was from Turkey.'

'He said he helped nurse her.'

'He sat and held her hand, no doubt in the hope of a fat inheritance. The Macmillan nurses and I cared for her.'

'Mr Dowd, was your wife on any medication towards the end?'

'She refused. Being lucid was more important to her than pain relief. She was incredibly brave. Only morphine during the last few days. It really is hard to believe Dennis is her child.'

'Okay. Thank you for your time.' Ashley had a final thought before she hung up. 'Mr Dowd, I was just thinking, I've seen his criminal record, and it's concerning.'

'Are you asking if he's capable of murder?'

'I suppose so.'

The line was quiet for a moment.

'Under enough pressure, aren't we all?'

35

The more Ashley thought about that comment, the more she didn't like it. She'd expected him to say no. Cecil offered to attend a Sheffield police station the next day, to give a full statement. He said he would do so with relish.

Ashley had received a report on the records for Dennis's mobile, which were as he said: lots of calls to Katrina's number, then no more shortly before she died. Then there was a lot of communication with Jasmine's phone, even though they could have shouted over their decking railings to each other. After they stopped, which she assumed was the end of their relationship, calls to an unregistered number picked up.

Ninety minutes later, Ashley was cursing the traffic as she and Barry inched along the A149 to Hunstanton. They wouldn't be home until late in the evening now. Hector had a prior arrangement, and Sal and Emma wanted time with their families. Ashley felt herself slipping into a foul mood with the delay. Luckily, Barry hadn't mentioned anything about liking her again, or she'd have stopped the vehicle and beaten him to death with the car jack.

Barry was on his mobile to an investigator in the HOLMES team. Ashley heard him double-checking transactions. When he finished the conversation, Barry whistled.

'Cecil was right. He is getting five grand a month straight into his account. The mad thing is, he's spending it.'

'What the hell on? Cecil Dowd said he was paying the bills at the lodge.'

'Mostly gambling. A few hefty cash withdrawals. Some scary deposits to various poker sites. I can only assume he's not a skilful player.'

'We're back to him needing money again. Okay. Custody are going to release him at five unless they hear otherwise. I want to be near his lodge when he gets home. Let's see how he acts when he returns.'

'Aren't you always warning me about unauthorised surveillance?'

Ashley laughed.

'Officially, we'll be there for further interviews with Verne and Bertie and the two fitness bunnies. I wonder if he's been borrowing money all over. What was Jasmine's bank account like?'

'As you'd expect. No major cash withdrawals or transfers, just regular spending patterns.'

'Maybe the real reason he dumped Jasmine was because she wouldn't lend him anything. That might have been the same reason he split up with Katrina.'

'I'll ring Percy. See if he's heard any negative rumblings about Dennis, and I'll chase up our caravan. We could always sleep in it if Percy gives us a nice one.'

Ashley shook her head in mock disgust as Barry laughed.

By the time they turned into Paradise, Ashley's eyes were gritty. The site was surprisingly busy, with many more cars around the reception area than previous visits. Numerous people queued at the desk.

Ashley stopped the car and let Barry out while she checked her emails. He was back two minutes later. He had grey suit trousers on and a crisp white shirt. He appeared relaxed and full of vigour. Ashley felt and looked as if she'd just climbed out of the dirty laundry basket.

'Percy said he's got a caravan for us.' Barry pointed at one near the entrance gates. 'It'll be cleaned for tomorrow, then we can have it for as long as it takes. He reiterated he wants this solved as fast as possible, and he'll do anything to help.'

'Percy seems keen on helping all of a sudden. Has he heard gossip about Dennis?'

'He said not, but he's flat-out processing people who are leaving early, and the phone is ringing off the hook with worried holidaymakers.'

Ashley checked her watch. She had arranged for a response vehicle to return Dennis to Hunstanton, but they'd get caught in the traffic she and Barry had.

'We have time to visit Alfie Hook's wife, Jackie. I want to spring this weed angle on her, hear what she has to say, but her home will need to be searched after.'

'Are there any CSI vans available now?'

Ashley was interrupted by the ringing of her phone. It was the crime scene manager, Gerald.

'Speak of the devil,' she said to Barry, then accepted the call.

'Hi, Gerald. Have you discovered a confession?'

'Almost, Ash. We've got at least two good finds.'

'I'm a minute away. We'll come down. I need to talk to you about needing another search team.'

'Joy. See you soon.'

Ashley and Barry drove through Paradise and reached

Diamond, parking next to Verne and Bertie's lodge. The couple were grinning, sitting in deckchairs, holding large orange cocktails. They were on the side of their decking when they could have been out of sight at the rear. They both waved.

Ashley wasn't sure how old Gerald was. She suspected with his greying hair and stoop, he was quite close to retirement, but he probably looked like that when he was thirty too. Although he might have passed for two hundred as he staggered from Dennis's place.

'You okay?' asked Ashley.

'Getting a bit ancient for working seven days on the bounce and not getting much sleep.'

'Think about the fishing.'

'I'll be fishing off a cloud if I'm not careful.'

'Update me quickly then, before it's too late.'

'You're all heart. First up is the pond. We have, in no particular order, a pair of new trainers, some expensive-looking grey silicone oven mitts, which also appear new, and a hammer with a red handle. There's a whole load of other crap which we've kept, but I've given you the pertinent items.'

'I don't suppose the hammer has a bloody clump of hair on it.'

'No, but the great news about whoever threw the hammer is it landed on a pizza box.'

'It wasn't submerged.'

'Correct. We might even get fingerprints off it.'

'And the trainers?'

'Brand new. Why would you throw a perfectly good pair of runners into this pond? Again, we'll have them tested.'

'What size?'

'Not to be presumptuous, but they appear to be men's trainers. Size ten is clear inside.'

'Right. Maybe the person walked on the decking and was concerned they'd left footprints.'

'It's possible,' said Barry. 'But don't you reckon they'd suspect we'd search the nearby swamp after someone's been killed?'

'Most people wouldn't know police procedure,' said Ashley. 'Although I have to say it's been a professional job so far.'

'Unless they panicked,' said Gerald. 'As you mentioned earlier, many murders are assaults gone wrong. Perhaps they meant to return for them and never had a chance.'

'And the oven gloves?'

'I was involved in a murder thirty years ago, not long after I first started. The wife had been strangled. She'd fought like mad. All her false fingernails came off. The detectives were checking hands, thinking whoever was responsible would be covered in scratches. It turned out to be the neighbour, who confessed in the end. It was an impulsive crime after lusting after her for many years. He put her oven mitts on and throttled her before finally taking what he'd coveted.'

'A charming and informative story. Right, there's unlikely to be fingerprints, but we can check for DNA in the mitts.'

'Exactly. They're also in pristine condition. Why throw them away? I admit if the killer was smart, they'd have worn thin gloves before they put the mitts on, but that's not the case with the final item, which we found right at the death.'

Gerald puffed his chest up.

'Is it gold star time for Gerald?' she asked.

Ashley wondered if she'd stepped over a line, but Gerald nodded eagerly. She didn't know him well, but he'd proven funny with a slightly childish sense of humour. He was fitting right in.

'There was nothing untoward in Dennis's lodge. We were finished, but one of the CSIs noticed a slight gap at the edge of the seats, which something could have fallen through. We had to unscrew and remove the entire table area, which is why we're still here.'

Gerald called over a technician, who brought the bag over to Ashley. She held it up to the light.

Inside was a diamond-studded gold-leaf earring.

36

Ashley understood the implications of the discovery immediately.

'It's got to belong to another woman,' she said.

'Agreed,' said Gerald. 'Jasmine's place had nothing of any value. She clearly led a simple life.'

'I suppose it could have been in there a while.'

'Her husband was wealthy. So maybe he bought her fancy jewellery as part of his controlling behaviour.'

'Remember, her ears aren't pierced.'

'No, they were, but they've closed up. Everybody's different, but it's plausible they healed up in the last year.'

'Surely the first place anyone would check for it was in the hot tub. I'll have the team go through her social media feed to see if her or a friend are wearing it.'

'We found a photo album from around ten years ago, judging by how old Jasmine appears in it,' said Gerald. 'I had a flick through, and she doesn't wear similar jewellery.'

'You still get a star, though,' said Ashley. 'We won't get much from the earring in the water, whereas this one will talk to us.'

'Yes, it's bound to have DNA on it. At the least, we should know if this was Jasmine's or not. I've also taken the liberty of collecting samples from Katrina's lodge, which seems to be untouched since she died. I assume she didn't leave a will, and it's tied up in probate.'

'Correct and good thinking.'

'I assumed that if there was nobody to inherit, all her things, toothbrush included, would still be present.'

'Perhaps the earrings were hers.'

Gerald gave her a tired thumbs-up.

A muddy police diver trudged over carrying her flippers and a towel.

'We're all finished here. Gerald will have our report, but we've found nothing else.'

'With the sun, I bet it's been like a spa day,' said Barry.

The woman shook her head at him and plodded away.

After she'd gone, Ashley observed Gerald's guys as they packed up their things. A sergeant who introduced himself as being in charge of the search team on the park explained they'd finished too.

'We drew a blank on everything until we reached the fence beyond the meadow. Someone's used wire cutters to cut through the bottom half of one of the sections.'

'Which means someone could sneak out of the park without using the main entrance.'

'Easily. From the number of kids I've seen carrying boogie boards and towels, it's a well-known shortcut to the beach.'

'Brilliant.'

The sergeant chuckled.

'There are fibres on the sharp edges, so we've removed them. The maintenance guy knew about it. He's fixed it countless times, but they keep cutting it. In the end, he gave up.'

When the sergeant had gone, Ashley tutted.

'How come that's the first I'm hearing of a maintenance man? He'd have access to all areas with a range of tools, and would be familiar with the residents and the area.'

'You can't do everything in one day,' said Gerald.

Ashley nodded. She appreciated the gesture, but caretakers had been key to many cases in the past.

'Gerald, I need a team to search a residential property.'

'What, now? No chance.'

'It's Alfie Hook's house. Seems he was selling cannabis and who knows what else. How about tomorrow morning?'

'Okay. I'll have a team there, assuming I wake up. Email me the details.'

Gerald and his group drove away. The sun was beginning its long descent, but it was still a glorious day. It was quiet in Diamond and she was really starting to understand the attraction. Imagine no traffic thundering around you and everyone in the holiday mood for eleven months of the year. Would it be heaven? Ashley suspected if you were young, you'd end up going stir-crazy, but for retirees it would normally be safe, relaxing and peaceful.

Ashley watched Glory walk over to Pip's lodge and knock. Pip opened the door with a smile and welcomed her in.

Verne and Bertie were still sitting on their deckchairs. Observing their drinks were now red, she knew they were at least on their second round. Bertie was a similar age to Ashley, and he seemed to be relaxed, despite what had happened. Ashley wandered over to join them.

'Having fun, guys?'

'Yes, it's so lovely to watch the sun go down,' said Bertie, who was clearly the worse for wear. 'We had a different plot when we first arrived, but we love it on here. It's more secluded and the people are our sort of people.'

'How so?'

'Well, some residents try to live in your pockets. You show them manners, then they're constantly knocking around. The folk on Diamond are polite, but they know we like to be by ourselves. If I want to talk to someone, I'll go to the bar.'

'I see you've managed to put the deaths to one side,' said Ashley, gesturing to their full glasses.

'Well, not really,' slurred Bertie. 'That's probably why I'm drinking so fast. We'll miss the sunset at this rate because we'll be unconscious in bed.'

'No work tomorrow?'

'I haven't been sleeping with all that's gone on, so work have agreed to give me some time off.'

Ashley recalled Pip's career.

'Did you know Pip when she was at the hospital?'

'Yes. She was a well-respected paediatric doctor. I'd book her operations sometimes. We didn't chat, but would say hi to each other if we passed in the corridors. It was funny when we arrived here and she was leaning on her gate.'

'And Glory's husband is there, too, isn't he?'

'Yes. He's infamous. We don't get too many gunshot victims.'

37

Ashley almost had to wind her jaw back up. Glory had definitely not mentioned that.

'What?' she managed.

'Yes, it's a terribly sad story, even though, if I'm honest, I haven't heard it first-hand. A little birdie told me they were robbed on holiday in America, and he got shot in the head. Luckily, he and Glory had money so they could afford for him to be flown back.'

'Interesting,' said Ashley. 'And Glory's never mentioned it to you, despite the fact he's in your hospital?'

'No. I find her a bit intense, but we do have a chat about the weather and the news, that kind of thing. She's cool.'

Barry was almost snarling as they walked over to Pip's lodge and Ashley heard him mouth something about liars as he trudged through the gate and knocked on the door. A large black and white cat sat outside. Pip appeared with a big smile and a bigger wobble, and the cat raced in.

'Hey,' said Pip. 'We were just going to watch a movie, then enjoy the sunset with a Disaronno. Welcome to join.'

Ashley laughed. 'Tempting. Barry and I were chatting about the case, and we've come up with a few discrepancies.'

'Like what?'

Barry walked into the lodge, sat next to Glory, and smiled.

'Would you mind telling me about your husband's car accident in America?'

Glory imperceptibly edged away from him. She put her cup of coffee down.

'It was a brain injury while he was in a vehicle.'

'From a bullet?'

'Does it matter?'

'Not being told the truth matters to me.'

'What difference does it make? He's a cabbage. I hate talking about it. If I say he was shot, everyone wants the gory details.'

'What are the gory details?'

'See!' She glowered at him. 'Who told you?'

Glory's angry eyes switched to Pip, whom Ashley had to admit looked guilty. It seemed they'd identified the gossiping birdie.

'You bitch!' said Glory.

'It wasn't me,' said Pip.

'You're the only one I told. It can't have been anyone else.'

'I'm sorry, Glory. Really, I am. I don't remember.'

Glory's eyebrows furrowed and her nostrils flared. She smiled coldly at Ashley.

'Pip's been screwing Dennis.'

Ashley's jaw dropped for a second time.

'My God,' muttered Pip with disbelief.

'A lot! And everyone knows. Even Dennis's new girlfriend.'

Pip frowned.

'How does she know?'

'Because she turned up, and you were both here, the sounds of pleasure echoing from your lodge.'

Pip's eyes blazed with worry. Ashley wasn't sure why she was so concerned.

'And Pip's still happily married,' snarled Glory.

Glory turned and sneered at Pip, which was a mistake. Pip was close enough to slap her face. A loud crack echoed around the room. Glory grabbed the closest thing to hand, a wine bottle, and lifted it up high.

She gasped when it didn't move. Barry had caught it. He plucked it out of her hand. She turned, seized his arm and dragged it down before he twisted the bottle away. Barry put his arm around her and tried to manoeuvre her behind him as Pip came hurtling forward. Ashley could see Barry struggling to control Glory, so she stood in Pip's way.

'You fucking cow!' roared Pip, trying to push past Ashley.

'Screw you, Pip, and screw this goddamn place,' bellowed Glory, deftly dodging Barry after giving him a small shove. Then she stepped out of his range. Glory turned at the door. 'I'm going to ask them to move me as far from Diamond as possible. I can't stand it any more. You're all fucking mad.'

When the door slammed shut, Pip let out a sob and dropped onto the sofa and placed her head in her hands. Barry massaged his arm, took his pocketbook and pen out, then began writing. Ashley sat opposite Pip and spoke quietly.

'What you did is an offence called assault by beating. If you've marked Glory, it would be actual bodily harm. Be honest with me now, because you could be in a lot of trouble.'

'Okay.'

'Have you been sleeping with Dennis?'

'Yes,' whispered Pip.

'How long for?'

'Six months, probably longer.'

'So, all the time he was seeing Katrina and Jasmine and even his new girlfriend, you were meeting up.'

Pip nodded.

'And you're not separated from your husband.'

Pip shook her head.

'Why?' asked Ashley. 'Why not tell us the truth?'

Pip looked up through bloodshot eyes.

'I lied to myself. It started off one evening when I was drunk. I'm lonely here. My husband's old. He just wants to sit in his comfy armchair and watch World War Two documentaries. Dennis came around with some wine and we had a one-night stand. After, he said let's be friends with benefits, which suited me.'

Ashley checked Barry was writing everything down and waited for Pip to continue. The cat jumped onto Ashley's lap. Ashley was more a dog person. She always had the feeling cats were judging her, and she came up wanting. She gently stroked its head. It blinked twice, then leapt off and sat next to the door.

Pip sniffed and exhaled deeply.

'You developed feelings,' stated Ashley.

'Yes. I'd forgotten what it was like to be wanted and feel sexy.'

Barry delivered the telling question.

'How did it make you feel when he was sleeping with those other women?'

Pip's face crumpled in on itself. Barry gave her a minute, then hit the bullseye.

'Were you here the night Dennis was having sex with Jasmine in the hot tub?'

Pip couldn't help her teeth clenching, and her hands turning into claws. Ashley contemplated taking out her handcuffs, then changed her mind.

'Come on, Pip. Come back to the nick with us. We'll record a statement and take our time. Get a good account in place.'

Ashley watched her expression as they took her outside.

Pip was definitely extremely worried about something.

38

The cat sat on the railing with its head cocked to one side as Ashley locked up Pip's lodge. Barry guided Pip into the back of their car and her head hung low, almost to her knees, when she was sitting inside. Barry slammed the door shut, but Pip didn't react. Outside the vehicle, Barry stretched his arms and winced as he rotated his shoulder.

'Crazy hellcats,' he said.

They decided to head to King's Lynn for interview, which was the closest nick with cells.

Pip was the first person with a clear motive for killing the women: plain old jealousy. It didn't explain the death of Alfie Hook but maybe the link between the two murders was a red herring. Dennis being a complete snake hadn't helped, but he wasn't breaking the law by embellishing his career, short of wasting police time.

With perfect timing, a patrol car pulled into Diamond.

Ashley couldn't help herself. She went over and stood near Dennis's gate, so he had to walk past her. Dennis left the vehicle and plodded over.

'Dennis. I've a couple of questions for you.'

'No comment.'

'Just tidying up some loose ends.'

'Go away,' he said as he walked around her.

'What size shoe do you take?'

'What?'

'It's a simple question.'

'A ten. Nine and a half in trainers.'

'Who's your current partner?'

'I'm single.'

'That's not what we've heard.'

Dennis stopped with his key inserted into the lodge door. His head snapped back.

'It's fucking gossip. Ignore it.'

'Her car was seen here. A beautiful woman, apparently.'

'I said I don't have a girlfriend.'

'We found her earring.'

Dennis froze, then pushed his door open and stepped inside. He turned around.

'I don't know anything about any missing earrings.'

Ashley recognised concern on his face as he closed the door and locked it. Ashley was starting to feel as if her head was going to explode. She returned to the pool car, and Barry drove them out of Diamond. Verne and Bertie waved as they passed. Ashley called Control and gave them their movements: one en route for questioning at King's Lynn.

Ashley allowed herself a few minutes to get her head straight before she rang Kettle and relayed the news before peering over her shoulder at Pip.

'Have you lost any earrings?'

Pip glanced up with a weary expression on her face.

'I only wear studs. Look, you can drive me home. Take me to 99 Tennyson Avenue, King's Lynn.'

'We're not giving you a lift to collect your pyjamas,' said Barry.

'Come on, do you really think I murdered those people?'

Ashley checked Pip's face. Her fists were clenched white, but Ashley could see it was with worry, not anger.

'Where were you last weekend?' said Ashley.

'With my husband. Definitely when the poor man in the car park was killed. I got summoned back for a curry. I've never been a huge fan, but my husband, Rupert, loves it. The previous weekend, I was also with him. We had a dinner party with his stuffy brother and wife to keep up appearances.'

Ashley considered her gut reaction. She believed Pip, but she wondered what else she'd lied to them about.

'Were you more friendly with Jasmine than you made out?'

'Yes, I suppose. We kind of all hung around together with Deniz and occasionally Glory. I felt bad about sleeping with Deniz when he'd been seeing Jasmine, but he was like a drug I couldn't quit.'

Not bad enough, then, thought Ashley.

'We need proof you weren't in Hunstanton on those dates,' she said. 'You don't have to mention anything you've been up to at Paradise.'

Pip leaned back in her seat, understanding what Ashley meant.

'Let's get it over with.'

39

Pip directed them to the centre of King's Lynn, then down one of the plusher residential streets. Barry and Ashley left the car and helped Pip out. The detectives walked up a block-paved drive and knocked. Ashley noticed a curtain move at a downstairs window.

When the door was yanked open, Ashley flinched as loud gunfire came from inside. There was harsh German shouting and multiple explosions. Rupert had an empty bottle of wine in his hand. He was a huge, stooped man with tawny skin and a shock of grey hair around his bald head. He checked each face slowly, then kept his gaze on Pip, who was further back down the path.

'What's the meaning of this?'

'Pip's helping us with our enquiries,' said Ashley.

'Into what, may I ask?'

'Murder.'

Rupert's expression didn't change.

'I saw a bulletin on TV,' he said. 'About Paradise. I hope you haven't embarrassed me, Pip. I warned you about that stupid place. You can come in, officers. Wipe your feet.'

They followed him as he lumbered down the hall, shutting a

door to where the action was coming from. They entered a good-sized kitchen at the rear of the house. All the furniture and fittings appeared decent quality, but bland. The décor in Pip's lodge had been much more colourful and livelier.

Rupert didn't offer them a drink.

'What do you think Pip has done?' he asked.

'Where were you on Thursday night?' asked Barry.

'This Thursday night? The curry house down the road. We love it there, although I felt a bit rough the next day. Probably the wine.'

'And last weekend?'

'Let's see. Pip returned home and went shopping, then my brother came to stay. He's good fun. We stayed in both nights. Pip cooked. Did a decent job.'

'That fits with what she's told us. We'll need to double-check with the other people if that's okay?'

'I took a picture.'

Rupert leaned back in his seat and his meaty fingers prodded his phone for a minute.

'Here. I rested it on the sideboard and used the timer.'

Ashley studied the photo. Another tall black man, similar to Rupert but younger and slimmer, and a petite redhead were on either side of Rupert on a sofa. Pip was sitting on the arm. She was the only one not smiling.

Rupert put his phone away and laughed.

'Why would you think our Pip was a murderer? She's far from the killing type.'

Ashley glanced at Pip, who appeared capable of murder. Ashley let out a quiet groan as she realised what Pip was about to do. Pip sat in the seat next to her husband and smiled.

'You're unbelievable,' she said. 'Two women have died under suspicious circumstances, and it hasn't even registered in your brain. One lived opposite me. She'd been sleeping with a man called Dennis, who I also fell for. The detectives thought for a moment I'd killed her out of jealousy. You're right, though. I'm not the murdering type, but I am the cheating kind.'

Barry's head swivelled around to stare at Rupert at the same time Ashley's did. A small smile appeared on Rupert's face, which rapidly vanished.

'Pip, is this a joke?'

'No. It's a divorce.'

Rupert placed his large hands on the edge of the table.

'I'd like to leave now, officers,' said Pip.

Rupert swelled in size, and he was already huge. When he stood, his eyes widened. A thick finger jabbed in Pip's direction, then his clunking fist crashed down on the table.

'You'll get nothing. Nothing!'

Barry took a step forward and crossed his arms. Rupert immediately wilted and lowered himself back onto his seat. Ashley and Barry strode from the house to meet Pip outside.

As Ashley closed the door behind her, she couldn't hide the feeling she should be escaping down a beanstalk.

40

Ashley and Barry returned Pip to her lodge and took a statement there.

'We can arrange for an officer to be outside,' said Ashley afterwards.

'God, no. I just want to be left alone. Trust me. Nobody would dare mess with me tonight.'

'Is there a chance he'd head here?' asked Barry.

'No, he doesn't drive any more. I think he's agoraphobic. Apart from the newspaper shop, the library and the Taj Mahal, he doesn't venture out. I'll be safe here. Besides, he's like all bullies. All mouth no trousers.'

'Okay, but maybe a few nights in a hotel might be advisable in case he gets a taxi,' said Ashley.

'Yeah, you're probably right. I'll book into The Golden Lion tomorrow.' Pip's face fell. 'He'd never hurt me. Rupert and I had our first holiday there.'

Ashley left her phone number and told Pip that if she was even slightly concerned about anything, she should ring 999, and they'd send a patrol car.

'One last question, Pip. Did you ever lend money to Dennis?' asked Ashley.

'No, he never asked.'

Barry and Ashley stepped outside and paused at the railing. The sun was dipping in the sky. There were a few wisps of high cloud on an otherwise perfect expanse of turquoise. It was definitely the peace she would appreciate here, especially down this bottom part of the park.

Ashley blew out a long breath.

'God, what a day.'

Barry rubbed his shoulder.

'Yeah, I think I've strained something tussling with Glory. She was a piece of gristle.'

'So much for the site being full of oldies living out their days. When I pushed on Pip's stomach to stop her attacking Glory, it was like holding back a train. I feel pooped.'

'And now an hour's drive home,' said Barry. 'Fancy a cold drink and a bar snack first? I'm starving.'

Ashley couldn't imagine anything nicer.

'The Waterside Bar is close. We can watch the sun go down.'

'You're the boss.'

'Yes, don't forget it. Unless, of course, you fancy going for a quick ride.'

Ashley strode off and climbed in the car. Barry's simple brain couldn't walk and think, so he was quite a few seconds behind her. He looked sheepish when he got in, knowing that his juvenile mind had linked ride to sex.

'You're talking about the fairground.'

'Of course.'

It was only a few minutes' drive to the seafront. Barry parked up, while Ashley bought a ticket for two hours. After she slid it onto the dashboard, she found Barry staring glumly at the closed fairground.

The sun hung heavy over it, casting parts of it into darkness and lighting up the rest. Instead of the place being alive with booming music, exhilarated screams and delighted squeals, there was a sense of foreboding, even evil. Ashley imagined the fiery rays from the setting globe burning into the gloom around the quiet rides, but soon it would be nightfall, and the shadows would deepen.

She jolted Barry with her elbow, which made him jump.

'Come on. You've watched too many Stephen King films.'

When they reached the pub, Ashley stopped and poked Barry in the chest.

'This isn't a date, so don't mention it to anyone, which might be hard with you being a blabbermouth.'

'What's that supposed to mean?'

'Hector and his celibacy, and my not being able to have children.'

'I didn't know the Hector thing was a secret, and you're mid-forties, so not having kids is hardly a revelation.'

'Oh, dear. Just when you've moved into a net positive rating, you plunge back into the abyss. So you have to visit the bar and buy me a pint of Kronenbourg. I'll see if I can grab a table with a view.'

The Waterside was raised on the promenade and faced west, looking out on a shallow bay of the North Sea called The Wash. At the front of the building was a cross between a balcony and a conservatory, which gave a panorama of the entire beach. Hunstanton beach wasn't the best. It was quite stony, with little soft sand, and the tide came right into the sea wall. The sunsets, however, were unforgettable.

Every table was taken in the busy bar. She headed to the

conservatory just as a couple rose to leave. Ashley gave them a huge smile and slipped into one of their seats. She had a glance at the menu, which, apart from the prices, appeared to be one they'd printed in the 1960s.

The Waterside was a long-standing feature of the town and had once been the Railway Station Refreshment Hall & Waiting Room, dating back to 1892. The couple next to her might have been there when it first opened.

'Lovely view,' said the gent, touching the brim of his battered cap.

The food was good value, and her mouth watered at the memory of a lasagne she'd eaten there before. She settled on the ploughman's salad, a nod to her new attitude to health.

Barry arrived with two pints of Diet Coke, despite what she'd asked for. They were still officially on duty.

'Wow,' he said, gawking out of the windows.

Ashley shielded her eyes and peered out over the ice-cream hut in front of them across the wet beach, which shone from the dipping sphere. All along the beach, people had stopped as though captivated.

The slanting rays gave a red hue to the sand. As the burning fireball touched the water, Ashley half expected to hear it sizzle. There was a reassuring feeling of insignificance as the sea mirrored the orange glow, seemingly displaying a glowing path to heaven.

Usually, the calm feelings would last, but Ashley couldn't help picturing Jasmine in her hot tub as the sun went down. She found herself wondering if murderers paused to admire the night sky, or if they just took advantage of the distraction.

41

Pip opened a second bottle of wine, poured a large glass, then screwed the top back on. She'd done it. She was going to be free of Rupert and could move on with her life. It was a moment to remember and celebrate, not one to rue. Pip didn't care about his money.

She stepped out onto the decking and smiled as she caught the last of the daylight. The whole skyline ahead of her glowed like the dying embers of an old world. Tomorrow would bring a new dawn, and Pip would be waiting.

She couldn't help a sneaky peek over her shoulder towards Dennis's lodge. Stupid to think he'd be interested now she was single, but a girl could dream. His door looked half open, but nobody seemed to be about.

Pip felt her footing go but caught herself on the railing. The wooden surface was more slippery than usual. She must have spilled sun lotion earlier, so she kicked off her trainers and pulled over a deckchair. Bats often flitted through the air at dusk. Perhaps she'd sit awhile and watch them.

Pip was half dozing when her gate creaked. Her ears strained as steady steps approached. She twisted slightly and opened an eye. Maybe Dennis missed their secret rendezvous as much as she did.

All she could see was a pair of blue jeans surprisingly close to her head. She looked down at a pair of sturdy boots. A brief twist of silver flashed in her vision, then instant agony as metal viciously cut into her throat. She put her fingers up, but there was no chance of them getting under the wire.

Her feet slipped on the decking as she attempted to rise. She bucked in her seat, but the pain was agonising. Pip tried to gasp. No air escaped. She grabbed the gloved hand, but her strength faded as her eyes bulged. Pip gave a last desperate tug on it and the glove came off. She dug her nails into the hand underneath but found thin rubber instead of skin. A voice hissed in her ear.

'This is no less than you deserve.'

They were the final words Pip heard as her attacker dragged her backwards into the lodge, and out of sight.

42

Ashley was tired when she woke on Monday morning. A lot of driving, either at the wheel or as a passenger, always took it out of her. She just resisted mainlining toast and butter, although the microwaved porridge she gobbled down was a poor substitute.

A missed call from Hector was on her phone when she got out of the shower. She rang him back and put him on speaker when he answered so she could do her make-up while she talked.

'Morning, Ashley. How are you?'

'No need for pleasantries this early in the morning. Who's dead now?'

Heavy silence came over the line. She put her eyeliner down.

'What's wrong?'

'Sorry. I've been thinking about things and wanted to talk to someone about it.'

'You had all day yesterday.'

'I don't want other people's opinions. Just yours.'

'I think that's the nicest thing you've ever said to me.'

Ashley considered what his concerns were.

'Can't you speak to your mum and dad?' she asked.

'No, not at all. You've been like a mother to me.'

'Oi, cheeky. Enough of that. The benefits of staying are simple. Job security, rapid promotion, decent salary, camaraderie and you're serving the public. Simples.'

'Surely that's not why you do the job. I can earn more money elsewhere with fewer rude people.'

'Why do people like chess? Backgammon? Even crosswords?'

'The logic and reasoning, the challenge, the endless variation, the chance of victory.'

'That's why I'm a detective, but it's better than chess because there's more at stake.'

It took Hector a few seconds to understand. He chuckled down the line.

'So, what you're saying is that being a detective is the ultimate puzzle.'

'You got it. Now bugger off. You're making me late.'

Barry tooted his horn outside while Ashley stood in mismatched bra and knickers, neither of which were very new. The weekend's plan had been washing, not investigating.

When she went to grab one of her other two suits, she recalled sending them to the dry-cleaners. Ashley found the previous day's jacket on the lounge floor where it had slipped off the armchair. It was covered in sand, which she must have brought back after running.

She left her house finally, feeling as if the transition to mad cat lady was complete. All she was missing was the feline itself.

'Hey, lady,' said a voice from above, confirming it.

Ashley looked up to the bedroom of her neighbour. It could only be the eleven-year-old grandson who lived with his grandma while his mother worked in London.

'Morning, Oliver. How's the football?'

'It's not as good.'

'No.'

'It's getting too easy for me.'

'Oh, I see. Swelling heads eventually pop, you know. I hope you're taking care of your nan.'

'She's still in bed, but things are going to be perfect. Mum's moving back forever. She's gonna be a Cromer lawyer. I was wondering that, because you meet people in trouble, you could give them my mum's telephone number.'

'I'm sure your mother will be so successful I won't need to. Everyone will want the best.'

Oliver grinned at her.

'Have a good day, lady.'

Ashley grunted, 'Morning,' when she got in the car. Barry looked as if he'd just come back from a week at Champneys. He had a nice watch on and, even though he'd rolled up his sleeves, he gave off a smart air. She threw her bag with her running kit on the back seat.

'How do you look so fresh?' she asked.

'It's the age gap.'

'Shut it.'

'Okay. Did your mind solve the puzzle overnight?'

'Funny you should say that, but I think mine closed down. You?'

'Same. Should we exhume Katrina's body?'

'The suicide? Sal checked. Ashes to ashes, unfortunately.'

'Great.'

'Gerald's had Katrina's caravan sealed, so if we want to check further for DNA and prints, we still can, but the CSI teams are stretched as it is, so let's see what happens today. There are two strong lines of inquiry. We might strike gold with what we get back from the earring or the hammer. Uniform are going to meet us a street away from Jackie's, but I don't reckon we'll have any aggro. Sal's got a warrant just in case but Jackie isn't stupid enough to keep anything in the house.'

'No, it seems a waste of resource to search the whole property.'

'That's the problem with not solving these cases quickly. We end up burning time on pointless interviews and searches, while teams trawl millions of minutes of CCTV.'

'Surely not pointless if we solve the case,' said Barry with a straight face.

Ashley laughed. 'That's the spirit. No doubt we'll need more of that positivity by day's end.'

'I was thinking about the poker thing as well. Dennis is clearly crap at it. I used to spend money on those sites.'

'I think of you more as a bingo guy.'

'Piss off. Pubs used to do poker nights, which I enjoyed, but I started playing on my laptop. That led me into online fruit machines for a bit. Mostly lost but only twenty quid a night. I'd have spent miles more in an actual casino. But then I had a mad evening where I was drinking and playing, and I burned through three hundred quid. It was so easy. I couldn't believe what I'd done when I woke up, so I deleted all the apps and programs.'

'With his monthly income, we'd expect Dennis to play for decent stakes anyway, but what you're saying is he could easily spend more.'

'If he's addicted, he'll race through every penny he has, then search around for extra.'

'Pip told me Jasmine's husband was a business high-flyer, so she'd have inherited plenty of money after his heart attack. Her house is in Barnes, too, which even I know is an expensive place to live.'

'Let's double-check there aren't transfers to Dennis.'

'No, we've seen Dennis's account.'

'That was the one he gave us. Maybe he has a few.'

'True. She may have been withdrawing it from machines and giving him cash.'

'Jasmine's son might know something, although it doesn't sound like they have a functioning relationship.'

'I'll ring Scott Gorton now. He replied to my email yesterday saying Jackie didn't want to see him. Scott will also have Jasmine's son to deal with. I wonder if he's booked in to meet either yet.'

Scott's phone rang for a while before he answered.

'Ash. It's not even eight o'clock.'

'I didn't want you getting a better offer.'

'Unlikely. How are things?'

'Good, you?'

'Excellent. How's your investigation?'

'We're struggling with these two murders. It'd be a remarkable coincidence if they weren't related, but nothing's obvious.'

'I heard you had a suspect in for questioning, although he wasn't charged.'

'Yes. Dennis had a top-notch solicitor, but we didn't have anything damning anyway. We've got DNA tests due back tomorrow, which might help. I'm about to call on Jackie Hook. Seems Alfie was dealing on a low scale.'

'Ask her if she's changed her mind and would like me to come around.'

Ashley grinned. 'Ah, she fully declined your services.'

'It's too early to repeat the language she used, but yes. I'll give it another go.'

'Are you seeing Jasmine's son today?'

'Nobody's been able to get hold of him so far. He's the only next of kin, too. I might drive down there and talk to his neighbours, or see if I can track down where he works.'

'Pip said he's some kind of trainee at HSBC in London.'

'Cheers, that's helpful.'

'Do you remember a Katrina Lake who committed suicide?'

'Rings a bell. Wasn't that in a caravan park?'

'The same one.'

'Ah, understood. Not my case, but if my memory's right, there weren't any family or close friends to liaise with.'

'That sad state of affairs seems to get more common. Anyway, I'll let you know how it goes with Jackie this morning.'

Barry was grinning at her when she finished the call.

'Were you flirting with Flash?'

'Of course not. He was on good form, though.'

'I'm not surprised with that young girlfriend.'

Ashley gave him a tight smile.

Barry pulled up where a response van was already waiting with four officers inside and went over to greet them. Gerald had agreed to be here with his team later in the morning after he finished up the paperwork from yesterday.

Ashley had only brought the uniform presence as a precaution, but she felt a chill as they walked around the corner and stood in front of the unloved house. The grey drapes had been drawn. The knackered car that had been on the drive had gone. It was quiet. There was nobody else in the entire street, despite the promise of the early sunshine.

Ashley knocked. Nothing. She rapped again. She was debating whether she should ask one of the constables to fetch the big red key, when a bolt scraped across.

Jackie appeared with her hair standing up and heavy bags under her eyes. She wore only a vest top and pyjama bottoms. After a peek at Ashley, she half-heartedly tried to close the door. Ashley clocked a pair of wings tattooed at the top of Jackie's chest with her son's name, Lennie, below them, and Jackie's name above.

Jackie sagged, her stare far away. Ashley spotted the bloodshot eye, surrounded by purple and blue.

43

Ashley stopped the door shutting with her shoe, as Jackie turned and wandered down the hall as if in a daze. Ashley followed as Barry closed the door. Jackie walked into the lounge, sat in an armchair, and lit a roll-up. Judging by the dense smog in the room, it was far from her first.

'Everything okay?' asked Ashley.

'Peachy.'

Ashley didn't expect Jackie to grass on anyone, especially seeing as she'd already served eight years rather than blab. She decided to appeal to her sense of humour.

'Were you out clubbing last night?'

Jackie's bruised face didn't respond. Then a laugh wheezed out.

'Feck off, will ya? What do you want?'

'We're here to search the house.'

'You won't find it.'

'How do you know what we're looking for?'

'The only thing you'll discover in this gaff is nothing, which I assume isn't what you're after.'

'Are the boys on their paper rounds?' asked Barry.

'Morning, Barry. Have you got dance lessons later?'

Ashley followed Jackie's gaze to Barry's shoes, which were remarkably shiny.

'The lads have gone,' growled Jackie. 'You won't see them again, but they had zip to do with it, anyway.'

'To do with what?' asked Ashley.

'Alfie's drug-dealing empire.' Again, Jackie wheezed and chuckled.

'Was he in bed with the Mexican cartels?'

'The boys said he made about £50 a week. They told him it wasn't worth the arse ache, but he wanted a few treats in life. Fish and chips are bloody dear nowadays. And as I explained before, we were left with the bare minimum.'

'Was that why he was killed?'

'How the hell would I know? It's not what you think. Nobody kills anyone for a few bags of weed. I had an early visitor today, who I explained that to.' Jackie touched her face. 'Hopefully, you'll be more inclined to believe me.'

It surprised Ashley that Jackie was talking to her at all, although grief could drain a person of all resistance.

Jackie gazed into nowhere, then noticed how close to her fingers the cigarette had burned. She dropped it into the ashtray and rolled another.

'Does this concern Betty Brown?' asked Ashley.

Jackie chose not to reply.

'We can get you protected or moved if you want to talk.'

Jackie didn't laugh this time.

'You know that would be no life for me. And I reckon their reach is longer than yours. Fuck knows why my Alfie was murdered. I told them that. Maybe a pothead did it to save themselves twenty quid.'

'His phone and money were still in his pockets.'

'No idea, then. Neither do the boys. I said that to my visitors, too.'

'So, Betty came here.'

'Betty's long gone. You must know that. It's Elizabeth now, and she did not come here. She's wealthy and doesn't do house calls. You'll never get to her. I suppose she just wanted to make sure she wasn't implicated.'

'What did she threaten you with?'

'When you're done searching this place, I'll be off with the lads, too. They won't ever be back. This town's no good for them. They're safe, hidden in deepest darkest Lincolnshire. I'm a bit long in the tooth for change, so maybe I'll return, but those kids' futures are my priority.'

'You could tell me the truth off the record.'

'I reckon they're watching and seen you arrive, so I'm probably already dead. It doesn't matter where I go, they'd find me, which means I've nothing to lose, but I'll say it anyway. It wasn't anything to do with Betty. We made our peace a long time ago and, even though she barely kept her side of it, Alfie's death isn't on her.'

Ashley was inclined to agree. It would be a pointless risk to kill Alfie unless you were mad or desperate.

'If it wasn't Betty Brown, then who was the supplier?'

'The lads thought the dealer was foreign, but that's all they know. The suppliers wouldn't care. Alfie would have paid them up front, so what he did with it after was up to him.'

Ashley's mobile rang in her pocket. She struggled to hear the frail voice when she answered it.

'Speak up, please.'

'It's Helga from Diamond. We had a scare last night. Someone was trying to break into our lodge.'

44

Ashley took in Jackie's hard face and suspected finding out what happened to Jasmine in Paradise would be easier and quicker than discovering who was responsible for Alfie's death.

'I'll be there in ten minutes,' said Ashley, and cut the call.

Ashley beckoned Barry to come out to the hall.

'Who was that?' asked Barry when they were out of Jackie's earshot.

'Helga from the caravan park. She reckons they had someone trying to enter their lodge yesterday evening. I'll head down there and leave this place in your capable hands.'

'Why didn't they call the police last night?'

'God knows. I'll find out. Search this room, then let Jackie stay in here while CSI sweep the house.'

'It already looks as if anything of value and the youngsters' personal items have gone.'

'Yep. I'll ring Kettle after I've spoken to Helga. The full team is back today, so let's see if we get some direction with the intel and evidence we have. I'll start getting the caravan Percy's let us use set up as a base.'

Barry frowned.

'I've got the feeling this is going to be like nothing we've dealt with before.'

Ashley just nodded.

45

Ashley got in the car Barry had booked out and drove to Paradise. She stopped at the entrance and spoke to the uniformed constables stationed there.

'Any news?' she asked.

'No. We've had a word with everyone who's left and took details of their cars, but a surprising number were unaware anything bad had happened.'

Ashley carried on, parked up at Reception, then went inside. Percy's blue-haired stepson was oblivious as Ashley breezed past him and stood next to the girl who had been present the previous time, Gail. She looked apologetic.

'Percy's gone,' she said.

'Gone where?'

'He mentioned something about needing a holiday. He left this for you.'

The young lady handed over a Manila envelope.

'The keys to your van are inside. He said you can use all the facilities.'

'Who's in charge in his absence?'

Gail laughed. 'Surely you don't think Percy ever runs the site. He's not daft, but he's easily distracted and a little childish. His major fault is common to a lot of wealthy people.'

'Go on.'

'He's tighter than a gnat's chuff.'

Ashley couldn't help smiling as she left.

She'd try to contact Percy later, but he was low on her list of suspects. Ashley pootled down the road. It said 5 mph max on the signs, but the car wanted to stall going so slowly. It gave her a chance to check out the rest of the site, which seemed busy for a Monday morning. She supposed weekend holidaymakers were packing to go home. Ashley suspected she'd depart pretty damn swiftly if a dead body had been found under suspicious circumstances.

She slowed for a ball bouncing across the road. Young kids ran around in their swimming costumes. When she arrived at Diamond, it was a different environment. Ashley stepped out of the vehicle to quiet. There was an air of abandonment. Even the ducks had left the pond.

Ashley heard a miaowing and saw the tabby cat licking his paws outside Pip's van. She sensed movement at the edge of her vision and turned. Dennis sprinted up the road towards her.

For a moment, she tensed, not realising he was in his running gear. He slowed down as he passed her, but only stopped when he reached his decking, where he performed cooling-down stretches. Helga and Hans were leaving their lodge with a small suitcase each. They put the cases down at the kerb, then Helga went back inside. Hans stared over at Ashley, who strolled towards him.

'Morning, Hans. Everything okay?' shouted Ashley

'No, we feel rattled.'

'What happened?' asked Dennis, with genuine concern. He had strolled over and was listening.

'Last night, there were strange goings-on around our lodge. At least, I thought that's what they were. It sounded like a branch was scraping against the windows. So, I went outside.' His eyes narrowed. 'I took a carving knife.' His eyes widened. 'There was nobody there but also no trees close by to have made the noise.'

'That's it?' asked Dennis.

'No, five minutes later, I heard the slow stomp of someone walking on our decking. I think the handle was tried. The front door is opaque, so we can't see who's there. I'm sure a dark shape moved past, though. I grabbed my weapon again, but Helga wouldn't let me go outside.'

'Always trust a wife's instincts,' said Ashley. 'Call 999 immediately next time.'

'We locked ourselves in the en suite. I took the knife. Would have used it, too. I swear it.'

Hans jabbed with his hand, which reminded Ashley of Michelle's thrusting action. Sweat had broken out on Hans's forehead as he relived his ordeal.

'It's not safe here. We're leaving until they catch the evil psycho that's doing these things.'

'I would say that's a good idea,' said Ashley.

'Hans, do you want me to call you if anything happens?' asked Dennis, which surprised Ashley.

'Yes, you have my number, but tell Percy, too. He'll sort it out.'

Ashley doubted that but kept quiet.

'You should leave, too, Dennis,' said Hans. 'There's a malevolent presence down here.'

Ashley helped Hans and Helga move their coats and the perishable food items from their lodge, making sure nobody touched the door handle again. A taxi pulled up and took the elderly couple away.

'And then there were four,' said Dennis, who then turned and walked away.

He stopped when Verne lurched out of his lodge.

'Never again!'

'Rough night?' asked Dennis.

'I've been bingeing *Game of Thrones* and didn't realise how late it was.' Verne picked up on Dennis's tone. 'What did we miss?'

'Hans reckoned an intruder was trying to get in his lodge last night. Did you see or hear anything?'

'The amount I had to drink, someone could have entered my mind and I wouldn't have noticed.'

Ashley walked up to Pip's lodge and observed the deckchair on its side. She knocked on the door, then moved to the decking to peer through the windows, but the curtains were pulled.

'Anyone seen Pip?' she asked the other two.

'I've just jogged on the beach,' said Dennis. 'I think I spotted her much further up along the promenade going out towards Old Hunstanton. She sometimes does a long run on a Monday to blow away the cobwebs, so she might be a while.'

'Did I see Hans and Helga in a taxi?' asked Bertie, coming out to join them.

Verne told him what Hans had said.

'I'm glad we're leaving today as well, then,' he said with a visible shiver. 'I don't want to be the only ones here when the killer returns.' Bertie raised an eyebrow at Verne. 'Looks like I'll be driving after your performance last night.'

'Final person to leave needs to write under the Diamond sign,' said Verne. 'All ye who enter shall perish.'

Dennis was at his door when Ashley had a thought.

'Will you be vacating, too?' she shouted.

Dennis's face was hard to read.

'I've only got one place to go,' he said, 'and I don't like it there, so, no!' He opened his door and stepped inside. Before he shut himself in, he gave her a stiff nod.

'I'm here to the death.'

46

Ashley drove back to the park entrance and opened the door to the caravan Percy had allowed her to use. Gail had told her it was a mid-range one. Ashley found the price label in the window: £40,000 pounds. Better than she expected from Percy. After a mooch through the three bedrooms and the kitchen, she decided she'd nip to Tesco later and stock the fridge. Might as well get comfortable.

The caravan would be frequented by numerous officers when they realised it was there, especially if they knew they could grab a cuppa inside. Years ago, they'd have used it to store evidence, but not any more. Nowadays, they'd put up a map of the park, have staff meetings, and it would be a quiet place for a call or to email. The exhibits officer, who recorded all items of property seized during an investigation, would park his van beside it and use it as a base.

She returned to the reception area, where blue-haired Hamilton was chatting on the phone again. Gail was clearly running the show, so Ashley introduced herself properly and asked how things worked.

'Let me see,' replied the young woman. 'There are two part-timers who come in to make sure we're staffed until 8 p.m., but one's on holiday this week. Obviously, Hamilton here is an immense help.'

Gail rolled her eyes theatrically, but Hamilton didn't notice.

'I understand there's a maintenance person. I haven't seen him around.'

'Maintenance guy and a groundsman. They're both full-time. The groundsman does funny hours, but the grass is cut, and the bins are emptied, so I don't care what he's up to if he doesn't cause me any hassle.'

'Can I have their mobile numbers, please?'

'Of course.'

'Are they the murdering sort?' said Ashley, only half joking.

Gail took longer thinking about the question than Ashley expected and then merely shrugged.

'Some parks have proper security and a staffed barrier,' she said. 'I'm guessing Percy doesn't want to pay for that. We had a guy who used to drive around the park in a golf buggy at night with a torch, but he retired a month ago. Percy hasn't been looking awfully hard for a replacement. He says catching criminals is what the police are for.'

'Okay,' said Ashley. 'There'll be officers working out of the van Percy gave us this week in the hope we catch the culprit sooner rather than later, so you can direct queries to there or my mobile number. Have you heard any rumours?'

'No, nothing. We've had a few cancel their holidays because of it, but Percy doesn't give refunds this late, so most people will come.' Gail's face fell. 'Was Jasmine definitely murdered?'

'We think so. It's possible it was an accident, but unlikely.'

'She was always so friendly. Percy said Katrina's suicide could also be suspicious.'

'We're looking into everything, but Hunstanton is the land CCTV forgot.'

'As you might imagine, Percy cuts the odd corner. We used to have it all over, but the ones on the main road and entrance were vandalised a few months ago. Percy fixed the entrance camera, but someone broke it again the next week, so he didn't bother a second time.'

'Did the CCTV catch the vandals?'

'No, they must have known what they were doing, which makes me think it wasn't children. Saying that, we had a complaint this morning that some youths were causing trouble and making a load of noise last night.'

'Any descriptions?'

'No. The kids are often bored or hyper when they run out of money for the arcades, and they often get up to mischief.'

'Is there much theft?'

'No, not really. It's rare caravans or lodges are broken into, but stuff can get nicked if it's unattended.'

'Who complained about the children?'

'It was a woman from Four on Bronze. She's always complaining about the kids. There's a family on Bronze who have what I call energetic lads.'

Ashley checked her map, left Reception and walked over to Bronze. There were no lodges, just caravans. Most were well used, but none were falling apart. Ashley leapt back as she was about to knock, when the door was pushed open.

'Oh, sorry,' said the lady.

'That's okay. Were you expecting trouble?'

'Those bloody feral kids at Fifteen have been winding me up. Their grandparents own it, but the little shits come every week-end. It's reached the point where I'm thinking about not staying at the weekends.'

'That's why I'm here. My name's Detective Sergeant Ashley Knight. I'm investigating the suspicious deaths.'

'My name's Lil Doherty.' The woman frowned. 'It's bloody worrying. Have you found out who did it?'

'It's early days. The other incident was over on Diamond. A resident over there said someone was messing around outside their place last night and even tried their door.'

'Isn't Diamond the posh end with the expensive lodges?'

'Yes, that's right.'

'I wouldn't put it past these kids. They nicked my Kindle. I asked their gran, but she denied any knowledge, then suspiciously it made its way back to my decking. I suppose at least they returned it. Twenty-six found the oldest kid, Willy, in her caravan.'

'Nicking stuff?'

'No, he'd had a poo because his nan had gone shopping and locked their van. Said she'd never smelled anything like it.'

'Nothing was taken?'

'No. They're more naughty than criminal, but it's draining. I come here for peace and quiet, not to hear them burping and farting.'

'Are they still here?'

'No, but no doubt they'll be back on Friday afternoon after school's finished.'

'Okay, I'll have a word then. I suspect if I ask them, they'll just deny it, but maybe a visit from the police will be a shock.'

The woman sneered at Ashley and closed the door.

Ashley returned to what would now be called the police caravan and tried the telephone numbers Gail had given her, but one had a busy tone, and the other went straight to voicemail. Ashley rang her office number at OCC. DS Bhavini Kotecha picked up.

'Hey, Bee. It's me.'

'Hi, Ash. How did the search go?'

'I haven't heard from Barry yet. Jackie admitted she knew Alfie had been doing some dabbling on the side, but it's a leap to think Betty Brown was involved. She's living in obscene wealth, so we'd need more before pulling her in.'

'What's the plan? I feel like a fifth wheel after having a week off.'

'I'm going to stay here today until late. The site owner has let us use a beautiful caravan. Barry will return to OCC for his paperwork, and he can talk to Kettle and keep him on top of the latest finds. I want two more people here with me. Send Hector and Sal.'

'I just spoke to Sal. He said all that fieldwork has given him blisters, so he won't be keen. Sal's brilliant with getting all the intel processed here, so I'll come instead.'

'There's something not right here, Bee. I can't put my finger on what's going on, but someone incredibly dangerous is wandering around Hunstanton. So, do you think it's wise—?'

'Please don't say in your condition. I haven't told HR, so Hector and I will be leaving shortly.'

Ashley smiled at her disconnected phone. Feisty. She thought of Bhavini. Imagine walking around with another life inside you. Ashley would have wrapped herself in metre-thick bubble wrap the moment she found out.

It put Ashley in a tricky position. Bhavini was also a sergeant, and they had a great working relationship with both happy to take direction depending on who was responsible for the case they were dealing with. Ashley would talk to her when she arrived. It was a welcome distraction when there was a light rapping on her caravan's door.

She opened it to what she could only describe as a glamorous granny. The lady had the brightest red lipstick on and a stylish wraparound dress above strappy sandals.

'Are you the detective?' she asked.

'Yes, Sergeant Ashley Knight.'

'I went to Reception yesterday and told idiot boy that I'd seen someone dodgy walking around the site at night. He said he'd mention it to the police, but nobody's been in touch.'

'Dodgy?'

'Dodgy probably isn't the right word. I'd been at my salsa class, and a gentleman there insisted I join him for a glass of Sancerre, so I was late getting home. As I closed the curtains, I noticed movement among the shadows. There's a streetlight outside my caravan, so I saw him clearly. He was a hunched creature with a mean face.'

'What was he doing?'

'Carrying an axe.'

47

Ashley raised an eyebrow.

'What time was this?'

'Nearly 11 p.m.'

'Not normally the hour for chopping down trees.'

'No, it wasn't that sort of axe. This was much smaller. I suppose the kind Red Indians had.'

Ashley smiled. 'I believe you should say Native American now, but I get your point. You mean like a tomahawk?'

'Well, there were no tassels on it.'

'Hopefully no war paint, either.'

The woman grinned. 'You must think me silly or drunk, but I'd only had one because I was driving.'

'Not at all. I'll look into it. What's your name and where are you on the site?'

'Mrs Zabczynska. Twenty-six Bronze.'

'Ah, near the boisterous boys.'

'So you've heard about them. One of the cheeky little shits got into my van last summer, destroyed my toilet, then helped himself to two Magnum ice creams.'

'Willy?'

'Yes. My friend and I found him at my table flicking through *Cosmo*. You'd be amazed at the tiny gap at the top of a window that he managed to climb through. My friend asked him what he was doing. He said it was a dare.'

'Thank you. I'll talk with them at the end of the week. They don't sound like they'd be involved with murder, but it's possible they might have seen something. Can you describe this fellow with the axe?'

'He reminded me of Willem Dafoe.'

'Okay. Someone will take a statement at your caravan shortly. Give me your number and keep your phone on.'

When the woman had gone, Ashley decided that, while she was looking forward to meeting Willy, bumping into the actor who played the Green Goblin on a dark night would be unsettling. She set off for Reception to have a quiet word with Hamilton. There was another woman in the office with Gail, and they were both heads down over their desks checking files. Even the boy was doing something on the computer, which must have been complicated because he had his tongue sticking out of the side of his mouth as he typed.

'Hamilton. Do you know who I am?'

'Yes, you're the police chief.'

'Close enough. Did a smartly dressed woman visit here saying she'd seen someone with an axe?'

Hamilton's brow furrowed. Then it was as though the secrets of all creation had been revealed to him.

'Yes, she did. I think she said something like an actor had been walking around the site with one.'

'Did she say it was an actor, or was that your interpretation?'

His brow furrowed further. Ashley imagined black oil oozing out of his ears.

'I'm sorry, I don't understand.'

Ashley grimaced. It would be a turn-up if it were Willem Dafoe.

'Okay, forget it. Any more people with information like that send straight to my caravan. Now, I've tried to ring the handyman and the groundsman, but neither are picking up.'

Hamilton remained motionless and expressionless. Ashley could see Gail quietly laughing at her desk.

'Behind you,' she shouted.

The door opened and a man wearing a tool belt came in. He seemed young to Ashley, but he had a nice smile and thick black hair over a ruddy face. Ashley stuck out a hand.

'Hi, I'm DS Knight.'

'Tim.'

'Ah, like Tim "the Tool Man" Taylor. Tool Time.'

'Pardon?'

'Sorry. It's probably a bit before your time. How long have you been doing this job?'

'A year. I used to help on a Saturday, worked here after school, ended up staying. It's pretty simple. The same things go wrong, then I appear and fix them.'

'So, you're employed as opposed to freelance.'

'Yes. Percy pays me minimum wage to keep the site ticking over. Most work is blocked bogs, or loose drawers and cupboards. If the vans or lodges are privately owned, I charge as and when, which makes the money okay.'

'Have you seen any strange behaviour recently?'

'I'm always seeing crazy antics. You get all types here.'

'Anything menacing?'

Tim shook his head after considering the question.

'Spend much time on Diamond?'

'No, the lodges are all pretty new and well made. I did a job for a nice German couple a few weeks back and I fixed the decking gate for a friendly Turkish guy.'

'Dennis?'

'I think he pronounced it Deniz.'

'Okay. I've tried ringing the groundsman, but he's not picking up.'

'He lives here. He's not great at answering his phone, but there are blackspots all over the park.'

'Does he have a caravan?'

'Yes.'

Ashley glanced over at blue-haired Hamilton and wondered whether she could borrow the tomahawk when she discovered who owned it.

'Whereabouts is he?'

'He's up a drive at the top edge of Bronze. His caravan and an enormous garage are up there, where he keeps the lawnmowers and the trailers. I wouldn't go there alone.'

Timothy slowly raised an eyebrow, then tipped his head back and laughed.

'Stop it,' said Gail, fluttering her eyelashes. 'Ignore him, Sergeant. Lionel's quiet, but he's been here from when Percy's parents first ran Paradise. He's just a bit eccentric. We've never had a whiff of trouble in all that time, and he helps Tim.'

'Yes, that's true. He's a decent bloke, except for the baby eating.'

48

Ashley returned to her caravan, set up her laptop and began getting herself up to date. Percy, to her surprise, had left a welcome pack with details of the site's Wi-Fi. Then she realised it would have been Gail.

She rang Barry to ask Gerald to send one of his guys to take swabs and prints from Hans's door handle. Nothing had been found at Jackie's. Barry had also heard Jasmine's laptop had nothing untoward on it.

After two hours of calls and emailing, Hector and Bhavini still hadn't arrived. Ashley's phone beeped. There was a one-word message from Bhavini.

Potatoes!

Ashley assumed she'd hear what that meant later. She rang Kettle and relayed the latest developments.

'Okay, sounds like you're making progress,' he said. 'I've got a meeting planned for five. Will you be present?'

'No, Barry will attend. I want a feel for this place at night and to drop into the clubhouse. I don't imagine the killer has been hanging around in view, but the bar staff could know something. It might be quiet because the kids are at school still, but it's worth a shot.'

'What's your gut feeling about Betty Brown?'

'To be honest, I can't see it. Why risk a life of leisure and pleasure by taking out Alfie? Apparently, she goes by Elizabeth now.'

'Agreed, but sometimes idiots do stupid stuff. Either that or we're missing something.'

'Somebody's given Jackie a warning, judging by her black eye. My guess would be Alfie's death had nothing to do with Elizabeth, but she was worried her name might get dragged into things. Jackie has less to lose now her husband's gone, so maybe Elizabeth was concerned enough to send a stooge to put the frighteners on her. It looks like her visitors threatened the grandkids, which seems to have worked.'

'That makes sense, but there's no point in bringing Elizabeth in without concrete intel. Even then, she'll have the best lawyer money can buy, so any evidence would need to be strong.'

'I'll be in the office first thing tomorrow.'

'See you then.'

Ashley needed to speak to Lionel, the likely axe man, next. She knew Tim had been joking, but there was a risk in going up to his isolated shack alone. After all, individuals were dying. She called Lionel's number again but had no joy. She rang Barry at 1 p.m. for another update on the search at Jackie Hook's place.

'Any luck?' she asked.

'Nope. Gerald said he's never seen such an empty house, considering four people live here. The boys when they left could have taken things, and she wasn't long out of prison, but it feels like a dead end. Gerald's team are in the loft, then they're done unless you want the garden searched.'

'Check the garden. I don't think we need to dig it up.'

'Any news your end?'

Ashley updated him on the rest of the operation.

'Okay, I'll return to OCC straight from here and attend Kettle's 5 p.m. meeting. Shall I visit this Lionel fella with you?'

'You head off. I'll ask the search team to assist if Bee and Hector don't appear soon. Decent work over the last few days, Barry.'

'No closer to solving it, though, are we?'

Ashley ignored Barry's impatience, said goodbye, and cut the call. She received a text from Bhavini saying they'd be thirty minutes, so she set off for Tesco, which was just a few minutes away. She could have asked for a PCSO to fetch the items, but Ashley had always found doing the mundane sometimes unlocked ideas in her head.

Ashley ambled out of the park and, after a short stroll, saw the supermarket ahead. It was a glorious day. When the weather was like this, a British seaside was perfect. She enjoyed the heat on her face for a moment, then used the remainder of the walk to call the search team and the door knockers but there was no news. There was a slight breeze coming off the sea, but Ashley was desperate for a cold drink when she arrived at her destination.

She bought a copy of the *Daily Mirror* because it had the headline 'Death at Paradise Park'. The press had not been allowed on the site, so the article focused on the killing of Alfie. It seemed Kettle hadn't released the finer details, which made sense.

Ashley grabbed essential supplies. Four cheap porcelain mugs, plastic cutlery and plates, sandwiches, biscuits, fruit and crisps. She picked up a six-pack of Evian near the tills, which she regretted as she sweated on the way back.

As usual, just a five-minute walk cleared her head, and she pondered over a plan for the next few days. Modern techniques meant DNA and fingerprint results would be back swiftly. Nowadays, they could even scan a fingerprint at the scene and check it against the database.

The problem was this case was already getting older than she would like. Most murder cases were solved quickly, but Ashley didn't feel close to understanding why either of the victims had been killed.

It seemed all types lived and worked on caravan parks. Ashley thought of the people she'd spoken to so far.

Apart from Hans and Helga, it really could be any of them.

49

Ashley had just arrived back at the caravan when Hector and Bhavini turned up. Ashley brought them inside, and they started the picnic while they caught up.

'Didn't they do wraps or couscous?' asked Hector.

'I'm surprised she didn't buy pork pies and sausage rolls,' said Bhavini.

'Damn, I forgot about them. I got apples and bananas. That's progress,' replied Ashley.

'I brought my trainers. We could go for a jog later and burn off the excess,' said Bhavini.

Ashley raised an eyebrow at her.

'I'm pregnant, not having heart bypass surgery,' she replied.

Ashley's eyes widened as she glanced over at Hector. He grinned.

'It turns out two and a half hours trapped in a vehicle is long enough to bond.'

'What was the potato thing?' asked Ashley.

'A spillage,' said Bhavini. 'A load of new ones went over the road. We couldn't go back, so we had to wait. Eventually, another tractor came across the field and collected them up. It was sweltering in the car, and neither of us had thought to bring a drink. It was lucky I'd made him stop for the toilet just beforehand, or we really would have bonded. The traffic jam must have been ten miles behind us. I'm glad we're going home late because it'll take a while to clear.'

'Talking of which,' said Hector, 'I need to use the facilities.'

'Check first. I'm not sure the waste is connected.'

'You're kidding.'

'No, go across to the clubhouse and use theirs. I don't want one of your turds loitering in here while I work.'

'I'll bet you've kept worse company,' he said before making a sharp exit.

A few seconds after Hector had left the van, Bhavini smiled.

'Isn't he easy to talk to? I opened right up in the car. He did what no other man has ever managed when I've given them my problems.'

'He didn't try to solve them?'

'Yep. He listened. That's husband material. Shame I'm not a few years younger and less pregnant.'

Ashley chuckled.

'Poor Hector. He'll end up married to a pregnant woman before he's even had sex.'

A shadow passed over Bhavini's face as she recalled her predicament.

'Are you sure it's fine to stay at yours?'

'Yes, of course, or I wouldn't have said.'

'I spoke to another friend. Apparently, babies cry, a lot! All day and all night and for no reason. That's okay if it's your child, but you'll have a job to do in the morning.'

'No worries. We'll cope. It'll be fine, fun, even.'

Bhavini reached over the table and took both of Ashley's hands.

'You're a good mate.'

'Only good?'

'You might throw me out after a week, so we'll see. Talking of throwing out, I'm going to tell my mum I've found a place to stay, and I'm keeping the baby.'

'I take it she'll inform your dad.'

'Yes, but I want Mum involved, even if it's only for a sneaky coffee meet-up, so this gives her plenty of time to get her head around it. Or maybe she can strangle him in his sleep before it arrives.'

Ashley laughed.

'I shouldn't say stuff like that,' said Bhavini. 'He's a loving father and husband. Hardworking and fair, it's just his values are traditional.'

'I suspect fathers of any culture aren't overjoyed when their daughter gets knocked up by a married playboy.'

'Ash!'

'You need to tell HR tomorrow. It's not worth the risk.'

'I'd hate to spend the next five months behind a desk.'

Ashley shrugged, then gave Bhavini a quick update until Hector reappeared.

'Everything all right?' he asked.

'Ashley's confirmed she's happy for me to live at hers.'

Hector looked at Ashley for a few moments, then gave her a little nod.

'I have a theory about our killer,' he said. 'I think we should try the jealousy angle. The groundsman is perfect. You've hinted he's a bit strange, and he'd be on the site all the time. Perhaps he's been quietly going about his business and seeing these women throwing themselves at Dennis.'

'Why am I getting a vision of Quasimodo?'

Bhavini picked up the idea, so they'd clearly been discussing it during the journey.

'He fell in love with Jasmine or Katrina. From what Hector said, Jasmine was quite a soft-hearted person, so perhaps she was kind to the groundsman. Then when she so publicly slept with Dennis, she was not worthy of his affection and had to go.'

'So, in your theory, Lionel is running around killing all the fallen women who chose Dennis over him.'

'That's right.'

'It's not a terrible theory. If he was smart and left no trace, Dennis might even be blamed.'

'Exactly,' the pair said at the same time.

'Although he's taken quite a risk. If Dennis has an alibi, or we can't find a motive, or any evidence he did do it, which is where we are now, we'd start casting our beady eyes elsewhere. It wouldn't be long until we headed to the troubled groundsman's dark and mysterious dwelling secreted at the edge of the park.'

'Maybe he's not too bright,' said Bhavini.

'Let's hope that's it, and he hasn't planned a grand finale.'

50

Hector, Bhavini and Ashley left the caravan and headed towards Bronze. Hector rang Control to relay their movements as they walked.

Bronze was full of life. There were mothers and prams, toddlers tottering around, a lady chasing a dog that had slipped its lead, and two men laughed over a barbecue. Only a younger woman, sitting on her step and smoking a cigarette, stared at them. Did these holidaymakers not know about the deaths, or was being a few hundred metres away far enough not to care?

If Ashley hadn't known there was a lane up to Lionel's, she'd have missed it. The trees and shrubs at the side at the entrance were trimmed but had been allowed to grow, so it seemed hidden. They headed down the track. Once they'd rounded a bend, it was as if someone had transported them to the middle of the countryside. The path stretched about a hundred metres ahead of them, then twisted to the right.

The only sound was their footsteps on the gravel. Two seagulls screeched by overhead and there was an ominous rustle in the bushes next to them. Ashley grinned as she felt adrenalin enter her veins.

'I'm glad it's not dark.' Bhavini laughed.

'Why does it feel like we're walking towards Grandma's place, and she's already inside the wolf?' asked Hector.

Ashley was half expecting some kind of *The Hills Have Eyes* type dwelling, listing dangerously to the side as black smoke poured out of a wonky chimney, perhaps with a row of scalps on the washing line, but Lionel's place, when it came into sight, was clean and modern and the surrounding area tidy. It was a bit of a let-down.

Yet the sun felt different here. It beat down with an intensity that had them all perspiring. There was a sense of being watched. A familiar black and white cat crept out from under the caravan and purred against Ashley's leg.

She rapped on the door. There was no answer, so she edged to the side where there was a window without blinds or a curtain. Steam or condensation concealed whatever was inside, perhaps from a kettle, making it seem murky. Ashley leaned closer and peered through the glass. A pair of black eyes stared back.

A few seconds later, the door eased open, and a man appeared in green army-type fatigues. The T-shirt was tight and showed off a toned figure, even though the hair above the sunglasses was grey and thinning. Apart from two deep laughter lines, he didn't resemble Dafoe, but she supposed with street lighting he might have done.

'Sorry, you scared me. I thought it was that bloody kid again.'

'Willy?' asked Ashley.

'Yes. He's pretty harmless, but he'll wander around your caravan given half the chance. I can't shut him up asking me questions, neither.'

'You're Lionel,' said Hector.

'That's correct.' Lionel swelled with confirmation and straightened his shoulders. 'Head groundsman.'

'Are there other groundsmen?' asked Bhavini.

'No, but I don't tell anyone that.'

Ashley imagined Lionel's mother sitting in his caravan in her favourite chair in front of the TV right this moment, having died of old age ten years ago.

Lionel smirked at them in a way Ashley struggled to interpret. His eyes bored into hers.

'Do you have a problem for me to sort?'

'No, we're detectives.' Ashley showed her card, as did the others. 'We sort the problems.'

'Lionel Bates. Only groundsman. I've got nothing to tell you.'

'We have some questions about how the park runs and your role within it,' said Hector. 'Would it be okay to talk inside and take notes?'

'Nope.'

Lionel stepped back inside and closed the door behind him. Ashley rubbed her temples. After a minute of knocking and shouting and feeling as though she could remove the door with her teeth, he opened up again.

'Do I have to talk to you?'

'Most people want to help the police.'

Lionel stepped back, allowing them and the cat inside.

'Tea? I just boiled the kettle, although I only got green tea.'

Bhavini and Ashley declined. Hector looked as if he was going to accept until he caught Ashley's expression.

'No, thanks. Take a seat please.'

Bhavini guided him out of the compact but tidy kitchen area. The lounge, where they were sitting, was also neat except for cat hairs on the armchair. Ashley smiled when Hector didn't notice and sat on them.

'Comfy?' she asked him.

Hector's eyes narrowed.

'That's the cat's seat,' said Lionel, sitting opposite him. 'Even I don't sit there.'

Hector slowly rose, twisting in horror to see his hairy suit trousers.

'That moggy looks the same as the one I saw over near Pip's house,' said Ashley.

'It is the same one,' said Lionel, remaining standing without a cup but still with his shades on. 'She stole him from me.'

'How did that make you feel?' asked Bhavini, who had her pocketbook out.

'Oh, that's okay. I treat the cat like a prince, so if he'd rather stay at Pip's, she must be providing caviar.' Lionel chuckled.

Hector was puzzled as he tried to pick up on Lionel's thick Norfolk accent.

'Can you confirm your date of birth, please?' asked Hector.

'It's 1 November. I'm sixty.'

'Are you aware of what's been going on the last few days?'

'Like what?'

'The strange things. You must have heard.'

'Jasmine was found in her hot tub.'

'Yes. Did you know her?'

'Yeah. Percy asked me to help her put the hot tub together, but it didn't need much more than standing up. I think she was lonely, but there are a few here like that.'

'Did you know Katrina?'

'The suicide? Yes. The same, I guess. Bit more maybe. She had a tree above her van that seemed to grow daily, so I'd cut it down regular. She drank green tea, too.'

'Do you enjoy your job?'

'I love it. The modern world makes me uncomfortable, but I

can keep to myself here. I don't need much money, so that's okay, and I don't have to leave the site. I do go for fish and chips twice a week, Tuesdays and Fridays.'

'What time on Fridays?' asked Bhavini.

'Near closing. Sometimes Tony gives me the fish he was keeping for himself.'

'Anything different last Friday?' asked Ashley.

'My fish was pretty small for a change. Also, once a week, I go to Tesco, on Sundays just before they shut. It's empty then, because I don't like busy, and you can find sandwiches ever so cheap. Even the prawn ones. The cat loves the prawns. I swear that's why he reappears on a Sunday.'

'Do you live with a partner?' asked Hector, who leaned forward with concentration as he listened.

'No, it's only me here. Always has been.'

Lionel turned his head towards Hector and removed his glasses. 'I keep my distance. It suits me living alone.' He placed his shades back on.

'Isn't the park busy?'

'In what way?'

'You don't like Tesco when it's crowded, but it must be chaos on here during the summer holidays.'

'Yeah, that's right, but I work the hours I want. Mr Percy pays me for the job, and I can do it whenever suits me, so I often nip around first thing, or the evening up to dusk. That's how I cope when it's manic.'

'You must notice interesting things.'

'Yes, mostly because people don't see me. I'm just the man in the green clothes. It's like I don't exist. People have massive arguments as I walk past. You know, holiday rage, and they don't even stop shouting at each other. I'm invisible. It's a brilliant job.'

'Does your position pay well?' asked Ashley.

'I suppose it's okay. He gives me two hundred pounds cash every Friday morning. Lovely it is, but soon goes.'

'What do you spend it on?'

'Fish and chips and arcades, mostly. I love the arcades.'

'You gamble?'

Lionel smiled widely. 'No, not the penny pushers. Games! I call them Space Invaders still, but they're so good nowadays. Thrilling, you know?'

'You go into town to the amusements, as well as Tesco and the chippy. Anywhere else?'

Lionel's face fell. Ashley's skin prickled.

'What is this? You're beginning to annoy me.'

'Just checking who you might see on your travels. The arcades must be busy.'

Lionel's face remained tense.

'I go when they open, so it's quiet. Percy won't pay for the best ones here. A lot of my money goes on them.'

Lionel looked up at the ceiling as though there were something to read up there.

Ashley caught Bhavini's eye and gave her a slight nod.

'I just need to use the phone, Lionel. Is there a good signal here?'

'Oh, no. You'll have to walk back down the path.'

'Okay, I won't be long. Ten minutes, hopefully much less.'

Lionel cocked his head to one side, but his eyes crinkled.

'I bet she wants the toilet. I don't like going in other people's vans either.'

'Someone saw you walking around at night with an axe,' said Hector.

Ashley's heart began to pump faster. That wasn't what she'd have asked at this point, but they did need to keep him talking. Bhavini would be down the path for a background check and to call for backup if necessary, having had the same alarm bells ringing.

Lionel smiled at him but didn't reply.

'Is that true?' asked Hector.

'Could've been. When?'

'Friday night, I think.'

'Yes, maybe. I'm often out during the evening. I've got one of those hats with the built-in light. Fabulous they are.'

'So how long have you worked here for?' asked Ashley.

Lionel linked his arms behind his head while he thought. They were tanned and full of muscle.

'Forty years.'

'Wow, so long. You must have seen lots of changes in that time.'

Lionel considered that. 'Not so many, you know? I think that's part of the attraction of the place. I wish my wages changed faster.'

'Your money's still the same?'

'No, it was a hundred per week at the start, but things are expensive now. Mr Percy employed my father back then, and I only helped. They paid me cash. Then my dad got ill. I took over, but they carried on paying me the same way. You know how these things tend to drift. Mr Percy did give me this lovely caravan. The old one was falling down. This one's nearly new.'

'Do you have any favourites on the site?' asked Hector.

'Vans?'

'People.'

'Oh, erm, there's a few. I talk to most of the older people who are on their own.'

'Are they lonely?'

'Some of the younger folk seem to be the loneliest. The older single ones are usually women who enjoy bingo in the clubhouse and go to the owners' barbecue. They like the fact they can then head home without their husbands having made a mess. That's what they tell me.'

'Are most of those you speak to female?'

'All of them, really.'

'Any favourites of those?'

Lionel took his glasses off again, but his eyes weren't smiling. They were ice blue. Lionel swallowed.

'Erm, I enjoyed the company of those two you mentioned earlier. Jasmine and Katrina. I'll miss them, and Pip is fun.'

'Have you seen Pip lately?'

'No, she can't be here because otherwise the cat would be with her.'

'Do you have any family?'

'No, none left.'

Ashley heard the sound of a heavy vehicle trundling up the gravel path.

'I like Deniz, too, but he's a naughty man, and the kids are mischievous. I shout at them, but they just laugh at me.'

'Why is Deniz naughty?'

'He has lots of different girlfriends.' Lionel's grin was back. 'Often at the same time.' His smile faded. 'He needs watching.'

Bhavini knocked on the door and walked in. She left it wide open.

'Everything okay?' she asked.

'We're calm here,' said Ashley.

'I'm going to invite these people in, Lionel,' said Bhavini. 'They're my colleagues.'

Lionel put his sunglasses on and rose from his seat.

'Lionel,' said Bhavini. 'Have you ever been in trouble with the police before?'

51

Lionel, who was nimble for an older man, leapt back as if buzzed with a cattle prod. His mouth twisted into a howl of pain, but no sound came out. Then he roared a reply.

'I only talked to them, so I'm staying. You can't make me leave!'

Two female constables were soon in the caravan. Lionel waved a fist in one of their faces, then backed up against a wall and slid down it. He sat with his hands over his eyes, which was handy for the cuffing officer.

Ashley knelt down and cautioned him in a stern but quiet voice. She gestured for Hector to come over and help.

'Let's get you up,' she said to Lionel, while thinking of the traffic jams back to Norwich. 'The handcuffs are just a precaution, so nobody gets hurt. We'll take you to the station in King's Lynn to clarify everything.'

Lionel struggled to his feet, resisted for a moment, then went limp. Ashley and Hector guided him to the police van, which was parked outside. A male officer placed Lionel in the rear seat, then sat next to him. The door slid shut.

'Process him and be careful on the way,' said Ashley to the two women. 'I suspect he's stronger than he looks.'

'Is he the double murderer?'

Ashley glanced around the tidy camp. She saw a small axe buried in a sawn-off tree trunk, wandered over, and crouched beside it. The blade glinted in the sunlight, but the edge was reddish-brown. There was a toolbox on the decking. Inside was a set of spanners, which had red handles similar to the hammer they'd found in the reeds.

'He could well be. What was his previous?'

The officer looked over at Bhavini.

'Sexual assault, wasn't it, Bee?'

'Yes. It was a long time ago, though.'

'How long?'

'Over forty years.'

Ashley nodded. Murderers often started off with sexual crimes, which escalated, although it was rare for someone not to have re-offended for so long. But who knew what Lionel had been up to out here, skulking around the park at night?

The cat left Lionel's caravan and sat next to the door, cleaning his paws. What had Lionel said? Pip must have gone away. Ashley's stomach rolled.

'Are further units arriving?' she asked Bhavini.

'One's coming here. There's another at the site entrance.'

Ashley instructed the police van to leave and take Lionel to King's Lynn. She'd follow, but first she wanted to check on Pip and Dennis.

A police estate raced up the lane, spitting pebbles out of the way. A young pair leaped out.

'Relax, gents,' said Bhavini. 'The drama's over. You just need to protect the scene.'

Bhavini explained what she wanted to the two new arrivals. Despite their youth, they were on the ball.

'Come on,' said Ashley to Bhavini and Hector. 'Let's walk to Diamond. We can ring this in to Control and Kettle on the way.' Ashley scanned the area. 'Gerald's never going to have been so busy.'

Ashley stopped off at Reception en route and spoke to Gail.

'Is the handyman, Tim, about?'

'He's on Gold doing a leaky roof. Number thirty-two. It's at the far edge of the site. What do you want him for?'

'I might need entrance to a caravan.'

'Whose van?'

'Four Diamond. Patricia Dilley.'

'I can help. We keep a key for all of them in case of gas or water leaks. Hamilton, would you go with—?'

Gail stopped talking and frowned. Hamilton had his head bent down and was giggling to himself.

'It'll be quicker if I come myself rather than explain it to that bell-end,' she said.

It was the first crack in Gail's professional veneer. She went into Percy's office and returned a minute later with a key.

'We'll walk, so I can get some fresh air. He's been winding me up all morning,' she said loudly to no effect. 'I'll be twenty minutes, Hamilton.'

She received a small wave.

When they were outside, Ashley couldn't help probing.

'Why does Percy put up with Hamilton's indifference?'

'Percy doesn't pay him. It's work experience, apparently, as a favour to Percy's ex. Percy's been trying to sneak back in her good books, but she's awful and just using him.'

'Is Percy a good boss?'

Gail slowed down as she thought, then speeded up.

'Yes, in a way. He can be hilarious, but it was a nightmare when I first started because he's so disorganised. The team is efficient now. All the women who work Reception with me are slick. They live on site and do it for pin money, but they had high-powered careers, so it's easy for them. I make sure they get paid properly through the books.'

'Unlike Lionel.'

Gail gave her a brief glance.

'Yes, I told Percy he needed to pay Lionel officially because it was illegal, but he was surprisingly resistant. In the end, he said not to mention it again, and it benefited Lionel.'

'But you didn't know why it was to his benefit he was being underpaid and, in effect, being exploited?'

'Nope. Lionel's great. There are a lot of spinning plates here. That includes him and Tim, but we never have problems with either of them. So, I stopped hassling Percy about Lionel and took the easy option. Sorry. Has it caused a problem?'

'Maybe. We'll get it sorted. You aren't in any trouble, but Percy might be.'

Gail knew the site like the back of her hand. Instead of following the path, she weaved her way through the myriad caravans and lodges, while smiling and greeting people by name. Ashley chuckled at a mum laughing at her giggling daughter slapping the water then shrieking in a small paddling pool.

'I can't wait to have kids,' said Gail.

Bhavini, Hector and Ashley kept quiet.

When they reached Diamond, it was as if they'd come to a different planet. The weather was the same, the sky was clear, but again it was so quiet. Even Gail looked around with surprise. Ashley walked up to Pip's gate, putting gloves on before she opened it. All the curtains were still closed. She knocked hard three times.

'Pip!'

There was no letter box to shout through, so Ashley wandered down the lodge, knocking on the panels. She noticed a glass had rolled to the edge of the decking behind the upended deckchair. Ashley thought back to Lionel's comments and decided there was enough risk for her to ask Gail for the key.

As Gail passed it over, Dennis came out of his lodge and stared over with a quizzical expression.

'Have you seen Pip?' Ashley shouted.

'No, but she can't have gone far if her car's still here.'

Ashley gave the key back to Gail after unlocking the door. She pressed the handle and it opened. There was nothing untoward in the hall, but the bedroom and bathroom doors were shut. Then she noticed dark-red speckles on the carpet. Ashley tiptoed to the ajar lounge door and nudged it wider. Pip was lying on the sofa.

Ashley cursed. The pool of blood beside Pip gave little cause for hope.

52

Ashley took a few seconds while her experience kicked in. She crouched next to Pip's swollen face, but she was clearly long dead. Ashley poked a bare arm. Rigor mortis had set in to the cold flesh. What had Michelle said? More than eight hours and less than thirty-six. Ashley thought back to the fun woman she'd spoken to, who'd been so alive less than twenty-four hours ago.

She rang Control and informed them, double-checking they'd notify the team escorting Lionel. Ashley had a brief image of the van being found later with the officers' throats slit, but handcuffs were an incredible handicap, despite what the movies suggested.

The scene was controlled and there didn't seem to be anyone else in immediate danger, especially with Lionel soon to be in a cell. Ashley hovered near Pip, whose clothing was drenched in blood. There was no other word to use for the instrument of death than a garrotte. Whoever had done it was strong enough to have broken the skin. The wire had been left in place, stuck in the flesh, with the handles dangling to one side.

Ashley rang the mortuary at Norwich and Norfolk hospital. A

technician answered and said Michelle was beside her. She put Michelle on.

Ashley gave her the news about arresting Lionel and described the scene at Pip's. There was a low whistle down the line.

'Wow. I've not done one of them before. Are you sure it's a proper garrotte, not just a piece of wire?'

'It appears to be professional kit.'

'I'm coming. Where are you? And please don't say Hunstanton?'

'Hunstanton, and a lorry shed its load earlier.'

'Okay, ask CSI to send me as many photos as soon as they can. I'll see the body when it's brought in. Describe the area for me. Is there evidence of a fight?'

'There's a chair knocked over outside. Blood splatters through the entrance. Then the victim was placed on the sofa. The wire has cut deep into the flesh.'

'Is it a wire with two wooden grips?'

'Yes, like a cheese or pottery cutter, although the handles are better made.'

'Okay, I'll have a look as soon as the photos come through. I knew someone in London who had a lot of experience with this sort of thing. Do you have a suspect in custody?'

Michelle would submit a swifter report if the clock was ticking on holding time.

'Yes.'

'I'll do some prep before the poor woman arrives. It would have been a horrific death, but mercifully fast. Let's hope you already have the killer behind bars because the thought of a person capable of a crime like that being on the loose is absolutely horrifying.'

53

Ashley slowly analysed the deceased from all angles, then the carpet and lodge. She glanced at the decking as she left, but there was no blood visible. Perhaps the attack started outside, and Pip was dragged inside to be finished off. Shouting for help wouldn't have been possible.

She rang Kettle, but Control had already informed him. Ashley could hear the approaching sirens as she completed the update.

'Okay, this Lionel character is concerning,' said Kettle. 'Do you reckon it's him?'

'For Pip and Jasmine, maybe. Not for Katrina, and not for Alfie. It makes no sense to me. We're back to that missing link between these deaths.'

As she was talking, Ashley could see Hector helping Dennis up off his decking steps and inside. Dennis was a decent actor if he was involved.

Kettle quietly swore.

'One of the other teams had a full read of Katrina's file and found correspondence from an old friend of hers who was in touch with the coroner by mail from Hawaii,' he said. 'She said Katrina's letters had been maudlin of late, and she'd become concerned.'

'So Katrina's death was likely suicide, but Pip and Alfie are even less connected than Jasmine and Alfie.'

'What do you think about shutting the site down until we know what we're dealing with?'

'It's not as easy as that. People live here nearly all year round. I suspect quite a few will have nowhere else to go.'

'How large is Paradise?'

'Pretty big. Two hundred dwellings. There's a clubhouse, a few parks and a washing and shower centre.'

'Access?'

'Just one road in, but a hole-ridden mesh barrier or a head-height fence separates the surrounding area, so the place is porous to anyone on foot.'

'Which means if this Lionel Bates character isn't the culprit, the person responsible might be long gone, or living quietly in Hunstanton.'

'I would have thought so.'

'What do you suggest?'

'Flood the area with uniforms tonight. Continue with a check-point on the main gate until it's over. The flow in and out is pretty light during the week, with it being out of high season, so there won't be a bottleneck. I'll ask DS Kotecha to remain here and manage the scene with CSI while I attend King's Lynn to grill Lionel. She can share any discoveries as they're made.'

'Right. Starting tomorrow, we explain to everyone on the site and anyone arriving that there's been a murder on Diamond. If they want to stay, that's up to them. We've spoken to some owners and guests with the list Percy provided when we discovered Jasmine's death, but many people don't answer calls nowadays if they don't recognise the number, so it was a time-consuming process, and we got little out of it.'

'Let's hope Lionel folds during his interview. I'll take Hector with me.'

'I heard about the traffic situation. You can always bring Lionel to OCC later.'

'Yes, but I'd rather we kept as much resource here as possible. It'll take custody a while to put Lionel through close analysis, and he'll need to have the opportunity to speak to the duty solicitor. I want to contact his boss, Percy, first. We'll prepare for the interview in the car.'

'Okay. Lionel stays in overnight. The park goes into lockdown. No social club, no tennis or charades. Folk stay in their vans. We'll patrol tonight and make a further judgement in the morning. If we don't like it, let's discuss more site restrictions.'

'At least that will grab Percy's attention. I suspect he'll be hard to reach otherwise.'

'Anything else I can help you with now? Do you need more people?'

'No, let's see what Lionel has to say. If it's not him, we'll do a full background analysis on Pip, starting with her husband, although I think it's a remote possibility he's responsible.'

'Why is that?'

'They're estranged as of a night ago, but he appeared in poor health.'

'Shall we pick him up now?'

'No, he lives in King's Lynn, so I'll be nearby if necessary, but we didn't bond when I met him, so arrange for the death message to be delivered by King's Lynn officers. He isn't the type to run, and if he did it, I don't believe anyone else is in danger.'

'But he isn't likely to be responsible for Katrina or Jasmine?'

'Not at all, nor Alfie. If Rupert killed Pip, then it's possible we have two or more killers, and Hunstanton will be swiftly on its way to being the murder capital of the UK.'

54

Ashley and Hector returned to his car and began the drive to King's Lynn.

'This muddies things,' said Hector.

'Yes. Linking Lionel to Alfie Hook isn't easy, and I suppose Jasmine's death isn't clear-cut, but there's nothing remotely accidental about Pip's murder.'

'Let's forget Alfie for the moment and strip the rest down. What have we got?'

'Three dead women. Perhaps it's a misogynistic killer.'

'Yes. A person who kills women. Lonely women.'

'That's a scary thought. Dennis confessed he bought the drugs for Jasmine. Maybe that wasn't true, and he was trying to cover for her. Perhaps Alfie was dealing to Jasmine direct. Alfie arrived and saw Jasmine with the person who drowned her. Whoever the murderer was took Alfie out so he wouldn't talk.'

'We could cross-check Alfie's movements from the delivery company against—'

Ashley let out a deep breath.

'What is it?' asked Hector.

'I was going to say the site booking records, but many are here all year except for the closed month.'

'It's another angle. If the killer is someone from the site, then it's more likely they're permanent because they've so far kept under the radar. Unless it's someone who visits a lot. I'm confident we'll crack it now there's been a third death.'

'Agreed, which makes it damage limitation until we do.' Ashley rubbed her eyes for a moment. 'Shit. Dennis told me he spotted Pip running on the promenade this morning when she was already dead.'

'You're now thinking it was a sneaky deflecting tactic.'

'Actually, he said he thought he saw her. I suppose runners from afar look similar, but I'll have Bhavini interview him again. He'd need to be pretty loopy to kill three women in spitting distance of his own lodge when he's been romantically involved with all of them.'

'We should get hold of Glory as well.'

'God, yes. If we're dealing with a woman-killer, she might be next. The papers will call it The Diamond Killings, where deaths are forever.'

Hector groaned.

'I bet you've had that prepared for days.'

She smiled. 'Gail told me that Percy wants to credit-check people, so he knows which part of the site to put them in.'

Hector shook his head with disgust.

'I can believe it. Okay, we'll ring Hans and Helga, Glory, and Verne and Bertie, none of whom I assume will be rushing to return in the short term.'

They didn't hit traffic until five miles from the Hardwick roundabout, then it was nose to tail, which was usual approaching rush hour. Ashley called Percy but he didn't answer. She imagined the little weasel sweating as he stared at the caller ID, so she texted him to say they were considering closing the site and needed his help. Glory and Bertie's numbers both went to voicemail. She left a message for them to ring her.

Helga picked up her phone and assured Ashley they wouldn't be returning to Hunstanton until it was safe. They had booked a week on a bus tour around the Lake District instead.

Ashley emailed details for Patricia Dilley and her husband, Rupert, to Scott Gorton, the FLO. Uniform would attend to break the news to Rupert tonight. Hopefully, Scott would be free to visit him in the morning, by which time Pip's body would be ready for him to confirm identification. Lionel would have been spoken to, so Scott would know how to frame the conversation with Rupert. She thought it improbable Rupert had been to Hunstanton, but she supposed it was possible he'd got someone else to do it for him. Maybe that brother.

Ashley was pondering the unlikelihood of that when her phone rang.

'Percy. Good of you to call me back.'

'What's this rubbish about shutting the site down? You can't do that. People live there. Would you empty a half-mile residential street if there was a murder at one end of it?'

Ashley decided to ignore his questions. 'We seem to have a problem with Lionel.'

The slight pause told Ashley all she needed to know.

'Yes, what's that?'

'He's at King's Lynn police station to help with our inquiries.'

'Right.'

'What do you think of that?'

'He's been an exemplary employee. Hardly any problems at all.'

'What do you mean by hardly?'

'A few things over the years. Nothing serious. He's over-friendly at times, so he occasionally freaks people out.'

'What does over-friendly mean?'

'You know, hanging about their vans a bit too much, saying hello too often. No touching or anything. I just nip it in the bud.'

'Where are you?'

'I've not long left Norwich on the way back to Hunstanton. Traffic's terrible.'

'I want you at Paradise's reception tomorrow at midday. We need a full statement around this. You might be in a lot of trouble.'

'It's about the thing before, isn't it?'

'You tell me.'

'His sexual assault where he went to prison.'

'You've also been paying him a derisory amount off the books for decades.'

'Our insurance wouldn't have liked knowing he was on the site with a recent conviction like that, so we kept it quiet. It kind of rolled on over the years.'

'Midday, Percy.'

'Okay, I'll be there.'

As Ashley cut the call, another came through, this time from OCC.

'Hey, Ash, it's Emma.'

'Hi, what have you got?'

'The details on Lionel Bates' offence. It's not as damning as we first thought.'

55

Ashley groaned.

'Hit me with it.'

'The case is ancient. The sexual assault of a child over the age of thirteen by touching. Lionel was eighteen, the girl fifteen. They gave him twenty-six weeks' custody, which seems harsh. The file record's been scanned, but it's not complete. It looks like alcohol was an aggravating factor, but I doubt we'd give him a custodial nowadays.'

'And nothing since?'

'Nope. Not even a speeding ticket.'

'Well, I've spoken to Lionel's boss, and something's not right. We'll be talking to Lionel within the hour, so I'll keep you posted. I'll be in the office first thing tomorrow. Those DNA tests should be back then, although we're going to be waiting on a load more. I assume you've all been chatting about the case. Any hunches?'

'No, which is rare.'

Ashley clicked her tongue as she finished the call. Exceedingly rare. They pulled into King's Lynn police station, and an hour later Lionel was sitting in front of them in a snug tracksuit with the duty solicitor next to him. After the tape was rolling, Ashley smiled at Lionel, who didn't smile back.

'Do you know why we brought you in?' she asked.

'You think I'm responsible for the deaths of those nice people.'

'They are all women you're familiar with.'

'Yes.'

'Women you talk to regularly.'

'Yes.'

'Those you visit at their homes in the park.'

Lionel closed his eyes for a few moments. Then he stared at the table.

'It's more that I meet them as I go about my business.'

'You have favourites.'

'I like some more than others.'

'Let's start on Friday night. You went for food at eight thirty. Was there a queue?'

'Two couples before me, but they were served quick. A spotty kid arrived as I was leaving. Tony gave me extra chips because he said I needed feeding up. It's a joke because I'm bigger than him.'

'Did you see this man in there?'

Hector passed over a photograph.

'Lionel Bates has been shown a picture of Alfie Hook.'

Lionel peered at it. 'No. I do recognise him, though.'

'Who is he?' asked Hector.

'The PSST! delivery guy.'

'Have you spoken to him?'

'I've seen him around the park a few times. Red or a blue van. He's only supposed to deliver to Reception, but he goes on the site.'

'Did you tell him off?'

'No, that's Percy's job. I shouted at him to slow down, which he did.'

'Where did you see him?'

'A couple of places.'

'At Diamond?'

'Yes, and driving about. Once he was making Jasmine laugh at her lodge.'

Ashley paused.

'Do you often find yourself at Jasmine's lodge?'

The solicitor cut in.

'He doesn't need to reply to that.'

'Okay,' said Ashley. 'Lionel. Did you spot him that night before you went for chips?'

'No.'

'How about in the car park behind it?'

'I don't use the car park.'

'Have you ever had an argument with him?'

'I don't recall so, but it's annoying when people don't follow the rules.'

'When did you last see Jasmine Green?'

Again, Lionel closed his eyes for a few seconds before answering.

'It's hard to say. Each day blends into another. If it wasn't for the fish and chip and arcade routine, I'm not sure I'd know what day it was.'

'About a week?'

'Maybe.'

'Did you speak to her?'

'No,' he replied firmly.

'Why not?'

'My client won't be answering that at this point,' interjected the solicitor.

'Fair enough. Are you okay to continue, Lionel?' asked Ashley.

Lionel smiled at her. 'Yes.'

'Did you used to chat with Katrina much?' she asked.

'The one who killed herself?'

'Yes.'

'Yes, but she was a little scary.'

Ashley widened her eyes. 'Scary in what way?'

'Powerful, I guess. Judgemental.'

'What about Pip in Diamond? Was she nice?'

'Yes, she was friendly. Sometimes really chatty, although she often couldn't remember our conversations when we spoke again, which was odd.'

'How about Glory next door?'

'No, also frightening. Occasionally she'd tell me to fuck off.'

'Why?'

Lionel scowled for a moment. 'I don't know.'

'Have you ever been in Katrina, Pip or Jasmine's lodges?'

Lionel looked at the ceiling. 'No, never. It was my dad's rule.' He glanced back at Ashley and waved a finger at her. 'You don't go on the decking.'

'How do you feel about violence, Lionel?' asked Hector.

'I hate it.'

'Lionel, you seem worried. We're just trying to find out what's happened, or is there something you need to explain?'

'I was in trouble before and I hated it.'

'Tell me about your spell in prison,' said Ashley.

Lionel shook his head. 'I didn't like that at all, but it was a long time ago.'

'Sexual assault is a serious offence, especially against a child. Why did you do it?'

Lionel met Ashley's stare.

'It was an accident.'

56

The solicitor asked for a quick break, which was fine with Ashley and Hector.

'What are you thinking?' asked Hector.

'That we should play Lionel at three-card brag,' replied Ashley.

'Yes, he's no wily nemesis. The solicitor seems bored. He clearly believes Lionel isn't involved.'

'Maybe *he's* the wily nemesis.'

'Touché.'

'If that axe is bloody, he's got some explaining to do.'

'Especially seeing as we haven't found anyone with an axe injury.' Ashley pulled a face.

'Right, let's ask him for the details on the sexual assault and why he seemed so guilty when we spoke to him. We've got more than enough to keep him while we wait for CSI to check the axe and see if he was inside any of those holiday homes. If he was, then we know his unusual presentation is probably him lying, and this "keeping off the decking" story is bollocks.'

'Yes, which blows the rest of his defence apart because we have a motive of sorts, some history, and the park is his home.' Hector curled his lip.

'What?'

'It's all rather flabby. We need to find some blood on his clothes. That garrotting would have been messy. What was he wearing if he did it? Did he hide those clothes?'

'Perhaps we can pick Lionel up on CCTV in town, proving that he's lying about where he goes. He's displayed no anger yet, so let's prod him a little. Whoever choked Pip to death damn near cut her head off. That makes me think of rage and strength. We know he has the latter.'

'Fair enough.'

'I understand where you're coming from, though. He's an unusual guy, so let's take things easy.'

Ashley reconvened the interview fifteen minutes later.

'Okay, Lionel. You were walking around the park with an axe later on the night you had chips at eight thirty. Why?'

'It was windy. A tree had blown onto the road, so I took the small axe to chop the little branches off, then I carried the bigger branch to the woodchipper.'

'That's a reasonable explanation.'

'It's the truth.'

'Why were you so upset when we arrested you?'

'I love this job. I don't know what I'd do if I lost it. My life would be over.'

'Have you been bothering the women on the site?' asked Hector.

'That's what Mr Percy sometimes says, but I only chat to them if they talk to me. As soon as he says don't speak to her again, that's it. I stop.'

'Can you understand our concern with your previous offence?' asked Ashley.

The solicitor leaned forward. 'I'll answer that to save time.'

'Okay.'

'My client is not a man of guile. He has nothing to do with these ghastly offences because he would never jeopardise his job. You can see how he could be accused of being over-friendly. Lionel was just eighteen when that got him into trouble, and he has been incredibly cautious around women ever since. He respects their personal space and never enters it unless permission is crystal clear. He touched a fifteen-year-old girl's breasts under her jumper. A group of them were drunk in the park, and they were having some fun with him. Lionel thought she wanted him to be her boyfriend. The police were called. Her father was a judge, so she blamed it all on Lionel, who told the truth. Yes, he'd been drinking, yes, he knew she was fifteen because she went to the same school, and yes, he touched her breasts without permission, and yes, he grabbed her hand. No one cared that she was hugging and teasing him and saying he was sweet.'

Ashley had investigated similar cases herself. Few reached court. Some of those charged received conditional discharges, others jail time.

'There's been nothing in over forty years since,' said the solicitor. 'I assume you'll be checking his background. My client is more than happy to provide a DNA sample to exclude him from these offences.'

'Not leaving DNA doesn't mean he wasn't there.'

'Of course not, but it doesn't confirm your suspicions, either. You need much more to charge him, and you simply don't have it. Lionel assures me he isn't responsible, and that you won't find anything.'

'It's going to take us a while to process his caravan and surrounding area. Where will he go if we release him?'

'His girlfriend's place.'

Ashley coughed to disguise her surprise.

'Lionel. You said you don't have a partner.'

'I don't. She's my girlfriend.'

'Where does she live?'

'At Paradise, but she has her own caravan. Mrs Lil Doherty.'

'Wait. Isn't that the older lady from Bronze who keeps complaining about young Willy?'

'Yes, that boy drives her scranny, too,' said Lionel.

'How long have you been dating her?' asked Hector.

'Two years. We were friends for ages beforehand. I think she was lonely when her husband died, and she found it comforting to have me around.'

Ashley could feel the energy draining from her.

'You seem a placid man, Lionel. What upsets you?'

'People steal things on the site, like my tools.'

'Which tools went missing?'

'Quite a few.'

'Was it a saw, or a hammer, maybe some spanners?'

'Yes, I lost my best hammer. It was annoying because it was part of a set.'

'Can you describe it?'

'It had a red handle.'

'I bet you'd like to have words with whoever stole it,' said Hector.

Lionel glanced up and nodded.

Ashley searched her memories of the last few days. Who would upset Lionel? She recalled his comment about Dennis needing watching.

'Is Dennis also a friend on Diamond?'

'Yes, but you need to keep an eye on him.'

The way Lionel growled his reply, even made his solicitor glance at him.

'Why?' asked Ashley.

Lionel's eyes bored into hers. A vein throbbed at his temple.

'He's in all the women's caravans. I told him if I saw him in Lil's caravan, I would be upset.'

Ashley concluded that nobody would like Lionel when he was upset.

57

Lionel was taken down to the cells for the night. Hector followed to arrange an assessment by the doctor. It was hard to say whether he was vulnerable or just a bit eccentric.

Ashley met Hector in the car park ten minutes later, and they set off to Hunstanton. When they arrived, they could see the rumours had spread because people with cars full of luggage passed them when they reached the site entrance. A constable held up his hand for them to stop and Ashley showed her warrant card.

'How's it going?' she asked.

'Lots of folk leaving. Seems to have sunk in with the latest death. We're taking names, addresses and telephone numbers from them on the way in and out and asking them a set of questions, but no one's given us anything so far.'

'Anyone suspicious?'

'No, it's mostly families with young kids who don't want to take any chances. A few of the oldies have walked out, but they're only going to The Honeystone pub because the clubhouse is shut.'

'Keep up the good work.'

'Will do, Sarge.'

Hector drove through to Diamond, which was a hive of activity. Judging by the wording on the side of one of the CSI vans parked up, they'd collared help from outside of the area.

The officer with the scene log recorded their entrance at the outer cordon and they found Bhavini sitting on the steps to Jasmine's lodge swigging from a bottle of water.

'Anything?' asked Ashley.

'Nope. CSI are taking their time at Pip's and will be back tomorrow and the day after if they don't get more help. I spoke to Gerald. He was glum.'

'Because?'

'He hoped to have a place similar when he retired. This is popping his dream somewhat. Michelle rang as well and wants you to return her call. She has another angle.'

Ashley smiled.

'That's what we need. Did you speak to Dennis?'

'Yes, I took a detailed statement from him. I thought you said he wasn't helpful.'

'He wasn't with me. What did he say?'

'Plenty. He admitted to dating lots of women here. It went to his head. All these pretty ladies, throwing themselves at him, but he began to feel guilty. He reckons he has an alibi for when we think Jasmine died because he was with a woman he really likes, but she lives with someone else and messes him about. He seemed genuinely shaken by Pip's death.'

'Did he provide details of his alibi?'

'No, he wants to speak to her first. There's a huge issue with her partner. Dennis said he'll be here tomorrow and should be able to give us her name then.'

'My brain's mush,' said Ashley. 'Let's go home.'

'So much for my jog around the park to see what the atmosphere was like,' said Bhavini.

Ashley shrugged, but it was a shame. The clubhouse was closed now too, so they would learn nothing there except interviews with the bar and kitchen staff.

With all the bright lights and people, it was not dissimilar to leaving a funfair. Ashley usually had a headache then, too.

Once they got back on the much emptier main roads, Ashley rang Michelle and put her on speaker.

'Hey, Ash. Long day, uh? Anything else to tell me?'

'No, but I heard you had a theory.'

'It's a loose one.'

'Give it to me.'

'When I was doing my PhD, we had a lecturer who came in to talk about the victims of trained killers.'

'Like soldiers?'

'Yeah, or specialist police, or just nutters. Basically, anyone who knows what they're doing. He explained it's pretty obvious when an experienced killer is involved, because there's a lack of emotion or drama in the deaths. There are no obvious clues. Most murders are messy, noisy affairs with the evidence dripping off people's faces. Or by the time the authorities arrive, the shifty and sweaty culprit's house smells of bleach and the washing machine is on a hot cycle.'

'With their computer's file cleaner running in the background.'

'Exactly.'

'You have none of that here, but also think of the methods of dispatch.'

Michelle remained quiet, so Ashley assumed she wanted her to repeat them.

'Alfie, knife wound direct to the heart.'

'A stiletto knife would do the job. It's a perfect kill. Three plunges in and out. Alfie died so quietly he still had a piece of fish in his mouth.'

'Jasmine drowns in the tub,' said Hector. 'Fractured skull, but also a quiet end.'

'Yes. Again, no noise, no mess. If it hadn't been for the cover being pulled over and leaving the fish on the side, a simple slip and fall would've been believable.'

'Abandoning a fish doesn't sound professional.'

'I rang the guy who taught us this afternoon. Cal's a professor now back at Harvard. He believes it's potentially brilliant but scary. A body in water could have gone undetected for a while. Jasmine lived alone, so maybe the killer left it to make sure she was discovered.'

'That level of planning or thought would be concerning.'

'He said with Jasmine high on drugs, the hammer that was found probably wouldn't have been necessary. A person held down like that who wasn't expecting it would drown fast, anyway. Knocking her silly beforehand made it easy.'

'Why leave the hammer and oven gloves there if they knew what they were doing? I know we said it might have been because of panic, but you're now saying our guy is a cool killer.'

'The professor thinks they were left deliberately. If there is DNA on either, then they could be red herrings.'

Ashley scowled at the prospect of an adversary capable of such cold plotting.

'Great. More fish. Let's see what testing brings back.'

'Which brings us to Pip,' said Bhavini.

'Yes,' said Michelle 'A garrotte. There would have been a bit of a struggle, but not much because getting out of that kind of attack is only possible in the first few seconds. You have to spin and strike the eyes, or, better yet, the groin of the assailant.'

'Why the groin?'

'With the kind of agony and instant incapacitation you get from a wire tight around your throat, you pass out quickly, but you'd lose cognitive skills even faster. Gouging the assailant's eyes might not get the attacker off quick enough if they scrunched them up. A firm slap or knee to a man's testicles would loosen his grip, perhaps enough for escape.'

'Pip was tiny,' said Ashley. 'I can picture it. She'd have had little chance with a heavier foe, who could then drag her back into the lodge, spilling blood on the carpet in the hall, before pulling the handles so tight, her head nearly came off.'

'No person has the power to decapitate in that way. There's too many muscles and ligaments in the neck, not to mention the spinal column. Even gouging the skin like in our victim wouldn't be easy with brute strength.'

'But method might. Maybe a sawing technique.'

'Yes, that's why I wanted to send the prof a close-up of the wire and handles, but I need to remove the garrotte here for that. I sent him what was emailed to me, and he thinks it's definitely been made for killing. Let's not forget Katrina. How did she die?'

'Overdose,' said Bhavini.

'In other words?' asked Michelle.

'Poison,' said Hector.

'Yes, so, based on all evidence presented, the professor is confident that if one person is responsible, a single description fits.'

Michelle didn't need to say it.

The word was assassin.

58

The next day, the meeting was pushed back to ten o'clock while they waited for test results to return. Ashley stood ready at the front to deliver an update as various teams and departments made their announcements. She'd noticed that morning the inquiry had begun to move into what her old boss in Sheffield called rolling thunder. It was how he described the detailed and progressive way the investigation picked its way through the personal lives and backgrounds of everyone implicated, and the longer the case remained unsolved, the more people got sucked in.

Ashley had been mentally and physically exhausted when she reached home the previous evening, but it was always amazing what a night of solid sleep could do, and she was raring to go.

Ashley updated the room as succinctly as she could, then brought Lionel into the equation near the end, noting many eyebrows rising as the circumstantial evidence against him mounted.

Finally, she delivered the feedback from the Harvard professor and assassin theory. There were more than a few nods.

'Now, having considered Dennis, Lionel and Percy as possible suspects, describing any of them as contract killers for hire is a leap, even for Barry.'

Chuckles rippled around for Barry, who enjoyed the attention.

'As Michelle's old lecturer said, that sort of thing is much more common in America. We're the most surveilled western country on the planet. We live in a digital country with ninety-nine per cent mobile-phone coverage. Because of that and the location, I believe this killer will already be present in our investigation or on our systems.'

Ashley was about to continue when a beautiful redhead entered at the rear. Gabriella had been on secondment to the Suffolk force for the fraud inquiry and had taken some personal time before that. Normally, she ran the admin team in Norfolk and was brilliant. Barry had nicknamed her Gingerpuss, which was probably one of the reasons she'd turned down his many offers of dates.

Gabriella reminded Ashley of a geisha with her pale complexion and open expression, but today she seemed particularly wide-eyed.

'Sorry to interrupt, but I thought you'd want this hot off the press. We've received a detailed testing report, which is on HOLMES. My team tells me most of it is confirmation of people having been where we already knew they were, except for a couple of titbits. I only got involved this morning, but I know you were waiting on two items in particular.'

The room went completely quiet.

'They found a partial print on the hammer that was discovered in the pond, which brought up approximately two hundred close matches. They worked backwards in time order, which is why it took a while, but they are ninety-nine per cent sure one of the last people to wield that tool was none other than Lionel Bates.'

There was a buzz as people commented.

'The reddish brown on the axe, though, was only rust.'

A few people moaned. Gabriella held up her hand.

'That's not the surprise.'

Ashley looked for Hector. Lionel had told them his tools got stolen. Was that him getting it in before they discovered the weapon because he knew he'd thrown it in the reeds and had since seen the divers searching in there, or was it genuine? She couldn't imagine him being so calculating. Hector was staring at Gabriella and oblivious to anyone else.

'The final piece of evidence we received back concerns the earring. Analytically speaking, there was plenty of DNA recovered, which means the margin for error is virtually zero. There was an exact match for a known criminal residing in Norfolk. It belongs to a woman already linked to the case.'

Gabriella double-checked her sheet.

'Betty Brown.'

59

To stunned silence, Kettle returned to the front and stood next to Ashley with a smile.

'It couldn't have belonged to a nicer woman,' he said. 'Although I must admit I didn't see that coming.'

'We heard evidence of what might have been her,' said Ashley to the room. 'Verne and Bertie, Dennis's neighbours, mentioned he had a new girlfriend with an amazing car. Dennis told us yesterday he had an alibi, but he'd need to check it, so let's assume for a minute it's Elizabeth Brown.'

'The married-to-a-billionaire Elizabeth Brown?' asked Ally Williamson, still shocked.

'Sal, explain at the front, please?'

Sal rose from his seat and joined her.

'We did detailed background research on Elizabeth because of her involvement with Jackie Hook from nearly a decade ago, but it does seem as though she's clean now. There are a few discrepancies. We can't find a marriage certificate, so she wasn't married in the UK, but potentially abroad. She hasn't taken his name.'

'Is she still Elizabeth Brown on all official documentation?'

'Yes. That's not to say she isn't his partner. Emma found photographs in *Hello!* magazine from not long after they first met. He didn't seem to care about her background, even mentioning rags to riches. It frankly seems ridiculous she'd get involved with petty drug offences when she's firmly attached to a millionaire. Married or not.'

'Not billionaire?' asked Kettle.

'No, but Abraham's net worth, according to *Forbes*, is two hundred million dollars.'

'Does that mean his wealth is mostly US rather than UK?'

'Yes.'

Kettle rubbed his hand over his bald head as he thought.

If it was true, Ashley reckoned the affair being made public would infuriate Abraham. But was it something he knowingly turned a blind eye to due to his age and health, or would it enrage him?

Ashley suspected the latter, especially with Dennis wanting to speak to his 'alibi' before he revealed where he'd been. Elizabeth would not have wanted him using her as proof of his innocence, but now she'd been put at the scene, her involvement was guaranteed.

'Back then, Elizabeth had a reputation for volatility,' said Ashley, playing devil's advocate. 'Remember, we're dealing with people who believe the rules don't apply to them. So could she, in a spate of jealousy, have arranged for three women to be taken out because they were after her lover, the irresistible Dennis?'

Kettle chuckled.

'Yes, that's a leap, but it was her earring in the filter.'

'I reckon Jasmine either let Dennis use the hot tub or they sneaked in when she was elsewhere, and in the throes of passion it fell off Elizabeth's ear,' said Ashley. 'For those who weren't aware, Dennis was seen making love to Jasmine in that hot tub by at least one neighbour, so he has form.'

'Maybe it was a threesome, although you'd have thought someone would have mentioned it,' said Kettle.

'I guess that's possible, but the earring is heavy. You'd know if it wasn't swinging from your ear any more,' said Ashley.

Sal nodded.

'And it's worth a lot of money. At the bottom or in the filter would be an obvious place to search.'

'Unless they were disturbed. Possibly by Alfie,' shouted Barry.

Kettle glanced at Ashley.

'Blackmail?' she said incredulously. 'So, someone with her claws in one of the country's wealthiest men has knocked off Alfie because he saw her and Dennis in the tub? It's an idea, but she knows the Hooks. She could have bought them off easily.'

'Love makes people do strange things, and secrets like that rarely stay secrets,' said Kettle. 'She has a lot to lose, so she could have paid someone to do it. It's possible Alfie or Jackie wanted revenge and wouldn't take money.'

Ashley shook her head.

'Jackie Hook's a realist and just out of prison. She'd have taken cash. Perhaps the Hooks demanded too much?'

'No,' said Barry. 'Jackie would have found a price. They're desperate for money.'

'What are the alternatives?' asked Kettle. 'Think out of the box.'

There was quiet until Gabriella put her hand up at the back.

'Maybe this old fella, Abraham, got wind of the affair and set his wife, or Dennis, up. Perhaps both of them. He's ancient, so he doesn't care if he gets caught. Some wealthy and powerful people hate to believe anyone's had one over them.'

Kettle pondered her idea.

'No. He wouldn't want to spend his final years in HMP Norwich with the other old-timers on the geriatric wing. I agree it's more plausible that he's responsible than his wife, but someone that affluent is highly unlikely to get his hands dirty.'

'Remember, he's super wealthy,' said Jan. 'If he hired a killer or killers, they'd be professionals. Nothing would link back to him.'

'It's an interesting angle,' said Ashley. 'People make mistakes, they're sloppy. The further this is away from Abraham, the less his shadow would hang over those involved. There'll be a chink in someone's armour. A call that wasn't anonymous or a text that wasn't deleted. Remember the guy who kept his burner phone because he'd taken a video of his girlfriend on it?'

'Abraham might be so ill he has only weeks left, so being caught isn't important,' said Hector.

Kettle let that apposite comment sink in, then clapped his hands together.

'It's old-school policing until you hear otherwise. Interview everyone. Put them under pressure. This powerful guy's going to be upset if we arrive and he's blindsided. Perhaps he'll do something daft. If he hired a killer, whose bank account is the money going to or leaving? If Elizabeth is involved, how concerned is she with Abraham finding out?'

Kettle paused as the energy in the room grew.

'Ashley, put together a plan and see me in my office in an hour.' Kettle looked around. 'Bodies are piling up. We're not dealing with anyone reasonable here. If they're backed into a corner, they'll lash out given the chance. Everyone who seems to be involved is middle-aged or older, so a prison sentence will be for the rest of their lives.'

Kettle scowled for dramatic effect.

'With that in mind, I suspect the only life that has value to them will be their own.'

60

Ashley collected her team together in a meeting room and picked up a whiteboard pen. Jan, Bhavini and Barry were on one side of the table and Sal, Emma and Hector on the other.

'We're going to visit Abraham's estate and speak to Elizabeth Brown. Some of you are old hands at doing this sort of thing, others new to the game.'

'Hector,' coughed Barry.

Ashley ignored him.

'We certainly have enough to bring Elizabeth in for questioning because her earring was in the hot tub of the deceased. We have cause to arrest her if she refuses to explain why her earring was under a dead body. The evidence implicating Abraham is much more tenuous. His connection is Elizabeth. Perhaps he found out about the affair. That's not enough of an angle to force him to attend. His brief might accept us talking to him for a short time. That's okay, as long as we get him away from the house.'

'He could be one of those wealthy people who loves to talk,' said Emma.

'Let's hope so,' said Sal. 'Or maybe all this is news to him, and, like Kettle said, he'll be furious enough to let things slip.'

Ashley suspected Abraham didn't attain his wealth by letting situations fluster him.

'Let's not pin our hopes on anger or Alzheimer's,' she replied. 'Let's analyse the risks so we're prepared if they happen. Shout them out.'

Ashley pulled the top off her pen as replies came thick and fast.

'We turn up and they've already gone.'

'We can't get in.'

'They're aggressive.'

'Nobody talks to us.'

'There are more people there than we expected.'

'They try to hide or destroy the evidence.'

'The goons shoot at us.'

'The old guy has a heart attack.'

'They don't lie or complain,' said Hector.

The team chuckled at first, then realised he'd flipped their thought processes.

'Explain,' said Ashley.

'I attended private school, but the kids still got in trouble. They caught a friend of mine with some stolen clothes. His parents panicked when officers came to arrest him. They weren't used to the police coming into their homes and they threatened to sue and all sorts. Abraham is a different kind of uber-rich businessperson who probably doesn't make rash decisions. He might decide once we're there to let us get on with it, especially if he's not involved, because he'll want to learn what we know.'

Ashley smiled because nobody, even Barry, made a derogatory comment about Hector being posh. Hector was well on the way to being accepted.

'That's good, isn't it?' she asked.

'He lives on acres of land with multiple properties and has a staff of unknown size. To do this safely and efficiently, we'll need to direct a considerable resource towards investigating his life, and tie it up for days, if not longer. Shouldn't we be searching elsewhere if we don't think they've done anything?'

'Said like a trainee superintendent,' said Barry.

'You're spot on, Hector,' said Ashley. 'But it's not a waste of time if we eliminate them from our investigation. So we do it right, then we won't need to go back.'

'Yes, but what will Abraham do when he understands what's going on?' said Jan. 'It could create a different problem.'

'Noted. We might have someone with unlimited funds who wants to punish Elizabeth or Dennis.'

Ashley turned to her list.

'Two detective teams will be enough. Four members from ours and four from Ally's. We'll also need uniforms. Four vans minimum. Elizabeth returns here, assuming she's present. She'll want to get out of there. Abraham might become difficult and make threats, but we ignore them. We'll request authorisation to check her mobile phones and bank accounts, which we'll arrange in advance. There'll be CCTV in the house and grounds, which we'll also need permission from the courts to look at.'

'You'll need a warrant for entry, too,' said Sal.

'Agreed. There was a locking mechanism on the front gate which we can batter, so it's best to have it approved beforehand if they don't let us in. A 4 x 4 will push the gates open if necessary. The security guards will know better than to talk, but we can try. CSI enters when the place is secure. Elizabeth Brown is clearly our target. It's doubtful she'll reveal anything without representation, which I assume will be on speed dial, but she'll be detained overnight while we finish the searches and CSI start their work.'

'We won't have long enough to process the whole scene before their holding time expires,' said Jan.

'I know. His solicitors will attack any search warrants as an invasion of privacy and our evidence inadequate, but, hopefully, the picture should be clearer by then. We can release them on police bail if necessary. Someone as visible as Abraham won't want an Interpol entry hanging over him, so bail conditions not to leave the country should suffice. How they respond will affect our approach. Kettle can make the final decision on whether we need any armed response, but it's not likely. Sal, remind Hector about the rules on the public having weapons.'

'Since Dunblane, all guns have to be registered and a firearm certificate obtained. You simply can't get one if you don't have a good enough reason for having one, and home security is not even close.'

Hector nodded.

'So, if we found a gun, we could arrest the lot of them.'

'Correct. His goons wouldn't open up on the police. That's the biggest risk if it escalated, but I don't see that happening.'

'Didn't you say there was a guy with a rifle?' asked Bhavini.

'There's a gamekeeper at a cottage on the estate,' said Sal. 'He has shotguns and a small-bore rifle, pest control, but he's been licensed for thirty years without issue. I'd be more concerned about the dog you heard.'

'I'll take my spray,' said Barry.

'Spray any animals, and I'll spray you,' said Ashley. 'The hound will be fine. In my experience, anyone with a dog like that uses it purely as a deterrent for intruders. I bet the owners love it more than each other. They'll know if it attacked a visitor, especially a police officer, it would be destroyed, so they'll keep it on a tight leash.'

'Okay, we'll let Ally's team secure the evidence and we manage the suspects and security with uniform as backup,' said Barry.

'Yes. There'll be somebody around to talk to, even if Abraham and Elizabeth aren't present, because those estates always have round-the-clock guards. Once everyone's left the premises, CSI can start with the property and vehicles. As for the grounds, that's a lot of acres to fingertip search. Kettle will decide if he wants to pay for that kind of expenditure, but I suspect he'll consider what to spend his budget on after we've seen how helpful they are.'

'CSI should be finishing at Paradise,' said Sal. 'Do we keep the same level of police on the site, or do we divert the officers to Abraham's?'

'Let's see what Abraham and Betty have to say. Retain the same presence at the park tonight and we'll adjust first thing tomorrow.'

'An inquiry came from HOLMES not long before the meeting started,' said Jan. 'A Cecil Dowd was supposed to head into Woodfield's police station in Sheffield yesterday and provide a statement. He never showed.'

'Cecil Dowd is Dennis's stepdad,' said Ashley for clarity. 'I'm surprised he didn't attend because he seemed keen to help. Jan, can you chase him? I still have a niggle about Dennis's involvement. Bhavini, you be our link to Kettle and the custody suite. Sal, you have enough admin to do, so, Jan, I want you to check into Abraham's background and assist Sal. Someone so successful might have skeletons. Try to find a bio from where he came from. He is pretty old, so he could see Elizabeth as a gangster's moll type.'

'Any final points?' asked Ashley. 'Is this overkill?'

'No,' said Bhavini. 'If a pair of us turns up and they refuse to open the gates, chances are they'll disappear by the time we go back. They could vanish to the Caribbean for months.'

'Do you think we'll need an ambulance at the scene on standby, just in case anyone wants to test my karate?' joked Barry.

A few of those present smiled, but the tension in the air was palpable. The team was about to enter the unknown, and the risks were real.

61

Two hours later, Ashley and Hector were heading towards Abraham's private estate. Kettle decided against an ARV, deeming it unnecessary. Due to stretched resources, uniformed units were meeting them at the location from as wide an area as Cambridgeshire and Lincolnshire. CSI teams were on the way, but would only enter when the residents had been removed.

Kettle's plan was to go in with considerable numbers and secure the properties. Once the people present had left, they would start with the buildings. Sal back at OCC could begin looking into Elizabeth's phone and bank records. There would be a walked search of the entire area the next day if necessary. CSI would continue the following morning depending on what occurred or was revealed.

Ashley was driving a 4 x 4 Land Rover with Hector as passenger. Barry was behind with Jan and Emma in a similar vehicle. The traffic flowed well for a change, and the sky was clear. Ashley pulled down the sun visor.

'We haven't had the chance to speak much lately,' she said.

'No, but don't worry, I'm still perfect.'

'Still enjoying it.'

'Yes. I'm learning at a rate.'

Ashley smiled at Hector's choice of words. She was certain she hadn't been so focused and serious at his age. Hector had let slip to her that he'd received a new job offer from a university friend. It wasn't due to start for a while, but Hector felt he'd been sold short about what a career in the police was like nowadays.

'Have you thought about your plans?' she asked, glancing over at him.

'So, that was Gingerpuss,' he said, changing the subject.

'Yes, lovely, isn't she? Great at her job, too, which is obviously more important.'

'Where's she been?'

'Helping out in Suffolk, and a family thing which isn't public knowledge.'

'Is she single?'

'I don't know much about her. She's had a lot of time off. Barry will probably have her shoe size if you're smitten.'

Hector shrugged. 'Just intrigued.'

'Call it what you like.'

'And she blew Barry out when he asked her for a date?'

'She's blown everyone out.'

Ashley suspected a smile slipped out of Hector, but she was navigating a roundabout and couldn't be sure.

'You shouldn't call her Gingerpuss,' he said.

Ashley slowed for a phalanx of silver-haired cyclists.

'No, I suppose not. Although Barry says she loves the nick-name because it's a take on Glamourpuss. She reckons it's a bit James Bond.'

Hector rolled the idea around his head for a few seconds.

'Remind me to tell you something about Barry when this is all over,' he said. 'It's childish, but so is he. He deserves a dose of his own medicine.'

'I'll look forward to it, although I wouldn't advise sinking to his level,' she replied. 'He's been operating down there longer.'

They slipped into silence as they neared the scene. Ashley rang Control as they approached the lane where everyone was to meet. When they went in, Abraham's security would have a minute to open the gate, or uniform would force entry. All the warrants were in place. Hector chewed a fingernail as Ashley parked behind the first of the police vehicles to arrive.

'Are you nervous?' asked Ashley.

'A little. You?'

'Apprehensive. But that's good. It gives you focus. Let's talk about something else.'

'All right. Do you mind if I ask you a personal question?'

'Okay. Although not if it's insulting.'

'It isn't. How many sexual partners is it normal to have had?'

'Are you wondering what's average?'

'Something like that.'

'What you're asking is, after all my stories about previous relationships and travelling, how many have I had?'

'If you don't mind.'

'I haven't kept count. Definitely less than forty.'

'Forty!' said Hector.

'I see you feel that's plenty.'

'It is quite a lot, and fancy not knowing exactly.'

'Are you implying that I've been around more times than Dougal and Ermintrude? If you think about it, I lost my virginity at fifteen, then, considering my age, that's less than two a year. That's hardly rock-star levels of sluttery. I was wild in my travelling days, but I'm not going to look back with any regrets. Whereas you might.'

'That's fair enough. Now I'm out in the real world after university, I realise how sex dominates people's lives.'

'The hunting for, finding and maintaining relationships.'

'Yes.'

'It was you who said being human is about connection, and I'm glad you brought it up. I think that is going to be our best angle here. Unless we find something on phone or bank records that links either to a crime, then good old-fashioned interviewing is our only tactic.'

'Our arrival should be a surprise.'

Ashley nodded, suspecting neither Abraham nor Elizabeth was the type to like surprises. 'Yes, that moment is when we might learn the most.'

A quarter of an hour later, everyone was present, briefed and ready. Ashley drove past the police convoy and headed towards Abraham's estate. After five minutes, she pulled over, then stepped out of her car and pressed the button above the flashing green light on the intercom at the gates. She checked her watch: 15:01. At 15:02, she nodded at the uniformed sergeant who was standing further up the road with the big red key. It was time to batter the gates open. He strode forward. When he was in position, there was a click, and they began to open.

Ashley and the officer returned to their vehicles and drove at a steady pace down the drive. It was vastly different from the mist-filled avenue they'd encountered on their first visit. A beautiful wood stretched out of sight, with birds flitting in and out of view, and she could see deer behind a mesh fence on one side. Sunlight filtered through the branches and foliage of the deciduous trees, which lit up the way ahead.

Ashley parked at the front of the main house. She walked up the steps, then turned to wait for everyone else to arrive. There were no vehicles outside the triple garage, and the up-and-over was open to reveal an empty space. It was peaceful, with chickens scrabbling down a track that led further into the estate.

The door opened behind her. It was the sinister squat security guard. His suit fitted better this time.

'Abraham is waiting for you in his office.'

Ashley's face fell as she understood.

Abraham was expecting them.

62

DC Emma Stones spent most of her time in the office with Sal, but she was a great asset in the field. Emma stamped up the steps towards the entrance, then stared down at the short man as she stood next to him. He peered up at her uneasily, then cleared his throat.

'Abraham said to tell you only he and I are in the property. He's happy to give you any assistance you need in his office.'

Ashley's sinking feeling sank further.

'Okay,' she replied, turning back to her team. 'Barry and Hector, you know what to do. Emma and I will have a word with the boss. We'll be out shortly. This gentleman here will be your first customer after he's shown us to Abraham, but that might be all the people present. The gamekeeper may be elsewhere on the estate.'

Barry cursed loudly, having also realised money had once again bought protection.

'He's straight down the hall, then through the lounge,' said the guard. 'Follow me.'

Ashley and Emma strode inside. Emma quietly whistled at the

place, taking her pocketbook out as they reached the lounge. There was a door at the back of it, which was open. They walked into another enormous room where Abraham was sitting behind a desk with two large monitors on the top, which seemed to be controlled by one keyboard. There was another, more ornate desk in the opposite corner with a laptop resting on it.

Abraham rose slowly from his seat, arms outstretched magnanimously, but Ashley could see he was unsteady.

'Afternoon, Officers.'

'Mr Englebert. Were you expecting us?' asked Ashley.

'I prefer to be ready for all my guests. How may I help you?'

Ashley struggled to keep her irritation hidden, then decided the time for nice was over.

'It seems your wife has become embroiled in an extremely serious investigation.'

'I can only assume you're referring to the murders at the caravan park. How does that concern my partner?'

'Are you married to Elizabeth Brown?'

'I'm sure you have more important questions than that.'

'Where is Betty?'

'Elizabeth isn't here at the moment. She's gone to a friend's. She'll be back tomorrow morning.'

'We need to talk to her now.'

'I could try to ring her, but I doubt she'd pick up. You know how women are when they're chatting.'

'We're here to take her phones and computers and check your CCTV footage. I assume you want to co-operate?'

'*Mi casa, su casa.* Although, I'll save you a lot of expense. We have in-house CCTV, so if you give me the timings you're after, I'm sure I can prove Elizabeth was here. Snooping was complicated years ago, but it's all so simple nowadays. It's as easy as watching TV.'

'Is everywhere in your home covered?' asked Emma.

'Yes, but only the man you met at the door and I know there is CCTV inside all the rooms. I've found it helpful to keep it that way.'

'Fair enough. We're interested in the last two weeks.'

'Specifics, please. I'll prove Elizabeth wasn't killing people in Hunstanton.'

Ashley walked over and stood beside him at the desk.

'Two Saturday evenings back, around sunset.'

Abraham sat down and used the cursor to select the day, then the hour. The screen sprang to life in brilliant HD. At 8 p.m. Elizabeth Brown was in the lounge watching television. The playback sped up, reminding Ashley of old silent movies. A butler brought Elizabeth in a tray of snacks at high speed, but she didn't move. Abraham appeared to be asleep in a recliner opposite her.

Abraham upped the pace further. Neither he nor Elizabeth moved from their seats for an hour. He glanced across at Ashley and smiled.

'Last Thursday evening, around the same time,' she said.

'I was out at a business meeting in Norwich at the Maids Head Hotel in their AA rosette restaurant, but my darling was here. She rarely goes out, except on Friday afternoons when she heads to a cards game arranged by the same hotel.'

Abraham found the time slot and showed Betty walking up to her bedroom with her phone in her hand and not leaving. If the video was genuine, Elizabeth was not present for the murders.

'These could have been doctored,' said Ashley.

'Before you came? Why would I? Surely I couldn't guess what you'd ask, or did I doctor them all? My arthritis wouldn't have enjoyed that, I can tell you.'

'Those were the times we suspect people died. Although one of the incidents occurred the week before.'

'Okay, when would you like me to search?'

'Look at the previous Saturday around 6 p.m. onwards.'

Abraham almost hid his surprise, but it was clear to Ashley he was thrown by the date. No, it wasn't shock, it was concern.

'Let me see. I was away that weekend in London. In another hotel and later at The Ivy, but my partner was here.' Abraham grimaced for a moment. 'I recall ringing Elizabeth, who said she was poorly and having an early night. My butler would be able to confirm, but he's gone on holiday, too.'

'Show me the footage of that call, please.'

A slight sheen of sweat rose on Abraham's forehead as he operated the mouse. He leaned back in his seat and exhaled when he found Elizabeth in the hall on her phone. She was pacing up and down, not appearing terribly ill.

At six thirty, she finished the call and applied lipstick in the hall mirror. The butler appeared. She spoke to him briefly, then slid a folded note into his top pocket. The butler nodded, smiled, and strolled away. An enormous Doberman, full of muscle, padded menacingly into the room. Elizabeth crouched and stroked his head, checked in her handbag and retrieved a set of keys. She adjusted her hair one last time, admired her reflection, then walked outside.

Ashley glanced at Abraham, who took a slow, deep breath through his nose. His eyes shifted up and to the left and met Ashley's.

'What do you have to say about that?' she asked.

His hands became fists, but he spoke calmly.

'My assistance is almost at an end.'

Abraham had received a surprise. He had sincerely believed Elizabeth was at home. Would he want to help? She kept her reply neutral with a hint of promise.

'I think we both want to find the truth,' she said. 'Come to the station and we can discuss it.'

Abraham stared hard at her for ten seconds, blinking rapidly as he thought. Abraham rose from his seat and moved to the door much quicker than she expected. Hector had been right that if Abraham was surprised by their questions, he would want to know what they knew.

Ashley followed him outside. The game was on.

63

Three hours later, Ashley and her team had a meeting at OCC to prepare for Abraham's interview.

'So, you didn't find anything untoward at the premises?' asked Bhavini.

'No, he'd clearly got wind we were on the way, so the place was quiet and empty.'

'How would he know we were coming?' asked Hector. 'We only had a rough idea this morning.'

'Not everyone here's as noble as you, Hector,' said Barry. 'I fucking hate rats. We had one before when I was in uniform, but when we nicked the guy who he'd been feeding intel to, he gave him up. Both went to prison, but the officer received longer.'

Ashley thought back to when Abraham implied that wealth could put you above the law. Police starting salaries weren't great. People were struggling all over the country with increased costs, from housing to food. It wouldn't be the greatest surprise if someone had sent him a warning text.

'I hear Abraham's solicitor was here before he was. That's money for you,' said Sal.

Ashley grumbled, but they had to move on.

'We secured two phones,' said Barry. 'Abraham's and the gamekeeper's. Both were happy to hand them over as proof of their innocence. The guard said he didn't have one. Barry and Emma will talk to him and the gamekeeper, but I had the impression the latter is oblivious to anything except his job, and the guard hasn't spoken since we left the property. Abraham's phone has barely been used.'

'Abraham doesn't strike me as the type of guy who orders people to be killed,' said Hector.

'He seemed exactly the sort to me,' replied Barry.

'He's also too intelligent to spill any beans. How are we going to play the interview?'

'I suspect he is a Machiavellian type,' said Ashley.

'What's that mean?' asked Barry.

'Someone who is manipulative, callous, and indifferent to morality,' said Hector.

'Right,' replied Barry.

'But he was surprised when he watched Elizabeth on his CCTV sneaking out for her secret rendezvous,' said Ashley.

'He probably likes to give the impression nothing surprises him at his age, but we'll see. Maybe Elizabeth is his Achilles heel.'

'Hopefully, he'll be angry,' said Hector. 'Gabriella is right. Powerful men don't like feeling they've been taken advantage of.'

'Exactly. Abraham might talk. His staff won't. They'll be more afraid of him than they are of the police, but Abraham will believe he's cleverer than us.'

'He probably is,' said Barry.

'No doubt, which is why we'll need to be sneaky.'

'There is something else,' said Bhavini. 'Sal had the admin team research Abraham's past using US websites. There wasn't much for the last ten years, but he had a merciless reputation for a long time. The media were always gossiping about him, and they often saw him out and about with pretty women, which got him in magazines. An article suggested a few of his competitors came to untimely ends, others mysteriously pulled out of deals, although no charges were ever made against Abraham or his associates.'

'They say nobody innocent becomes really rich,' said Jan.

'I don't suppose his rivals were garrotted or killed with a stiletto?' asked Ashley.

'One drowned for reasons unknown. Another left the third floor of his building via a window. A third sliced his wrists open, but no stilettos or garrottes.'

'All suicides?'

'One of the articles Sal read said the man's wife admitted he was stressed and depressed about his failing business, but she was surprised about his chosen method if it was suicide. He hated heights. All the deaths were investigated, but they found no evidence of wrongdoing apart from the partners stating their husbands weren't the type to take their own lives.'

'Wasn't that what they said about Katrina?' asked Hector.

Ashley nodded as another layer of complication settled on the case. She checked her emails and noticed she had one concerning Lionel's DNA and fingerprints. Neither were at any of the scenes, nor could he be linked to the oven gloves. Lionel had been picked up on the reception camera on Thursday night walking towards his caravan a bit before nine, swinging a bag that probably held his fish and chips.

Detective Superintendent Zara Grave had also emailed Ashley to give her a quick ring, which she did. After a pleasant greeting, Zara got right to it.

'It's come to my attention retired MP Cecil Dowd is close to this case. Could you please tread carefully concerning him and keep me informed?'

Ashley frowned as Grave immediately finished the call. What the hell did that mean? Was it a warning, or just a useful piece of advice from someone who was probably a bigger politician than Dowd? Perhaps it was just Zara covering her arse somehow.

Thirty minutes later, Ashley started the interview. Abraham appeared relaxed, but his eyes couldn't disguise he was finding it tiring. His lawyer wore wire-framed glasses with a sensible suit and haircut, and looked nineteen years old.

'Apologies for the delay,' said Ashley. 'Hopefully you'll help us, and we can get you out of here.'

'No problem. I'm kind of enjoying it all. You don't experience many new things at my age.'

'You've been in trouble before, Mr Englebert,' said Hector. 'Prison time, too.'

'Call me Abraham, boy. That was sixty-five years ago. After a night on a cold floor and some stiff whacks with a truncheon, I confessed. It was the clever thing to do, seeing as I was guilty, and it was worth it. The money I made from the things I stole enabled me to start my first business when I got out of jail. Everything followed from there.'

'You grew up in Norfolk. Is that why you came back?' asked Ashley.

'Yes, I lived in Baja, California, for years, but I missed the British seasons. I enjoy the bleak and lonely coast here, the sunsets and the memories. Like one of the Great Train Robbers once said, sometimes you just want to go for a stroll in the drizzle.'

'Interesting you compare yourself to them,' said Ashley.

'You aren't daft, so you'll know I had nothing to do with whatever's gone on in Hunstanton. I'm beyond all that. My largest firms are in America, so I'm not involved in the day to day any more, but the managers fly over once a month to give me a full update. I adore long business lunches where I can look them in the eye.

These days they're more lunch than business, but the managers humour me, and they enjoy the posh hotels and top restaurants as much as I do. I want to spend what years I have left with intelligent, interesting company, which I wouldn't jeopardise by getting tangled up with petty revenge.'

'What makes you think it's revenge?'

'Isn't it always?'

'Sometimes it's love turned to anger. Other times it's business,' said Hector.

Abraham smiled widely, showing the teeth of a twenty-year-old.

'Then it's revenge on whoever stole their partner, and all's fair in business.'

'I've found it's usually men who kill women.'

'Yes, although this case clearly isn't usual, or simple. If it were, you wouldn't be wasting your time talking to me.'

'I wouldn't be speaking to you if I knew where your wife was,' said Ashley.

'I'm not married.'

'Elizabeth is your partner, yes?'

'Yes.'

'Where is she?'

'I told you. She went to see a friend.'

'With her dog?'

Abraham laughed. 'Something like that. My solicitor has reached her, and he'll bring her to the station in the morning. What time would suit you?'

Ashley smiled at his control games.

'I'd prefer her here now.'

'I find women are often late.'

'And sneaky, judging by the CCTV you and I saw.'

Abraham chuckled to himself.

'I love the mystery.'

'I'm surprised you're laughing. Aren't you let down and irritated? Angry, even?'

'Not especially. Disappointed perhaps, but I expect the worst of people. Life has taught me that. I won't beat around the bush with you. Elizabeth is a beautiful young woman. I'm eighty-six. I wish I could tell you I was still chiselling notches in bedposts and swinging from chandeliers, but I'm not.'

'And you don't mind if someone else takes your place for those tasks?'

Abraham stared at the desk for a moment.

'No, not really. Elizabeth is untameable and full of life. I can't match her passion, but she returns to me every night. Love is different in your eighties.'

'But not enough love for marriage?'

'I'm going senile, not crazy.'

Ashley smiled. 'So, she's impulsive.'

'She makes me feel alive, even when I'm dying.'

Ashley watched a shadow pass over Abraham's face.

'Are you dying?'

'My powers are fading. I can't tie the laces on my shoes now. At least, not when I'm wearing them. Maybe I should have picked a slightly calmer girlfriend.'

'I'd say Elizabeth was thinking of leaving you,' said Hector.

Ashley hid a smile because there was a tiny twitch at the side of Abraham's mouth.

'I doubt it.'

'What would you do if Elizabeth had killed people?'

'Say goodbye. There is no shortage of ladies who want to live like a queen.'

Ashley could see being with Abraham would soon become more a gilded cage than a comfy throne.

'Why not choose someone more refined?'

'Because I dated girls like Elizabeth when I was young. She reminds me of my first romance. The way she talks, the way she walks, even down to the way she lies. I used to take my teenage sweethearts to The Mariner over at Old Hunstanton. We'd get drunk and make love in the dunes. Those simple times are some of my best memories. My strongest ones, too.' Abraham scratched his chin. 'They are vivid still. It's the others that fade.'

'Money, in the end, means nothing,' stated Hector.

'Having loads of it certainly causes its own problems. I have to pay people to protect it. If you can believe the price, I spent sixty thousand pounds on a guard dog. Saying that, he's proving more loyal than most of the other things of similar cost.'

'A problem many can only dream of.'

'Security doesn't come cheap, young man. People try to burgle my house. The Doberman invokes more fear than my men, yet I could give him an egg to put in his mouth, and he wouldn't break it.'

'We'll keep digging until we find the truth,' said Ashley.

Abraham's shrewd eyes switched to Ashley's. He analysed her face.

'Elizabeth didn't do what you think she did. I know her, and I know women like her. She's heartless. She's calculating, yes. But she's fearful of returning to where she once was. There's a reason people like her and I claw and scrap our way out of the gutter.'

'And what's that?'

'It stinks down there.'

'And you'd do anything to keep out of it?'

'You don't risk falling back down. Her type survives and turns the other cheek, if that's what it takes.'

'Sometimes you have to fight fire with fire.'

'Not if you get fried as well.'

'Do you believe in revenge?'

Abraham smiled, but it was cold.

'Revenge is emotion. I believe in taking care of business.'

Ashley realised being close to Abraham and crossing him would be a foolish move. But people like Elizabeth made mistakes. She was seeing Dennis. He was the same. Perhaps there was a gap to Abraham's story, but Ashley wasn't sure what it was.

'Did you buy Elizabeth some gold leaf-shaped earrings?'

Abraham couldn't disguise his annoyance this time and crossed his arms.

'I lent them to her. Encrusted with diamonds. They cost a cool ten grand. Men and women's jaws dropped when she walked past, but she misplaced them.'

Ashley didn't reply, knowing she had him on the hook. She slid a photograph of the earrings across the desk to him. He nodded.

'You found the earrings at the scene. That's the connection.'

She had to give him credit, though. He was still a swift thinker.

'Elizabeth is implicated.'

Abraham shook his head. Ashley smiled and spoke quietly.

'Perhaps she'll tell us something different.'

Abraham's veneer broke. His reply was a rapid snarl.

'If Elizabeth does what she's told, she'll tell you nothing at all.'

Abraham swallowed before steeling himself.

'That's enough for one day. Check my phone. There's nothing on it. I'll stay locally and come back in the morning to pick Elizabeth up. You'll be finished with her by then.'

Abraham's hands trembled when he put them on the table to leave. Ashley realised, as she terminated the interview, that his solicitor hadn't uttered a word.

64

Ashley drove home with another banging headache. She suspected it was dehydration. One of the common problems with the early stages of a major inquiry was the loss of regular mealtimes and drinks. Your health suffered living on service-station snacks.

The detective team at King's Lynn had spoken to Lionel about the claw hammer. He'd confirmed it had gone missing a few weeks before, and he had a receipt for the replacement. They'd suggested to him he'd done it deliberately so he could then use it as the murder weapon, but he'd struggled to even understand the concept. His concerned girlfriend, Lil, had turned up at the station. Lionel had been given conditional bail to her main property in Castle Acre on condition of not visiting the site until he was cleared. Paradise would have to cope without him.

As Ashley parked up outside her house, she thought of the families of the people who'd died, but also those like Lionel and his girlfriend, who were probably innocent. Their lives had been upended, too.

All the kills had been so personal. What type of person could carry on as normal, having been so up close to their victim? What were they thinking as their victim desperately struggled to survive? She found it hard to believe that people like this existed. Yet, she knew they did.

Whoever had committed these crimes had taken quite a risk. Perhaps that was the thrill? Maybe they were looking for a psychopath. If the victims' only connection was that they were all on their own, that nobody was watching, then more women in Paradise were in danger.

Ashley was glad she wasn't in a caravan in Hunstanton, but she didn't fancy going into her empty house, either. She saw Arthur's lounge light was on. They'd lived beside each other for years without exchanging more than a few words, but they'd become friendlier of late after Ashley had offered to drive him to the supermarket on Wednesday evenings.

Arthur opened the door with a sheepish smile and beckoned her in. When Ashley stepped past him she saw why. Joan was sitting on the sofa with a small glass of something dark red. She wore a pair of pink slippers.

'Hi, Ashley, good to see you, hen,' she said, with her thick Scottish accent.

'And you. I've been seeing quite a bit of you fleeing the scene of the crime,' replied Ashley with a wink.

'There's been crimes all right,' replied Joan, following it with a dirty chuckle.

'Cup of coffee or a port?' asked a blushing Arthur.

'I'll have a quick coffee,' said Ashley.

She waited for Arthur to leave. There were two candles burning in the fireplace, filling the room with a soft lavender smell, which intermingled with something meaty roasting in the oven.

'So, Joan. I finally allow a man into my life, and you sneak in and steal him. When did all this happen?'

'That afternoon, when we all went drinking and came back here after the football, I fell asleep in his spare room, cheeky mare that I am. I'd had a few. I woke up all shifty in the morning, but he was good as gold. Made me mackerel for breakfast, which to be honest I had to force down. We got to talking and had a great laugh. When I left, I said I'll take him out to make up for letting me stay, and he asked, is that a date?'

Joan smiled as she recalled the moment.

'And I said, yes, it is. Arthur's a real gent. I think we were both lonely. It's strange to be as ancient as I am and feel loved up.'

'Enjoy every minute,' said Ashley.

When Arthur returned, he and Joan asked about the case. Ashley skirted around the details but mentioned they were struggling to link the three deaths in Paradise with the chip-shop murder, although it was early days.

'If there are women dying, it'll be a bloke,' said Joan. 'I watch enough detective shows to know it'll be a jealous man.'

'Sounds more like a woman scorned to me,' said Arthur.

'I often wonder what happens if you guys can't figure it out,' said Joan. 'Do you just pack your stuff up and start on the next case?'

'It's quite rare with this kind of crime for us not to solve it, even if it takes a long time. Killers are human, they make mistakes, or people finally talk, maybe on their deathbeds. Others boast about their crimes or fall out with their accomplices. The odd one develops a conscience. Taking another life is no small thing for most of us.'

The word *most* lingered in the scented air.

'I assume everyone lies to you at the start,' said Joan.

'Yes, many do, which makes it hard as the rules state we don't have long to hold someone unless we have, or are waiting for, confirmation of damning evidence. Usually the DNA, CCTV, number-plate cameras or fingerprints we gather puts a person at the scene, and that's enough to blow their alibi out of the water.'

'Ah, I see,' said Arthur. 'If they say, "I wasn't there, guvnor, and never have been," but you can prove they were, it's the beginning of the end for them.'

'Exactly. What we will do is keep going. A suspect's version of their relationships might change, which gives us leverage when we interview them. More developments should come to light as the pressure builds, especially if they are guilty.'

'Scary to think there's such a callous killer on the loose,' said Joan.

'Very much so, and sometimes killers resurface and attack other victims. That's the way many are caught.'

'It almost sounds like you're waiting for someone else to die,' said Joan.

Ashley smiled, but unfortunately there was some truth in it.

'I might not be able to take you shopping tomorrow, Arthur. But I reckon I'll be free on Thursday.'

'Don't worry, Ashley. I'll take him,' said Joan. 'It must be tough when you have these cases. I suppose the first week is important.'

'Yes, crucial. Details are fresh in people's minds. The memories of eyewitnesses get hazy after a few days. Evidence is washed away, or bins are emptied. So, it's full on, and we obviously don't receive prior notice, so if you were supposed to be taking the kids to karate, or had a celebratory meal booked, it all gets cancelled. That's why we're all single or heading for divorce.'

Ashley drank her coffee and made her excuses, feeling as though she was intruding. Joan gave her a hug as they said goodbye.

'You look after yourself. I'm always happy for a phone call or a beer.'

Ashley left the lovebirds to it and went home.

It was a mild evening, but her house was cold and still.

65

Ashley tried to do a few yoga stretches, but she wasn't feeling it. She laid out her exercise gear for the morning, then took a camomile tea up to bed. Three hours later, she lay in the dark while her heart thudded in her ears. It was a solitary place to be.

As ever, when sleep was slow to come, Ashley's mind wandered to the future. She knew people who'd reached her age and simply accepted they would be single forever. Was that her destiny, too?

She cursed when she rolled over and it was gone four and she'd barely slept a wink. Her alarm jangled seemingly five minutes later, but after beating it into submission, she still heard a ringing sound.

She staggered downstairs and found her phone where she'd left it on charge. Two missed calls. Both from Control. It was a quarter to six. That did not bode well. She returned the call.

'DS Knight. You called me.'

'Yes, there's been an incident at Paradise caravan park.'

'What kind?'

'Arson. A firebomb launched at a lodge.'

'Whose place was it?'

'A Dennis Turner. We had a response vehicle parked up close by and they heard a smash. They were at the scene within a minute, but nobody's been apprehended.'

'Was he inside?'

'The smashing glass woke him, and he escaped.'

'They say the devil looks after his own. What about anyone with him?'

'There are no reported injuries or fatalities.'

'Any other incidents in the park?'

'No. The fire brigade has arrived, so everything's under control but it did a fair bit of damage. I contacted the on-call detective, DC Barry Hooper, and he's en route. DC Hooper said you'd want to know straight away and to keep trying you. He'll be in touch when he has more to add.'

'Okay, thank you. I'm interviewing this morning at OCC, but I'll head down later.'

'Confirmed, also can I have a quick word, Sarge?'

Ashley paused, then realised the Control voice was that of Jenny Groves, who Ashley met when she came to their department for a look around.

'Of course. Pardon me, Jenny, I'm still half asleep.'

'It's my last day.'

'I'm sorry to hear that.'

'No, it's fab news. I start my police officer training next week. You inspired me. I just wanted to let you know.'

Ashley had walked back upstairs while she was talking. She gave her running kit a rueful glance as the call ended, put on her black suit and a light yellow shirt and went to hunt for her car keys. She was no longer tired though, and drove to the office with a smile on her face.

Ashley was first in, beating DCI Kettle by a few minutes. He came straight over.

'What are your thoughts?' he asked.

'Clearly, there's been an attempt on Dennis's life.'

'And we both know who's most likely to want him silenced.'

'Do we?'

'A jealous attack ordered by the rich Abraham.'

'Hmm. Elizabeth Brown might want him dead.'

'What do you mean?'

'The noose has tightened around her neck. I was going to fetch Dennis in today and attempt to prise the details of their affair out of him. If Dennis was dead, she could accuse him of taking advantage of her. Or say Dennis was blackmailing her in some way.'

'Ah! So, she tells her partner, Abraham, it was all Dennis. They only met up a few times. She gets off the hook, keeps her relationship intact and therefore continues to live in the manner to which she's become accustomed.'

'Maybe. It's also possible someone else has taken the opportunity to do away with Dennis. He's pissed a fair few people off, and it's a significantly cruder method of dispatch than the other murders. Ultimately, it's the only one that's been unsuccessful.'

Kettle scratched his head. 'Perhaps the killer attempted it knowing the spotlight was elsewhere.'

'Exactly. I find it hard to believe Abraham would order something as basic as that, shortly after leaving a police station.'

Hector had arrived and was listening.

'I've another theory,' he said. 'Elizabeth has been doing all the killing, maybe with Dennis's help, but likely without. If she's smart, she could waltz in and blame him for them all.'

'But he's not dead,' said Kettle.

'She might not know that. Even if he was alive, she could come in and point the finger. Getting in first, so to speak,' replied Hector.

'He'd deny it, or perhaps accuse her,' replied Kettle. 'We wouldn't know who was lying and we'd still have no proof.'

'I can't see Elizabeth sneaking around any lodges with a flaming firebomb in her hands,' said Ashley.

'Good point,' said Hector. 'She will have the best lawyer as well.'

'But remember Dennis's brief was also top-drawer.'

Ashley had a deepening frown. None of these solutions rang true to her. The person committing the arson was taking a considerable risk seeing as the police were already present, even if they knew the park layout intimately. Surely Lionel hadn't returned and done it.

Kettle was staring at her.

'What is it?' he asked.

'Do you get the feeling we're being played somehow?'

'In what way?'

'That someone's manipulating the investigation.'

'Are you referring to the mole in our department?'

'That could be an element, but, no, something else. We're like headless chickens being led from one suspect to another. Can you remember a case with so many victims that's such a complicated mess, where we still don't have a clue what's going on?'

'No, I can't.'

'Look at the first murder.'

'Alfie Hook.'

'No, he was the second. Jasmine was already dead in her tub.'

'Right.'

'We've struggled with this because the link between Jasmine and Alfie is tenuous. It's hard to think why anyone would hurt either, much less kill them both.'

'Are you saying Alfie Hook's death was just a distraction, or Jasmine's was?' asked Hector.

Kettle whistled.

'That's a pretty high-stakes play.'

'Yes, it is. The culprit, if we ever find them, will spend the rest of their days in jail. Their freedom would be gone forever. The stakes don't get any higher.'

'I suppose not, and you have to say whoever it is has been near faultless so far, or we'd be closer to pinning it on them.'

Ashley clicked her fingers.

'What a great choice of words,' she said.

'What is?'

'High stakes.'

'So?'

'Think card games. Think winning. Who likes poker?'

'Dennis had sites downloaded onto his computer,' said Hector.

'Yes, but Elizabeth loves the buzz,' said Ashley.

'Bloody hell,' whispered Hector. 'Perhaps it's not money that gives her the ultimate thrill.'

66

Kettle smiled.

'Interesting angle.'

Ashley's mind was racing.

'It still seems like madness when she's due here this morning.'

'Maybe it's purely down to money,' said Hector. 'Dennis lost a large amount, or borrowed some and couldn't repay her. It's certainly possible.'

'Dennis must be panicking,' said Ashley. 'Scared people talk.'

The office door opened, and Emma walked in.

'Elizabeth Brown has arrived. The lawyer is the same as Abraham had yesterday. It looks like they're doing some final heated prep in the car.'

'Interesting,' said Ashley. 'Maybe Elizabeth has been told to toe a certain line.'

'A woman who we know doesn't like to be told what to do,' said Hector.

'Okay,' said Ashley. 'We'll start at nine. Emma, can you ring Barry? He should be at Paradise. Tell him I need Dennis Turner back at OCC this morning, even if he has to drive him here himself.'

'Will do, Sarge.'

'Come on, Hector. Let's discuss how we're going to handle Elizabeth.'

At nine-fifteen, the preliminaries were complete, and Elizabeth Brown and her solicitor were seated in front of a prepared Hector and Ashley. Ashley tried to gauge Elizabeth's mood, but her make-up was so thick it was even hard to judge her expression. She appeared as if she'd popped in on her way to Royal Ascot.

'Thank you for coming in to see us, Elizabeth,' said Ashley after the formalities were over.

'Did I have any choice?'

'No, but we'll make this quick and painless for you. I'll dive right in. Are you having a relationship with someone on the site?'

Elizabeth leaned forward and whispered her reply.

'The young man next to me says you have nothing on me, so why don't you make it really easy and let me go?'

Ashley found most interviews went better if she was polite, focused and didn't condescend, but she knew Elizabeth of old. The key was to rouse her anger.

'We have your jewellery in the vicinity of two murders.'

Elizabeth's eyes narrowed. Her voice was louder.

'You have a pair of earrings someone left at a friend's house.'

'Did you lose your earrings?'

'I lost one at Deniz's lodge, so I left the other until I could find it.'

'One of those earrings was recovered from the hot tub where a woman was killed,' said Hector.

They all knew Elizabeth was a good actor, so Ashley watched closely for a flaw in her performance.

'You what? Why the hell would it be in the neighbour's hot tub?'

'You tell us. It's all rather cosy. Did you all clamber in together?'

'I don't do hot tubs. They dry my skin out. It's hard enough fighting the years as it is.'

'Perhaps you didn't get in the tub, and were merely next to it,' said Hector.

'I've been nowhere near any fucking hot tubs.'

'Could you explain how your earring was found inside one, then, please?' he asked.

Elizabeth flicked her hair back, then gave her solicitor an incredulous glance. Her eyes were blazing when she returned her glare to Hector. She spat the words out.

'Because, you bloody fools, someone stuck it there.'

Hector smiled.

'Okay, so who placed it there, and how did they get it?'

'What do you mean?'

'You must know who had it to put it in the hot tub.'

Elizabeth paused and glowered slightly. She exchanged a glance with her solicitor, who gave her a tiny but obvious nod. Elizabeth took a few breaths as she composed herself.

Ashley leaned back in her seat. This wasn't going the way she expected. Elizabeth had been told to talk. Which meant either she had a brilliant cover story, or she wasn't involved.

'I removed my earrings when I was at my friend's lodge because they were heavy,' explained Elizabeth, talking deliberately. 'It was a few weeks ago. I left and forgot to put them back on. When I returned, the useless cunt had lost one.'

It always surprised Ashley when a woman used that word. She immediately recalled Verne and Bertie telling her they'd overheard a female using foul language. That must have been when

Elizabeth went to fetch her earrings, which were a present from Abraham, and discovered there was only one.

'And your friend is Dennis Turner, lodge One, Diamond,' stated Hector. Elizabeth picked up on the name. She released a brief chuckle.

'That's right.'

'Friend or lover?'

'That's not important.'

'Are you close friends?'

'We have a shared interest. That's all.'

'Would that interest be poker?'

For the first time, Elizabeth lost her composure, but she didn't look guilty.

'Yes,' she said, slowly. 'How did you know?'

'We're beginning to build a picture of those involved,' said Ashley, nodding. 'Each day, more people slot into place. Now would be the moment to tell us where you fit in.'

Elizabeth glanced over at the solicitor, who bobbed his head again.

'I love poker. I always have. It's fun, and it's a challenge. I enjoy the sneaky aspect of it, the bluffing. For me, the gambling is merely how you see who's won. I have enough money not to be focused solely on that.'

'You enjoy the feeling of bettering someone in something that you see as a game of skill.'

'Exactly.'

'Does Abraham give you an allowance?'

'Let's just say I'm taken care of.'

'And what if that ended?'

'I'm a resourceful woman. I'll cope.'

'In the gutter?'

'What?'

'Abraham said nobody wants to go back down to where they were, because it stinks.'

'Did he now?'

Ashley smiled but didn't reply. Elizabeth clenched her fists.

'Well, that's not too much of a surprise. He's always saying that sort of thing.'

'So, you had an affair with a younger man?'

'Dennis is a friend.'

Ashley realised the relationship was important to all this. She again wondered if Elizabeth chose to sleep with other people with Abraham's permission, or without it. No doubt Dennis, when Barry got him here, would be singing from the same song sheet that they were just friends. Which would mean Elizabeth would have no motive to hurt his ex-girlfriends if that were true.

'Did you visit Dennis's to play together?' asked Hector.

'Pardon?'

'Poker. Is that why your earrings were at his lodge?'

'Yes, I wore them to his place once.'

'And took them off during, or before, playing together?'

Elizabeth scowled at him.

'As I said, they're heavy. Abraham loves to see me wearing them, but they aren't comfy. It feels like I'm turning into a lop-eared rabbit when they're in.'

Hector chuckled, then smiled nicely at her. Ashley was impressed.

'They're so expensive,' he said. 'Weren't you worried about losing them?'

'They'll be insured. Anyway, it was Abe who adored them. He wanted to see me wearing them; he didn't give them to me.'

Ashley felt her heartbeat increase. They were getting somewhere.

'Abraham thinks you wouldn't jeopardise your living standards by doing anything that would upset him.'

'I know.'

Elizabeth let out a deep breath, which made Ashley suspect that whatever came out next was going to be the truth.

'Abraham was old when we met, but he was in amazing nick for his age. He had drive, charm and charisma. Now he has charm and charisma, and I love being with him, but the spark and energy have gone. I still have mine. He could live for another decade, swanning off to his fancy lunches and falling asleep in the car on the way home. But I don't want to live like that. Not full-time, anyway.'

'Does he know this?'

'I reckon he does, but he doesn't want to admit it. At least not to me. I haven't even been that subtle about my movements.'

'Are you perhaps forcing the issue? You want to get caught?'

Elizabeth stiffly shook her head.

'He's a strange choice,' said Ashley.

'Abraham?'

'No, Dennis.'

'You might think so, but Dennis is attractive. More importantly, I understand his morals and how he's come to be how he is. I've been down there. He got a hand up with an inheritance, but he'll play what he's been given badly because that's what people like him always do. Dennis is the binman who wins the lottery and is back on benefits five years later. He's lucky his mother knew that and gave him a monthly income as opposed to assets to burn through, but he'll borrow against it as soon as he realises he can. He may already have.'

'Is he rubbish at poker?' asked Hector.

'No, he's decent. But he's careless because he knows more money is coming, which is why I usually beat him. Do you play?'

'No,' said Hector. 'I don't think I could hide my thoughts.'

'It's great. It only takes a second to say, "all in", and you can lose everything. Or win big.'

'Do you worry about losing too much?' asked Ashley.

'You're as bad as Abraham. I was already forty-five when I met him. I've got plenty of my own cash.'

'From your businesses beforehand, when you worked with Jackie Hook?' asked Hector.

Elizabeth remained stony-faced and made no comment.

'I'll be talking to Abraham again,' said Ashley. 'It'll be interesting to see if his story matches yours.'

The solicitor cleared his throat.

'Mr Abraham has had a rough night at the hotel, as you'd expect for a man of his age. He won't be cooperating with any interviews. If you wish to charge him, go ahead.'

Ashley took a deep breath.

'Has he come back here?'

'Yes, he's in a waiting room.'

'Does he know what Elizabeth has said this morning?'

'Of course, and he's happy for it to be on file.'

Abraham's opinion as to what went on file was inconsequential, but Elizabeth's head jerked to the side. It had dawned on her that she wasn't as in control as she believed.

'Hopefully we'll talk to Dennis again, Elizabeth,' said Ashley. 'See if what he says matches with your story.'

'I don't care if it doesn't.'

'Do you think Dennis put the earring in the tub to incriminate you?'

'He wouldn't be so stupid.'

'So you do trust him?'

'The guy is a career liar. His word means nothing, and any half-decent barrister would destroy him on the stand.'

'Is he to be thrown to the wolves?'

'I don't understand what you're getting at. Dennis is a distraction. He's a fit young man who's served a purpose. I won't be seeing him again. Ever. We're done.'

Ashley toyed with the ace she'd been holding for the entire conversation, then laid it down.

'Last night, a petrol bomb was thrown through Dennis's lodge window while he was inside.'

Elizabeth's face fell. 'What? Are you for real?'

'Yes. Our people are at the scene now.'

Elizabeth's mouth opened and closed. Then she braced herself. Ashley was intrigued. Elizabeth hadn't been taking any of this seriously. She finally understood this was no longer her game. It was someone else's. And she might not survive it.

67

Ashley cut the interview to give Elizabeth a break and for the news about Dennis to sink in. When Ashley returned ten minutes later and they started again, she smiled.

'Luckily, Dennis has survived. He should be with us shortly and we'll ask what he thinks of all this. Dennis can back up your story about heavy earrings and innocent poker play.'

Elizabeth was distracted though, and Ashley's words didn't register.

'It's all wrong,' she said.

She glanced from Ashley to Hector, then jabbed her finger at Hector.

'This is bullshit. It's a trick.'

'What do you mean?' asked Hector, holding his hands wide.

'I haven't killed anyone, and neither has Dennis. Someone's playing you lot, and they're cleverer than you are. I can't make any sense of it. I'm betting you can't either. They've led you to me and Dennis, which means you're searching in the wrong direction.' She slapped her hand down hard on the table. 'You should be looking for them!'

Elizabeth frowned as she slumped in her seat. She swallowed deeply as the implications of what she had said sank in. Her gaze strayed to Ashley, who saw the dilated pupils and trembling lips.

'I haven't got a clue what this is,' whispered Elizabeth. 'But it isn't over.'

Ashley at least agreed with her about that, but Elizabeth was no innocent.

'Do you believe Abraham breaks the law?'

'My client has nothing further to say,' said the solicitor calmly.

Ashley glanced at Elizabeth one last time, but she had her hands over her face. What else did she know?

After another five minutes of fruitless questions, Ashley and Hector returned to the office. The entire team was in except for Barry. They didn't even have the chance to sit down before more unwelcome news arrived from Jan.

'Barry rang in while you were out. It's Dennis. He's gone.'

'You're kidding. Gone where?'

'He was hungry and went to Tesco for food and a hot drink, then never came back.'

Ashley was about to moan, but she supposed they wouldn't have arrested the victim, which would mean he was free to come and go as he pleased.

A knot of worry gathered in her stomach.

'I assume Barry has gone to search for him.'

'Yes, but he wasn't surprised Dennis had vanished. He'd been acting nervously all morning as you'd expect. Barry took a statement, but there was nothing in it that was any help. Dennis is convinced someone's trying to knock off everyone in Diamond.'

Ashley shook her head. That didn't explain Alfie or Katrina.

'Perhaps it was Dennis who threw the petrol bomb through his own window, then pretended he just woke up,' said Hector.

'That way, we rule him out. He even had you considering whether someone was planning to kill everyone on Diamond.'

Ashley smiled at the way Hector's brain worked, even if she did reckon it unlikely.

'It's possible, but he loves it there. It really is paradise for him. All this is too complex for him to be the ringleader. He has a point, though. Six lodges, two dead and one attacked. That only leaves Glory and the two couples. I think we should check up on them in person. Make sure they're safe.'

'Shall we ring them first to say we're coming, or surprise them?' asked Sal, with a wink.

Ashley considered whether the owners of the other three lodges could be involved.

'It's not going to be Hans and Helga, but they might have remembered something now they've had a few days away. I suppose we need to put the magnifying glass over Bert and Ernie, and Glory. Everyone else's story works out to a certain degree.'

'Do you mean Verne and Bertie?' asked Hector, innocently.

Ashley laughed.

'Yes, sorry. I had an awful night's sleep where I basically snatched a few minutes. My mind was telling me the same thing Elizabeth said to us in the interview just now.'

'Which was?' asked Hector.

'That someone smarter or at least more cunning is playing us all for fools.'

'Do you think Elizabeth is involved?' asked Jan.

'Not in the killings, no. I suspect someone planted her earring in that hot tub to lead us to her. They only put one in. Perhaps they knew the DNA would get washed off, which is why they left the other in Dennis's lounge.'

'Killing Katrina and making it appear a suicide was sneaky,' said Hector. 'If that were the case. Knocking Alfie off in the corner of a quiet car park was smart to distract us at the beginning. Hiding the other earring so well was genius, knowing our CSI would find it.'

'It would mean they'd been in Dennis's lodge,' said Sal.

'Unless Elizabeth was lying about that,' said Ashley.

'Pip's been killed. Dennis's beloved lodge is burned out. We're running out of suspects,' said Jan.

'The firebomb doesn't fit,' said Ashley. 'Michelle used the term assassin. A professional killer wouldn't use something so crude. How did they know Dennis was inside the property? Even if he was home, he'd probably have been at the rear in bed and able to get out.'

'Perhaps they were going to shoot him as he escaped,' said Jan.

'Maybe, although there was a marked car about a hundred metres away,' said Hector.

'That's what's got me worried. Is it another distraction? What does the person who's doing all this want?' asked Ashley. 'What's the end plan?'

Her team remained quiet.

'Sal, where do Hans and Helga live?' she asked.

'Swaffham.'

'That's not too far. Emma and Jan, one of you speak to Abraham again this morning in the improbable event he's changed his tune about talking to us, then both of you head to Swaffham. It's possible the Germans have had family or friends stay in their lodge, or there's another twist we haven't considered. Bee, you stay here and orchestrate.'

'Yes, boss.'

She gave Ashley a smile and a certain nod that made Ashley suspect she'd told HR about her condition and was accepting of her not taking any unnecessary risks.

'Sal and Hector, drive to Thetford and do the same with Verne and Bertie. Then return here and start doing the hard yards. We need to look at recent and historic offences, past criminals, in particular anyone who's committed serious crimes at caravan sites. Start countywide, then all of England. I'm heading to Paradise. I want to see this fire first hand, then I'll take Barry with me to King's Lynn and surprise Glory. She has a flat there, and she visits her husband in the hospital. I'll check that out too. Scott Gorton emailed me to say he's visiting Pip's husband this morning. Let's rule Rupert out.'

'Someone should have a word with Gail and Hamilton in Reception,' said Hector. 'They must meet everyone at some point.'

'Good idea. I'll do that. Keep trying to reach Dennis, but, as far as I can see, he has little money and nowhere else to go but back to his stepfather in Sheffield. Has his stepfather shown up yet or attended his local station?'

'No,' said Emma. 'Although his phone rings. We could have the signal triangulated. You think he might be involved?'

'No, but he's going to get an unwanted house guest arrive, because Dennis is skint and homeless. Sal, put the registration of Dennis's Toyota into ANPR. Let's see if we can pick his car up and track it back to Sheffield and Cecil Dowd.'

'Ask local CID to grab him?'

'Yes, although I'd like a conversation with this Cecil myself. Dragging him to Norfolk isn't ideal at his age. Video calls don't give you any feel, either.'

'If you're seeing Glory in King's Lynn, you're already an hour closer if you fancy a personal visit,' said Emma. 'We'll keep trying and let you know if he picks up. I'll leave a more forceful message, perhaps saying if he doesn't get in contact, we'll have to bring him to Norwich.'

'Great. If Cecil won't allow Dennis in, what will he do? Elizabeth has washed her hands of him.'

'And all his exes are dead.' Jan chuckled.

'Yep,' said Bhavini. 'The papers are going mad for the story. It's all over the national news. Murders like these are guaranteed to get you caught sooner or later.'

'I agree,' said Emma, 'but that might be a problem in itself. This killer is efficient and intelligent. They won't want prison, so they must be nearly finished. They might just vanish.'

Ashley blew out a long breath.

'I'm getting the dreadful feeling it's almost a game to them.'

'Perhaps it's not a game,' said Hector. 'It's a challenge.'

68

Ashley checked her emails, then had a series of meetings with Kettle and the other teams involved in the investigation before she left. CCTV had been no help at all and the group monitoring the images was despondent. Those checking bank accounts and call records had come up blank, too.

Abraham declined any further comment and the solicitor indicated Elizabeth wouldn't answer any more questions either, knowing the police would release them if no further evidence was discovered at Abraham's estate.

As Ashley was leaving OCC, Barry rang her.

'The fire chief has let CSI into the lodge, and they've found a weapon on the floor.'

'What kind?'

'Gerald called it a flick knife. It resembles one, but it looks a thing of real quality to me. One of the team from the brigade, Jennifer, is a knife fan. She's looking at it now.'

'Do you think it was in there with Dennis, or thrown in by whoever put the petrol bomb through the window?'

'I haven't been inside yet, so I'm not sure. Are you heading here?'

'Yes, I'll be just over an hour, traffic permitting. I want to talk to the guys at Reception, all of them. There are two part-timers to meet.'

'Okay. There's something else.'

'Go on.'

'You know the handyman?'

'Tim.'

'Yeah. Tim was working on a leaking pipe under a caravan at Thirteen Bronze when he noticed someone he hadn't seen before. There are fewer people on the site at the moment, and those that are about don't dawdle if they head outside, so this man stuck out a bit.'

'Dodgy?'

'Tim described him as a guy with a hat on who mooched around. He knows it's a bit of a cliché, but the bloke reminded him of a private detective. Later, Tim saw him talking to Hamilton at the desk. Then he spotted him knocking on a door down Silver.'

'Did he give you a description?'

'Man in a trilby-type hat and thick-framed glasses, wearing a three-quarter length lightweight coat like a windcheater. His hair was long enough to show despite the headwear.'

'Sounds like a western gunfighter.'

Barry laughed. 'I said he sounds like a cowboy. Tim reckons he had that air about him, but it was broad daylight, and he kept his pistols in their holsters.'

'Very funny. What about his face? Was he tall, thin?'

'He said he didn't notice any features, although he thinks he was old. His hair was mostly grey, and he had a biggish nose.'

'We could have an identity parade of all the criminals in

Norfolk who satisfy those criteria. I'll need to ring Carrow Road and ask if we can use the stadium to fit them in.'

'I do like a bit of humour to ease the tension,' said Barry. 'Look, if we have a word with Gail at Reception, she might point him out on CCTV. I saw what I thought was the groundsman, Lionel, on his mower and asked him if he'd seen him.'

'Surely Lionel hasn't returned?'

'No, it was Percy, pretending to be Forrest Gump. Percy reckons he saw this cowboy last weekend.'

'After Jasmine was discovered?'

'Yes, but, more interestingly, he'd noticed him before that. It seems he's a man people remember, but struggle to describe his face. We'll discuss it when you arrive.'

Ashley finished the call and dismissed Percy from her likely suspects. She'd not been able to do the midday interview with him as she'd hoped yesterday, so one of the other teams had spoken to him. Their feedback had been that, if Percy was the criminal genius who had them all confused, they should all consider whether they were in the right job.

Percy was also still around, which lessened the chance of his involvement. The prospect of hiding in plain sight would likely be beyond him, unless his bumbling buffoon act was a ploy.

Before she left the office, she asked Jan and Emma to follow her to Hunstanton after they'd visited Hans and Helga. There would be a new wave of holidaymakers to talk with who had just arrived at the park. Maybe regular weekenders. Ashley raked her hands through her hair. What were they missing?

After half an hour of driving, the lack of sleep caught up with her. She wound down her window, but she needed a break. When her phone rang just before Fakenham New Cemetery, she took that as a sign to stop but the ringing stopped before she had a chance to answer it.

A vehicle followed her into the gravelled entrance where there was little room, so she drove through the gates to the spaces at the other end. She checked her rear-view mirror and saw the maroon car was still following. Sunlight glinted off the windscreen, so Ashley couldn't see the driver's face. After reversing next to a tree, she rubbed her eyes. The driver of the maroon vehicle, when she stopped checking her make-up and finally prised herself from it, could have passed for Barbie. Ashley had half been expecting a gun-toting Jesse James.

The call record gave her a mobile number, but it was new to her phone. She returned it.

'Hello?' said a mature voice.

'Hi, I just had a missed call. It's Detective Sergeant Ashley Knight.'

'Hello, Sergeant. It's Cecil Dowd here.'

The man who was supposed to attend a Sheffield police station on Monday but hadn't and who'd not been answering his phone.

'Thanks for ringing me. How can I help?'

'I rang to apologise.'

'What for?'

'For not giving that statement.'

'Okay.' She let the silence hang.

'I suppose it was guilt. Dennis is a slimeball, for want of a better description, but his mother loved him. She made me promise he would always have somewhere safe to stay.'

Ashley smiled.

'So, you felt disloyal giving the police a statement about his underhand ways.'

'Correct. Although if I had held to my word, I wouldn't have told you the truth when I spoke to you before.'

'That he was a thief and a liar.'

'Yes.'

'I doubt she'd have wanted you to lie to us.'

'She would have.'

There it was again. The strength of a mother's love.

'Even when people were dying?'

'That's why I'm ringing you now, because he is a total scoundrel, and I saw someone else had died.'

'Do you believe he's involved?'

'I would have said no, but this year when Paradise was closed, he stole from my house when he stayed here.'

Ashley pondered that for a moment, but her thoughts were interrupted.

'You're probably wondering why he's stealing if he has a guaranteed income for life.'

'No, some people can never have enough, and with others, money becomes an addiction. They'd rather take things than spend their own cash. And if gambling's their thing, then no amount of dough is enough. Think of the trouble pro-footballers find themselves in.'

'Ah, you do know what you're talking about.'

Ashley laughed. 'Sometimes.'

'Dennis has had all the addictions at one time or another, but he shook them off. Except one. We all have something similar that we do. It's how we survive. We need a thing to escape the worries of life.'

'And his is gambling.'

'Yes.'

'And stealing to pay for it.'

'Yes.'

'Or perhaps doing whatever's asked to fund it?'

As soon as her casual comment slipped out, Ashley recognised the seriousness of its implications.

Cecil stayed quiet on the phone. Ashley pondered whether now was the time to tell him Dennis's lodge had been seriously damaged by arson and Dennis was probably on his way to Cecil's place.

'Are you willing to give us a statement, then?' she asked first.

'I'm not sure. I don't want to go to the station.'

'What if I had someone come to your house?'

'No, I don't want the police here.'

Ashley knew she had to ask.

'What if I came?'

There was a pause.

'I think that would be okay. That boy has used up his final life with me. I can't have him in the house again. He'll need to spend his money more sensibly and find somewhere else to live. What he stole last time had great sentimental value. I'm too old to be dealing with such annoyances, whatever his mother wanted. He's on his own from now on.'

'You might need to tell him sooner rather than later. It seems there was a fire at the lodge, and it's uninhabitable.'

There was a heavy pause.

'Oh, God. He's heading here?'

'We're just checking where he might be. It only happened last night.'

'Was it an accident?'

'We don't think so. What will you do if he turns up there wanting to be let in?'

The silence was longer.

'I'm not sure. If you're coming to see me, I'll be at home for the rest of today. Goodbye.'

Ashley left the vehicle for a stretch and some fresh air. It was a mild day, with thick white clouds and a gentle breeze off the farmland behind her. She took a deep breath and wandered around the edge of the graves.

The cemetery's gravel path wasn't in great condition, but the graves were well tended, and the grass cut. Her mind casually pondered whether the world could become a better place if people expressed as much affection towards the living.

Ashley read a few of the names and dates. Most of the deaths were relatively recent. Upon second thought as she ambled around, it was a lovely spot. Ashley often found peace and strength in cemeteries. Every person buried in one would swap places with her in an instant.

She had hope, where they had none.

Her phone buzzed again.

'Hey, Sal. What's up?'

'Ally's team has been on ANPR. They've tracked Dennis's car all the way back to Sheffield from here.'

'Shit. Is he at his stepfather's place?'

'No, Cecil lives in Stumperlowe, which is south-west. Dennis is somewhere north in the city. There are plenty of cameras around there, so we're fairly sure he hasn't moved. We're analysing the area to see if there's a place where he could be. Shopping centre, that sort of thing.'

'Okay, good work. Anything else?'

'The woman fire investigator with an interest in knives had a look at the object they found. It's rare. American-made and high end.'

'Deadly or for show?'

'Her exact words were, it's a blade for killing.'

69

Ashley arrived at Paradise at two o'clock. It was eerie seeing the place so devoid of life. There was one car in the car park for customers and three in the staff area. She parked next to a small blue Renault, which had a sticker on the back stating the inhabitants of the vehicle were on their way to the Blue Lagoon. No prizes for guessing whose vehicle it was. The sun's rays made the two-seater BMW beside it sparkle.

When Ashley left her car, she was stunned by the silence. It reminded her of when a heavy blanket of snow fell and hushed the world. She tried to imagine evil skulking between the caravans, but it wasn't easy with such bright light.

Before she went inside, she noticed two laughing people approaching.

'Afternoon, Detective,' said Tim.

Percy was with him. He gave her a bashful smile.

'Afternoon, gents,' replied Ashley. 'Any developments?'

'No, I was just saying how I prefer it quiet. There'll be fewer toilets to unblock. Percy reckons the opposite will be true.'

Ashley laughed out loud at the thought of the remaining holidaymakers being very nervous. Maybe Percy did have hidden qualities.

Not everyone was chuckling, though. They all turned towards the shouting, which was coming from Reception. Ashley strode over and opened the door.

'You're getting fuck all, cos he pays me fuck all.'

'It's work experience.'

'What is this? 1990? It's child exploitation.'

'You're an adult. Go if you don't want to be here.'

A woman who Ashley hadn't seen before shook her head at Hamilton, stomped into Percy's office, and slammed the door.

An exasperated and confused Percy had followed Ashley in.

'See what I have to work with?' he said.

'He's just trying to bone my mum again.' Hamilton pointed a finger in Percy's direction. 'He doesn't know she has a boyfriend.'

Percy's face turned a strange purple colour.

'You're fired.'

'How can you fire me if I'm not paid anything?'

'Enough!' said Ashley. 'Percy, I need another look at your CCTV.'

'Which one? They're all over the site.'

'Gail said most were vandalised.'

Percy licked his lips.

'Some are. There's four or five left. Here, outside the public toilets, the play park, the bar. Oh, there was another one near Gold, which got smashed a few weeks ago. You'll need to see Gail or Valerie to work the machine.'

'Was that Valerie?'

'No, that's Marie. Gail and Val are in London at a show. Back tomorrow.'

'Don't you know how to view it?'

'Nope.'

Ashley bared her teeth in disgust.

'I do,' said Hamilton.

'You do?' said Ashley and Percy, perfectly synchronised.

'Of course.'

'Maybe you should watch him, Percy. Learn something,' said Ashley.

They stood behind Hamilton, who cracked his fingers theatrically.

'When and where do you want?'

'There's been a guy walking around who doesn't live here. Kind of mysterious bloke in a hat.'

'The cowboy?'

'Yeah. You know him?'

'I don't know him, but he came in here for a chat.'

'Who was he?'

'Said he was a friend of Glory's and she'd recommended the site. I told him where her lodge was.'

'When was this?'

'A few days ago.'

'Then he'll be on your CCTV.'

'Of course. Reception is the only place where the coverage and quality are excellent. Percy's more worried about his safe being burgled than his customers getting robbed.'

'That's not true.'

'Quiet, Percy. Can you search for him, please, Hamilton?' asked Ashley.

After a few minutes of lightning-speed mouse-work, which even Percy's eyes widened at, Hamilton leaned back. They watched a man walk into the office. He kept his hat on. Even observing him through the camera lens, Ashley could tell he had an air about him. His hat was angled in just the right way to keep his face in shadow.

'Can you describe his manner?' she asked.

'Kinda cool and charming. Spoke like a movie star.'

'Did he have an American accent?' asked Percy.

'Hmm, I don't know. I think there's a woman on Bronze who sounds American. His voice was quiet, but it sounded more normal.'

'What do you mean, normal?'

'I wouldn't say he had any kind of accent.'

'Was he British?'

Hamilton shrugged. 'Probably.'

'Did he ask for anyone or anything else?'

'He asked a lot of questions. Opening times, how busy we were, access to the site, security, that sort of thing. In the end, it felt like a grilling, so I passed him a brochure. He came back a few hours later and wanted Glory's home address. Said her lodge was shut up, so he hadn't spoken to her. He didn't have Glory's details on him, but he wanted to send her flowers.'

'Please tell me you didn't give it to him,' said Ashley.

'No, I'm not daft. They taught us about data protection at school.'

'Good.'

'I gave him her mobile number instead so he could ring and thank her.'

'You didn't,' whispered Percy.

'I liked him. My grandad had similar crinkly eyes!'

'That's a criminal offence, Hamilton.'

'He said they were close friends!'

'Then he'd already have her phone number, and he'd know her address, wouldn't he?' asked Ashley.

It was Hamilton's turn to have a red face. His reply was barely audible.

'Oh, dear.'

70

Ashley drove down to Barry at Diamond. He looked pensive.

'You okay?' she asked.

'This case is ruining some of my happiest memories. My nanna had a caravan on a similar site. It was a respite from my mother when I visited her.'

Ashley kept a blank face, but she was intrigued. Barry never mentioned his family, except a sibling who had a good job in Manchester.

'Does she still have it?'

'No, lengthy story, but my mum died, Dad had long gone, and Nanna had to raise me and my brother. She couldn't afford it to keep it on.'

'I'm sorry.'

'Don't be. She was brilliant. Every day with her and Gramps was a holiday after my mother's chaos.'

'Do you still see her?'

'Yes, all the time. I'd be lost without her.'

Ashley wasn't sure how to reply to that, so she told him about the Cowboy. Barry's eyes widened. Then he laughed when she mentioned Hamilton giving out Glory's details.

'That lad's a keeper.'

'To be fair, he whizzed round the computer. I suspect he'd be a decent employee with a bit of training, assuming his attitude changed at the same time. He's going to have a hunt through their coverage from when we think Jasmine was killed. I get the impression he watches it because he's bored.'

'Haven't we already seen all the CCTV?'

'Yes, but he'll be aware of what's unusual and what isn't, like vans going in when they aren't supposed to. He also told me something interesting.'

'Oh, yeah?'

'The CCTV in Diamond was vandalised long ago.'

'Yeah, we know that.'

'Yes, but the next section, Gold, had a camera that led to an area where the fence isn't too hard to climb over. That one was broken recently.'

'Which is about the time this cowboy fella showed up.'

'Yeah.'

'We're miles off the pace,' said Barry with a shake of his head. 'There's something sinister going on. What sort of person would want to knock off everyone in Diamond?'

'This mysterious guy walking around with his hat on has me really concerned.'

'Assassin or psycho?'

'Perhaps both, killing to order.'

'Maybe Abraham does have Alzheimer's or something similar and has lost his mind. When he suspected Elizabeth of cheating, he had her followed and found out about Dennis.'

'So, he hired a professional to dispatch all Dennis's ex-girlfriends, before an amateur attempt at smoking Dennis himself?'

Barry smiled. 'CPS wouldn't be too keen on that hypothesis.

Especially when we say he killed Alfie Hook because he and Dennis were friends.'

Ashley groaned as the conundrum made her brain hurt.

'Could Alfie have been murdered to confuse us?'

Barry whistled.

'Now that would be ruthless, although if you want to come over and speak to Jennifer, the scary knife lady, it might not be as mad an idea as you think.'

Barry escorted Ashley over to a folding table that had been set up outside Barry's scorched lodge. The rear window was smashed, and flames had licked up and discoloured the metal panels, but the damage didn't seem extensive. Ashley peered through the hole and saw the fire-damaged upholstery and carpets and the blackened ceiling. The eye-stinging stench of burnt plastic was ubiquitous to all the arsons she'd attended.

Ashley shivered despite the hot sun beating down on her back.

She turned to the table. Gerald and a short woman had just taken their hoods and masks off.

'Morning, Gerald,' said Ashley. 'We're keeping you and your team busy.'

'No, you're killing me. It's lucky I'm young and fit. Now, this fire tells quite a story, and we've enjoyed coming to our conclusions. This is Jennifer, by the way. She's the fire investigator and also a bit of a knife aficionado. She'll give you the rundown.'

Jennifer smiled and shook Ashley's hand. She had large front teeth and wide blue eyes, making Ashley think of Bugs Bunny's pretty girlfriend, Lola.

'Hi,' she said. 'We don't believe this blaze was a serious attempt to kill anyone. So, unless it was children or someone who doesn't know much about how things burn, I would say it was meant to scare.'

Ashley thought of Willy, but surely he'd be at school during the week.

'If you look at this exhibit here...' Jennifer raised a bag with some broken glass in it. 'Notice the curvature of the container that held the petrol. It's thin glass and fairly small. Think 500ml.'

'Like a pint bottle,' said Barry.

'Exactly, which is a traditional Molotov cocktail delivery system for this kind of attack, even though glass bottles of milk are rare now. The windows on the lodge are toughened. Even thrown with force, the bottle would just break outside and set the window on fire.'

'Definitely petrol?' asked Ashley.

'It burned like petrol. You can still smell it.'

'They broke the window first,' said Barry.

Jennifer turned her mesmerising eyes on Barry and beamed at him.

'Excellent. We think they threw a large flat ornamental stone with some force. We found it inside. The person was strong because the object ended up behind the sofa on the other side of the room. Then they chucked the bomb in, which smashed on the coffee table. The petrol ignited, burning the laminate flooring but not setting it on fire. The liquid splashed the sofa, because it's also burnt, but they're fire-resistant nowadays, so, again, once the petrol was consumed, it would merely smoulder.'

'We don't think there was much accelerant in the bottle,' said Gerald.

'So, even if Dennis had been in the room, it's unlikely he would have perished.'

Jennifer gave Barry another enormous grin.

'Correct! The only risk of death was if he'd been hit by the stone.'

Barry laughed, which made Jennifer giggle, too.

'It's a warning,' said Ashley.

'Yes, that seems likely. It could have been an insurance job, but if it were, it was a poor one because, while it's not habitable, the damage is mostly superficial. We've taken a video of the surrounding areas for footprints or dropped items, which we'll compare to the recording Gerald took for the analysis of Jasmine's death, but there's nothing obvious. The evidence is plain to see, anyway.'

'Any chance of prints or DNA on the stone?'

'Perhaps DNA.'

Ashley glanced around. The arsonist could have easily escaped through the trees before the police came back, and Dennis was the only one left on Diamond. Two residents were dead, and the other five had gone home.

'Which begs me to ask who would want to scare Dennis, but not kill him like the others?' asked Ashley, thinking out loud.

'That's a good question,' said Jennifer. 'It might appear at first glance as a bodge job, but if it's to frighten Dennis, then it's sophisticated. The final part of the incident is the most exciting. For me at least.'

Jennifer's eyes glistened as she held up another bag with a black knife handle in it.

'This,' she said, grin widening, 'is a Grant & Gavin Hawk Deadlock. It's the perfect hitman's blade.'

71

Ashley took the evidence bag and felt the weight of the weapon. It was a solid bit of kit. She looked at the mechanism on the side.

'It's a flick knife.'

'Yes, but not just any flick knife. These babies retail at well over a thousand dollars. This is a Deadlock model C. They only came out two years ago.'

'They're American?'

'Americans call them OTF knives. Out the front. Useful, depending on what you want it for. If, as you're starting to suspect, you have a professional killer on your hands, this is the perfect weapon.'

'I suppose you could approach a victim with it in your hand, and they wouldn't see you were armed.'

'Exactly. Most OTFs have the same problem. The blade comes out the front, but the mechanism is inside, giving play in the blade. That makes it weak. Not with a Grant and Gavin Hawk blade. No play at all, and they're sharp as hell.'

'I was telling Jennifer about Alfie Hook's passing,' said Gerald.

'She read online he was stabbed but expected the weapon to be from a kitchen. I'm guessing this is the tool that killed Alfie.'

Ashley glanced back at the lodge.

'And the knife was in Dennis's lounge?'

'Yes. It could have been thrown in with the flaming bottle to incriminate him,' said Gerald.

'More cunning.'

'Yeah, but Jennifer said this one costs a grand. It's the type of thing someone would cherish. Would they lob it in and leave it behind?'

'A valid point. A rich person might. Although we found it on the floor near the television in the middle of the room, which is an odd place.'

'It could have fallen out of Dennis's pocket as he ran away.'

'If it wasn't thrown in, then it had to be his knife because he lives alone,' said Barry.

'Come on,' said Ashley 'Dennis isn't daft. What sort of idiot would be so careless with a murder weapon? We've been all over him. There's no way it was in the lodge before because CSI searched here. It would even be risky bringing it back into their home when the police were still around.'

'We have form for coming back for second looks,' said Gerald.

'Surely you'd bury it somewhere if you couldn't bear to part with it.'

'Gerald can test the knife, anyway,' said Jennifer. 'He might have some success with that. One of the features of these types of knives is the hole in the front of the handle for the knife to come out. All manner of things collect in there. Dirt, fluff, lint and potentially specks of blood. The eject mechanism means if you dismantle them to clean the insides, they can be hard to put back together, so people don't bother. Although in this case it's easier because the tool is so well built.'

'An expert wouldn't struggle,' said Barry.

'Precisely,' said Jennifer with another smile.

'And they're American made and desirable,' stated Ashley.

'Yes, even with the high price, there's a waiting list.'

'A moneyed person who used to live in America springs to mind,' said Barry.

Gerald held the evidence bag with the knife inside up to the light.

'We might have luck tomorrow testing it regardless,' said Gerald. 'I think I can see blood on the handle.'

72

Ashley decided it was even more unlikely Dennis would leave blood on the murder weapon and then place it in the middle of his lounge for the police to find. Someone had thrown that knife in to incriminate him. More sneaky tactics designed to obscure and confuse.

She took her phone out and tried Dennis's number. To her surprise, he answered.

'Dennis speaking.'

Ashley smiled at him giving up the pretence of using Deniz.

'Hey, Dennis. Sergeant Knight here.'

Ashley heard him softly curse.

'Okay, I'm sorry for driving off,' he said.

'Why did you leave? You knew we'd need to talk it through with you.'

'I'm scared. I might have died if I'd been asleep.'

'We believe the intention was to scare, not kill. There wasn't that much accelerant used, and you have little combustible material in your lodge. Do you have an idea who did it?'

'It's gotta be Elizabeth's partner. She said he's wealthy and powerful.'

'Didn't you consider playing around with the girlfriend of someone that rich to be dangerous? Why give yourself the aggro? Seems you were busy enough without her.'

'Life was different with Elizabeth. I wanted to spend all my time with her, but that horrible old git stopped her going out. Abraham's a control freak. It's domestic abuse. I read about it. She's not allowed friends or money, and he keeps her stuck in that big house. I bet he's responsible for killing Pip and Jasmine.'

'Why would he do that?'

'To warn me. Leave his woman alone.'

A cheer erupted in the background from Dennis's end of the line while Ashley was digesting his theory. Abraham killing Jasmine and Pip made no sense to her. Surely, it would have been easier and more satisfying simply to kill Dennis.

There was another roar from down the phone.

'Are you in a betting shop?' she asked.

'Somewhere I hope my luck might change.'

'We need to talk to you right away.'

'I won't be back there until all this is over. I don't know what my plans are. When I rang Elizabeth and told her what happened, she said she never wants to speak to me again. I thought we loved each other.'

Ashley heard emotion in Dennis's voice that hadn't been present before. Love came easily for Dennis at Paradise, but Elizabeth hadn't come running when he clicked his fingers.

This time oohs came down the line, and Dennis swore.

'Will you return to live with Cecil?' she asked.

'Yes, I can't afford a hotel until the first of next month. Trust me, I have no choice.'

Ashley was concerned for Dennis's safety and well-being. If

she warned him Cecil might not want him there, though, he might disappear. If he went back to Cecil's house tonight, that was great because Dennis had to be interviewed about why that knife was in his lodge. They probably had enough to hold him until the blood was checked if he was less than forthcoming, but people with no money rarely vanished for long.

'Will you go into one of the Sheffield police stations to give a statement?'

'What for?'

'There's been a serious arson incident. We have procedures to follow. If you're not careful, there'll be an arrest warrant with your name on it.'

'I'm the victim. I've been inconvenienced enough. Look, I've gotta go.'

Ashley stared incredulously at her phone, having been cut off. She almost dropped it when it rang again.

'Knight speaking.'

'Hi, Ash. It's Sal. We think Dennis is in the Hillsborough area of Sheffield if that means anything to you.'

Ashley racked her brain, having lived not far from the area.

'I've just spoken to him. It sounded as if he was in a bookmaker's. Wait a minute. Is there a casino in the vicinity? I'll bet he's there. If we nab him inside or outside, it'll save us waiting until he shows up at his stepfather's.'

'Is he likely to visit Cecil?'

'Yes, that's what he said. Ring the detective team in Sheffield, who've been assisting at their end, and ask them about the casino. If they find him, they can take him to the closest nick with a custody suite. I'm heading over to King's Lynn now to see Glory. Then I'm probably going to Sheffield. Do you know how Scott got on when he visited Pip's husband?'

'He was in earlier and wants you to call him. Rupert had a medical event the night he was told his wife had been killed.'

'That doesn't sound good.'

'No, Scott said he's visiting another client, but his mobile will be on.'

'Has the team reached the other owners from Diamond?'

'Hans and Helga are on their way to the Lake District. Verne and Bertie have friends in London and are going to stay with them for a while. They leave tomorrow. Neither couple had heard about Dennis's lodge being torched. Their responses were authentic according to Bee and Jan. Verne and Bertie's paranoia levels were off the scale now they'd thought about things.'

'Okay, at least they're all out of the way. That just leaves Glory.'

'Yes. I'll let you know when I've liaised with Sheffield police. If Dennis isn't at a casino, shall I ask them to wait at Cecil's place for him?'

Ashley took a moment to think. 'I'm worried about spooking Dennis. He seemed close to the edge when I spoke to him.'

'I agree. And if he's involved, there's no telling what he might do.'

73

Ashley got into Barry's car and took her phone out so she could make some calls while he drove. She was about to ring Scott but stopped because her mind kept coming back to the mystery man.

'I don't like the sound of the Cowboy,' she said.

'I have to agree it's an unwelcome complication.'

'Abraham told us he lived in the States for many years. Perhaps he used this cowboy guy over there in the past. Now he's brought him here to do his dirty work.'

'Which is killing shitloads of loosely connected people?'

'Good point. One of whom might have been a suicide months ago.'

'He's probably just a nosey sod.'

'No, he's been asking after Glory.' Ashley rubbed her eyes. 'I couldn't sleep last night with the hired-gun angle going through my head.'

'Get real. Would a highly paid contract killer come over for this kind of performance?'

'You've answered your own question. Yes, enough money buys anything you need.'

'But whoever did this is familiar with the area. They know the caravan park well, or they wouldn't have got away with it.'

'Which means we need to know who the Cowboy is, *and* who's been helping him.'

'Perhaps he's a PI.'

'That's not a bad idea. Abraham was suspicious of Elizabeth and asked him over to check up on her. Maybe he trusts him, having worked together in the past in America.'

'Then why is he interested in Glory?'

'He must know something we don't.'

'That's why Abraham flew him over. He's better than us.'

Ashley blew a raspberry at Barry.

'Don't fret, Hoops.'

'Piss off.'

'Chill. We're getting there. Remember, the villains have no paperwork to complete or rules to follow. It's not even been a week since we got involved. Someone could have been planning this for months.'

'True. It's possible Abraham already had this guy over here doing other dirty work.'

Ashley wondered if Abraham would fess up if she challenged him about the Cowboy. First, they urgently needed to talk to Glory.

The traffic was light heading away from the coast, so they made good progress. Ashley rang Scott.

'Hi, Ashley. Thanks for calling. No real news to report. King's Lynn police informed Pip's husband. He told them to leave, but to let him know when the body was at the mortuary. Apparently, he had a medical event after they'd gone. It could be a stroke. He managed to ring for an ambulance, which took him to The Queen Elizabeth Hospital. I rang them just now, and he's just regained consciousness. He's in the ICU.'

'How did you get on with Jasmine's son?'

'Even over the phone, he was another cold fish. I half wondered if he was responsible, but he was in Frankfurt with work. He asked me to email him the details over, saying something like that was bound to happen with her lifestyle.'

'Is he sorting out the funeral?'

'No idea. He said he wasn't sure when he'll be back. I'll call him as soon as we release the body. How's the investigation going?'

'It's a complicated case, but I think we're finally closing in on the people involved. Dennis Turner seems to be at the heart of it. Either someone's setting him up, or he's taking part by choice. One of the other owners, Glory, has become another person of interest with questions to answer.'

'Okay. I read the file notes. It really does seem like the MO of a professional killer. Makes you wonder what they were doing in Hunstanton.'

'Assassins need a break, too.'

Scott laughed.

'Maybe he's having a busman's holiday,' he said. 'I reckon whoever it is will be from around these parts. And it's interesting you mention Glory's name, who used to live here many years ago. Some people can hold grudges, even for decades. All the people in this case are aged forties upwards, so that fits.'

'I suppose people who buy in these places tend to be at least middle-aged, but a historic connection is definitely a possibility. I'll ask the crew at OCC to look into it.'

'I'm almost at the office now, so I'll have a chat to whoever's in and get them to do a full check on Glory and further look into Dennis's history.'

'Glory is a bit older than most of her neighbours, but having a search into her background might tell us where she's lived and what she's been up to. Let's hope Glory talks, because she's been a closed book up to now.'

There was a pause on the line.

'When I think of a hitman or woman running around a caravan park, fox and henhouse spring to mind.'

Ashley weighed his words as they said goodbye, and she cut the call.

'Barry. You strike me as a man who watches a lot of American movies with killing in them.'

'What makes you say that?'

'Do you?'

Barry shifted in his seat.

'Yeah, a few.'

'It's the land of the contract killer, right? There are guns all over the place. There's a long history, from *The Godfather* to Jimmy Hoffa. Concrete overcoats, cheese wire, car bombs, stiletto blades. What if Glory is a hired gun?'

'You don't get many female contract killers.'

'God, you men can be so stupid.'

'I wasn't being sexist. You just don't.'

'Remember, the only contract killers we know about are the ones we catch. Haven't you considered women might just be better at evading justice?'

Barry's lip curled, but he struggled for a reply.

'Most killers are male because more men are criminals,' he finally said without conviction. 'They are also more violent, driven by testosterone.'

'That's true. You only have to see the make up of our prison population to understand that. Maybe testosterone makes killers impulsive, which leads to their capture.'

'We've been doing this long enough to know the person responsible could be anyone, but the odds are it's a man.'

'Did Glory appear a psychopathic serial killer to you?'

'Nope.'

'That's another thing. Being a psycho would help with the mental side of things, but hired killing is a business. Professionalism is needed. If the murderer sees it as a job, they might be able to go about their lives with a relatively free conscience.'

'And if they did it for a long time...'

'They'd be experts. Glory is in her early sixties and this cowboy is apparently older too.'

'But it's so difficult to get away with murder in this country,' said Barry. 'The UK is covered with cameras, both CCTV and number-plate recognition. MIT has the use of the latest technology and access to banks, mobile-phone companies and social media accounts. The HOLMES computer is constantly making connections for us to follow up on.'

'Yes, but that all takes time, meaning someone could be in and out.'

'I suppose so. America is a much larger place, with state border lines and less surveillance.'

'So, if our killer is a professional, their contract might be complete, which means...'

'They'll be out of here.'

'Yes, hang on.'

Ashley grabbed her mobile and called Michelle, the pathologist.

'Afternoon, Ash.'

'Hi, Michelle. Do you reckon you could give me the email or phone number of your expert from Harvard? I want to ask him about contract killings in the States.'

'I'll forward Cal's email to you. He's one of their foremost experts on that sort of thing, having helped the Chicago and Detroit police forces for a while.'

'Brilliant. Let's catch up for a drink soon.'

'Yeah, are you with the new guy?'

'No, sadly, I'm stuck with Barry.' Ashley put her Mr T voice on. 'Which obviously sucks really bad.'

Barry mock scowled as Ashley finished the call.

'Very funny,' he said. 'Here we are. Ouse Avenue.'

Barry pulled up in front of a row of small terraced houses, some of which were run-down.

'Which number?'

'Two. It's on the right at the end.'

They were both gawking at the shabby house with the peeling door when an upstairs light blinked on.

'Not the type of place I imagined Glory living,' said Ashley. 'The devious sod told me she had a flat.'

'Come on,' said Barry as they left their vehicle.

'You had a tussle with Glory when Pip was trying to attack her. She seemed a bit of a handful,' said Ashley, following him to the door.

Barry nodded. 'I think she deliberately poked a nerve because my shoulder ached for a few days after, and I didn't have control of her.'

'Met your match?'

'I wasn't prepared for a fight, that's all.'

'Did she feel strong?'

Barry glanced at Ashley.

'She was hard as iron.'

74

Ashley raised her hand to press the doorbell, then paused, wondering whether they needed backup. She caught movement out of the corner of her eye and glanced across to the houses opposite, but no curtains were twitching. A car screeched away much further up the road.

Ashley gave the doorbell a quick ring, then she and Barry took a step away as they heard heavy footsteps from inside. The door creaked open like something from a horror film.

It revealed a small cheerful chap in a cheap grey suit.

'Greetings, I'll have to fix that. Can I help?'

'We're after the person who lives here.'

'The place is vacant now.'

Ashley peered past him down the empty hall.

'When did they move out?'

'I met the lady here this morning to take the keys off her.'

'What was her name?'

'What's this about?'

Ashley and Barry showed their warrants.

'Do you have ID?' asked Barry.

The man gave them a crumpled business card. Chris Hain. Lettings manager.

'We want to speak to the tenant, Glory,' said Ashley.

'If you mean Gloria Trubell, she's gone. She said she'd be heading home soon.'

'Do you know where home is?'

'She didn't say.'

'What does she look like?'

'Gloria? I met her four or five times. Check-ups on the house and once to give her the keys and once to take them back. I thought she was a pensioner at first. Grey hair, few wrinkles, no make-up, but she exuded good health and was often in tight sportswear. My boss reckoned that he'd— Sorry.'

'We get the picture,' said Barry. 'Did she pay monthly through the bank?'

The letting agent shrugged. 'No. She paid cash. A year up front.'

'You must have taken ID and references.'

The man smiled. 'What's she done?'

'It doesn't matter what,' said Barry with a lowered voice. 'I'm going to need you to be more helpful. ID and references?'

'Yes, I've just been through her file to close it. She provided a driving licence, although it was old.'

'How old?'

'If I remember right, the person in the photograph had brown hair and no wrinkles. She'd been living abroad.'

'References?'

'No, she paid extra because she wanted a place sorted quickly. Her husband had been in a car accident and was at the Queen Elizabeth, so she was desperate. I saw the paperwork for him, so it wasn't a lie. Although I did notice he had a different surname.'

Ashley didn't bother to ask whose pocket the extra cash went in.

'Can you remember what it was?'

'Sorry. She was a great tenant. The house is spotless and smells incredibly clean. I think she's painted as well.'

Ashley's phone rang again. She answered it while Barry took details of the shady letting agent.

'Hi, Ems. What's going on?'

'South Yorks police attended the local casino, but he wasn't there. They spoke to a manager. Customers need to sign up because all purchases, including buying chips to gamble, are made through a membership-card system. She checked if he'd been in, and he had. Dennis was there for an hour and spent over two hundred quid.'

'Lost two hundred?'

'He didn't cash any chips in, so yes, that's likely. We have a BOLO for him and his car, but he hasn't triggered any cameras so far.'

Ashley gave her the news about Glory Trubell's house.

'It sounds as if Glory's about to play her last card as well.'

'Yes, let's organise a BOLO for her, too. We need a warrant to get her lodge searched. Anything from the background checks?'

'Sal's been cursing, so I assume that's not promising. I'll put him on.'

'Hey, Ash,' said Sal. 'Glory's a bit of a ghost. I found her driving licence, but it's not been updated for over thirty years. I've checked the electoral register. She's not on it and hasn't been for decades. No tickets, no crimes. She's been out of the country for ages, at least under that name.'

'I bet she's been living in America. Try Interpol and Europol.'

'You reckon she's the killer?'

'I'm considering it.'

'Could she have killed all of them?'

'I'm not sure. Let's forget about who or why, and focus on how they were done.'

'They're all professional hits except for the fire. Dennis escaped. There were two police units nearby anyway, so he was always likely to survive.'

'That's my point. She didn't know if he was in it or not. I think she just torched it.'

'To warn him?'

'No, to destroy it. I reckon Dennis also had a fling with her, but she didn't take being dumped as well as the others. She probably knows he's a gambling addict and cash is tight.'

Sal caught up fast.

'It would have been messy to storm the lodge and kill him, so she scares him and makes his place unliveable. You're right. Jesus! So sly.'

Sal didn't need to say what that meant. It was a clever ruse making Dennis's lodge uninhabitable.

Now he only had one place to go. And Glory would know that too.

75

Ashley waited for Barry to finish with the letting agent, who swiftly departed. She gave Barry a smile.

'Fancy a road trip?'

'Sheffield?'

'Yep.'

'How far is it?'

'Bit over two hours from here. I want to be in the thick of things. If we go to Cecil Dowd's house, we can interview him and Dennis.'

'Dennis, who might have dropped the murder weapon on the lodge floor.'

'That's the one. You're right. It's best to get Cecil out of there.'

Ashley's phone beeped. It was a text from Kettle.

Ring me. Extreme caution.

She showed Barry.

'That doesn't sound good. We might need an ARV as a minimum, but I'm wondering if it's more Dennis who's at risk than us.'

'You believe either Glory or the Cowboy will be waiting for him?'

'It makes sense. Maybe both. We need to speak to Cecil and Dennis face to face but it's also our job to protect the public, remember?'

'Oh, yeah. I keep forgetting that. I'll check on my phone for the latest traffic. There's a shop over there. We'll want drinks for the journey.'

Barry headed over to the store, which was called Polska, while Ashley checked her phone and saw the email from Michelle with the Harvard professor's details on it. She spent a few minutes composing a message to Cal Johns explaining what she was interested in and included the vague description of the Cowboy who numerous people had seen at Paradise.

After some consideration, Ashley added they were investigating a case where a flick knife, garrotte, staged suicide and a drowning were used as methods of dispatch. She also asked him about the occurrence of female contract killers, then hit send. After checking her watch, she realised he'd be in bed with the time difference.

As they drove away, Ashley rang Kettle, who would be running the operation back at OCC. He was up to speed on the Dennis situation.

'So,' he said. 'Dennis has gambled his last few coins, and now he's probably going to Cecil's. You think he's been set up? It wouldn't have been easy to attack Dennis in a locked lodge with police at the park, so the killer has flushed him out with only one place to go.'

'That's right, but Cecil has explained he doesn't want him back in the house.'

'Okay. Zara looked into Cecil's past in case there was anything dubious there, but as politicians go, he was genuine and squeaky clean.'

'Good to know.'

'What's Dennis's mental state?'

'Fragile.'

'And Glory has vanished and is involved somehow?'

'Yes. She's vacated her rented house in King's Lynn. You could smell the bleach and fresh paint from outside.'

'Reception gave us the key for her caravan,' said Kettle. 'It's also spotless. I'd be surprised if we can't get DNA out of it, but it'll take time, which it sounds like we don't have.'

Ashley thought for a moment. DNA might be the difference between a loose charge and a concrete conviction.

'Do you remember the argument where Barry and I separated her and Pip?'

'I read the report.'

'They were drinking, and Pip's van was a bit of a mess. Check the prints and residue CSI would have taken from the wine glasses, or perhaps from the door handles and frames. If you exclude Pip's markers, what's remaining could be Glory's.'

'I'll get someone on it. We've got Pip's details in the machine. The Communication Centre has been prepared and will link in with Sheffield. What does the response team up there need to consider?'

'I'm heading over with Barry, but it's likely we won't arrive in time, so they'll need to check in with me via mobile if they have questions. Right now, it makes sense for them to head to Cecil's house immediately and take Cecil to a police station. That way, he's safe. It feels to me like this is the finale.'

'Which plays out how?'

'Glory kills Dennis, taking her final revenge, then heads back to America. She'll believe her tracks are covered so she can escape. Who knows where or who the Cowboy is, but, if he's involved and brilliant at his job, he'll be looking to disappear. It's still possible Dennis is involved.'

'Okay, well, I have some concerning intel. The National Crime Agency have been picking up some traffic on the dark web over the last few months around rifles.'

'That's concerning.'

'Someone's been offering good money both for guns and ammo. It sounds like the order has been fulfilled.'

'Bloody hell.'

'Yes, it could be the gunfight at the OK Corral.'

'I was wondering about an armed response vehicle anyway, but that might not be enough if Glory, or anyone else for that matter, has bought a gun. They're going to need a tactical firearms unit if a rifle is in play.'

'I've already arranged for an ARV. Hang on, Ash.'

Ashley could hear an officer speaking to Kettle in the background. He came back on the line.

'Dennis's Toyota Rav4 is on the move, triggering a camera quite a way from the casino. He must be keeping off the main roads. We've got all eyes searching for him, multiple vehicles heading in his direction.'

'We have to assume he's making his way to Cecil's house. What's his ETA there?'

There was a pause, with more chatter in the background. Kettle must have been talking to Control up in Sheffield.

'Traffic is building with rush hour, but he's close. Approx six minutes.'

'How long for the ARV?'

'Sixteen minutes.'

'Brilliant. Tactical?'

'Nowhere near. We can get a marked car there much quicker. In fact, there's one only five minutes away.'

'They'll have to race in there, knock on the door, grab Cecil, and leave in case someone with a gun shows up. Other units should stay in the area if they arrive, but keep clear of the road until armed response is in position. It could be dangerous as hell for the team that collects Cecil. The killer could be waiting.'

Kettle growled down the phone, then she heard him giving orders.

Barry slowed their vehicle for stationary traffic ahead, and they came to a halt.

'What's the satnav say about our arrival time?' she asked.

'We should arrive by midnight.'

'What?'

'It's not quite that bad, but there are numerous tailbacks. Whatever happens in Sheffield will be occurring without us.'

'You still there, Ashley?' asked Kettle.

'Yes, sir. I'm going to pull over so we can concentrate. We're too far away to be of any use otherwise. I've got a decent signal here.'

'Great idea.'

'I'll ring Dennis now. He picked up to me earlier, so he might answer. Hopefully, he'll stop or at least slow down so the first unit has time to collect Cecil.'

'Would making him suspicious aggravate things?'

'I'm going to ask him about Glory. Imply something's not adding up and see what he has to say.'

Kettle was quiet for a few seconds.

'Okay, give it a go.'

Ashley cut the call to Kettle and rang Dennis. She was about to hang up when he answered. She put him on speaker.

'What do you want?'

'I had a question. Where are you?'

'I'm driving to Cecil's house.'

'Can you pull over, please, so there's no danger of you crashing? I've got a few questions about Glory. Just a few minutes, then I'll leave you alone.'

Dennis tutted, but she could hear the sound of an indicator.

'Make it quick. I barely have enough fuel to get back.'

'We've had some confusing information around Glory. How well do you know her?'

'Reasonably well. We had the odd chat. Sometimes jogged together. Had a few drinks if we saw each other in the clubhouse bar. I think she fancied me.'

'Did you like her?'

'Are you asking if I had sex with her?'

'Yes.'

'Okay, yes. Once. It was unusual, but enjoyable.'

'In what way?'

'Intense. She was in fantastic shape, but the whole experience was cold. You know those movies where there's a robot sex doll?'

Ashley sensed Barry grinning next to her.

'It was like that. Effective but emotionless.'

'Why didn't you see her again?'

'I'd been seeing Elizabeth on and off, but she was messing me about, and I hadn't seen her for weeks. Glory came around, and we did the deed, but Elizabeth turned up as she was leaving. I pretended Glory was just being neighbourly, but Elizabeth was suspicious. It made her keener for a bit. A few days later, Glory popped over to take me for lunch. I declined, because Elizabeth and I were giving it another go.'

'How did she take it?'

'Again, it was weird. Glory asked if there was anything she could do to change my mind but her voice was pretty emotionless. I said no, and she just said it was a real shame.'

'Right. I don't suppose you know where she lived before the lodge.'

'Yeah, King's Lynn. Ouse Avenue. Said she and her husband bought it as a bolthole twenty years ago. I thought she'd live in a posh area. She reckoned they had a lodge at Heacham before and spent most of their time there. They were away a lot on business, until her husband got hurt.'

It was more half-truths and lies from Glory. Her other half in the coma had slipped to the back of Ashley's mind.

'Excellent,' she said. 'That's helpful. It's sad about her husband. Were they happy?'

'They were before his accident, and she still cared. She visited him all the time, so she was only at Paradise half the week.'

'That's King's Lynn hospital, isn't it?'

'I assume so. Look, I'm tired and hungry. Can I go?'

Ashley thought about the fact they hadn't been able to get hold of Cecil. She didn't want to spook Dennis while he was in his car in case he drove elsewhere.

'Dennis. Be careful, okay. We don't really know what's going on.'

'Sure.'

Ashley finished the call to Dennis and rang Kettle back.

'Ashley,' he answered.

'Dennis stopped while I spoke to him. He's moving again.'

'Yes, his vehicle has been located. He has an unmarked car behind him. You've bought us five minutes. Well done. Does he sound unstable?'

'Not at all. Have the officers got Cecil Dowd out?'

'They're at the door now.'

76

PC Jane Scoffings braced herself as the police estate car screeched to a halt fifty metres from Cecil Dowd's property. She glanced up the steeply sloped street. There were only half a dozen cars and a van in sight. Jane had worked in Sheffield for fifteen years and five before in Rotherham. She loved her job and lived for days like these.

The woman next to her, Daniella, was a probationer. Admittedly near the end of her two years of training, and she'd driven well to arrive so quickly, but Jane noticed how hard Daniella gripped the steering wheel.

Stumperlowe was a nightmare location for the police. It was one of the nicest areas in Sheffield, but was on a hillside like most of the city. The roads wound around and circled back. Gardens were massive. Entrances often gated. There were hiding places everywhere. Jane had chased two teenage burglars out of a property years ago. They'd run down the hill through people's gardens and easily given her the slip, and she'd been a lot fitter then.

'Park at the entrance,' she said to Daniella, who did, but almost stalled the engine.

Jane focused. The road to the left had a small white Berlingo van parked a hundred metres up. On the right was a red estate car, which a grey-haired man was getting into. She peered back at the house.

A wide, open drive led to a large modern building with pillars. It resembled a Spanish hacienda more than a British home. There were huge double doors in the middle of the property. The lights were on upstairs and downstairs.

'Drive in and park right outside the front door.'

'We're knocking now,' said Jane to Control.

She put the radio down.

'Okay, Daniella. We grab him, escort him into the back of the car, and leave.'

Jane opened her door, then opened the rear door on her side so she could shove Cecil straight in. Daniella had her PAVA spray in her hand. She pressed the doorbell. Jane felt her pulse pick up and imagined the seconds until Dennis arrived were racing along at the same pace. She adjusted her stab vest, stepped forward and tried the door handle. It opened and she pushed it wide.

'Mr Dowd, police!' she bellowed.

Jane advanced inside. The door to her left was ajar. She drew her Taser and edged towards it. A sonorous voice echoed from elsewhere in the property. A familiar crime scene smell filled her nostrils. Steeling herself, she nudged the door fully open with her boot, to reveal a red puddle. She poked her head into the room.

Jane pressed talk on her radio.

'IC1, elderly male, found in lounge armchair, left of house, surrounded by blood. Two gunshot wounds. Extremely deceased.'

Jane shuffled backwards. Her and Daniella's eyes flicked up at the ceiling as they heard a thud above them. Their ears strained. Their noses twitched at the scents of death that permeated the air. There was a further slight creak a little distance from the thud.

Jane whispered into her radio.

'There's someone here.'

The controller's reply was instant.

'Get out of there.'

Daniella was already outside. Jane not far behind.

77

Dennis checked his rear-view mirror. The silver car was still behind him. They'd dropped back a bit, but he was definitely being followed. Dennis didn't care. The time for running was over. He was even looking forward to seeing Cecil. The old fart was rude, but at least he was consistent. He often paid for the odd takeaway for them to share, too.

Who knew? Maybe in a different world they could have been friends. Dennis chuckled to himself, but it turned into a sob. Cecil understood what Dennis was as much as Dennis did.

Dennis knew he was a wrong 'un. He lied and stole even when there was no reason to. Every opportunity had been afforded him, but he was lazy and prone to addiction. He was always enthralled by something. This time it had been women, then it had become Elizabeth.

Yet, even with her, he almost stole the earrings she'd left on his shelf. Elizabeth had panicked when she'd realised a few days later and raced round, but one was missing. Dennis knew she thought he'd nicked it, but he hadn't. She'd told him to find it or else. It was him who'd gone crazy hunting for it afterwards, but it was gone. Then he'd lost the other one. The only people who'd been in his lodge were Glory and Jasmine, but he often forgot to lock it. He'd suspected Glory was responsible until it turned up in Jasmine's hot tub.

He pictured Glory's face after he'd told her he was getting back with his ex. Maybe it was Glory after all, and she'd put it in the hot tub to implicate Elizabeth. Despite the air con being on full blast, he started to overheat. He was about to indicate to turn into Cecil's drive when he noticed the front door was slightly ajar. He felt the hairs on his arms rise.

Instead of driving straight in, he slowed and parked by the kerb, then stared across at the entrance. The huge driveway was entirely block-paved, so with the precise lines, he could detect the wobble of the front door when it moved. It was as still a day as he could remember, so something was moving it.

Dennis nearly wet himself with relief when a furry head poked its way through the gap. It was their neighbours' scrawny old cat, which must have been pushing twenty years old. It was a grumpy, aggressive, stubborn thing, but had often spent time with his mother. Maybe it had found shared values with Cecil.

Dennis's eyes narrowed as he saw the cat leave dark footprints on the porch. Little bugger must have knocked something over. He left his vehicle and glanced behind him. The silver car had stopped thirty metres away up the road in front of a work van. The driver was flashing his lights at him. That was weird. He imagined if the police were there, they would leap on him the moment he stepped from his vehicle. Why would they not get out of their car?

As he thought that, the passenger of the police car opened the door, half stepped out and beckoned him to come over. The young officer appeared very concerned, almost frantic.

The door of the house being open puzzled Dennis. As he turned to stare at it again, there was a loud noise. A car had backfired. He peered back at the vehicle that had followed him. The officer who was half out had turned to check as though they'd been rear-ended.

There was nothing behind them except the white van, which hadn't moved, although one of its rear doors was half open. Dennis saw an orange flash and the inside of the van lit up, following by another bang. The windscreen of the silver car shattered. A bullet zipped by Dennis as he stared aghast at the damaged vehicle.

A black glove came through the broken windscreen as the driver punched a hole in it. The standing officer leapt back in. There was a screech of tyres, then the car hurtled past Dennis, passenger door swinging. It left a puff of dark-grey smoke and the smell of burning rubber in the air.

Dennis felt his bowels weaken. He stared at the blackness inside the van, imagining the person inside reloading. On wooden legs, he twisted around and tottered onto the driveway. His legs failed to respond to the signals to run. He thought of Elizabeth and how he'd finally met someone who understood him, because she was just the same.

The relative safety of the front door was metres away. The centre of his back itched where he imagined a target to be.

Dennis didn't hear the ricochet of the high-velocity bullet as it hit the stone column in front of him. There were no dramatic jerks, despite it having passed through his chest. He collapsed onto his knees. His head hung low. He saw the blood pooling underneath him. Quietly and slowly, he tipped over onto his side.

There was no pain. Dennis's final thought was that when the police returned, the van, and the shooter, would be gone.

And so would he.

78

Fifteen minutes later, Sal rang Ashley and gave her a brief outline of what they knew had happened so far.

'Do we know Dennis's fate yet?' she asked.

'No, but I can't imagine it's good news. The armed response units aren't trained to deal with what might be a professional sniper, so we've held them back, even though the shooter might escape. The last thing we want is someone else shot. Tactical should be there in fifteen minutes and the helicopter at the same time.'

'Didn't the unit that got shot at give us anything to go on?'

'There were two vehicles in the street with one person noted. A grey-haired man we suspected might be the Cowboy, but his car checks out. It seems unlikely that the cowboy has been living in Stumperlowe for ten years. There was a Citroen Berlingo van as well, which we're looking into. The shots may have been fired from there. We've got a ring of police around the area, but it's an absolute warren.'

'Okay. Let's assume it's Glory, and she slips your net. Where would she head next? She might be planning to return to King's Lynn to say goodbye to her husband.'

'Kettle put an armed guard on the coma ward this morning, and there's another one at each hospital entrance.'

'I can head there now. We're not far away. It's pointless us carrying on to Sheffield.'

'Okay. Kettle already requested permission to access medical records. It should be authorised by the time you reach there.' Sal let out a deep breath. 'This woman has pulled nearly all of eastern England's armed resource into Norfolk, and the north of England's resource is heading towards Sheffield.'

'It's the audacity I'm struggling with. I hope this means it's over.'

'We know who she is, and we have a motive. Kettle's instructing the news channels. Shortly, everyone in the UK will be aware she's alive and dangerous, probably in Sheffield, and they'll have an easily accessible picture on their phones.'

'Have you made any progress with her history?'

'Not much. It seems she emigrated for good a long time ago. We're checking flights into the country over the last year for a Gloria Trubell and variants of, starting with those from America, but that's not a small job. She may be travelling under a pseudonym or a married name. Once we identify who her husband is, things will move rapidly.'

'Is Elizabeth still in custody?'

'No. Emma rang Abraham's home saying she wanted to make sure they got back okay, but she was really just checking everything was fine there. Abraham informed her they would be visiting the Devon and Cornwall area in the next few days while this settles down.'

'Was their only bail condition not to leave England?'

'Yes. It's promising that he's still communicating.'

'Unless it's more lies. What about Glory's car on ANPR, or any sign of the Cowboy in Paradise?'

'Neither. If this Glory is a professional, she'll have hired vans or cars or bought them cheap, and maybe put on false plates.'

'I assume Border Force is checking flights out.'

'Of course. It's all in hand. Hang on. Kettle wants a quick word.'

Her boss came on the line.

'Hi, Ashley. We've had a helpful break. Now we have authority, the hospital has told us the bloke in the coma from a gunshot wound is a Tony Lerner. There's a team in London who deals with our friends on the other side of the pond, so they're also probing into all of this. I suspect Glory went over there and married this guy, but didn't change her name back here.'

'It's hard to believe this murderfest started over Dennis dumping her.'

'I know, but you said she was a cool customer.'

'Cool, not frozen.' Ashley frowned. 'Christ. Do you know what else just dawned on me?'

'What?'

'Glory's speech was peppered with Americanisms. They only half registered at the time. She said phrases like no clue, vacation, real shame and godawful, which aren't common over here.'

'It's easy when you know what to look for.'

'I suppose. I'll talk with the nurses on the ward. See if any of them picked up information we don't have.'

'Good, then go home. There'll be a meeting here at ten in the morning. She's probably heading to an airport or port as we speak.'

'She'll have changed her appearance.'

'Yes. Relax, Ashley, we're on it. You sound tired. Don't spend long at the hospital. Hopefully, this will all be sorted by the time you wake up.'

Ashley put her phone back in her pocket and told Barry what Kettle had said.

'Let's hope so. A few days off would be nice.'

Ashley nodded at him, but she suspected Kettle was just trying to get her to have a good night's sleep to be ready in the morning. He'd know, as she did, there were too many loose ends for this to be tied up quickly. Glory would be aware the authorities would monitor all methods of leaving the country.

Would she attempt to leave in disguise, or would she go to ground?

Perhaps her contract wasn't yet fulfilled.

79

Twenty minutes later, Ashley and Barry pulled into the hospital car park.

'Maybe we could go out for a meal this weekend,' blurted Barry.

'Why don't you ask that Jennifer out? She thought you were such a clever boy.'

'She's not my type.'

'That's an insult to me, seeing as she's young and pretty.'

'I'm not keen on the knife-wielding killer-bunny vibe.'

Ashley couldn't stop barking out a laugh. 'Is that a thing?'

'Who knows? If it is, it's not mine.'

'Barry, you know when a pigeon hits a glass window, and you go outside and look into its eyes?'

'Yes.'

'That's like talking to you sometimes.'

'If you want to change the subject, just say so.'

Ashley checked emails on her phone.

'I've received the paperwork here for the hospital. Have you been on one of these coma wards before?'

'No, have you?'

'Yes. Once in Sheffield. You'd think they'd be deathly quiet, but they aren't.'

'Really?'

'Some sing whole songs in their sleep. Others do high kicks.'

'I never knew that.'

'I was joking, bird brain. Come on, let's head in.'

Ashley had a quick word with the officer near the entrance. There had been no sign of Glory. At the main reception, they were given directions. Ashley received a text from Emma, which she showed to Barry.

Dennis Turner. Deceased. Single gunshot wound to chest.

An image of a relaxed and smiling Dennis running a hand through his hair materialised in Ashley's mind. She pushed it away and carried on to the coma ward. They walked through a long, straight corridor before they reached a door on the right that was locked. Ashley pressed the buzzer.

'We're here to see Tony Lerner,' said Ashley into the intercom, but the door was opened by a police officer.

'Everything okay?' she asked.

'Church quiet,' he said.

Ashley knew him and said if he wanted a five-minute break, now was a good time.

A nurse in blue scrubs appeared. It was hard to age her due to the thick make-up and long fake eyelashes. Ashley wondered what she looked like without all that on.

'Visiting hours are over,' said the nurse.

Ashley and Barry showed their warrant cards.

'Ah, sorry. The day shift mentioned some detectives might

come in and I should accommodate them. I'm on my own here at the moment, so you'll need to be quick.'

They walked into a smaller reception, where the nurse sat down and indicated for them to do the same.

'I'm Ingrid Hart. How can I help?'

'We'd like to hear about Mr Lerner, please. What's wrong with him? How long he's been here. Who visits? His prognosis, and anything else you think important.'

'I've been a nurse here for three years. I do six 'til six nights, so I know Tony well. He was transferred here about a year ago after a bullet wound to the brain.'

'The move was from America.'

'Yes. I've spoken to his wife frequently. She said they were on holiday, but I got the impression they lived there as well. Either way, they paid to fly him back to the UK. There were some signs of brain activity for a few months. Glory came daily. Then he slipped into something deeper, which is where he's remained. Glory visits in the early evenings when I start my shift, and leaves when we close the ward at eight.'

'Is he likely to wake up again?' asked Barry.

'No, not now. Tony can't breathe for himself and has virtually no cognitive function. After a year of no change, it's usual for the trust to approach the courts to withdraw feeding. Tony could live for twenty years, but the chance of him waking up and having any quality of life is zero. It'd be the kindest thing to do.'

'Does he have other visitors?'

'No, just Glory. Although, I read in the log she came with a friend this week during the day. Glory is quiet and respectful. She talks to him while holding his hand. The patients often struggle with phlegm in their throats and fluid on their chests, which we don't believe is uncomfortable for them, but it sounds awful for the visitors. We give them medicine to help, but Glory sometimes has to suction his throat if I'm flat out. She even offered to do it to the man in the bed next to him once, which obviously she isn't allowed to do.'

Ashley and Barry exchanged a glance.

'When was Glory last here?'

'She hasn't been in for a few nights. Hang on, I'll check the observation book.'

Ingrid went to the reception desk and grabbed a thick notebook. She opened it. Her eyes widened as she read the contents.

'Oh, that's odd. She came before I started today. After five minutes, she left a thank-you card on her husband's bedside table for the staff, then disappeared. The card said she was moving abroad and might not be contactable for a long time, so it was a goodbye if his condition deteriorated in the meantime.'

'Does that coldness surprise you?' asked Ashley.

'Yes, although it's not unheard of. While the person lives in this minimal state, the family has to continue. It can be soul-destroying for them to enter this environment with no end in sight. There's no hope, yet still they come. A few eventually decide they can't carry on so they leave to start again elsewhere. Who are we to judge?'

Ashley raised an eyebrow at Ingrid, but her words rang true. She supposed it took a certain kind of person to do the job Ingrid did. Imagine spending all day on a ward with the living dead.

'Wait a minute. What time was Glory's visit today?' asked Ashley.

'A little over two hours ago.'

80

Ashley did the maths and realised it was highly unlikely Glory could have been responsible for shooting Dennis in Sheffield. There wasn't enough time for her to have made it over there and got into position. Again, Ashley considered whether there was more than one killer involved.

Ashley took her phone from her pocket and showed the dated photograph she had of Glory Trubell to Ingrid.

'Is this her?'

Ingrid pulled her glasses down from her forehead.

'Yes, that's her. She's much older now, and she has darker hair.'

'Isn't it grey?'

'No, it's black, but she never wears make-up. I was a bit scared of her at first, but in time I considered her a friend.'

Ashley was definitely getting an unusual air from the woman.

'Are you sure it's her? Do family members need ID to visit?'

Ingrid smiled.

'They should show identification every time they come, but after so long, we don't bother.'

Barry tilted his head at Ashley.

'Can we go through to the ward?' she asked.

'Of course. Let me find masks for you.'

When she returned, they put the masks on, followed her to another door and washed their hands with the gel that was provided next to it. Ashley knew her day was about to become more surreal.

They walked into a small ward with eight beds in it, about three metres between each one. Ashley heard a quiet gargle, then a groan. Most of the patients appeared to be on ventilators, which hissed in the background.

'Do some breathe on their own?' she whispered.

'You can talk normally, Detective. We'll be running and screaming if anyone sits up and tells us to keep our voices down.'

'Sorry,' said Ashley in her normal voice. 'Some aren't on ventilators.'

'That's right. We tend to move those patients into nursing homes faster because they're easier to care for. After six months, we try to transfer all of them if possible. There are always more on the way.'

'Car accidents and strokes?'

'Yes. Many types of accidents, viruses and illnesses can cause comas. This is Tony.'

Barry clicked his fingers and checked his notebook.

'What drugs do they give to coma patients?'

'All manner. We might use muscle relaxants like vecuronium bromide to aid ventilated patients. Phenytoin sodium for seizures. Hyoscine butylbromide is what we give for the rattling in the throat.'

Barry nodded at Ashley.

'What are the side effects of an overdose of that?' he asked.

'It depends. A really dry throat would be one. It's used as a date-rape drug in some countries because in excess it makes you pretty mindless, and certain people become susceptible to suggestion.'

Ashley looked down at the wasted soul in front of her. He seemed tiny. She could discern his expression, despite the ventilator mask. Even in perpetual sleep, he wore a scowl.

'Did Glory ever tell you anything personal? We need to talk to her, and we don't know where she's gone.'

Ingrid cocked her head to one side, then shook it.

'Thinking about it, she never told me anything private. She did say recently Tony was breathing only to survive, but it's not living, so what's the point?'

Ashley was listening until she saw Tony's finger move.

'What is it?' asked Ingrid, noticing Ashley's expression.

'His finger moved.'

'That's common. The bodily functions still occur, even the bowels perform properly in some. A few grumble a lot. If the damage is from a significant impact, the brain sometimes tries to rewire itself. I had a patient once who often gasped the word *yes*.' Ingrid smiled sweetly at Ashley. 'I nearly needed to change my underwear the first time she did it.'

Ingrid reached over and patted Tony's hand.

'Tony's my favourite. Never ever any trouble.'

Ashley stared down at the bare arm above the sheet.

'Is that a bruise?' she asked.

'The skin gets papery. Infections are common. Blood pools in odd places, bruises occur with us constantly turning and washing them.' Ingrid winked at Barry. 'We don't hit them, if that's what you're thinking, even if they really misbehave.'

Barry's face dropped.

'You must have CCTV in here,' said Ashley.

'The one in the ward isn't great. After all, nobody's likely to climb out of bed, and visitors have to buzz the door and sign in. If you want to see the footage from the hospital entrance, you'll need to put in a request with the security manager, but he'll have gone for the day.'

'Can you show me Glory arriving and leaving the ward?'

'Sure.'

Ingrid took them to the nurses' station and logged in to the ward monitor. She found the time when Glory arrived. Ashley and Barry leaned in. The quality was a little grainy, but they could see the woman arrive and stare down at the bed for a moment. She had her back to the camera, so it was hard to see what she was doing and saying, or if she was just standing there. She put the card on the bedside table and left.

That was the best view of Glory, if it was her. They watched it numerous times. This woman had thick black hair, which didn't seem right for someone her age. Large sunglasses and loose clothes completed the look.

Ashley glanced at her watch.

'We'll be in touch for the rest of the CCTV footage tomorrow morning. I'll take the card now. Can you send this recording to me?'

Ingrid shook her head, so Ashley recorded it on her mobile. That would have to do until the morning. She'd send it to the team back at OCC when they left the ward.

'Should I be worried about anything?' asked Ingrid.

'I doubt Glory's coming back in the short term, but the officer will be here. Ring us immediately if you have any contact with her at all, even by phone.'

Ashley handed Ingrid her contact details.

'No problem. I'll take diligent care of Tony until Glory returns.'

Ashley and Barry both took deep breaths. When the PC returned with a coffee to take up his position, they left the stifling heat of the ward.

Outside, Barry placed his hand on her arm.

'If I ever end up in there, kill me.'

81

Ashley and Barry were wilting when they reached the car, and they had an hour until they got back to Cromer. Ashley remembered her vehicle was still in Hunstanton so she decided to get it tomorrow. Barry could pick her up in the morning.

She spent the journey on the phone to Kettle, who confirmed Dennis had been shot through the chest on the driveway and was discovered presumed dead by the tactical unit. Camera footage from the vehicle following Dennis showed the van at the side of the road, which the shooter likely used. It had disappeared but not triggered any cameras, so they were still searching the vicinity. Other than that, they had no fresh leads.

Glory Trubell, or Lerner, appeared to have vanished and there had been no sign of the Cowboy.

When they reached Cromer, Barry pulled in next to a line of closed shops in the town centre.

'Where are you going?' she asked.

'I'm just seeing if Cromer Gift Shop is open still.'

'It's a bit late.'

'I've known Jeff and Jayne for years. If they're in there stocking up, they'll let me in. I need to buy my uncle a sixtieth birthday present.'

'And you're getting it from Cromer Gift Shop?'

'Yeah. They do these mugs with warts on them, and it says, "You're my favourite carbuncle".'

Barry popped out, leaving Ashley open-mouthed.

He returned a few minutes later and chucked three boxes of Penny Lane fudge onto the backseat.

'Your opinion of me must be sky-high if you thought I'd give him a comedy mug.'

'I knew you were joking.'

'Yeah, right. He's mad for that fudge. They don't sell it where he lives.'

Barry stopped outside her house, and she got out with a wave goodbye, both too tired to say the words. When she reached her kitchen, she realised it was shopping night. She had a box of salad in her fridge, but it was more like soup when she opened it. In the end, she cooked a Lidl frozen sourdough pizza and went to bed.

The next day at six thirty, she stepped outside in her running gear. She loved fresh mornings with stiff breezes. There were only a few clouds hurrying across the sky. The smell of the sea was in the air. Arthur leant against his doorway, cup in hand.

'Beautiful morning, Ashley.'

'Sorry about missing our supermarket trip. It's been a crazy week.'

'Yes, I saw the news. The world's gone mad. Two people were killed in Sheffield yesterday, too.'

'I heard. I'm going to organise another meet-up when I next get a chance to breathe. Drinks or food?'

'A meal would be great.' Arthur pointed up to Ashley's left. 'Our neighbour's not doing so well.'

'Oliver's gran?'

'Yes, I spoke to Oliver's mum a few days ago. I'm afraid it's terminal. Three months.'

'I'll go around as soon as I can. Offer my help.'

'Oliver's mother quit her London job, so she's able to live here with him. She's joining a local firm with a plan to become a partner when Oliver starts senior school. I offered my babysitting services. She was grateful and said she'd let me know.'

'Look at you. Whirlwind romance and now babysitter extraordinaire.'

'Is it still called that when they're eleven?'

'Who knows?' Ashley chuckled as she left.

She walked towards the Overstrand Road, then bounded up the path to the lighthouse. The early golfers waved as she made her way beside the course. She turned right and loped along the clifftops down towards the village. At the café, she turned left and trotted down the slipway and ran hard back along the beach to Cromer.

She considered poor Oliver's grandmother. She was thirty years older than Ashley, but mid-seventies didn't seem so far away. Doing a police officer's job meant you were constantly exposed to how fragile life could be. Ashley had decided by the end of her run to apply for the upcoming Inspector assessment day.

She was doing some of the job anyway, so she might as well be paid for it. If she was successful and she had to go back to uniform, then so be it. Ashley was grinning by the time she returned home. Finally, she was controlling her life, rather than life controlling her.

After she'd had a quick shower and a bowl of porridge for breakfast, Barry picked her up. She said little on the journey with her mind on the case. The jog had cleared her head and she could see a picture forming. Glory had to be responsible. A wig was an easy disguise for a woman.

Ashley also now believed that Glory wasn't working alone. Maybe the best way to catch Glory before she escaped was to treat her as a professional. She could plan and think strategically, with seemingly no moral concerns at all. The million-dollar question was, had she finished? Was Dennis the final clinical act?

Ashley thought of Elizabeth Brown. Could Jackie's release from prison have something to do with things? Did Dennis's fire link Alfie to the kills, or was it Elizabeth? Dennis said Elizabeth had turned up at his lodge when Glory was leaving. Wouldn't that have made both women angry? If Glory was murdering Dennis's other girlfriends, would Elizabeth be next? Unless, of course, the women were working together.

All seaports, railway stations and airports were under surveillance but if Glory was some kind of master of disguise, it wouldn't be impossible for her to slip through the UK's porous borders. She'd be taking a risk, though. Ashley suspected Glory would lie low. She clearly had patience.

Ashley recalled the incident where Hans said someone had been trying to break into his caravan. They had assumed it was the killer, but Glory hadn't been at her lodge, or at least she'd said she wasn't. Could it have been her accomplice? If so, who was that accomplice?

At OCC, Ashley nodded to her team, who were all in except Emma. She sensed an energy that events like the previous day's horrors often created.

'Morning, Sarge,' said Sal. 'Glory Lerner flew into the UK with her husband on a medical flight. The airport keeps its CCTV footage forever. It's definitely her. We haven't caught her yet, but her time's up. We'll have her soon.'

Ashley looked around the office. Faces were grim but determined. They all knew if Glory escaped, the case would haunt them for the rest of their careers.

82

Ashley had just checked her inbox and found a message from Michelle's Harvard professor when Kettle called her for a chat before he took the morning meeting. She scanned the information Cal Johns had sent her, then followed Kettle to his office where he explained his plan.

At ten, everyone shuffled into the meeting room, and Kettle gave them the latest before handing over to Ashley. She delivered an update and took questions. Everything was in motion.

'Okay, final points. DCI Kettle is doing an interview for all the major channels at lunch. We'll have the nation's eyes looking for Glory. She's gifted at disguising herself, but we have a recent picture from when she arrived at customs last year. The American authorities will send us all they have on Gloria and Tony Lerner. I'm going to ring Elizabeth Brown and Abraham Englebert today. I'm concerned she might be next, although Abraham has on-site security and they are planning to go to Cornwall. Even a hired killer would be put off by that journey.'

A ripple of laughter went through the team, but they were quickly focused.

'I think it's plain this murderer has many skills.'

There were quite a few ironic smiles at that statement.

'I've been speaking to a professor via email about serial killers and contract killings in America. I mentioned the methods used and wondered if there was a pattern that fitted with anything over there. He emailed last night to say there are a couple of things that might match, and he knows of a rumour concerning the Cowboy.'

That caused a response in the room, but, again, they were soon quiet.

'Before you get too excited, he said most of the intel he has on him is thirty to forty years old, so even though that fits our guy's age bracket, it's a leap.'

'Is their cowboy wanted for murder?' asked Kettle.

'I don't know. With the time difference to the US, the bloke from Harvard has offered to get up early to talk to me, but that will be 1 p.m. here. I'll update the file immediately with whatever I find. Anything else?'

'We're chasing our tails with this killer,' said Morgan from Ally's team. 'She seems to know exactly what we're planning to do and when we're going to do it.'

'I agree. We have to assume this killer is brilliant. Plan to be one step ahead of where we normally would be. It's no big secret how we, the police, operate. Our manuals are online. You can watch hundreds of shows which aren't far from the mark, and a few are right on the money. Not only that, we have rules, laws and procedures to follow, whereas the person we're after is prepared to break every principle known to man.'

Ashley paused and glanced from face to face.

'It's also pretty obvious that information has been leaking out of this department, so keep your eyes peeled and your ears open.'

There was no point lying about it, so she told the truth.

'There's an enemy within.'

83

Kettle brought the meeting to a close, then asked her to stay behind.

'I'd rather you had mentioned that to me before you said it.'

'Sorry. I thought it better off out there.'

Kettle smiled at her.

'Fine. I think you should visit the Abraham place today, not wait for tomorrow.'

'Fair enough. Should I let them know I'm on the way?'

'I'm not sure. This cowboy guy might be there if he's working for Abraham.'

'I'll go this afternoon with Barry and Hector. If the leak was in the room, at least they won't know we're coming today.'

'True. Maybe Glory is heading there next, or it's possible she's working for Abraham. Perhaps he's developed some kind of paranoia and has ordered everyone killed who dared interfere with his life.'

'Let's hope that doesn't include us,' said Ashley.

Kettle's expression was hard to read. 'It is possible.'

'I reckon it'd just be unlucky timing if Glory were there.'

'Agreed. Attacking a private estate with security isn't a smart move.'

'What I don't want happening is us arriving at an empty house after our mole has given them the heads-up.'

Kettle scratched his chin.

'Let's see. Money buys information. Abraham has a lot of cash and not much time remaining to spend it. I believe he's got this cowboy investigating, but I also reckon Abraham has bought himself an officer or two.'

'He's probably fully aware of Dennis's gambling problem and all about Elizabeth's affair. I still don't think he'd order a killing, do you?'

Kettle shrugged.

'Who knows? Let's find our suspects, then we'll focus on which officers have gone bad. Are you sure Glory wasn't the woman who was at the hospital leaving that note?'

'Not certain, but remember, Glory's really smart. If it was her, she'd have made it more obvious, and the camera would have clearly seen her face. No large glasses and loose clothing would have been necessary. I suspect the person was whoever Glory brought with her to visit her husband this week. That must have been a recce. Maybe she paid them to help. The person appears shifty and nervous. I'm hoping they made the mistake of driving there yesterday and we'll find her that way. There's CCTV all over the entrances and car parks.'

'Good thinking. Should we send an ARV to Abraham's estate with you?'

'No. Abraham has security and they'd be prepared for all eventualities. His gamekeeper shooting the police would be idiotic.'

Kettle nodded and returned to the incident room. The rest of the morning Ashley spent at her desk catching up on forms, inputting, organising, chasing and delivering instructions. The HOLMES system had churned out tasks. Ally Williamson's team headed to the hospital to retrieve the CCTV footage. Others were watching various traffic and council cameras in real time. Another group set off for Sheffield. More reports came back, for DNA, laptops and phones, which all began to hint at Glory's involvement.

Ashley decided the fair thing to do would be to warn Elizabeth that she might be a target. Ashley ended up ringing four times without an answer, so she sent a text message asking her to call asap. At midday, when she was about to try Elizabeth again, she received a reply.

What do you want?

Ring me. It's about your safety.

A few moments later, Ashley's phone rang.

'Thanks for calling, Elizabeth. How are you?'

'Worried. What about my safety?'

'I think whoever is responsible for the murders could be interested in you, too. Have you seen what's happened in Sheffield?'

'No. There's drama here. Abe cleared off and wouldn't tell me where he was going apart from it was south-west. Told me I have until tonight to move all my stuff out. He said the relationship has run its course, and I'm on my own. I reckon he was trying to make me panic, but, as I told you, I don't need his money to live well. I've realised luxury is lovely, but not if it comes at too high a cost. He was furious, though. Told me to ring him when I'd gone. Said I'd made him look a fool.'

'To be fair, you probably have.'

'I told him there's no fool like an old fool.'

Ashley wondered if that was wise, but let it go.

'Are you sitting down, Elizabeth? I have news.'

'Just tell me.'

'Two people were killed in Sheffield. One was Dennis's stepfather, and the other was Dennis.'

After a few seconds, Elizabeth sniffed and whispered, 'Who did it?'

'We were wondering if you could help us.'

'And why is that?'

'We're eager to talk to a Gloria Lerner. Do you know her?'

'No.'

'She was one of Dennis's neighbours.'

'Which one? I heard the women were all dead.'

'Grey-haired lady who lived at number five.'

There was a pause.

'I think I saw her once when she was talking to Dennis. Funnily enough, she was vaguely familiar. Are you certain it's her? I'm pretty sure Oddie could handle her.'

'Is Oddie the guard who looks similar to Oddjob?'

'Yes, it's my pet name for him. Abe told him to stay with me to make sure I left safely.'

'At least that's something. If I were you, Elizabeth, I'd get out of there fast and go somewhere safe.'

'Tonnes of my stuff is here. I need to bring it all down to the parlour, so he knows what's mine. He'll send it on later. I have loads of expensive jewellery here, too, which I won't be leaving. The gamekeeper has also been told to hang around the estate, just in case. I'll be fine.'

'You don't appear that upset over Dennis.'

'I'm not, he was just a bit of fun.'

'He loved you.'

'He was a needy thief and a liar. I reckon he hid my earrings with the intention of selling them, but I guess we'll never know. Trust me, nobody will lose any sleep over him. You have to look after number one in this world. See what's happened to me now? Thrown out with barely a day's notice.'

'Are you angry?'

'No, I'd have done the same thing to him if it was my place, the wrinkled old fucker.'

Ashley took a deep breath.

'Okay. Consider yourself warned. Phone me if you receive any unexpected visitors. Before you let them in! Or call 999.'

'Wait. Did you say Glory, or Gloria?'

'She was christened Gloria. Does it ring a bell? She was married to a Tony Lerner, but her maiden name was Trubell.'

Ashley listened to silence. Ten seconds later, Elizabeth replied.

'That does ring a distant bell. I'll see if I can remember while I carry on packing. Goodbye.'

The line was dead. Ashley smiled. She suspected their investigation now had their connection. The centre of the wheel wasn't Dennis, it was Elizabeth. All this would have started because of her, and would likely end with her, too.

Ashley was wondering again whether they should request armed officers to attend Abraham's estate, at least until Elizabeth left, when Emma rushed over.

'Glory's car. It's on the move.'

84

Ashley leaned back in her seat and took a deep breath.

'Where is she?'

'She's triggered a camera in Chapeltown, Sheffield, then another on the M1 going north towards Barnsley.'

Ashley knew the road and the area well. It was always busy on that motorway during the day, so put Glory more than three hours from Elizabeth, which probably made her safe for the moment.

There were traffic police all over that stretch of motorway. It wouldn't be long before they had her in their sights. Maybe she was hoping to flee to Scotland, but she wouldn't get there.

'Okay,' she said. 'I'll ring the Harvard specialist, then I'm going to visit Abraham's estate. I don't think Elizabeth is the perpetrator, but I believe she's the motive. If I see her face to face, I can get her to tell me what happened in the past.'

'You don't reckon it's a nutter killing Dennis's girlfriends and then Dennis?'

'No. I think Elizabeth's history has caught up with her. She knows Glory better than she's admitted. Let me know when we have eyes on Glory's car.'

'Will do.'

'Glory would also understand getting out of the country in a conventional way would be hard after everything she's done. She would plan for it. That means she'll have another base sorted out nearby and probably one further afield. It's also likely she has multiple cars. All of this would cost money. Lots of money. Where has she got hers from?'

Emma shrugged.

'America?'

Ashley picked up her phone again and called the professor.

'Cal Johns speaking.'

'Hi, Cal. Ashley Knight here. Sorry to be abrupt, but you said you have something interesting for me.'

'No problem. I can imagine the pressure you're under. The whole serial-killer phenomenon is a bit of a hobby for some of us over here due to having so many, especially for people in my line of work, but I've always been interested in guns for hire. I studied it when I was in England, too. So it piqued my interest when your email mentioned a cowboy, although I'd guess you can go back in history for millennia and find examples of mercenaries and assassins in cultures all over the world.'

'I'm sure there are, but I'm keen to hear what you have to say about this particular cowboy.'

'Here we go, then. There was an urban myth circulating in Texas and Arizona in the eighties. There were four suspicious deaths in about as many years of disreputable businesspeople, but they could have been suicides. The authorities looked into it, but it was hard to discern either way. Investigations were more basic. All the fatalities resulted from accidents or overdoses of some kind. All four families stated their loved ones weren't the type to kill themselves. No way.'

'And nobody was ever charged?'

'No one was ever arrested. In three of the cases, the police wanted to speak to a mysterious stranger who had a hat that made people who'd seen him use the word cowboy, although I prefer the term drifter. Two of the deaths occurred in the Texas area, so many rumours flew around. Have you visited Texas, ma'am?'

'No.'

'There are a lot of cowboy hats. I also found an old article, which I'll send to you. It casts doubt on the theory. It suggests this guy had been asking questions because he was actually a private investigator, and the folks who died had got themselves in business trouble. There were backhanders involved and dicey loans littered around like confetti.'

'The Mafia?'

'Perhaps.' Cal put on his best Godfather voice. 'I like to think he made them an offer they couldn't refuse.'

Ashley chuckled.

'You reckon he might have forced them to kill themselves?'

'Could be. It's ancient news, so any or none of it might be true.'

'The guy we've seen is old, so that fits, but has there been nothing since?'

'Nope. Perhaps he retired, or maybe he really was just a myth.'

'Or perhaps he improved at not being noticed.'

Cal chuckled.

'Left his Stetson at home. They were different times, too. Law enforcement over here was fragmented and there was poor CCTV and no mobile phones. People vanished across state lines. Nearly 185,000 cases of homicide and manslaughter have gone unsolved here from 1980 to 2019 – two per cent of those being done by guns for hire probably errs on the side of caution.'

'Christ. So many. We have nothing remotely similar here, although the problem does seem to be getting worse. We used to solve ninety per cent of murders, but that figure is slipping.'

'You guys float around six hundred murders a year.'

'Yes. That's why cases like these are so unusual.'

'There must be something in the Norfolk air after what happened on Cromer beach.'

'You read about that, then?'

'Of course. It was an amazing tale. What I've done for you is pull up the US stats and list by method. It won't surprise you that most of it is gun and knife crime. There were few of the ways that your guy used against your victims. Precision knife kills aren't common, and professional garrottes are exceedingly rare. What did strike me as unusual was the fact you've said the casualties aren't linked in any way except by location.'

'That's right. When we can't find a connection, it's a struggle to find a motive, but we now believe our case might be connected to a woman who has historic crime links.'

'That's what gave me a thought. There have been murders in many of the southern states for a long time where they've suspected a contract killer has been used.'

'How did they reach that conclusion?'

'Some incidents were linked to the Mafia in the past, often around big business. That still holds, but it's the corporations now that are corrupt. The motivation can be to do with getting huge building contracts, or things like planning permission. We're talking serious money.'

'Which means they could hire expensive people.'

'That's right. A person within an organisation that benefitted folded under investigation. She reckoned a contract had been ordered, but that's all she knew. There had been multiple victims, which the police and the feds investigated, but only one of the dead was connected to the business involved.'

'Which means, like us, they couldn't find a link.'

'Exactly.'

'Are drugs ever involved?'

'Not so much. The bosses who run drug cartels employ foot soldiers, who are expendable. They don't care if their underlings are caught afterwards.'

'I was thinking about the money. Getting away with murdering someone is possible if you're clever and lie low after, but you need to be rich. I read somewhere that the average hit in the UK is only about £15,000, which doesn't go far.'

'It's different over here. Larger country, bigger firms, and massive profits equals huge bounties. A hundred thousand dollars isn't unusual.'

'Wow, then that makes sense. We believe a woman could be involved in these kills.'

'The FBI gave the murderer a nickname. Obviously, they thought it was a man, but there's no reason it wasn't a female. The killer had to be brilliant, because they never left a print or DNA, but they almost caught them.'

'Almost? And did you say them?'

'Yes, a man was spotted acting oddly. A local guy chased him down an alley where someone else knocked him out. Those responsible disappeared although the car was identified on CCTV, which quickly showed up burnt out. They traced the vehicle to a disreputable dealer who'd sold it for cash in a place called Phoenix. He hadn't taken any details, but he said an older woman purchased it. Extra was paid for no questions asked. The feds re-examined other similar kills, and there seems to be the possibility a woman was involved, so they made the name a plural.'

'That sounds promising. What was the nickname?'

'The FBI called them The Distraction Killers.'

85

Ashley finished the call, saying she'd keep in touch. Cal said his contact in the FBI was interested, and he'd communicate through his normal route, whatever that meant. Ashley assumed he would go through the Home Office.

She spent thirty minutes updating the file with the latest intel, then hunted for Kettle, but he was in a meeting with the chief super. Barry was resolutely catching up with his paperwork, so Ashley asked Hector to accompany her to Hunstanton. She walked into the command room, expecting it to be filled with relaxed expressions as the net closed in on Glory, but faces were pinched.

'What's going on?' she asked Sal, who was staring at a large screen on the wall.

'Traffic were waiting for the car two junctions up. The vehicle didn't show. She must have taken the one before, so we sent multiple units after her, but she's not moving at the moment, or, if she is, it's not on the main roads. It's almost like she knows where the cameras are, or she's been warned somehow.'

Ashley whispered so only Sal heard. 'Sneaky bitch.'

'You think it's a distraction?' asked Sal.

'Yes, we're idiots. Come on. She wouldn't drive up one of our busiest, most surveilled motorways in England after all this. It's too risky. She'd keep clear of the cameras, lie low. It's probably not even her.'

'I guess not. Unless she's taunting us.'

'Collaring the accomplice now would be almost as good as finding Glory. What the hell kind of person would willingly assist her?'

'There's more bad news,' said Sal. 'Two kids were shot early this morning in London, which won't help with any requests for armed police, and a guy in Lincoln has pulled a gun out on his balcony.'

'Brilliant.'

Kettle returned to the room and Sal told him what they knew.

'You still want to visit Elizabeth?' he asked Ashley.

'Yes. I'm only going to be there for an hour, so we'll be unlucky to bump into anyone else. If Glory's there, she'd shoot at a helicopter, so that's no help. The armed response vehicles aren't equipped to deal with someone with sniper skills. Short of sending in a full tactical unit, which we don't have the intel for even if one was available, what other resource do we have?'

Kettle gave her a grim nod. He didn't need to tell her to be careful.

She booked a car out for the trip and reiterated her concerns to Hector, giving him the chance to stay at the office.

'No way. I'm in. We can catch up on how my month with Sal and Emma went.'

Ashley drove, and they were soon behind a tractor.

'Doesn't this annoy you living out here?' he asked.

'It's like working with Barry. You learn to tolerate it.'

'Feels personal. Like they're lurking in the fields, ready for when I appear.'

'Consider the Tube in London. It's a ridiculous state of affairs for anyone who lives outside the M25, but people become used to being so close to thousands of others and being herded like cattle.'

Hector smiled as the tractor turned into another field thirty seconds later.

'How has it been with Sal and Emma?' she asked.

'Excellent. They complement each other so well. Sal really is a freight train, trucking to the end. Emma is so organised and a veritable force of nature.'

'I know. I'm always surprised she puts up with her partner.'

'Ah, the one she threw out on Monday night?'

Ashley took her eyes off the road for a few seconds to look at Hector. 'No way. Good for her.'

'She said she physically threw him out of the front door when he refused to go. Apparently, he weighs half as much as her.'

Ashley laughed. She'd met Emma's husband only once. He'd been polite, but he was small and slim. 'It's funny how couples are often opposites.'

They discussed the case for the rest of the journey. Hector was intrigued with The Distraction Killers angle.

'Killing more people than ordered is so hard-hearted. It's amazing someone can behave like that, then continue their lives without beginning to mentally crumble.'

'That's the nature of a contract killer. It distracts from the reality of the service you're actually buying. There's a sanitising effect.'

'Like buying cocaine? Customers don't link it to the lives ruined back in Colombia and all the folk, some of whom are children, who are killed by cartels.'

'Exactly. Or wearing your new T-shirt with pride even though a twelve-year-old worked a fifteen-hour shift to make a hundred of them and got paid less than a dollar.'

'I hate fast fashion,' said Hector with a shake of his head. 'Purchase quality and it lasts.'

'Think of how we buy our meat. Four pork chops neatly lined up in plastic sit in our fridge innocently enough, but the real story is literally a traumatising slaughter.'

'Would you eat pork if you had to kill the pig?'

Ashley gave the question some consideration. 'No, probably not.'

'Then you've hired a contract killer.'

Ashley grimaced. 'What a lovely thought. Let's change the subject before you ruin one of the few pleasures I've got left. Are you still fawning over Gingerpuss?'

'Who told you I was?'

'Just a guess. I'm going to organise a meal at Bann Thai when this case is all over. You know, invite everyone who went to The Welly on that Sunday. Maybe even ask Barry if I'm feeling generous.'

'Sounds good.'

'Should I ask Gingerpuss?'

'No, I'll ask her.'

Ashley was chuckling when her phone rang. Hector grabbed it from the drinks holder and answered. He said okay a few times, mentioned they were about five minutes from Abraham's place, then cut the call.

'What's happened?'

'Glory's car has been found abandoned in a Sheffield back street. It seems she drove it in a circle, then ditched it. They're on the lookout for her, but it's a huge residential area.'

'Bollocks.'

'If Glory was the driver, she's hours from Hunstanton.'

'If it was her,' repeated Ashley. 'It's another way of diverting our focus, resources and attention.'

'There's some better intel. Glory's debit card has been used at a shop in King's Lynn. A convenience store called Polska where nobody answers the phone.'

'That's more promising. There was a shop with that name near where she lived. You know, it felt like I was being watched. Perhaps she's staying with a friend nearby. Maybe she's the one who's been helping her. It was a deprived area, and despite what she told Dennis, Glory's been there a year. She could easily have groomed someone over that time, getting them to be increasingly helpful with more serious crimes by offering extra money.'

'Units have been dispatched. If Glory made that purchase, she's still an hour away from here.'

'Okay, ring Kettle, tell him what I just said. I bet the shopkeeper knows everyone.'

Ashley pulled up outside the gates to Abraham's estate as Hector rang OCC.

'Are we going in?' he asked after he'd finished the call.

Ashley tutted.

'Would Glory use her own bank card in a shop in King's Lynn knowing we'd be tracking her spending?'

'No.'

'I don't think so, either.'

Ashley grabbed her phone and stepped out of the car. The forecast had predicted the hottest day of the year. She rang Control and informed them of their arrival and their intentions. She walked towards the tall gate. Then she paused.

Her blouse stuck to her back. Sweat trickled down her sides, but she stood there for a full minute letting the details of the case wash over her. She again felt as if she was being played. Ashley glanced across at the intercom. The light that had flashed the previous time they visited was now dark, and the birdsong that had been there before was elsewhere.

Ashley walked a few paces forward. The gravel crunched loudly under her feet. She stared through the bars as a small animal scurried across the lane. Two crows fled out of a birch tree to her right, startling her.

Ashley called Elizabeth's mobile number.

As it rang, she heard the sound of a large dog's bark.

86

Elizabeth picked up before the third ring. Her speech was fast and garbled. It sounded as if she was rushing.

'I was thinking about calling you,' she said.

Ashley waited for a solitary car, which was travelling at speed, to pass behind her.

'Is everything okay?' she asked.

'No. Well, I don't know. Something's not right.'

'Like what?'

'Oddie is behaving strangely.'

'Like he's going to hurt you?'

'No, he's nervous.'

'I take it that's not normal for him.'

'Not at all. Spartan keeps barking, too. I've been out to settle him twice. And I haven't seen the gamekeeper for at least two hours. He's supposed to be keeping an eye on me.'

'Where are you?'

'I'm walking to his cottage. I'll be mad as muck if he's asleep on the sofa.'

'Why don't you just get out of there?'

'I need to finish packing. Abe won't ever let me back in, so I need to do it now.'

'What's brought your panic on?'

'You had me worried when you mentioned Tony Lerner's name earlier.'

'You do know him?'

'Yes, he was a debt collector, who I sometimes hired. That was over thirty years ago. He had a craggy face with a hooked nose, scary-looking, so he was good at getting people to settle their bills. I used him a lot, but he met a girl and got above his station.'

'Okay.'

'Are we off the record?'

'No, Elizabeth. We're investigating multiple murders.'

Ashley heard Elizabeth's footsteps slow down, then the tap of something on glass, then a curse under Elizabeth's breath. Spartan was still barking.

'He's not here, and his van's gone.'

'Didn't you notice him leave?'

'The rear of the estate is open except for a locked five-bar gate, which he has the key for. He could drive through the lanes and disappear if he wanted to, without anyone knowing up at the main house.'

'Doesn't that mean others might get in that way?'

'I suppose, but few people know about it. It's through a maze of fields with no proper roads.'

'So, it's just you and Oddie.'

'Yes, and he's Abraham's man. He's edgy about something, which is strange because he was special forces. Nothing's supposed to bother him. Maybe Abraham *has* paid him to knock me off.'

'I thought he simply wanted you to leave.'

'Yes, but I bet that was so he could disappear without me

hassling him about my things. Abe said he often had unexplained hunches that over the years had kept him from making mistakes, or protected him from something terrible happening, and he was having one. It was telling him to vanish.'

'Elizabeth, leave!'

'Okay. I'll just fetch my jewellery. Shall I hang up?'

'No, keep talking. How did Tony Lerner get above his station?'

'I used to pay him a percentage of what he collected, but he began asking for a fee. I said I'd end up out of pocket if he didn't collect any money. He laughed and said not to worry about that.'

Elizabeth's breathing was laboured as she hastened back to the house.

'He was right. I'd pay his fee, and Tony never let me down, but I still finished our arrangement.'

'Why did you stop using him?'

'He was too violent. I wanted the cash they owed me, not the debtors in hospital. It was low-level stuff and not worth it. Then he did something insane.'

Ashley heard a crumple and a clatter.

'Shit, I fucking tripped on these heels. Where are you?'

'We're at the gate.'

'Wait there. I'll give you a full statement at the station.'

Ashley didn't want to stop her talking.

'Tell me now.'

Ashley's eyes narrowed as the dog's volume increased. Ashley heard it through the phone as well.

'What was insane, Elizabeth?'

'Okay, okay. Someone ripped me off for a large amount. I was furious. They were laughing at me, so I agreed Tony's charge and sent him round. The guy who owed was never going to cough up. He thought I was the scum of the earth. Next I hear, the guy's received a bullet in the back of his head while he's eating his breakfast on the patio in his garden. All hell broke loose. I scarpered and ignored Tony's phone calls.'

'Did you pay his fee?'

The clacking of trotting heels stopped as a howl echoed around the countryside. Ashley heard the intake of Elizabeth's breath. Then nothing.

Something had silenced the dog.

87

Ashley shouted down the phone.

'Get in your car, Elizabeth. Go now!'

'There was a strange noise.'

'Don't worry about that.'

'Hang on, I'm just fetching my handbag. I'll open the gates so I can drive straight out, and I'm going to ring Abe about his arsehole staff.'

The line went dead.

'Did you get the gist?' she asked Hector, who had come to stand beside her.

'Kind of. Are we going in?'

Ashley heard machinery grinding into action and the high metal gates creaked, then clunked into life. Another noise echoed out from beyond the wood.

'Did you hear that?' she asked.

'Sounded a bit like someone hitting a book on a table.'

'Or a silenced gun?'

Ashley's mind raced through what she knew of Glory.

'We could go in and fetch her,' said Hector.

'Maybe. It's better she drives out. Ring Control. Tell them suspected gunfire at our location.'

Ashley listened as Hector made the call. Her brain was telling her to get out of there, but they had to bring Elizabeth with them. Her phone rang. It was Elizabeth.

'Where are you?' asked Ashley.

'I rang Abe in a panic. If Glory's here, it's only for one reason. Look what she's done. I told him she was here and to get his people to protect me.'

'What did he say?'

'He cut the call.'

'Bastard.'

'The dog's still quiet. I'm going to check on him.'

'No, wait until we have support. Come to the gate.'

'I can't leave him if he's been hurt. I'll put you on speaker.'

Ashley listened as Elizabeth bellowed out for Oddie.

'Bloody Oddie's disappeared.'

'Maybe he's left as well. Get out of there. We can save the dog afterwards,' shouted Ashley.

Elizabeth's run this time was more solid, so she must have changed her shoes. The next sound to come from her mouth was an anguished shriek.

'No-o-o!' she screamed, which petered out into a sob.

'What is it, Elizabeth?'

'Someone's shot him.'

'Oddie?'

'No, Spartan. There's a huge dart in his side.'

'Where's Oddie?'

'Poor baby.'

It sounded as though Elizabeth had crouched beside the dog and was stroking it.

'Elizabeth. Return to your car. Now!'

This time, there was no mistaking it. A blast from a weapon. It echoed through the trees like the blast from an artillery shell. Birds flocked out of the trees, squawking in protest.

Elizabeth's feet pounded the ground as she ran. Ashley heard a car door open and close. She listened to the frantic attempts to insert a key into the ignition. The click as the key turned. The following silence was almost as deafening as the gunshot.

They heard the car door open again, then footsteps fading into the distance. Elizabeth had left the car with her phone still in it.

'Back in the car, Hector.'

She and Hector ran to their vehicle, and Ashley started the engine. She opened the window, and they stared down the tree-lined avenue. A wild running figure appeared at the end of it.

Elizabeth jerked her head to peer over her shoulder. She staggered as she lost her balance but managed to keep her feet. Ashley imagined their eyes connecting as Elizabeth increased her leg speed, even though they were nearly a hundred metres apart. The handbag in Elizabeth's right hand swung and banged against her thighs, but still she powered on.

Ashley's eyes searched for dangers. She debated whether to drive in and shorten Elizabeth's sprint, but Elizabeth was moving fast and would soon be out of danger.

'Come on, Elizabeth, come on!' shouted Ashley.

She froze. Once again, the gate machinery had creaked into life.

88

Ashley put the car into gear and drove through the closing gates, smashing them open. Elizabeth was close enough for them to see the tension and effort on her face. Her form was ragged as her legs tired.

A spark of orange lit up the gloom at the bottom of the drive. An explosion roared between the trees and Elizabeth staggered. A red spot blossomed on the centre of her white shirt. She hit the ground. Ashley put her car in reverse, but Elizabeth dragged herself to her feet, still clinging to her handbag.

Hector reached over behind the driver's side to open the passenger door so Elizabeth could dive in. With a hand out in desperation, eyes wild, she lurched towards the safety of the car. There was another huge crack of fire behind her. A puff of red mist sprayed out of the top of Elizabeth's head as she fell.

Ashley's tyres screeched, gravel sprayed, and the engine roared as she reversed back through the entrance. Hector's long arm just managed to pull the passenger door shut in time as they hit one of the gates. Ashley spun the car to point it down the road.

She didn't take her foot off the accelerator until they were over a mile away.

89

Ashley braked and pulled into a lay-by. Hector was already on the phone to Control, reporting what he started off saying was a change in circumstances.

Ashley rested her head on the steering wheel, but her pulse soon returned to normal. She put the car back in gear and drove towards Paradise.

Hector finished the call.

'Aren't we going to stop the traffic?' he asked.

'Just the two of us?'

Hector blinked rapidly as his brain struggled to process what he'd seen. Ashley didn't bother reminding him that the power to stop traffic required an officer to be in uniform.

'There's no point,' she said, quietly. 'Uniform will arrive shortly and sort all that, but only armed police will dare approach that gate. It's over, anyway.'

'You think?'

'Yes. This has to be what it's all about. I can only assume Glory and Tony Lerner fled the country after they murdered Elizabeth's debtor all those years ago. They didn't get paid, and no doubt it festered. In America, they created new lives. Tony was a debt collector in this country. Perhaps the leap to enforcer or contract killer over there was easy.'

'Must be nice to possess transferable skills.'

Ashley laughed. 'That's one way of putting it. If they were The Distraction Killers, they could have made some serious dough.'

'But why return to England?'

'He got shot in the head. People come home when things go wrong. Maybe it was cheaper to pay for repatriation to the UK than long-term healthcare in a pricey US hospital. Then Glory bumped into Elizabeth again outside Dennis's lodge and she decided to lance that festering wound.'

'What about the Cowboy's role in this? What about whoever's helping Glory?'

'I suspect Glory's killing spree is over. Now she'll be focused on evading justice. We need to find her before she leaves the country.'

'It'd help if we could identify her accomplice or accomplices.'

'Yeah, you'd think your average person wouldn't get involved. Perhaps she worked together with this cowboy fella in the States.'

'So that's our next step. We look for both of them.'

'She might have more than one helper. People are struggling at the moment. The lure of instant cash can lead to terrible choices. If Glory got her hooks into a desperate mother, they'd likely help. Particularly if it meant just driving around in Glory's car for a while, using her bank card, or dropping a letter off at a hospital. That wouldn't trouble many people's moral compasses if they didn't know about the murders, especially if their kids were starving and the bailiffs were knocking. If Glory and her husband were making hundreds of thousands over the years in the US, then something like ten grand won't mean much to her, but it could be a life raft to someone else.'

Ashley realised Hector wasn't listening. He'd slipped into a thousand-yard stare. Hearing about people dying and seeing the aftermath in the Cromer Beach case would have hardened him up somewhat, but they'd just seen a woman die in front of them in cold blood. Poor Oddie and the dog wouldn't have stood a chance, either.

Ashley reached over and squeezed his arm.

'Take deep breaths. Focus on that.'

Hector was certainly on the fast track now. She hoped his destination wasn't a rapid burnout.

If it had been Barry and her in the car, she'd have hung around and waited for the firearms team and uniform. Ashley had seen people die in their cars after accidents, while they waited for the fire brigade to cut them out. Barry had attended a domestic where, shortly after he'd arrived, the wife had knifed her husband. Ashley knew that, like her, Barry would be able put it to one side, at least until later.

Unfortunately, Hector would be a liability until he put it behind him, because he wouldn't be able to concentrate.

To his credit, Hector zoned back in as they reached Paradise Park. It was hard to believe it had only been a week since all this started. The site was busier. Long-weekenders, she guessed. Then tomorrow the parents with schoolkids would arrive. Funny how easily people ignored the most terrible of things if it suited them.

Ashley knew she'd need to come back to Hunstanton the next day. Abraham's entire estate would have a fine-tooth comb run over it. There was no way Abraham would want that, but she also suspected there would be no chance of contacting him now except through his solicitor.

Ashley parked outside the caravan Percy had given them, and they went in and worked off the park's Wi-Fi. The hunt was on for Glory. Three full teams were monitoring every aspect of her life. Kettle was running operations back at OCC.

Ashley needed time away from it all to clear her head. Tomorrow, she'd organise a brainstorming session where they took each contact and possibility from Glory's history and looked to rule it in or out. It was likely Glory had met the person or persons who were helping her since she came back. Any Americans would have stood out as the Cowboy had done.

They were going to need door-knocking teams where Glory had been renting if the shopkeeper was no help. The area where she discarded her car would also require similar. She emailed Kettle to check he was setting those things up, and arranged a meeting for the morning. Abraham's estate would have to be made safe before CSI and the rest arrived, but Ashley was hoping for a break elsewhere.

Glory had proved so expert that Ashley was suspecting anyone and everyone of helping her. Had Hans and Helga innocently let her stay at their house? Were Verne and Bertie in a secret debt nightmare and was she their only chance of salvation?

She rang Abraham's mobile number, then his solicitor's, before finally ringing the company's landline number. All three went immediately to voicemail. She checked her watch. It was gone six.

'Come on, Hector. Let's finish up and get going. Do you want to stay at mine tonight? We can have a bite to eat. Talk what happened through, or chat about something else. You shouldn't be alone.'

Hector smiled.

'Yeah, sounds great.'

It was 7 p.m. when Ashley returned to Paradise's reception to tell them they were leaving. Hamilton was long gone. The woman who was staffing the front desk reminded her of Glory. Mid-sixties, slim, grey hair in a nice style, laughter and frown lines. Ashley realised it wouldn't have been hard for Glory to find someone to use as a decoy. This holiday park was full of them.

90

Ashley found her car where she'd left it the day before and set off to Cromer with Hector following in his vehicle. She stopped at Suffield Park and bought two cod, chips and peas from the chip shop and they ate them on a bench while watching three young kids play on the roundabout. Well, Ashley ate hers.

'You okay?' she asked.

'I don't know.' He let out a small laugh. 'I'll have to be.'

'Take some time off. Kettle will allow whatever you ask for.'

'How can you carry on, regardless?'

Ashley blew on a chip as she considered his question.

'I've always been able to compartmentalise.'

'Nice word.'

'Thanks. I keep all the horrible things together, both those that affected others and the ones that happened to me. They're all locked away in a box where they can't hurt me.'

'What if I can't do that?'

Ashley decided that it wasn't a good time to mention his job offer.

'A prison officer told me they lose nearly fifty per cent of all trainees in their first year. They struggle to cope with the violence and the hopelessness, the constant noise, anger, arguments and fights. The feeling nobody, and that includes the staff, is completely safe. Faces appear when they close their eyes at night. But there's no shame in that. If you can't create your own box, then live a life where one isn't necessary.'

'Don't you have to open your box when you're investigating crimes like these? Don't you need that experience?'

'Clever boy. Yes, occasionally you look inside, and some slips free. The key is not to let it all fall out.'

'How do you ever sleep? My mind continually races through every possibility.'

'That's your brain's method of protection. It's trying to prepare you, so you're able to respond to whatever occurs.'

'It could be a thousand different things.'

'Yes, and that's why you're awake all night. Going round and round. Do the job long enough, though, and there are rarely surprises. It's just another murder case, and you'll solve it with your team.'

Ashley's phone rang. She threw the remainders of her food into the bin next to them and took the call from Kettle.

'Evening, sir.'

She listened for a few minutes, then looked over at Hector.

'I think he'll be okay. We'll be in at eight tomorrow. I'll spend the rest of the day in the caravan at Paradise, so I'm close to Abraham's estate if I need to attend. It's interesting what the shopkeeper from Polska said. I'll see you in the morning.'

'What did he say?' asked Hector when she'd put her phone back in her pocket.

'The guy from the store knew Glory although she wasn't in there often, but all her neighbours regularly popped in the shop. There was a woman, Janine, who was always skint. Two kids, no partner, social, you know, really struggling. He'd known her for years, even caught her nicking nappy cream when one of the kids was a baby. He let her keep it.'

'And?'

'It seems she recently had a change of luck. He even asked if she'd had an inheritance.'

'Have they found her?'

'Her house, yes, but she wasn't there. Another neighbour was watching TV. Janine had paid her fifty quid to babysit her kids because she was going to Sheffield for the day.'

'There's the accomplice.'

'Not so fast, my young apprentice. This woman was early thirties and whippet-thin with light brown hair.'

'No way.'

'Yep. Glory must have more than one person on the payroll.'

91

Ashley and Hector watched game shows on TV for a couple of hours when they got back. She had a stiff G & T, but managed to stop at one. Hector had four drinks. All herbal teas. He finally dropped off on the sofa, so she put a blanket over him and left him there.

When she woke up after a strangely dreamless sleep just before seven and trotted downstairs, he was cleaning her kitchen.

'You don't have to do that,' she said, wondering where he'd got a pair of Marigolds from at that time in the morning.

'I do if I don't want to die of botulism. I woke up hungry at five, then came in here to the land that Domestos forgot.'

'Where did you find the gloves?'

'Morrisons opens at six. I was waiting.'

'Couldn't you sleep?'

'I did, oddly, but when I woke up there was no chance of any more. I bought muesli, berries and natural yoghurt if you fancy some.'

'Any bacon and buttered white bread at Morrisons?'

'Do you want to be a contract killer? I purchased a live piglet instead. He's out the back if you fancy doing the business,' he said, handing her the carving knife from the block.

'I'll be having public schoolboy's meatballs on toast if you're not careful.'

'Merely lifting the veil.'

They had a quiet breakfast and a quick shower each. Hector had also purchased underwear and a shirt from Morrisons but still complained about putting his suit on for the second day in a row as they left the house. Ashley had done the same without even thinking about it.

'So, Glory's finished and trying to escape,' said Hector as they set off for OCC.

'Yes, and if we don't find out who her other accomplice is, we might struggle to catch her.'

'I suppose we can't stop every single woman between the ages of fifty and seventy from leaving the country.'

'No, she could head to Scotland or Wales and live off her savings for the rest of her life.'

'To a place she prepared beforehand. Maybe even somewhere where she has already created a new identity. Can't we freeze her accounts?'

'I'm assuming her money's hidden in separate places in different names, but we'll try that if we don't find her.'

'She's probably thought of everything.'

'Yes, so far. I would say if we don't locate her in the next few days, she'll be gone.'

Ashley had to unclench her grip from the steering wheel at that prospect.

The atmosphere was still subdued when they reached the office. By half past eight, the whole team was in. The break came as they were starting the ten o'clock meeting. King's Lynn police had been waiting outside the house of the young woman who'd helped Glory. She'd walked past their car. Two detectives were questioning Janine in her lounge.

Kettle postponed the meeting for fifteen minutes and left the room. Everyone took the opportunity to grab a coffee before Kettle returned and restarted.

'As we expected, Glory befriended Janine and gave her money. Eventually, she asked her to do menial jobs and drive her around. She was paid well for both. It was Janine who drove a set route north of Sheffield yesterday in Glory's car. Glory gave her the money for a taxi back first thing this morning.'

'Does she have any idea what Glory's plan is next?' asked Ashley.

'No. Janine knows nothing. She's apologetic. To a certain degree, her main crime is naivety. Glory's a hero to her for helping out. Apparently Janine is struggling to understand what's happened and the role she played in it.'

'I take it she wasn't the one who left the letter at the hospital,' said Barry.

'No, she knew nothing about that. Glory's lookalike is still out there. We probably have more hope of finding her than we do Glory, because, like Janine, Glory will leave her high and dry. She might be already dead. That person may have had a passport which Glory is planning on using. Glory is patient and calm and organised and not to be underestimated. Any thoughts?'

Ashley raised her hand.

'I'm going to call in at Reception at the caravan site. I want to take another look at the records of who's been staying at the site.'

'You think Glory might have recruited people at Paradise to help?'

'Perhaps. I had a glib thought about there being plenty of Glory lookalikes. It's the perfect hunting ground for her. She may even have stolen someone's passport there and left the UK already.'

'That's a worrying prospect,' said Kettle. He paused and took two deep breaths. 'Glory's face is on the front of every paper. Sky ran it last night on a loop. It's been on every website, radio, social media site and talk show in the land. The whole country hasn't found her. Why is that?'

He took another moment.

'We play the odds. She could be on the move and in disguise, whether she's getting out of the county or out of the country. We have every officer who can walk on duty today. The main railway stations have officers checking IDs for anyone who remotely resembles Glory. Roadblocks had been set up at various junctions. If I were her, I would keep away from railway stations, airports and ports, until things had settled down.'

'She was definitely near Hunstanton yesterday,' said Ashley. 'Probably on foot to approach Abraham's property.'

'Yes, I expect she laid low last night after the brutal murders of Elizabeth Brown and ex-decorated Royal Marine Barney Crisp, aka Oddie. Not to mention the injury to Spartan, the Doberman. You know my feelings about people who hurt animals.'

Barry raised his hand.

'If Glory's holed up somewhere quiet, she's not likely to leave until it's dark tonight.'

'That's a good point.'

Gabriella arrived and walked straight to the front, where she whispered to Kettle.

'Tell the room, please, Gabriella.'

'Someone named Hamilton has called 999. He says, and I quote, "The Cowboy is at Paradise."'

92

Ashley, Emma and Hector set off in one car. Barry and Jan in another. A small uniform presence remained on the site, anyway. Another two teams were going with Ashley's, but the hope was they would all be superfluous. Every police officer within thirty miles would be there before them, and the helicopter would be over Paradise in ten minutes.

Emma was telling Ashley about wanting to give Pilates a try when Ashley's skin contracted.

She knew who'd been helping Glory.

Ashley rang Kettle at the OCC while Emma was still talking.

She gave Kettle the name.

Ashley could see Hector staring wide-eyed at her in the driver's rear mirror.

'No. That makes no sense,' said Kettle.

'That's why it was so utterly perfect. Let me explain.'

93

The Cowboy shuffled his feet towards Two on Gold. That blue-haired idiot at Reception had provided him with the details when he'd given him the name of the woman he suspected had been helping Glory and had booked this caravan in her name. A woman who'd been playing more than one hand. Victim and villain.

The lad had mentioned something about data protection, then told him anyway with a smile. For a moment, the youth almost recognised him, but it clearly couldn't have been this very old man.

Two was a convenient location next to a knackered fence. Even at his age, the Cowboy could have kicked his way through it. Then it was into the new housing estate, which had cars parked up all over the place anyway so nobody would notice another one, and you were away. It wasn't far from the campervan he'd been staying in himself.

The Cowboy circled around the back of the caravan and waited. He didn't wear a windcheater today, instead he'd dressed like a ninety-year-old. His suit hung off him, and he had large, comfortable beige loafers on, all purchased from a local thrift shop. Even his walk was different.

It was funny how his reputation had grown from the gait of a nervous, bolshy twenty-year-old trying to look cool on his first job all that time ago. A kid who had no idea about life, or the seriousness of what he was about to do, and the terrible damage it would cause to him and others. There had been a lot of water under the bridge since then. Shit, he'd been retired ten years.

When nobody came out of the caravan, he took out the small knife he'd bought from a memorabilia store. It had been a useless thing, but it was good steel, so now, sharpened to a fine point and in the right hands, his hands, it was a deadly weapon.

They were probably onto him, so he needed to finish his job. He didn't want to get caught holding the knife, but, with it being less than three inches long, he could say it was for personal use. The blue pill was an entirely different thing. He'd probably be better off taking it himself rather than the police finding it.

The Cowboy was about to try the door handle when it opened. He lunged up the step and pressed the blade tight against the woman's throat.

'Back up, lady,' he snarled, and pushed her inside.

The caravan was impressive inside, and it looked pristine. There was a fixed seating area with a narrow table. He shoved her into the seat and sat opposite her.

'Hands in front of you,' he said.

'Who the fuck are you?'

'I suppose today I'm retribution.'

'What? Piss off, you weirdo. I'm on holiday.'

'Abraham says hello.'

The Cowboy nodded at the look of understanding that came across her face.

'Does he now? Is that it, or is there a message?'

The Cowboy reached into his pocket and withdrew a ring box. He pushed it over. Her hand hovered over the box for a second. Then she prised the lid open. Inside was a thick blue pill. She lifted it out.

'You're kidding me?'

'Nope.'

'Why should I? I might as well scream and let you slice my throat. I'd be dead, but you'd be finished, too.'

'You've got yourself a nice, quiet spot here. A two-second shriek won't do anything. But your last few minutes on this earth will be much, much worse than slipping away with that pill. Instead of the newspapers discussing your life, they'll be talking about the state you were in when they found you.'

'And how did you find me?'

'Abraham's money and influence have an incredible reach. I stupidly did something for him a long time ago, and he paid well. But when I told him it was a once-only deal, he explained those decisions weren't mine any more. I ended up working for him for damn near thirty years. When he retired back here, he finally let me go. Until recently.'

'Wow. Abraham blackmailed his own contract killer.'

'He's as sinister as they come.'

'Why didn't you just take him out?'

'He knew who I really was. Knew all about my kids. This time he'd heard about my first grandchild. Abraham's well protected. If I failed in an attempt to take him out, he would make certain I never saw her again, because she'd be dead.'

'You made a pact with the devil.'

'Sure did.'

'Kill yourself. That'll put an end to it.'

'I told him that. He said if I did, my family would suffer the same fate shortly afterwards.'

'Jesus. Now's the time to strike, then. I hear he's currently short on protection.'

'Abraham has enough of everything. He gave me plenty of inside information when I arrived. I came and sniffed around. Spoke to people. I suspected you'd have an extra base here, because that's what I'd have done. Rented it out under a pseudonym after the first murder, so nobody was suspicious, then hid in plain sight. Impressive leaving men's trainers and those oven mitts in the pond. Not to mention the earring in the hot tub.'

'You're well informed. Why do you suppose I did all this?'

'I know exactly who you are. Heard about your husband's so-called accident. I'd even guessed The Distraction Killer was two people. You see, I was the best. It seems I've still got it.'

'Pride comes before a fall.'

'Abraham rang me yesterday and confirmed what I had already guessed.'

The Cowboy decided he'd heard enough. He considered himself a heartless creature for the things he'd done, but this woman was different gravy. He picked up the pill and placed it in front of her.

'Take it.'

'I won't be taking that. You might.'

The Cowboy felt a shimmer of something that he hadn't experienced since he'd run away from home and his own father when he was sixteen. Real fear, the kind that turned your bones to jelly. He knew he would be too quick for her if she made a move, but something was wrong. Nobody who was about to die was that cool. He should know. Which meant he'd made a mistake.

Maybe she didn't understand. This was the end for her.

'I'm afraid you won't be visiting your husband at the hospital any more.'

She stared at him without interest.

'In his coma,' he said.

'That's not a problem. My husband's dead.'

The Cowboy frowned. 'You've just killed your husband?'

'Ah, sorry. You're talking about Glory's husband.'

'What? No,' he gasped.

'Yes, I'm Jackie Hook.'

94

The Cowboy stared into Jackie's hard eyes and understood it was all over. He would never see his wife again. The poor woman knew nothing of his murderous past. His children would lose a father. And a beautiful baby with a kiss of blonde hair would never know her grandfather because he'd shortly be choking on the lethal dose of fentanyl that Abraham had told him was in the blue pill.

'She's behind me, isn't she?' he whispered.

Jackie nodded.

He turned around, but there was nobody there. The sound of ripping tape filled the caravan. His head snapped back, but he was too late. Jackie pointed a snub-nosed pistol from under the table at him. They held each other's gaze for a few moments until a helicopter swooped low overhead and broke the moment.

'It turns out you *were* the best. But you got old and didn't realise this mad world has moved on,' said Jackie. 'The rules haven't changed. They've ceased to exist. It's just as well because I'm not ready to go quite yet.'

The Cowboy's gaze dropped to the blue pill. He grimaced, but he was out of choices. He was out of time. It seemed fate did have a sense of irony.

'Do it. Or I'll empty this pistol into your face,' snarled Jackie. 'Let your family know what you really were.'

'They'll hear you on the other side of town with that thing. You'll never make it out.'

'I don't plan to escape.'

The Cowboy picked up the pill and opened his mouth. Jackie cleared her throat to distract him, just before he popped it inside.

'Unless, as you yanks say, you want to cut a deal.'

95

Ashley spent most of the drive on the phone to Kettle. They were five minutes away from Paradise when she finished the call.

'Have they caught anyone?' asked Emma.

'The armed police are outside a caravan on Gold. They've evacuated the immediate area and sealed that section off. There's at least one person inside because they saw movement through the window. Hamilton let it to a J Cook on Tuesday. The payment went through, of course. Hamilton, being Hamilton, didn't notice the name on the card was slightly different.'

'That boy deserves a kicking,' said Emma.

'To be fair to Hamilton, it was him that clocked the Cowboy when he came into Reception even though his appearance had changed. He was dressed much older and had a flat cap instead of that trilby. Hamilton half recognised his crinkly eyes because, when he first came in and asked for Glory's details, they reminded him of his grandad, but he also noticed the longish grey hair.'

'It's funny how something like that can swing a case,' said Hector.

'We were on it. I'm sure we'd have spotted a J Cook on the site register eventually, if not today.'

'Hamilton's a hero.'

'Kind of. The Cowboy asked him if there was anyone with the name Jackie Hook at Paradise. Hamilton remembered there being a J Cook and gave him the caravan number to get rid of him. Then he rang us. It took fifteen minutes for the ARV to reach Hunstanton. Officers on site couldn't approach unarmed, knowing who we're dealing with. Tactical are minutes away. If whoever's in there comes out shooting, they'll be taken out, otherwise Tactical will put a canister of tear gas through the window when they arrive and end it that way.'

'I don't understand. Why would Jackie Hook help Glory after she killed her husband?'

'She had a black eye, remember, when I visited her. I thought it was Elizabeth making sure Jackie knew never to mention anything about their past. Instead, I bet Glory threatened to kill Jackie's grandkids and probably her. Jackie would have folded immediately. She'd just done eight years for them. Although I'm guessing there was also a financial sweetener to keep Jackie onside.'

'But Glory murdered her husband,' said Hector again. 'It's unfathomable.'

'Hector. This is all part of your learning curve. Some people don't think like you or me. They are amoral. I expect Jackie took a pragmatic view. After all, Alfie was already dead. There was no correcting that wrong. If she could make a few quid out of it, I'm sure she would.'

'Wouldn't Glory be concerned Jackie would switch sides?'

'That's why I think there'll be money involved, the bulk being paid on completion.'

Hector paused.

'There's no way Jackie was ever going to get away with helping Glory. She has eight years to serve of her original sentence. Her feet won't hit the floor, and she'll receive extra jail time for conspiracy to murder. She will die in prison.'

'If you add to that she's recently lost her husband, it makes her a seriously dangerous person.'

'So this investigator cowboy guy, on behalf of Abraham, has tracked Glory down in his search to find out what the hell's going on. Maybe he guessed Jackie has been helping Glory, and he's interrogating her for Glory's location.'

'I think he would have been expecting Glory in there and planned to kill her. Glory has desecrated Abraham's home, remember? Killed his girlfriend.'

'Ex-girlfriend.'

'Hurt his dog. Shot his man. He'll want revenge. I bet the Cowboy is out to get it for him.'

'But we don't know if it's Jackie, the Cowboy or Glory in there.'

'No,' she said. 'Let's hope it's all three.'

Ashley's mobile rang.

'Yes, sir,' she said into her phone. She listened for thirty seconds. 'Understood. I'm only a few minutes away.'

She cut the call.

'Everyone's in position. They've got a loudhailer and ordered them to come out with their hands up.'

Hector laughed.

'Like in the movies?'

Ashley smiled. They reached the entrance to Paradise. Cars were being redirected away. She wound down her window and showed her warrant card to the PC.

'I assume you're checking everyone who's leaving.'

'Yes, nobody fitting the description has come through here, but we're aware of how unsecure the site is.'

Ashley carried on to the edge of Gold where she was stopped by an officer wearing a bulletproof vest and an earpiece and carrying an automatic rifle.

'This is as far as you can go. A person has stepped out of the caravan.'

'I'm the deputy SIO, so grab me when it's clear. I'll park up.'

Ashley had just put the handbrake on when he strode to her window.

'Head down to number Two. Only one individual has come out, but they've searched the rest of the van and it's empty.'

'Do you know who came out?'

'Only that it was female.'

Ashley, Emma and Hector walked down to Two. A woman was cuffed with her back to them on the decking. Ashley couldn't tell if it was Jackie or Glory from the rear, but up close, her suspicions were proven right.

She tapped the woman on the shoulder.

'Jackie Hook. I'm arresting you for conspiracy to commit murder.'

Ashley finished the caution. She explained to the sergeant in charge of the tactical unit she was going to take Jackie to the caravan that Percy had provided for them. They didn't have time to question her back at a station with a custody suite. It wasn't ideal, but it would suffice.

'Emma. Stay here and check the van for anything that could lead us to the Cowboy or Glory. We might not have long to find them.'

The sergeant shouted out to Ashley as she was leaving.

'A neighbour saw an old man go in the caravan, so he was definitely in there. He can't be far because he wouldn't have got out in his vehicle.'

Ashley looked up as the helicopter hovered overhead, thought of who they were dealing with, then looked back at the sergeant.

'His appearance will have changed again. Challenge all males over thirty.'

Barry and Jan's car was arriving when Ashley returned to the entrance. There were still people milling around, both police and tourists. The team went into the caravan and placed Jackie on a chair in the middle of the room. Hector set up the recording, while Ashley re-cautioned Jackie and reiterated she had the right to legal advice.

Jackie smiled.

'They would need to be a pretty good lawyer.'

Ashley sat opposite her. Jackie had heavy make-up on, no doubt to cover up the black eye, although Ashley could see that if she wore large sunglasses and a hat, she'd resemble the woman who left the card at King's Lynn hospital.

'Why, Jackie? You only just got released.'

'You must know what's going on now to have caught me.'

'Yes, we do. Tell me about your relationship with Glory.'

Jackie nodded. 'Both boys would die if I didn't do as she said.'

'We could have put them in a safe place until this was over.'

'It'll never be over. Not until Glory's dead or inside with me. If she gets wind I've grassed, she'll be back, and the lads will be shot before you've noticed.'

'Help us to catch her, then.'

'Did you find the old guy?'

Ashley shook her head. 'Tell me about him.'

'I don't really know anything. In a way, he was a victim in all of this as well. He was made to come here. We've all been forced to get involved.'

'Do you consider yourself a victim?'

'Yes, I do. What choice did I have?'

Jackie stared stubbornly at her. Ashley was incredulous.

'Five have died since Alfie was killed. They had names. They had lives and families. Dennis Turner, Cecil Dowd, Patricia Dilley, Barney Crisp and Elizabeth Brown. Their blood is on your hands. If you'd come to us straight away, your boys would have been safe, and we could have protected those people.'

Jackie looked away.

'And we still haven't caught Glory. If she escapes, how many more futures will she steal?'

Jackie scowled. Ashley could tell the devious woman's mind was churning.

'Help us, Jackie. She killed your husband. We can put her behind bars. Take your revenge. Do you believe you'll be safe in jail? Haven't you seen enough of Glory to understand how organised and efficient she is? When you least expect it, someone she's paid, or blackmailed, will thrust a blade between your ribs.'

Jackie grimaced. She sniffed, then blinked through tear-filled eyes at Ashley.

'I want the boys to keep the money that Glory owes me. Then I'll tell you everything.'

Ashley knew the chances of that were pretty much zero.

'I'll have to check. It's criminal property, so I can't guarantee anything. We need to know where Glory is now, though.'

'I want a guarantee, or I say nothing.'

Ashley felt like punching the wall as time slipped through their fingers. She stepped outside for a moment. Emma had raced back to report.

'What is it?'

'They've found two incriminating things in the caravan. One is a small revolver. No ammo. The other is a neatly folded pile of old men's clothes.'

'Shit.'

'Yes. I've updated Control and Kettle that the Cowboy has changed his appearance, but it's worse than that.'

Emma took her phone out and showed Ashley a picture of the clothes. Upside down on top was the flat cap. There was a ring of grey hair attached to it.

'Fuck,' said Ashley.

There were police everywhere, including the helicopter, but Ashley didn't fancy their chances of finding him after the amount of time that had passed. She racked her brain for what to do next. It wasn't just time slipping through their fingers, it was Glory and the Cowboy.

Hector stepped out of the caravan.

'Jackie wants to make a deal.'

96

Six hours later, Ashley and the team watched the large television in the command room. Multiple cameras hidden in trees observed the quiet, dark lane just outside Holbeach in Lincolnshire, near to the Norfolk border.

Ashley could make out the two forms in the front seat. The boys were to wait in this spot and Glory was to hand over £18,000. The payment was the balance of the twenty that Jackie agreed with Glory for helping her. It had been no surprise Jackie struggled to give up that amount of money. She said her grandsons were on their own now, and they needed a start in life. To Ashley, it was a paltry price for working with the killer of her own husband and their grandfather.

Ashley thought back to Jackie's change of heart about helping them. It seemed odd that she'd folded before Ashley told her whether the boys would be able to keep the money. All Jackie had asked for in the end was it be put on the record she'd assisted the police in bringing Glory to justice.

Jackie told them Glory had threatened her with a pistol fitted with a suppressor, which was likely the weapon that killed Cecil, but the word had stuck in Ashley's mind. Surely your average Joe would say silencer. Perhaps it was a word that Glory used.

Kettle cleared his throat.

'The Americans sent over some of the details of the robbery when Tony Lerner was shot in the back of the head. There were no witnesses. It happened in a quiet street with no cameras in an area where those things don't generally happen. Glory told the investigating officers her husband had just been diagnosed with the beginnings of dementia and acted impulsively trying to grab the gun that was pointing at his head. It went off and the thief scrammed.'

'Sounds plausible,' said Ashley.

'The investigating detective said it was the weirdest case he'd ever worked on. It was as if the villain arrived in mid-air, shot him, then vanished. There were no prints, CCTV, witnesses, nothing. Just a bullet that ricocheted off his skull and didn't quite kill. He said the wife of the victim was so calm, there was part of him that suspected she was the one who'd pulled the trigger.'

Ashley considered it for a moment and realised a partner in a contract killing business who developed dementia would be as much a liability as one who developed a conscience. Glory probably made a business decision and terminated the arrangement.

'This must be her,' said Kettle.

Ashley couldn't help experiencing a small piece of regard for Glory as a cyclist came into view. The woman was a callous but efficient machine. A terminator. She imagined Glory cycling at speed over the flat fen landscape, face emotionless.

Ashley suspected Jackie had driven Glory out of Norfolk before she was caught in the caravan on Gold. Sal had found the Hooks' battered Vauxhall Astra on a variety of ANPR cameras in places where it shouldn't have been. Jackie had played them for fools, telling them she was leaving Hunstanton to be with her grandsons.

On the screen, Ashley watched a woman with a backpack dismount from her bike and rest it on the verge behind the car. Ashley recognised the relaxed, fluid movements of Glory as she reached inside the bag and pulled out a too-long pistol and kept it close to her body.

'Looks like she has no intention of settling her bills,' said Emma.

Then they were all surprised as Glory glanced around. She slipped her backpack from her shoulder and removed a large envelope from it. The money.

'She's brought the balance,' said Ashley. 'Maybe she's being cautious.'

Glory didn't approach the side of the vehicle. She stood on the balls of her feet with the gun hand at her hip.

Jackie's black eye pinged up in Ashley's memory. It had been Monday when Ashley saw it, but she hadn't noticed it today under Jackie's make-up. That was possible, although they usually took a couple of weeks to heal, but Ashley couldn't remember seeing any redness or swelling, either. She considered the implications, then groaned.

'It's a set-up.'

'What is?' asked Kettle, looking worried.

'This. Jackie intended all along to tell us the meet-up was at this spot. She wanted armed police here, knowing Glory would turn up with a weapon.'

'Shit, you're right,' said Barry. 'It's suicide by cop, only Glory doesn't know it.'

Kettle looked back at the screen. 'What do you suggest?'

Ashley knew there was little they could do if Glory raised her gun. There was no sound on the footage, but Ashley imagined the trees rustling with the light breeze. Distant cars rumbling by. She wondered if Glory could tell something was wrong, or if she was still hoping the two brothers would leave their car and take the cash.

'Inform Tactical...' she said, but let her comment tail off. They knew what they were doing.

As the detectives watched, Glory raised the arm with the pistol and pointed it at the back window. She threw the envelope she was holding with her other hand at the rear of the old Vauxhall, where it flapped weightlessly in the air. It did not contain £18,000.

Of course, the two mannequins inside the vehicle didn't move. Glory took a step backwards and was crouching to pick up her bicycle when she jerked her head to the right.

Ashley imagined the tinny voice saying, 'Put down your weapon'. A spotlight lit Glory up in the dark. Ashley thought of the Cowboy, then the westerns on a Saturday afternoon that her dad used to enjoy.

Glory, like her name, would go down in a blaze.

Glory hovered in the crouched position, then raced towards the hedge where Ashley knew a sharpshooter had the other side covered. Glory shot her weapon into the bushes. Ashley counted the muzzle flashes, one-two-three-four.

She was almost at the hedge when her back arched. Glory twisted in an agonised pose. She spun around and let off two more blasts in the direction she was facing.

Ashley couldn't see where the next volley of shots hit Glory, but they lifted her off her feet.

97

Ashley and Hector sat across the interview table from Jackie, who'd told the duty solicitor to sling her hook. The tape was rolling with the rest of the department watching via the feed in another room. It was midnight, but nobody was tired.

'Is she dead?' asked Jackie.

'You set her up.'

'You were right. She wouldn't have let me chill in prison. I'd have spent the remainder of my days with one eye behind me. I couldn't live that way.'

'All these people dead, Jackie. What happened to you? The Jackie I knew wasn't without mercy.'

'Prison murdered the person I was, slowly. I served a long time. All those nights, filled with rage. Betty Brown set me up. Then she never paid a penny towards our upkeep.'

'You said she did the bare minimum.'

'She did nothing. Nothing at all.'

Ashley stared at the wild-eyed woman in front of her and realised she'd lost her marbles inside. If Ashley was careful, Jackie's anger would spit out the truth.

'Which of the victims did you kill?'

'None. That murdering psychopath Glory did them all. Can you see me doing a Lara Croft at Abraham's estate?'

'No, I guess not. But every step of the way, Glory had you helping her.'

'Yes, we were good together. Is she dead?'

'How did you two meet?'

'Tit for tat, Detective.'

'Yes, she's gone.'

To Ashley's surprise, Jackie deflated. Her head bowed, and she let out a long breath. It was as though her need for vengeance had puffed her up, but now it was satisfied, she seemed to sink into herself. Even her voice became small.

'Glory fancied that bloke on the site. She'd already knocked off one of his exes with a fake suicide, and hoped to give herself a chance with him, but then he started with two other women. Glory couldn't believe her eyes when she saw one of them was the woman who'd ripped her and her husband off over a debt collection decades ago. Glory did her research. Asked around, and my name came up.'

Horrified, Ashley realised Glory hadn't coerced Jackie into assisting her. They had been enthusiastic partners.

'She heard you also wanted to get back at Elizabeth.'

'Get back? I wanted her tortured and executed. Eight long years, and I thought of nothing else.'

'The black eye was make-up.'

'Yes, and vinegar in my eye, so it was bloodshot. I learned that from the girls in prison. If you want peace from your heavy-handed drunken other half, tell the police he's been whacking you around.'

'Why not kill Dennis and Elizabeth and be done with it?' asked Ashley.

'I think she just enjoyed her job.'

Ashley raised her eyebrows.

'Yeah. Bad news getting on the wrong side of someone like her. I reckoned I was frosty until I met her.'

Ashley rubbed her eyes.

'Yes,' snarled Jackie. 'She was too good for you.'

'What about Alfie? Glory killed him in cold blood. He was your husband,' said Hector.

Jackie smiled thinly.

'I was at Sainsbury's getting an alibi. Or at least someone who looked like me was, but you lot never asked, anyway.'

Hector's mouth fell open. Jackie had learned from The Distraction Killer.

'My God,' said Hector. 'He kept things going while you were away. How could you be involved in any way?'

'Don't be so dramatic. Alfie cheated on me. He was dying and in pain. I heard time after time how he didn't want to be here.'

'He looked after your grandchildren.'

'He let them rot on the sofa. Do you know how many times they visited me in eight years? Alfie came six times, the boys none. I forgave them, but I couldn't forgive him. Eight years of bang up. Sometimes twenty-three hours a day on my own, with only my anger for company.'

'You killed him,' said Ashley.

Jackie's face twisted so much she might have passed for a gargoyle.

'Only my rage kept me alive. Glory was a godsend, but she wanted to be sure of my commitment.'

'Set the record straight, Jackie. Who did what?'

'I'll have my day in court,' she replied, teeth bared. 'Yes, my life is over, but they've paid. They fucked with the wrong women. Now, we are even, and I will have some peace.'

98

Jackie waited at the gates after visiting the med hatch. They'd given her two paracetamol for a night of toothache. She kicked the gate to get the officer's attention. The woman who let her onto the wing gave her a disdainful sneer.

Jackie followed her down the landing, which was empty because they'd already banged everyone else up. It was quiet, too. When the door was closed behind her, she couldn't even hear any muffled TVs from the other cells.

Jackie had spent three days in the police station being processed and charged. Then they'd taken her to Norwich Magistrates' Court. Her licence had been revoked, and she'd entered a not guilty plea to the charge of conspiracy to commit murder.

Jackie wasn't sure why she did that when she was so clearly guilty. Maybe she wanted the world to know how she'd got even, but now she felt old and exhausted. Prison seemed different, too, smaller and even more depressing.

On her previous sentence, there had been light at the end of her tunnel. This time, her future just stretched away into the dark.

She wondered for a moment what had become of her, but

deep down Jackie understood. Revenge, unsatisfied for all those years, had eaten her up from the inside out. Everything good about her had been consumed. She'd felt nothing when she killed Alfie.

The one bit of peace she could cling to was she'd done right by those grandchildren. They would split the hundred grand she fooled out of Abraham for the information she gave him. It hadn't been easy playing him and Glory off against each other. She'd had to double-cross Glory at the end. Jackie smiled as she imagined Glory turning up in Lincolnshire with a big envelope to collect her money.

At least now her boys had an opportunity, but Jackie doubted they would seize it. People like her grandkids never did.

Jackie pulled the plastic chair over and sat down heavily. She was about to turn her TV on when she saw a matchbox on her table. There was no tobacco in prison, and Jackie hadn't even bothered with e-cigs since the ban.

She stared at the little box as if it contained a bomb. There was a picture of a dog on the front of it. A Doberman Pinscher. On the other side, someone had drawn a gravestone and her initials. She picked up the box and pushed it open.

Inside was a thick blue pill. She rested it in her hands. Abraham, in his thirst for vengeance, had sent her the last present she would ever need.

The gift of oblivion.

99

The Cowboy shuffled to the front of the queue for Delta Airlines flight 2526 from Edinburgh to Vancouver. He was dressed in smart chinos and a pressed khaki shirt.

After handing over his suitcase to the man behind the counter, he presented his boarding pass. He had checked in online. There was no eye contact from the assistant while he was processed.

The last few weeks had been horrific. It was as though Jackie's kindness in letting him live had destroyed his resolve. He was close to tears whenever he thought about what he'd almost lost, and the suffering his family would have gone through.

He'd worn running shorts and vest under the baggy suit, in case he'd needed a change of outfit. It was something that had worked before. He had run straight out of the entrance, only stopping to ask what was happening. They weren't searching for a fit bald jogger with wraparound shades. By the time they found his clothes, he was in his campervan and long gone.

He'd been back to visit Abraham twice. Once at a hotel in London, where he'd returned the blue pill and explained to him that Jackie had double-crossed them. She'd been feeding just enough information to each side until she decided the time was right to draw in the net. Abraham said he would take care of Jackie. He seemed more upset his dog had been attacked than about Elizabeth's untimely end. The second occasion he'd seen Abraham was at his home.

The Cowboy had demanded he be allowed to retire.

Abraham had laughed at him.

The airport security guard waved him down with the wand after he went through the scanners. He had a few lines ready if anybody asked him what he'd been to the UK for, but nobody did. It certainly hadn't been for pleasure.

After an hour that seemed to drag on for days in the departure lounge, he made his way across the tarmac and up the steps to the plane.

The flight attendant at the top gave him a huge red-lipsticked grin. He nodded back at her and tried to smile.

'You look ready to go home,' she said.

'I can't wait to see my first grandchild,' he whispered.

'How lovely for you,' she replied.

He lurched past her, staggered down the aisle, and collapsed into his seat.

Then he quietly wept.

100

The orderlies pushed the trolley bed towards the coma ward. The man glanced at his watch and smiled. It was ten to six, so this was his last job.

'What are you grinning at?' his colleague asked.

'I've got a date with some pizza and a movie tonight, and a certain sexy Bulgarian lady from Theatre.'

'Get you,' she replied. 'I have a weekend with three kids and their entire week's washing. It could be worse, though. My husband has to put our new shed up.'

'Give me the laundry any time.'

He was about to reach over and press the bell when the door opened, and a nurse came out.

'Hey, Charles, Hi, Mina. Ingrid arrived a few minutes early and said I could head off. She's in the ward, so go straight through.'

The woman held the door open, and the orderlies guided the large trolley bed through. The door closed quietly behind them.

'This guy doesn't smell so good,' said Charles. 'Washing him might have to be Ingrid's first job.'

'I assume you don't want to make it your last job.'

They both laughed, but their chuckles faded fast as they went through the second doorway into the ward of seven beds with space for one more. Charles always whispered within those walls, despite Ingrid telling him he was being silly.

'Evening, Ingrid,' he said. 'We heard you had a vacation at your posh hotel.'

'That's right. They've taken my Tony away to a secure place. They were worried someone would kill him now the world has found out what he and his murderous wife had been up to.'

Charles glanced around and knew Tony would have preferred death rather than eking out his days as one of the living dead. He handed over the file to Ingrid, who had a peek inside.

'Blunt force trauma,' she read.

'He can breathe on his own and he's made a few sounds and movements on the way over. Gasps and jerks, that sort of thing.'

'Okay, so there's a chance he'll improve, and we might not have him too long.'

'I'm sure he's in good hands,' said Mina.

Charles guided the trolley into the remaining space in the room and peered at the other beds. The atmosphere was heavy, even the smells seemed denser to him than elsewhere in the hospital.

'You on all night?' he asked Ingrid.

'Yep. Twelve hours straight.'

'Have a good one, if that's possible.'

'Oh, we will.' Ingrid winked at Charles, which made him look away.

'Okay if we go, Ingrid?' he asked.

'Sure. Pull the door so it locks. We don't want anyone interrupting our beauty sleep.'

After the orderlies had gone, Ingrid sat down and read

through the notes in detail and studied the new patient's Glasgow Coma Scale score, which was used to measure consciousness.

'Patient opens eyes to pain,' she said. 'Incoherent speech, withdrawal from pain, abnormal posturing. Next of kin. None. Partner deceased.'

She rose and stood next to her latest arrival.

'Well, Abraham Englebert. It seems you're on your own, but that's okay. You can be my new favourite.'

Abraham let out a long gurgle. She stared into his eyes, which appeared to focus and stare defiantly up at her.

'Oh, dear,' said Ingrid, stroking his head.

She gave the skin on his forearm a gentle pinch. Then she bent over and whispered in his ear.

'I hope for your sake that you aren't going to be trouble.'

101

Ashley was distracted by the phone call she'd received earlier, but it was time to go. Barry had driven to her house and was pulling up behind Hector's car. Hector had given Jan a lift.

Parking for the Thai restaurant wasn't straightforward, so Ashley said for them to leave their cars at hers just five minutes' walk away.

Emma couldn't make it, as her husband had asked for a meeting about their future. Sal was on call, although he didn't enjoy what he called foreign food, anyway.

That left Michelle, who was picking up Bhavini, and they'd meet them at Bann Thai restaurant at seven. Joan and Arthur, who were also meeting everyone there, had nipped into The Albion nearby for a couple of drinks beforehand.

Ashley found herself walking with Hector behind Jan and Barry. He picked up on her mood.

'You okay?' he asked.

'Think so. Did you hear about Jackie Hook's overdose?'

'Yes, is she going to pull through?'

'No, she died this afternoon. Kettle just let me know.'

Hector frowned.

'It's hard to think what to do with that. Horrible woman, obviously, but I can't help feeling a shred of sympathy for her.'

'Yes, she didn't have the easiest of lives, but she became an evil criminal.'

'I suppose she loved those grandsons. They'll be lost without Alfie or Jackie.'

'I wouldn't worry about those boys.'

'Why do you say that?'

'Don't you consider it odd the Cowboy got up to speed so quickly?'

'Yes. I expect the department mole helped him.'

'If there is one, I'm sure he did. We'll flush whoever that is out, I'm sure of it. But no, he had too much knowledge. Remember, Jackie was a survivor. Think of Abraham.'

'You reckon she was selling him information?'

'Yes, I do. I reckon she sold him the same story she fed to us. That Glory blackmailed her. Abraham was prepared to spend his money, so she'd have fleeced him, seeing as she knew exactly what Glory's movements were. Maybe he even got news that Glory was coming, and he left Elizabeth to her fate.'

'Not that it did any of them any good in the end.'

'No. You have to wonder if Glory was cycling to kill those grandsons and not pay them their balance, or if she'd turned up with that empty envelope to collect half of the money that Jackie conned out of Abraham.'

'No honour amongst thieves, nor murderers.'

'How do you think Abraham got his injury?'

'Falling down the stairs.'

'Do you reckon he was pushed?'

'You've a cynical mind, Ashley.'

'Not at all. In fact, you met him and saw his poor mobility. I wouldn't be surprised if he lived downstairs.'

'What are you hinting? That someone just brained him.'

'Not hinting, knowing. Kettle finally managed to check the estate's CCTV. Turns out he had a visitor the night he got injured. A guy in a cowboy hat had an argument with him, then hit him around the head with what looked like a rolling pin.'

'Christ. The poor person's baseball bat. I take it the Cowboy hasn't turned up.'

'Nope. We don't have a clear image of him or the name he's travelling under, so I'm not hopeful. Apparently it was touch and go with Spartan, the guard dog, for a while due to the massive dose he was given, but he's fine.'

They crossed the road to the restaurant but paused outside.

'I was wrong,' said Hector. 'About a lot of things with this case. I wasn't prepared for how low people could go. I've been more of a liability than an asset.'

'You played your part. We always need both sides of the story argued. Maybe next time we'll be solving crimes where the people involved have retained some of their humanity.'

They were interrupted by Kim, the owner, who'd opened the door to let a couple out with their takeaway.

'Hi, Ashley. Great to see you.'

Ashley ate there a lot. She had travelled through South East Asia as a young woman, and this place served the most authentic food she'd had since.

Two seats remained empty at their table of eight. Ashley chose the one beside Michelle, which Ashley understood too late was where Michelle hoped Hector would sit, and Barry's brief scowl told her he'd have preferred she sat next to him.

As usual, it was busy with all the restaurant's tables taken.

Ashley realised, apart from Joan and Arthur's beers, the rest had ordered non-alcoholic drinks.

'I see it's going to be a less rowdy time than our previous night out.' She laughed. 'Anyone want to share a bottle of red?'

There were no takers, so she asked for a bottle of Singha.

Everyone plumped for the set menu except Bhavini and Hector, who ordered a few different vegetarian dishes.

'I have some news from yesterday,' said Hector. 'I was in Paradise and spoke to Willy.'

The naughty toilet-destroyer, Willy, had been forgotten about in the arrest of Jackie.

'Was he the criminal genius Ashley led us to believe he was?' asked Barry.

'I felt sorry for him. I'm fairly sure he wasn't the full ticket. He admitted to snooping around at night and listening to people, but something seemed different lately, and he'd been scared. Although he doesn't leave Bronze because his granny said not to go any further.'

Ashley chuckled at the good-natured abuse that headed her way. She put her hand up.

'I also heard today the blood on the knife that was found in Dennis's burned-out lodge belonged to Alfie. I reckon it was Jackie who threw in the firebomb and lobbed the knife in after.'

'I agree,' said Jan. 'I think Jackie killed her husband as part of the deal, so Glory knew Jackie was in as deep as she was.'

'I said right at the beginning I bet Jackie did it,' said Barry.

'That's a horrible thought,' said Hector. 'I want to believe Glory killed Alfie, not Jackie.'

'I told you,' said Ashley. 'If people like Jackie and Glory see other people's lives as barriers to their own ends, they will consider them expendable. They made a pact in blood. That's why these crimes are so shocking. Normal folk simply cannot comprehend them. We'll never know now, so let's talk about something positive.'

'I heard Hector asked Gingerpuss out,' shouted Barry.

The attention all turned to Hector, who blushed profusely.

'Yes, it's true. Seems I need practice.'

'Or better looks,' said Barry, with a bit too much venom.

Ashley reached over and squeezed Hector's hand.

'Welcome to the real world. It's called falling in love!'

'And it rarely has a happy ending,' hollered Joan.

'I've got a joke for you,' said Hector. 'What's well fed, well groomed and well sad?' After a few seconds of silence, he delivered the punchline. 'Barry, who still lives with his mum!'

All heads swivelled to Barry, whose face now matched Hector's of a minute ago.

'I don't live with my parents,' he said, but nobody believed him, except Ashley, who had guessed he lived with his gran. She remembered Barry waiting at the top of his road in the rain for Hector to pick him up, no doubt so Hector didn't see where he lived. She wondered if his gran was the one who ironed his clothes. Ashley was wondering how to move the conversation along when Bhavini knocked her knife against a wine glass. Her face was grave.

'I also have news. Ashley wonderfully offered to put me and my baby up if I struggled for somewhere to live. I went home and told my parents straight. I was having the baby with or without them. And do you know their answer?'

A smile crept onto her face as she enjoyed her moment of tension. She grinned at Ashley.

'Ashley, you're off the hook. My father said if those were his two choices, he would choose to help.'

They all clapped and cheered, which attracted a few looks and smiles from the other diners.

'I was so surprised,' said Bhavini. 'Lucky I wasn't further along, or it'd have shot out with the shock.'

Ashley watched the others laugh and congratulate Bhavini, but it was as if she'd been kicked in the stomach. She caught Barry's eye – he also remained quiet.

'I'll share that wine with you if I can kip on your sofa,' he said.

'Deal.'

Ashley did her best to seem cheerful, but she couldn't help how she felt. Hers was the only plate not emptied. Although she emptied her wine glass many times.

Glancing around, she spotted Michelle laughing just a little too fast at Hector's jokes and Barry did the same to hers. That was life in a nutshell.

Pip, Katrina and Glory had chased Dennis, but he hadn't wanted them. Then Elizabeth and Cecil had discarded Dennis. She thought of Scott Gorton and imagined him giddily skipping along Cromer pier to a show with his young girlfriend.

It sometimes seemed that life for too many people was about wanting someone who didn't feel the same way. It was the carousel at the fairground where everyone chased the person in front, but nobody ever caught up.

Many tried to change. Percy, Betty and Dennis took new names in the hope of being someone else, but few escaped themselves.

After the group settled the bill, they trooped back to Mill Road in twos. Joan and Arthur were seemingly in a rush to reach home. Jan was trying to convince Bhavini golf was a fun sport. Michelle had finally collared Hector. Ashley and Barry were sneakily listening to their conversation.

'Did you always want to work with dead people?' asked Hector.

'No, I wanted to be a surgeon.'

'What happened?'

'The brutal truth is, I wasn't good enough. My hands are a little unsteady. It matters less with the dead. The blood doesn't squirt as far if you make a mistake.'

Ashley and Barry laughed when Hector peered down at Michelle to see if she was joking.

'Do you mind me staying?' asked Barry. 'I can call for a taxi.'

'It's fine, although I'm not going to read you a bedtime story.'

'That's a shame.'

Everyone was full and tired, soon said their goodbyes, and got on their way. Hector was the last to leave. Ashley waved as he drove off, while Barry gave him the finger.

'You know, you should get on with Hector, seeing as you have shared interests.'

'Such as?'

'An interest in overpriced clothes and smelling like ladies.'

Barry shrugged, oblivious to the jibe. 'He's not too bad, I suppose, despite being born with a golden carrot up his ass.'

Ashley opened the front door and let Barry in.

'Oh, no,' he exclaimed. 'Your house has been ransacked.'

'You'll be sleeping in the shed if your jokes don't improve.'

Barry and Ashley headed into the kitchen where the walls were thin, and they could make out Joan and Arthur laughing mischievously next door, followed by thuds on the stairs as the couple hastened up them.

'Nasty to hear,' said Barry.

Ashley chuckled, then almost sobbed. Barry smiled at her. Thoughts tumbled through her mind like falling leaves. Her cool work head vanished. She made an instant decision. Ashley took Barry's hand, then moved in for a kiss.

Tonight, at the very least, she wouldn't be alone.

AUTHOR'S NOTE

Thanks for reading book two of The Norfolk Murders trilogy. Book three, where all the storylines collide, is finished. The conclusion will be out next May. You can read the blurb and pre-order your copy of *Death in Bacton Wood* now so it arrives like magic on publication day, although the title might get tweaked!

I was hoping that after finishing the Barton series, I would do something simpler, but these plots and twists became so complex and interlinked that I'm surprised I haven't spent the last eighteen months with a nosebleed. Still, I've enjoyed writing the new team. They all seem like decent people doing their best. Very much like real life.

What's next? I (hopefully) hear you say. I've been tempted by another Barton. It will have been three years since he took his cushy desk job. Maybe they've found a strong enough trusty steed for him to ride back into town to save the day.

Or perhaps you'd like to hear more from Ashley in beautiful Norfolk.

Please leave a review and let me know.

ABOUT THE AUTHOR

Ross Greenwood is the bestselling author of over ten crime thrillers. Before becoming a full-time writer he was most recently a prison officer and so worked everyday with murderers, rapists and thieves for four years. He lives in Peterborough.

Sign up to Ross Greenwood's mailing list for news, competitions and updates on future books.

Follow Ross on social media:

instagram.com/rossg555
twitter.com/greenwoodross
facebook.com/RossGreenwoodAuthor
bookbub.com/authors/ross-greenwood

ALSO BY ROSS GREENWOOD

The DI Barton Series

The Snow Killer

The Soul Killer

The Ice Killer

The Cold Killer

The Fire Killer

The Santa Killer

DS Knight Series

Death on Cromer Beach

Dear at Paradise Park

Standalones

Prisoner

Jail Break

Survivor

Lifer

Chancer

Hunter

Milton Keynes UK
Ingram Content Group UK Ltd.
UKHW040049200424
441418UK00005B/86